A BORROWING OF BONES

A
BORROWING
OF
BONES

PAULA MUNIER

MINOTAUR BOOKS
NEW YORK

A BORROWING OF BONES. Copyright © 2018 by Paula Munier. All rights reserved. Printed in the United States of America. For information, address St. Martin's Press, 175 Fifth Avenue, New York, N.Y. 10010.

Pablo Neruda "Pleno Octubre," Memorial de Isla Negra © 1964, Fundación Pablo Neruda

Excerpt from "October Fullness" from ISLA NEGRA by Pablo Neruda, translated by Alastair Reid. Translation copyright © 1981 by Alastair Reid. Reprinted by permission of Farrar, Straus and Gíroux.

www.minotaurbooks.com

The Library of Congress Cataloging-in-Publication Data is available upon request
ISBN 978-1-250-15303-6 (hardcover)
ISBN 978-1-250-15304-3 (ebook)

Our books may be purchased in bulk for promotional, educational, or business use. Please contact your local bookseller or the Macmillan Corporate and Premium Sales Department at 1-800-221-7945, extension 5442, or by email at MacmillanSpecialMarkets@macmillan.com.

First Edition: September 2018

10 9 8 7 6 5 4 3 2 1

*For the Colonel, the alpha of our pack,
and working dogs and dog handlers everywhere*

. . . life is only a borrowing of bones.

—PABLO NERUDA

THURSDAY
JULY 1

CHAPTER ONE

GRIEF AND GUILT ARE THE GHOSTS THAT HAUNT YOU when you survive what others do not. Mercy Carr survived, and so did Sergeant Martinez's dog. Nearly a year after her best friend died in Afghanistan, she rose at dawn and took Elvis on another long hike through the Vermont woods. A tired dog was a good dog. At least that's what the sergeant used to say.

Good was a relative term. Mercy was not Martinez, and Elvis knew it. The bomb-sniffing Belgian shepherd missed his handler and his mission. Just as she did. Every morning they marched off their grief mile after mile in the mountains, where the cool greens of the forest could chase away the dark ghosts of the desert, at least until night fell.

But not today. Today the wilderness held a hush that unnerved her, the same sort of hush that Martinez always called a disturbance in the Force when they went out on patrol. Bad things usually followed.

The dog didn't seem to notice. He raced ahead of her and plunged through a swollen stream, a streak of damp camel-colored fur disappearing into a thicket of small spruce. Mercy considered going after him, but like most soldiers she preferred her feet dry. She hoped he'd circle back to her shortly, as he'd been trained to do. And would have done for his sergeant, no problem.

She sighed. They'd hiked nearly a third of the way up to Lye Brook Falls, following the old bed of a logging railroad, which rose along a steady 20 percent incline for some two and a half miles up to the falls. The woods were blessedly calm and empty of people so early in the day. Towering birches, beeches, and maples in full leaf draped the trail in shade. A downpour the night before had left muddy puddles in its wake, and her boots were smudged with dirt. She tramped on, dodging the worst of the mud and taking care not to slip on the wet rocks, her eyes on the slick stone-ridden path and her mind off her future, which loomed ahead of her with no clear goal in sight.

After that last deployment, the one where Martinez got killed and she got shot and Elvis got depressed, Mercy and the dog were both sent home. Still, even though Martinez's last words to her had been "Take care of Elvis," she'd spent six months pulling strings to persuade the private defense contractor into letting her adopt the dog. In the end she prevailed, and they entered retirement together. Two former military police—one twenty-nine-year-old two-legged female Vermonter with an exit wound scar blighting her once perfect ass and one handsome five-year-old four-legged male Malinois with canine PTSD—reclaiming themselves in the backwoods one hike at a time.

The terrain grew rougher, steeper, tougher. She adjusted her pack, which at less than fifteen pounds barely registered on her body, once burdened by nearly one hundred pounds of gear. She whistled.

Nothing.

In Afghanistan, Elvis's job had been to walk in front of his sergeant and their unit, scouting ahead and alerting them to danger. The only dangers here in the southern Green Mountains were the ubiquitous clouds of biting deerflies—and the occasional bear. Still, after about a quarter of a mile, she paused to listen for the sound of a lively dog diving into the scrub, scampering over downed trees, racing up the rocky trail—but all she heard was the rush of the nearby brook, the warble of wood thrushes, and the skittering of red squirrels.

Too quiet.

She stopped and closed her eyes, remembering one of Martinez's many stories from his parents' native Mezquital Valley in Mexico. This one was about a devout monk who lived in a cave and drew murals of saints and sinners on the walls. One day he painted a picture of the serpent Satan that seemed so real it literally scared him to death, the whisper of *El Salvador* on his dying lips. "Don't let your demons scare you," the sergeant told her. "Wait for the real devil."

Wait for the real devil. Mercy whistled again and waited.

The Belgian shepherd darted out of the scrub onto the path, his fawn fur stippled with dark splotches of sludge, his black muzzle muddy. Even dirty he was a pretty dog, a standard-bearer of his breed, far sleeker and smarter than any German shepherd, according to Martinez.

Elvis skidded to a stop right in front of her and jangled his head. In his mouth he held what looked like one of his squeaky toys.

"Drop it." She held out her hand.

The dog obliged, releasing the canary-yellow object into her open palm, his bright eyes on Mercy and his new plaything. She held it up and examined it in the light filtering through the trees.

"I think it's a baby teether," she told him. About five inches long, the teether was shaped like a plastic daisy with a thick stem, the better for a baby's grip, and a flower-shaped lion's head blooming at the top. Apart from dog drool, the little lion toy was clean, so it wasn't something that had been abandoned in the woods for long. She bent over toward Elvis, holding the teether out to him. "Where did you get this?"

Elvis pushed at her hand with a cold nose and whined. With another quick yelp he leapt back into the underbrush. Mercy tucked the baby toy into one of her cargo pockets and followed the dog, as he obviously meant her to do. She cursed under her breath as she sank into a marshy patch, mud seeping into the tops of her boots as she stomped through the mire after him.

Sometimes Elvis behaved erratically. Over the past few months, she'd learned to anticipate his triggers—slamming doors, thunderstorms, fireworks—at least most of the time. At other times, like today, the triggers eluded her; they were scents, sounds, and situations known only to the dog. But baby teethers had never been among them.

He barreled through the tangle of bracken and brushwood to a stream that paralleled the trail, a fast tumbling of water over a bed of rocks. He jumped, clearing the six-foot-wide current easily. Mercy splashed after him, not willing to risk breaking a leg or twisting an ankle in a poorly landed leap. The cold water came up to her knees. Elvis waited for her, his triangular ears perked and his dark eyes on her.

She clambered out of the brook and stumbled over the stones into a thick copse of young birch trees. There he dropped down on his haunches in the middle of a large blowdown area littered with tree limbs. This was his alert position, the posture he assumed when he sniffed out weapons or explosives. IEDs were his specialty.

"What you got there, buddy?" She squatted down next to him. Elvis looked at her as if to say, *Okay, my job here is done. Where's my reward?*

But Mercy wasn't sure if he'd earned it. She examined the ground in front of his paws. The forest floor was thick with dead leaves and twigs and pine needles, as well as mushrooms and moss and ferns and what looked like poison oak. No evidence of trespass here. No evidence of explosives. As far as she knew, Elvis wasn't trained to alert for babies—not that there was any evidence of a baby here, either. They'd glimpsed babies on the trail before, bouncing along on their parents' backs like giggling bags of potatoes, but not this morning.

On the other hand, the sniffer dog had an excellent track record. Martinez bragged that Elvis's was the best nose of any dog he'd ever met, either in training or in action. Elvis had rarely been wrong before. What were the odds he was wrong now?

"Good boy," she said, scratching that favorite spot between his ears. She slipped a treat out of her pocket and held it in her open palm, and Elvis licked it up.

If they'd been on a mission, the sergeant would have called in the team responsible for bomb disposal. He and Elvis never touched anything; the Explosive Ordnance Disposal techs took it from there. But here there was no team trailing them; they weren't wearing flak or body armor. Mercy wasn't even sure Elvis had alerted to explosives. Who would plant explosives in a forest?

Or maybe the shepherd had alerted to fireworks. It was the week of the Fourth of July holiday, after all. Apart from sparklers, fireworks were illegal in Vermont. Even supervised public fireworks displays required a permit. But if someone had bothered to bury fireworks in the woods, surely they would have dug them up by now.

Mercy rose to her feet and stood in the middle of the blowdown, wondering what to do. Elvis leaped ahead of her and darted into the brush. She headed out after him.

And that's when she heard it. A thin cry. Followed by another. And another, growing in volume with each wail. Sounded like her mother's cat Sabrina back in Boston, meowing for breakfast.

But she knew it was no cat.

CHAPTER TWO

ELVIS BELLOWED, ACCOMPANIED BY A BURST OF BAWLING. She broke through the leatherleaf and bog laurel and came into a small glade. There in the middle sat a squalling baby in a blue backpack-style infant carrier.

A baby girl, if her pink cap and Hello Kitty long-sleeved onesie were any indication. A red-faced, cherub-cheeked baby girl, chubby arms and legs flailing against an assault of deerflies.

Mercy hurried over and fell to her knees in front of the pack, swatting away at the swarm. The baby appeared to be about six months old, but that was hardly an educated guess. Everything she knew about babies was based on her brother's toddler, Toby, whose infancy she'd mostly missed, and the injured infants she'd seen in theater.

This little one seemed okay, but her tiny neck and face and fingers were dotted with angry red marks left by the mean bites of deerflies. Mercy reached for her pack and the bug spray but then thought better of it. Nothing with DEET in it could be any good for babies.

The baby kept on screaming, and the dog kept on barking.

"Quiet," she ordered, but only the dog obeyed. She looked around, but there was no mom in sight.

The baby continued to cry, an escalation of shrieks.

"Okay, okay." She unbuckled the straps on the carrier and pulled out the wailing child. The baby lifted up her small head, and Mercy stared into round, slate-blue eyes rimmed in tears and deerfly bites.

"'Though she be but little, she is fierce,'" Mercy quoted, and the baby scrunched up her face as if to screech again, but hiccupped instead.

Maybe Shakespeare calms her the way he calms me, she thought. Mercy cradled the little girl in her arms and stood, holding her against her chest as she pulled the ends of her hoodie together under the baby's bottom and zipped it up around her as protection against the flies.

Mercy bobbed her up and down until her sobs subsided. Within minutes the baby was asleep.

"Now what?" She looked at Elvis, but he just stood there looking back at her, head cocked, ears up, waiting for their next move.

One of the rules of the universe should be: Wherever there's a baby, there's a mother close by. But Mercy had seen plenty of babies without mothers.

"Where's your mommy?" she asked the sleeping child. Maybe she'd gone off behind some bushes to pee. "Hello," she called. "Hello."

No answer.

The last time she'd held a baby over there, the child had died in her arms. But this was no time to think about that. She shook off the memory, and kept on rocking the baby and calling for her mother. The little one gurgled into her shoulder. Maybe her mother had fallen or hurt herself somehow. Mercy walked around the clearing, eyes on the ground.

She could see the trail they'd left behind as she and Elvis had barreled into the glade from the south. But leading out in the opposite direction, she saw broken branches and rustled leaves and faint boot prints tamped in the mud. Mercy was a good tracker; Martinez used to say she was part dog. *Which part?* she'd ask. One of their little jokes.

Mercy and Elvis followed the markings into a denser area of forest thick with maples and beeches in full leaf and hiked through the wood. The traces ended abruptly at a rushing stream some ten yards wide. Too wooded and winding to see much on the other side. Too far to jump across. Too fast-moving to ford holding a baby.

She yelled again. The dog barked. She listened for the sounds of humans, but all she heard were the sounds of the water and the trees and the creatures that truly belonged here. The baby stirred against her chest. She'd be hungry soon and tired and cold and wet. And those nasty deerfly bites had to hurt. Mercy was torn; she wanted to find the mother or whoever brought the little girl out here. But she knew the baby needed more care than she could provide deep in the woods. And she'd need it sooner rather than later.

"We're going back." She shifted her weight onto her left hip, holding the baby tightly with her left arm, and pulled her cell phone out of her pocket with her right hand. She turned it on.

No bars. Coverage was spotty up here. She'd have to try again when they were closer to the trail. At least she could still use the camera.

Together she and Elvis retraced their steps, Mercy snapping photographs of the footprints and other traces along the route as they went. When they reached the baby carrier, she carefully strapped the dozing child into it. She looked so sweet that Mercy took some shots of the baby as well. There was a large zippered compartment on the back of the carrier; she rifled through the baby bottles and formula and diapers and wipes and extra set of clothes to pull out one of the baby blankets, covering the infant lightly in what was probably a futile effort to keep away the flies.

Mercy slipped off her own small pack, tying it to the big one with the baby. She hoisted the carrier up onto her shoulders. The fit was good. The baby couldn't weigh much more than fifteen pounds. Piece of cake.

If you didn't count the squirming.

"She's waking up," she told Elvis. "Home."

Now there was a command the dog actually obeyed every time. She never had to tell him twice to go where his bowl and bed were. He set the pace, blazing back the way they came. She stepped carefully in his wake to avoid jostling her dozing cargo. They headed for the Lye Brook Falls Trail, where she hoped her cell phone would work and she could contact the authorities.

Mercy wasn't exactly comfortable taking the baby, not knowing where her mother was. But she couldn't leave the child there, as someone else had obviously done. How or why anyone would do such a thing was beyond her. She knew that people were capable of all manner of cruelty. She just tried not to think about it these days.

They came to the blowdown where she'd first heard the child. Elvis trotted over to the very same place where he'd alerted before and dropped into his alert position.

"Again?" Mercy didn't know why he seemed fixated on this spot. Maybe he detected explosives there, or maybe that was where he found the baby teether. Maybe he was just confused, his PTSD kicking in.

Or not. Either way, she couldn't bet against Elvis and his nose. Martinez would never forgive her. And if he truly was now in that heaven he had believed in so much, he'd be watching.

Mercy took more photos with her phone. Then she unhooked her small pack from the baby carrier and pulled out the duct tape and her Swiss Army knife, the two tools she never left home without. She used the duct tape to rope off a crescent around the area Elvis had targeted, using birch saplings as posts.

"Better safe than sorry," she told him.

Elvis vaulted ahead, steering them out of the forest. When they reached the trail, Mercy taped the spot where they'd gone into the woods. She checked her phone again for service. Still no bars. They'd have to trek down to the trailhead for a stronger signal.

"Back to civilization," Mercy said with a sigh.

The shepherd took the lead. As they began their descent, a cloud of deerflies fell upon them. The baby woke up with a start, and the wailing began again. Mercy swatted away at the miserable flying beasts, quickening her pace. Elvis stayed up front but close by.

They had a long walk ahead of them, and the deerflies seemed to know it.

CHAPTER THREE

Vermont fish and wildlife Game Warden Troy Warner hated national holidays. Holidays brought the most uninformed and inexperienced nature lovers to the southern Green Mountains. If the term *nature lovers* could *really* be applied to city people whose idea of a hike was stumbling inebriated through the woods high on hot dogs and beer in the hope of finding a moose or a bear to pose with them for a quick selfie before cannonballing naked into Stratton Pond.

The long Fourth of July weekend brought out the most determined of these amateurs, along with the smattering of seasoned hikers and birders willing to fight the hordes of tourists and deerflies to climb to the top of the fire tower on Stratton Mountain, where they could gaze east out on the lovely Green Mountains that gave Vermont its name—and the White Mountains to the northeast, the Berkshires to the south, and the Adirondacks to the west.

So when the dispatcher Delphine Dupree called him about an abandoned baby, Troy was intrigued as well as concerned. He expected the lost hikers (usually found), the snakebites (usually nonlethal), the poachers (usually long gone), but a baby . . . well, that was a first.

"The hiker who called it in says the child seems okay," she said. "But who leaves a baby alone in the wilderness?"

"Sounds like a story out of the Old Testament," said Troy.

"Moses or Abraham?" Delphine was a good French Catholic who sang in the choir at Our Lady of the Lake in Northshire at the ten o'clock Mass every Sunday.

"Either way it worries me. We can't get a helicopter or a truck in there," said Troy.

"The hiker found her off-trail," Delphine told him. "So she's carrying her down to the trail to meet you. Just as well. There's a big pileup on Route 313 down by Arlington, overturned semi, lots of folks injured. Most everyone who's available has gone down there. That plus all the holiday nonsense means you're on your own."

"I'm on it."

"The sooner we get her to a hospital, the better."

"Roger that." Troy signed off and jogged back some fifty feet along the shoreline of Branch Pond, where an enthusiastic troupe of ten-year-old Boy Scouts hankering for a fishing badge waited for him. He'd been lecturing them on the brightly colored brook trout that made the lake their home.

But the dozen ten-year-olds were so busy playing with Susie Bear that they barely registered his return. The big black shaggy dog was leaping in and out of the lake, splashing the Scouts. She was a New-foundland retriever mix he'd adopted a couple of years ago, and named for the character in John Irving's *The Hotel New Hampshire*.

One hundred pounds of muscle and shiny obsidian fur punctuated by a thick pink mottled tongue that hung out of the side of her mouth like the holster on a cowboy's thigh. Everybody loved her. Which was good for Troy, who relied on his sidekick for comic relief as well as search and rescue. An important part of his job—the most important part, Captain Thrasher always said—was communication, and Troy was not a big talker. When he struggled to find the right words, Susie Bear stepped in and won over the crowd every time.

"Sorry, guys." He whistled for the dog. "We've got to go."

The Newfie mutt did her canine version of the twist, and the water flew from her fur, spraying the laughing boys. She bounded over and slid to a stop right at Troy's side, big wet paws slopping the tips of his boots. Together they hustled back along the trail to the government-issued dark green Ford F-150 truck, which served as his mobile office as well as his transportation. The front seat held his radio system and citation book; the backseat was loaded with food, water, and energy drinks, a 12-gauge shotgun, a semiautomatic patrol rifle, a Smith & Wesson M&P40 semiautomatic pistol, pepper spray, handcuffs, dart weapons, hunter orange, night-vision goggles, extra batteries, towels, and all kinds of paperwork, from extra licenses and lifetime-license applications to field-interview forms and hunting regulations. All in containers or neatly secured in order to leave enough room for Susie Bear, who commanded most of the space.

He jerked the door open for her. There was nothing she liked more than a ride in a truck, except maybe a dip in a lake. And she'd already had that this morning. The big lady hurtled her thick body into the backseat, damp fur soaking the thick Orvis seat cover that supposedly protected the interior of the truck.

Nothing like the smell of wet dog, thought Troy as they bumped along on the rough logging road that ran through the national forest, bordering the Lye Brook Wilderness. There were no roads inside the wilderness, so he parked at the trailhead. They got out, and he added the deluxe first-aid kit and an extra blanket to his pack and pulled it onto his back, then stocked Susie Bear's pack with more water and slipped it onto the dog.

Troy locked the truck and shouldered his rifle. "Let's go get that baby."

HALF AN HOUR of huffing up the mountain later, Troy sighted a huddle of living creatures up the trail. He pulled out his binoculars for a closer look, and zeroed in on an attractive young woman, a sleeping baby, and a good-looking Belgian shepherd.

"Heel," he said to Susie Bear, and jogged up to them, stopping about ten feet away on account of the dog.

The woman had seen him coming, and put the baby in a carrier and slung it onto her back. She was about five feet eight inches, but she seemed taller, thanks to a lean build and an erect carriage that spelled *military* in his book. Her chin-length hair was as red as a burning bush in October, framing a freckled, finely boned face that looked upon him with a mixture of relief and reserve. She did not smile.

"Stay," she said to the Malinois at her side, and walked over to Troy.

"Mercy Carr. I've got ID in my Jeep down by the trailhead." She held out a long-fingered hand, and he shook it. A firm and forceful handshake. Definitely military.

"Troy Warner, state game warden," he said. "This is Susie Bear." The dog wagged her tail in welcome, and the woman smiled. Troy got the feeling that she liked dogs far more than people.

She stared at him.

"'We need a good, smart bear,'" she quoted from the John Irving novel, so softly he almost didn't hear her. But loud enough so that he'd know she got the reference.

Troy smiled. She was a genuine New Englander. Who looked vaguely familiar to him, although he could not place her at the moment. But it would come to him.

"That's Elvis." She tossed her head over her shoulder in the direction of her dog. "And this is Baby Doe. She's taking a nap." Her voice held the warning of all females poised to protect sleeping children.

Mercy Carr turned her broad-shouldered back to him so he could see the baby for himself. He lifted the blanket and peeked at the dozing child, who looked content enough despite the fact that she'd been abandoned in the woods like some cursed child in a fairy tale.

"She's got some deerfly bites that need attending to, and she's probably dehydrated. I did give her a bottle and changed her diaper."

"Let me get her to the hospital," said Troy.

"You're alone?" She looked at him with blue eyes bright with disapproval.

"I was nearest to the scene," he said evenly. What he didn't say was that he covered three hundred square miles of Vermont woods on his own as a matter of course. Not to mention that most of Vermont's law enforcement was down in Bennington this holiday week. The Senator was in town with his family, and would be the guest of honor at the Fourth of July extravaganza at the Bennington Battle Monument on Sunday. Security was even tighter than usual. Add in that multivehicle collision Delphine had told him about, and they'd be lucky to get any help with babies or anything else until the holiday weekend had come and gone.

"We're coming with you."

"That won't be necessary, Ms. Carr."

"Call me Mercy."

"Troy."

Her blue eyes softened. "We found her, Troy, and we'll see it through."

Troy wondered if she were speaking in the royal *we,* and then realized she was talking about herself and her dog. He nearly grinned, as he was often guilty of the same thing. It drove Captain Thrasher crazy.

"Besides," she said, "you'll need to take my statement and come back to check out the scene. We can show you where we found her."

Military police, he thought. "It may take a while."

"Understood."

He didn't see as he had much choice. The first priority was the baby. Finding whoever left her alone was secondary. But Troy would find them.

"Is Elvis okay with other dogs?"

"Is Susie Bear?"

She was a prickly one, as his mother would say—and had said more than once about his estranged wife.

"My truck's down at the trailhead, too." He waved her ahead with his arm. "After you."

"Come," she said to Elvis.

Troy stood there with the Newfie mutt at his side and watched the comely trio of woman, baby, and dog waltz by them single file down the narrow trail.

Good-looking shepherd, Troy thought again, as he and Susie Bear took up the rear.

THEY MADE GOOD time. Mercy Carr was tough and fast and used to a quick march. Troy was impressed. She reminded him of Sarah Thibodeau, a resourceful and resilient game warden assigned to the northern district known for her dogged pursuit of poachers. Only Mercy was cuter, in a girl-next-door kind of way.

When the trail widened enough to allow him to step up beside her, he quickened his gait and then matched hers, stride for stride. She turned and smiled at him for the first time—and her pretty pale face brightened into a fine beauty.

Again he was struck by the feeling that he knew her, and again he could not place her. His confusion must have registered on his face, because she laughed.

"You don't remember me," she said.

CHAPTER FOUR

I'M TRYING. ARE YOU FROM NORTHSHIRE?"

"I was born here, and spent most of my summers here as a child."

"Is that a hint?"

"Yeah. Sort of. It was a long time ago."

She ducked to avoid a low-hanging branch, jiggling the baby, who slept on. "You were a lifeguard at the town pool. You and your friend Hunter Boggs."

A murky memory of a long-legged red-haired kid diving into the town pool over and over again drifted in and out of his mind.

"I was fourteen." She laughed again. "I had the biggest crush on you."

"Me?" He and his best bud had scored the sweet jobs as joint life-guards at the Northshire Center Pool the summer after graduation. But as always Hunter was the one all the girls swooned and stuttered and sillied over. Hunter was the gold to Troy's silver. They'd competed against each other for everything since they were freshmen—from grades to goals to girls. For every *A* Troy won, Hunter won an *A*-plus. For every hockey goal Troy scored, Hunter scored two. For every girl Troy dated, Hunter dated three.

"Most of you girls went for Hunter."

"Not all of us." She looked at him, her blue eyes lit with mischief. "He was so full of himself. Always checking himself in every rear-view mirror when he walked across the parking lot."

"That's true." Troy laughed. Hunter never saw a mirror he didn't like. "You were a very observant fourteen-year-old."

She shrugged. "Nothing to do but swim and read and watch the cool kids."

"Cool." Troy shook his head. "I was not so cool. But Hunter was."

"Only in his own mind."

He frowned. She sounded like his estranged wife. Madeline, the prettiest girl at the pool. Hell, the prettiest girl in the county. Who shocked everyone when she chose him over Hunter.

"Didn't you marry Madeline Renard?" Mercy asked, as if she could read his mind.

"Yes." The only time he ever triumphed over Hunter. She'd been Hunter's girl all along, until that summer. When she threw him over for Troy. Or Hunter threw her over for Harvard. Or some combination of both.

"I imagine she's as beautiful as ever."

"Yeah," he said, not trusting himself to say any more.

Mercy looked at him. "I remember the first time I saw her at the pool, she looked so . . . otherworldly, like something out of a story. Snow White in a pink bikini."

"Yeah." He remembered, too.

"I begged my mother for a bikini just like that one for years. But she refused. It was all one-piece racing tank suits for me."

"And now?" He imagined she would look pretty good in a pink bikini. Maybe as good as Madeline.

"Now I hike in cargo pants."

He nodded his approval as they approached the trailhead.

"Mine's the red Jeep." She pointed to the vehicle parked a couple of spaces beyond his Ford F-150. "I don't have a car seat. Do you?"

"No. We'll all have to go together in the truck." Troy rearranged the stuff in his backseat to make room for her, the baby in her carrier, and the Malinois. All that hustle and bustle woke the baby up, and she started to fuss. Mercy rocked the carrier gently, murmuring a lullaby, while he settled in front with Susie Bear. He strained to hear the woman softly singing what sounded like "You've Got a Friend in Me" by Randy Newman. *Toy Story.* Sweet.

The medical center was only three miles down the road in Northshire—a ride just long enough for the baby to fall asleep again and just short enough that conversation was limited to the Fourth of July traffic. When they arrived, Mercy hurried out of the vehicle with the baby; Troy brought along the carrier. They left Elvis in the truck and Susie Bear outside tied to a tree. Just in case the dogs took a sudden disliking to one another in their absence.

Once inside the hospital, Mercy turned Baby Doe over to the ER nurse with reluctance. The baby cried for her, and she insisted on waiting close by while the doctor examined the infant.

Dr. Sharma was a young, confident physician with a faint Indian accent who cooed at the little girl as he gently examined her.

"Very odd to be finding a baby in the woods," he said to them as he jiggled the baby's fingers and toes. The baby laughed, a sweet little gurgling giggle that reminded Troy of his niece Charlotte, who was about the same age. "Especially one who apart from this disturbing incident is seeming well cared for."

"That's what I thought," Mercy said.

"And you have no idea who the parents are, or why they are leaving her all alone?"

"No," she said. "I mean, I don't think so. We hike there most every morning, and we have seen hikers with babies from time to time, or at least heard them. But not today."

"She seems to be all right," said Dr. Sharma. "We will be treating the bites and making sure she is well hydrated. But we are running some tests to make sure she is as well nourished as she looks. We will be keeping her overnight for observation." Mercy appeared as relieved as Troy was that the doctor had proclaimed the baby safe and relatively sound.

"What will happen to her after that?"

"We will be contacting Child Protective Services," Dr. Sharma said. "If no one is coming forward to claim the child . . ." He shrugged.

"CPS. Right." The way she said it made Troy believe her experience with that organization had not been good. She turned to Troy. "Here's hoping that you find her family before that happens."

"I'm sure law enforcement will do everything possible to track down her next of kin," Troy said to both of them.

But unless someone had put out an AMBER Alert, odds were they wouldn't know who the baby was until he found the mother himself. The holiday weekend meant law enforcement was out in force to protect and serve and keep the drunks off the roads and the trails and the waterways—himself included. "I really need to get back to the scene. And I'll be keeping this." He pointed to the baby's yellow blanket by the carrier, which sat on a plastic chair in a corner of the examination room.

"Of course." The doctor nodded.

"Thank you," said Mercy, looking back at the baby before she walked away. Troy could tell she hated leaving the child here, no matter how nice Dr. Sharma was.

"We are taking good care of her," said the doctor.

Troy wondered how many times a day he said that to comfort people, and how often it actually worked.

"Bye, baby," Mercy said, and the little girl looked up and stared at her with those slate-blue eyes.

"Come on," Troy said softly, touching her shoulder gently. He led Mercy down the corridor and out of the building.

Without a word, Mercy headed right for his truck. This time, she sat in front, and the dogs shared the backseat amicably. At least so far.

The quick ride was a quiet one. He didn't want to push her; he'd save his questions for the scene. He wasn't worried about her forgetting anything; she had all the earmarks of a former MP and he was betting that behind those startlingly blue eyes was a well-disciplined and analytical mind.

Still, this seemed like one of those times when he should say something reassuring, but he wasn't sure what. What wouldn't sound trite—*the baby's going to be fine*—or lame—*she's in good hands*—or even patronizing—*you've done all you can.*

Captain Thrasher would know what to say.

"Do you have any children?"

The question took him by surprise. Involuntarily he looked at the fourth finger of his left hand, curled around the steering wheel but still showing the faint circle of lighter skin left by the wedding ring he'd worn for nine years. He'd finally taken it off a couple of months ago after he caught Thrasher frowning at it one too many times. The removal made him feel like a quitter, even though he knew his marriage was, for all intents and purposes, over.

And kids were one of the reasons for that. He wanted them. His wife didn't. Madeline preferred cats. Namely Tiffany, a moody Siamese who hated him, and proved it by clawing at him every time he moved within six inches of her.

Madeline threw a fit when he brought Susie Bear home. Dogs and kids are too much work, she told him. When she left, she took the cat with her.

"No," he said to Mercy, careful to keep his eyes on the road. "No kids. Not yet." That was the only good thing about his wife leaving. The possibility of children. Someday, with someone else. At least that's what his mother kept telling him. She never much liked Madeline or her cat. "You?"

"Not yet," repeated Mercy, and he could hear the catch in her voice.

"I have a niece about the same age as Baby Doe," he told her. "My brother's little girl. Charlotte. She's a pistol."

"My older brother has a little boy. Toby. He just turned two." She turned toward him and smiled. "He's just like my brother, hell on wheels, only shorter." Her smile faded. "I'm just trying to imagine the circumstances under which his parents would leave him alone in the woods."

"And?"

"All I can come up with is some kind of Hail Mary pass to save the child." Mercy shrugged.

"And you caught it?"

"Maybe."

Troy eased the truck into the parking lot at the trailhead. Nearly full now. The Fourth of July festivities were approaching full swing; there would be more people on the trail now. More people to muck up his crime scene.

"I taped off the scene," she said, again as if she could read his mind. It was a little unnerving.

He nodded, and for the second time that day, he and Susie Bear took up the rear as she and Elvis led them back up the trail.

But this time they were going uphill, along the steep incline that rose along the boundary between the Lye Brook Wilderness and the Appalachian Trail, before veering off into wilderness proper. It was nearly noon, and the sun was nearly straight above their heads. Mercy wore a blue Boston Red Sox cap now, covering most of her hair and shading her eyes. She moved with the steady rhythm of an experienced hiker, slim hips and long legs evident even under the loose cargo pants she'd tucked into her high-topped brown hiking boots. Troy was enjoying the view.

She stopped about ten feet beyond where he'd found her and the baby, and pointed to the tape she'd attached to the long hanging branch of a tall maple.

"This is where Elvis took me off-trail."

"Is it marked?"

"Yep."

This time, Troy and Susie Bear led the way, following the broken twigs and human and canine tracks in the muddy ground. Apart from their own footfalls and the panting of the dogs as they scrambled up and down the rocky terrain, the only sounds were the rushing of Lye Brook, the birds chattering in the trees, and the occasional distant shout of a happy hiker.

"Is this it?" he asked when they came to a clearing marked by the same duct tape Mercy had used along the trail.

"Uh, no."

"No?"

Mercy Carr stopped at the edge of the tape, and Elvis stopped, too, settling quietly at her feet. She removed her baseball cap and shook her head, red strands falling around her face. Her face shone with sweat, and she wiped her brow with the back of her hand.

"But you taped it off anyway. Why?" He looked at her with curiosity and waited for an answer. She didn't strike him as an alarmist, so he figured she must have a good reason.

She sighed and put her cap back on. "Explosives."

CHAPTER FIVE

Eㄨ xPLOSIVES?" NOW THAT WAS NOT THE ANSWER he expected
to hear. He stood very still and stared at the area she'd marked
off. The earth before him revealed nothing: no disturbed ground or
raised patches or subtle variations in the color of the soil significant
enough to indicate hidden explosives. At least not to his naked eye.
Susie Bear sensed his caution and trotted over to sit quietly at his side.

"Elvis alerted to explosives."

She said this casually, as if it happened every day. Maybe it did, for
her and Elvis. Or had, in the recent past. Troy waited for her to explain herself.

"Two tours in Afghanistan. Elvis here is a bomb-sniffer dog. EDD
extraordinaire."

"Explosive Detection Dog." Troy regarded the Belgian shepherd
with a new respect. He'd done a tour in Afghanistan himself, and knew
what important work these K-9 soldiers did. Good-looking dog, indeed. "And you?"

"U.S. Army corporal, retired." Mercy scratched Elvis behind his
ears. "We're both retired now."

"Retired," he repeated. "But you just happened to be searching for
explosives in the Lye Brook Wilderness."

"I don't know." She shrugged. "I mean, no, we were just out for a
walk in the woods. It's not like we were outside the wire on a mission, and he was sniffing out IEDs."

"And yet . . ." He let his voice trail off. He wanted her to explain
herself—and her dog.

"I really don't know what set him off." She ran her long fingers through her hair, pulling it away from her damp forehead. "I got worried. So I taped it off just in case."

"So you're not sure about the possibility of explosives."

"I don't know. Like I said, he's retired." Mercy looked down at Elvis and smiled. "He's a dog. He'll pick up the scent of a coyote or a rabbit or somebody's leftover lunch and take off after it."

"But this is different."

She crossed her arms, whether out of annoyance or aggression, he wasn't sure. The Belgian shepherd growled softly, sensing her change in mood. Susie Bear reacted in kind. Apparently their new friendship did not extend past the well-being of their handlers.

"Down," Mercy and Troy said in unison. Both dogs backed down.

"I'm listening," he said, knowing that even the remote possibility of explosives might trigger bad memories for both her and her dog.

"Look. Back in Afghanistan, when Elvis was doing training exercises or on patrol, he'd do what he's supposed to do. You know, when he got the right command."

"But you gave him no such order here today."

"Of course not," she said forcefully, causing both dogs to sit up straight again. "We left all that behind us."

Troy walked the length of the tape, staring at the ground again, and again seeing nothing that sparked any safety concerns on his part. But he was no bomb-sniffing dog. And neither was Susie Bear, who was learning to find shell casings when called upon to do so but had more experience looking for lost hikers or invasive species or illegally procured fish and game. People and plants and wildlife, not incendiaries.

"It's been a long time since Elvis got that order. Maybe he's just rusty."

"But you're not convinced."

"No," she admitted.

"Because?"

"Because he was the best," she said, her voice thick and her eyes shining with pride or tears or both. Again, Troy wasn't sure. He was usually better at reading people, but there was something about this woman that eluded him.

"The very best," she said, repeating herself.

He considered this. "Maybe somebody buried fireworks or lost a gun or—what's this got to do with our Baby Doe?"

"I don't know. Nothing, maybe."

"Weird."

"Agreed."

"Okay, I'll report this and have a team come check it out. Let's move on."

She pointed to the edge of the clearing. "We went this way when we heard her cry." She led them through the bramble where she and her dog had followed the siren song of a baby wailing in the wilderness. Ten minutes later they entered the small glade where Mercy and Elvis had found the child.

Troy scoured the ground. "Not much here." But on the other side of the opening in the trees there were footmarks.

"I followed those tracks to the stream, where they ended," she said. "That's when I decided to turn back and bring the baby in."

"Show me."

She took him through a scrub of young birch and small spruce to the stream. He lamented the fact that Mercy and Elvis had already been this way twice, and this second traipsing was obscuring what was already a trail growing cold. But there was nothing to be done about it.

An investigation at the stream's edge revealed nothing. He waded across, Susie Bear on his heels, while Mercy and Elvis waited on the opposite bank. But there were no traces of any human traffic here. Susie Bear ran up and down along the banks of the stream, trying to pick up the scent where someone may have exited the water. But apparently she found nothing. He and his dog splashed back, and she repeated the exercise along this side.

Nothing.

"Only one more thing to try." Troy pulled the baby's blanket out of his pack. "Here's hoping that the scent of whoever brought her out here is still on this."

"The baby's scent is on it, as is mine," she said. "And yours."

"I know. It's a long shot. But if any dog can do it, Susie Bear can."

He held the blanket under the Newfie mutt's nose for a long moment. Then he pulled it away and said simply, "Search."

She went to work, nose sniffing, clumping up to Mercy, and then over to Troy.

"Search," he said again, and gave the dog another opportunity to smell the blanket.

Susie Bear snorted, wagged her tail, and went back to work. Broad snout twitching, she lumbered along the edge of the stream for about a hundred yards, and then turned into another blowdown area littered with fallen limbs. Elvis, who'd been shadowing her along with Mercy and Troy, now bounded after Susie Bear.

"Call him back," Troy told Mercy.

"Sorry." She whistled for the Belgian shepherd, but he ignored her.

Troy ran after the two dogs. He could hear Mercy jogging after him. The marshy ground was strewn with rocks and branches, and he slipped and slid along the uneven surface. By the time he caught up to them, the energetic canines were playing together in a corner of the blowdown area lined with black raspberry bushes laden with fruit due to ripen in the next month.

Susie Bear was kicking at a pile of pine needles and debris. Elvis was digging around in the brush, spraying dirt and twigs as he clawed at the earth.

At the sound of his approach, the Newfie mutt dropped to all fours. She looked at him, her dark eyes lively, her black feathery tail whacking the forest floor and whipping up dead leaves with every *whomp*. Elvis ignored Troy, intent on his burrowing and the growing hole at his feet.

He realized that they might not be playing.

"What are they doing?" Mercy appeared at his side, slightly out of breath.

"I'm not sure."

"Your dog seems to be alerting to something."

"Yours is just making a mess."

They stepped forward together. He squatted down to take a closer look at whatever was preoccupying Susie Bear. He grabbed a stick and pushed around the loose soil, scraping away bark and brush.

"I don't see anything." He looked at the dog. "Nothing here, girl."

She whined, and wagged her long tail even harder.

"Always trust your dog," Mercy said as she turned her attention to Elvis. Troy followed her gaze, and watched the sleek shepherd nose a long bone from a slight mound of dirt and leaves, about a foot from where Susie Bear waited patiently for Troy to get a clue.

"That looks like . . ." She hesitated.

"A femur bone." He finished the observation for her.

"Come," said Mercy in a stern voice Troy suspected had kept wayward soldiers as well as shepherds in line.

Elvis trotted over to her.

"Drop it," they ordered in unison.

To his credit, the shepherd dropped the bone.

"Human," she said with confidence.

"Probably not."

She raised an eyebrow at him.

"Could be from a bear or a deer. Our bones are more like theirs than you might think." People were always calling in about bones they'd found in the woods or on their property, and nine times out of ten they were not human.

"Uh-huh." She was obviously not convinced.

"Let's take a closer look." He could feel Mercy's cool blue eyes on him as he retrieved a pair of plastic gloves from his pack and slipped them on his hands. Then he picked up the femur bone gingerly. He raised it up in front of him.

The bone was more than twenty inches long.

"What do you think, about twenty-two, twenty-three inches long?"

"Yeah."

"That's a tall person." Mercy tilted her head, challenging him to disagree with her.

He couldn't. She was probably right. The bone was most likely human. A tall human, given the fact that the average femur was a little shorter than this one. But he didn't say anything; he just waited to see if she could tell him why.

"Oh, I get it, this is a test." She grinned at him. "Okay, the distal condyles are asymmetrical, which means this creature walked on two legs, not four." She pointed to the bony projections at the bottom of the bone, which looked a bit like knuckles. They were indeed asymmetrical, unlike their counterparts in bears and deer.

"That's right." He wondered how she knew that. He was about to ask her when Susie Bear barked. She still lay at the edge of what Troy now suspected could be a shallow grave, her tail still whomping away. Holding the bone gingerly, he walked over to her. Mercy and Elvis followed at a distance.

"Good job, girl." He scruffed the thick fringe on Susie Bear's head and gave her a treat from his pocket.

"Always trust your dog," Mercy repeated.

Troy tossed a treat at Elvis, too, and the handsome boy caught it easily.

Mercy came up beside him, removing her cap and slipping it into her pocket. She leaned in close to examine the bone more carefully. So close he could have reached out and touched her hair, which smelled faintly of lavender and lemon.

She pointed to a clear marking on the bone, her forefinger fractions of an inch from the femur. "Looks like an old break."

"Don't touch it." He stepped away from her.

Mercy snorted. "I wasn't going to touch it."

Elvis growled at him. Susie Bear sat up, ears alert, and growled back at the shepherd.

"Quiet," she told the Malinois. He settled down, but still appeared ready to pounce at any moment. "Sorry. He can be a little high-strung sometimes."

"PTSD?" He knew that dogs could be as susceptible to PTSD as human soldiers. It would explain why Mercy was so protective of the shepherd, and why he alerted to explosives in a forest halfway around the world from the battlefield. Not to mention that Malinois from working lines were bred to be dynamic and driven dogs with a strong prey/chase drive.

"Yeah." Mercy stiffened. "But he's doing much better."

They say that the best working dogs are the ones that either want to chase the ball or kill the ball. The game warden knew that Susie Bear was the former and Elvis was the latter. Killing the ball was what he was bred and trained to do.

Troy also knew that some of these war dogs never recovered from their experiences—and never could adapt to civilian life once they were injured or aged out and were ready for retirement. Some remained so combative that they had to be put down instead. Maybe Elvis was still overly aggressive, too.

He wasn't sure about the dog. And he wasn't sure about his pretty handler, either. He wondered if she suffered from PTSD, too. He'd seen a lot of soldiers fall apart both on and off the battlefield. Either they couldn't handle what happened to them over there—or they couldn't handle what happened to them when they came back here. He'd have to find out more about Mercy Carr—and exactly where she'd been and what she'd been up to since that summer at the town pool a lifetime ago.

"That break might help us identify the victim," she said, changing the subject.

There was no *us* here, he thought. There was just him and his congenial dog in the woods with this woman and her unpredictable dog. He didn't know what to think. Too many variables and too little data. He sighed.

"Babies, bombs, bones." Troy looked at Mercy. "You and your dog have had a very busy day."

CHAPTER SIX

MERCY STOOD WITH ELVIS AT THE EDGE of the crime scene, behind the tape, as the Crime Scene Search Team sorted through the detritus of the forest floor for evidence. They'd roped off a large circle about sixty feet in diameter around the slight mound where the dogs had found the bones. At first they concentrated their efforts on that spot, but after coming up with only a couple of finger bones and hair, they'd widened the search area.

"Bone fragments everywhere," Troy was saying to the medical examiner, a short, cheerful woman of about fifty named Dr. Darling. "Some bear must have gotten to the body fairly early on."

"We may not find many more of the large bones left intact," said the medical examiner. "You know how much black bears love their marrow."

Mercy knew they were probably right. She'd spent many a summer helping her grandmother at her veterinary practice—and she'd learned a lot about animals, wild and domestic, in the process. Bears were omnivores that fed on nuts and berries and ants and honey, but they weren't above feasting on small mammals like fawn and moose calves, rats and rabbits and more, when the opportunity presented itself. But they usually didn't bother with bigger animals unless the prey was already injured or dead. When their superior noses led them to a dead moose, bears would rip through the thick hide that kept other scavengers out and binge on the meat inside.

They didn't swing their meal around like coyotes or wolves; they preferred to straddle the dead animal to protect it from rivals, or grab a big piece and go sit down, enjoy it, and then come back for more. Some even napped on the carcass between snacks. They especially liked the marrow, so they'd crush the bones to get at it, leaving not much but shards behind.

The question was, how did the victim die? Did the bear kill the victim—or was the victim already dead when the bear came along for a sweet postmortem snack? Black bears rarely attacked humans, and then usually only when protecting their cubs. From what she knew about bears and what she knew about humans, she'd bet money that human nature was to blame here, not Mother Nature.

"But the remains are strewn all over," said Troy. "Maybe we'll get lucky."

"We'll keep on looking." Dr. Darling squatted on the ground, sorting contentedly through the remains, her foghorn tenor easily heard across the clearing.

"This must be a fairly old burial site," he told her, "given the state of the remains."

"What we've found so far has been picked pretty clean, so they've probably been here awhile," she conceded.

Dr. Darling reminded Mercy of a pug. The game warden, on the other hand, was your classic Labrador, good-hearted and good-looking in the earnest and energetic way of retrievers. Martinez always compared people to canines—he'd called Mercy a pit bull, loyal, smart, and misunderstood—and she'd picked up the bad habit. But there was something to it.

She remembered the first day she'd seen Troy at the Northshire Center Pool all those years ago. She'd been sitting on a deck chair tucked under a blue umbrella close to the chain-link fence surrounding the pool area, down by the shallow end of the Olympic-sized pool, where the moms gathered with their toddlers on the steps. Away from the middle depths, where raucous prepubescent boys played water polo, and away from the deep end, where high school guys splashed high school girls sunning on deck chairs nearby.

Mercy was reading *Romeo and Juliet*, the play that obsessed her at the time, appealing as it did to her teenager's overactive romantic imagination. Damien Landry, the skinny, six-foot-and-still-growing fourteen-year-old and scourge of her existence, towered above her, casting a shadow over her pages. *O! I am fortune's fool . . .*

"Whatcha reading?" Damien grabbed the book out of her hands and held it up just out of her reach. "Shakespeare?" He snickered. "You are such a dork."

Takes one to know one, she thought.

Damien read a couple of lines aloud, stumbling over *With love's light wings did I o'er-perch these walls; For stony limits cannot hold love out . . .*

Mercy laughed out loud.

"What's so funny?" Damien slammed the book shut and backed up until he hit the edge of the pool. He straightened out his long bony right arm and dangled the slim volume over the water.

She jumped to her feet. "Wait."

"Don't even think about it." The lifeguard—the one named Troy—placed a large well-formed hand on Damien's shoulder and squeezed. "Give me the book."

Wincing, Damien handed it over.

"Go get yourself a Coke or something."

Damien strutted away, and Troy handed the book back to her with a smile. "You know he likes you, right?"

"If you say so."

He grinned at her. "Are you ever going to go in?"

"Sure." She watched him as he leaped back into his chair, and then she headed for the diving board. Whereupon she executed a perfect pike dive. When she came back up out of the water, Troy gave her a thumbs-up.

Classic Labrador.

He really hadn't changed much at all since then, Mercy thought. He'd filled out a little, but he still had the athletic build, that outdoorsy tan, those warm brown eyes. Although there was a hint of sadness around them now.

Elvis sat leashed at her side, ears up, watching Susie Bear, also banished to the far side of the clearing, her lead tied to a tree. The Newfie mutt's eyes—like hers—were on the game warden, although from time to time the big dog snuck a glance at the Belgian shepherd.

The doctor and the Crime Scene techs kept on sifting and sorting. Troy nodded at Dr. Darling, then strode over to Mercy. She wondered how he'd treat her this time. He seemed to alternate between liking her and questioning her every move. Not that she blamed him. She was the only common denominator in three very suspicious circumstances:

an abandoned baby, an explosives alert, and unidentified remains. Not to mention her erratic dog Elvis. Troy probably thought she was as mixed up as the dog.

"You should go on home," he told her.

"I don't think so." She didn't want to go, not really. This was the most interesting thing that had happened to her since coming home from Afghanistan.

"You've got to be exhausted."

"Not really." She petted Elvis's head. "We're fine."

"I could order you off the scene."

She knew he didn't really want to do that. She smiled at him. "Are you going to arrest me?"

He smiled back. "Okay, don't say I didn't try." Troy shrugged and turned away.

She could read the strain of the day in his shoulders. They'd both fed and watered their dogs with supplies from their packs, but not themselves. Elvis and Susie Bear were resting now, leashed but alert.

There was no rest for Troy or Mercy. Not yet. She knew he must be tired. And hungry. She certainly was, not that she would ever admit as much to him. She refused to go home until she was sure that there was nothing more she or her shepherd could do.

"Victory!" Dr. Darling's celebratory shout boomed across the clearing.

Mercy watched the game warden stride quickly over to the doctor. "What is it?" he asked.

She held up a dusty roundish pale object in her gloved hands. "An intact skull. More or less."

Troy said something in reply, but she missed most of it. His back was to her now, and he spoke quietly. She couldn't hear what he was saying to the doctor. She leaned forward across the tape. "Warden Warner!"

He turned to look her way.

"Come on!"

The medical examiner grinned at Mercy and raised her already re-sounding voice. "An adult male, shot in the head."

Troy held up his hands in mock surrender. "Okay, but watch your step."

"Stay," she said to Elvis and joined them in the circle.

Dr. Darling was on her feet now, cupping the cracked dome in her open palms. "You can see the entrance wound here." She pointed to a round hole in the crown of the skull. Long fissures radiated out from around its center in a telltale starburst pattern.

"I guess the black bears are off the hook." Mercy wasn't surprised. People were far crueler to each other than animals were to them.

"Yep." She smiled at Mercy and tipped the skull forward to reveal its back side.

"No exit wound?" asked Troy.

"No." The medical examiner beamed as she tipped the skull forward again. "Hear that?"

"You mean that scraping sound? What is it?"

"The bullet is inside." Mercy laughed. "That's wild."

"But a stroke of luck for us."

"Maybe," said Troy. "If we can find the weapon or the casing."

"Weird that the bear who crushed the other bones for marrow didn't crack the skull to get at the brains."

Troy gave her a sharp look. "Maybe the bear was interrupted."

"Who interrupts a bear?" asked the doctor.

"Poachers," said Mercy and Troy in unison.

"I'LL KNOW MORE when we get back to the lab," the medical examiner said. "But don't expect any answers too soon."

"All right."

"Everyone's taking off for the long weekend," she explained to Mercy.

"Right." Or pulling extra duty in Bennington. Troy was going to need her help up here, whether he liked it or not.

A tall, skinny man in a Tyvek suit approached them in a seemingly purposeful slow and steady gait that Mercy suspected drove the game warden crazy. She smiled.

"What do you have for us?" asked Troy, failing to hide the note of impatience in his voice.

"Bob," said the doctor pointedly, "this is Mercy Carr. Mercy, meet Bob, head of the Crime Scene Search Team.

"Pleasure." He did not look her in the eye or move to shake her hand.

"Hi."

Bob dismissed her and addressed Troy and Dr. Darling. "Not much left of the victim's clothes, and the boots are so common as to be useless in terms of identification."

"Any teeth?" asked the medical examiner.

"Just fragments. Any left in the skull?"

Mercy knew that teeth were often the easiest way to identify a victim, thanks to dental records. And the fact that even if DNA couldn't be found anywhere else, it could usually be retrieved from inside the teeth.

"A few. But that's not all we found left in the skull." Dr. Darling told him about the bullet, which Bob acknowledged without comment.

"You didn't walk all the way over here to tell us about teeth fragments," said the game warden.

Or to meet me, thought Mercy.

Bob held out his gloved hands, palms open. There revealed in his cupped fingers was what appeared to be a tarnished pewter belt buckle.

In unison the three of them leaned toward the ornament for closer inspection.

"Is that a pine tree?" asked Dr. Darling.

"Yes, set against the mountains," Mercy said. "One of the classic symbols of Vermont."

Troy peered at the buckle and read the words that ran underneath the pine tree, still so grimy Mercy could barely make them out. "'Freedom and Unity.'"

"Interesting," said Dr. Darling.

"That it?" asked Troy.

"For now," said Bob. "I'll bag this and get on with it."

"Thanks."

"Later," he said.

They watched him amble back across the crime scene.

"I'll be wrapping up soon," Dr. Darling told them. "See you back at the ranch." The medical examiner tapped her forehead in a casual salute and went back to her work.

Troy ushered Mercy back to Elvis. "Now you really do have to go home."

She didn't say anything. But she didn't move, either.

"Look, there's nothing more to do here." He frowned. "The crime scene techs are about finished, and the bomb squad says they haven't found any explosives."

"Nothing?" She stared at him. "I find that hard to believe."

He looked down at his boots. Same tell as Martinez. Mercy knew he was lying, or at least not telling her the whole truth. "What aren't you telling me?"

"Look, I've already crossed over the line here." Troy straightened up and looked at her with those warm brown eyes. "Besides, it's out of my hands. The Vermont State Police are running this show now. It's their crime scene."

"But you're still here."

"I'm not a civilian."

You're not a detective, either, thought Mercy. But she didn't say that. They'd found these bones, and there was a responsibility that came along with that. Whether you were a game warden or a civilian.

"'Blessed be the man that spares these stones,'" she quoted quietly. "'And cursed be he that moves my bones.'"

"What's that supposed to mean?"

"Shakespeare."

"What's Shakespeare got to do with anything?"

"Somebody killed this man and then abandoned his body in the woods. Robbed him of the dignity of a decent burial. In effect failing to spare his stones and honor his bones."

"And cursing himself in the process. I get it."

"That curse begins with us." She stood a little taller and leaned forward. Elvis growled softly. He was on the leash now, sitting by her side, giving the warden his evil eye. Martinez used to say that your emotions traveled right down the leash from handler to dog, which is why Mercy knew she had to control her feelings, notably the negative ones. She made an effort to keep her voice steady and asked the question again. "What aren't you telling me?"

"What's wrong with your dog?"

"He's just being protective." Mercy willed herself to loosen her hold on the leash, a signal to the dog that she was calm so he should be, too. The fierce Belgian shepherd had always stood ready to defend his sergeant, but today he'd indicated he was prepared to defend her as well. Maybe he was settling in with her, after all. "Quiet, Elvis."

"Are you hungry?" Troy grinned at her. "I'm starving. How about we go back to town and grab something to eat? For us and the dogs. My treat."

She knew he was changing the subject, but she also knew an olive branch when she saw it. "Sure."

"I've got to drop by the hospital later anyway," he said. "And we can go over your statement."

And she could drill him over dinner.

CHAPTER SEVEN

MERCY STARTED GOING TO THE VERMONTER Drive-In out on Depot Street when she was just a kid. Famous for its sandwiches and milkshakes, the popular joint drew locals and summer people every day rain or shine during the season. All of Vermont went into mourning on November 1, when the place shut down for the winter—and celebrated even if the snow was still falling when it reopened on April 1.

She hadn't been back here in years. The place hadn't changed much. Calling it a drive-in was a glamorous misnomer; the restaurant was really just a glorified lean-to with a large window fronting the parking lot, where she stood in line with Troy and at least a dozen other folks to order. The dogs waited in their respective vehicles, Elvis alert on the front seat of her Jeep, dark muzzle jutting out the passenger window, and Susie Bear curled up on the backseat of the game warden's truck, obviously more confident that there was a burger in her near future than the ever-vigilant Elvis.

"Come on up, Warden." Lillian Jenkins, the owner, waved Troy up to the window. Everyone knew Lillian, an energetic and effusive petite brunette who'd been feeding the good citizens of Vermont in various capacities for decades. She ran the drive-in during the summer and the local book club the rest of the year. In a state where winters were interminable and access to cable and even satellite TV could be spotty, reading was a favorite pastime. Lillian also served on every committee in town, from the Friends of the Library to the historical society, and even authored a popular regional cookbook that was a New England indie bookstore hit. If there was anything of artistic note going on in southern Vermont, she knew about it.

"Hi, Lillian." Troy smiled, but he flushed and Mercy could tell he was embarrassed by the preferential treatment. "No need for this."

"Nonsense." Lillian turned to address the long line of patient customers in a voice far bigger than her person. "This is Warden Troy Warner, and he earned first place in line in perpetuity when he removed a rabid bat from the Porta-Potty out back before it bit anybody." She swiveled her attention back to Troy. "Who's your friend?"

"Mercy Carr," he said.

"I know you." Lillian gave her a long look. "You're a Fleury."

Mercy smiled. "Patience Fleury O'Sullivan is my grandmother."

"The veterinarian?" asked Troy.

"One and the same," answered Lillian, her eyes still on Mercy. "It's been a while, young lady."

"I was living out of state."

"Uh-huh."

"I'm back now." She knew those were the only words that ever placated a native Vermonter like Lillian, who could never understand why anyone would ever leave paradise.

"I went to school with Patience, up in Hyde Park." Lillian grinned. "You got your grandmother's good looks. But that red hair is all your granddaddy."

"Yes, ma'am." She waited for the inevitable red-haired and hot-headed comment.

"I hope you didn't get the O'Sullivan temper to go with it."

And there it was. Her grandfather had been the sheriff in Lamoille County for decades and as many people loved him as hated him. He'd died nearly twenty years ago, but memories in Vermont were long and hard, just like the winters.

"No, ma'am." She could see Troy holding back a laugh.

Lillian tapped her pencil against her pad. "Two cheeseburgers, fries, and chocolate shakes?"

"Make that four cheeseburgers, fully dressed," said Troy. "We got a couple of dogs to feed."

Lillian looked out into the parking lot and spotted Elvis. "That sweet shepherd yours?"

"Yes, ma'am." Again, Mercy waited.

"Now that's a Fleury for you." Lillian bestowed a warm smile on her. "Have a seat out back with the warden. And feel free to bring the dogs."

TEN MINUTES LATER, all four of them were gathered around the lone picnic table behind the burger shack that Lillian reserved for visiting dignitaries and such. At least that's what the laminated tabletop sign said. The weathered table had seen better days, but it sat at the edge of Lillian's potager garden, a beauty of knots and raised beds that produced a bounty of vegetables and herbs that made the Vermonter Drive-In menu justifiably famous.

Certainly Elvis and Susie Bear enjoyed their meals, which they gobbled down in ten seconds flat. The Newfie mutt plopped down at Troy's feet, ready to lap up any stray fries that might come her way. In stately contrast, Elvis dropped down into his classic Sphinx position, alert as ever.

"How's the baby?" Mercy knew Troy had received several texts, and she assumed that at least one of them concerned the infant she'd found.

"She's doing well. But they're still keeping her overnight."

"And then she goes into the system." She sipped at the chocolate shake to chase down the bitter taste that the idea of handing the baby over to Child Protective Services left in her mouth. "Will you even try to find her mother?"

"Of course. They've already got some volunteers doing a grid search of the area."

She jumped to her feet, startling Elvis, who scrambled up to join her. "We should go help."

"Sit down. If there's anything to find, they'll find it." Troy waved them both back to their meal. "You need to eat."

Mercy knew he was right, but she didn't like him telling her what to do. She stabbed a pair of french fries into the little paper cup of ketchup and popped them in her mouth. Elvis watched her, his eyes on the fries. She raised her forearm, palm up, toward the sky—the hand signal for *sit*—and the Malinois sat up.

"Do you turn everything into a training exercise?" Troy watched her as she rewarded Elvis with a french fry. Susie Bear watched, too, and promptly sat up.

"Give a dog a burger, but make him work for the fries," she said. Another one of Martinez's rules. "Besides, what he really works for is his Kong."

"Well, hell." Troy held his palm out to Susie Bear, offering her a fry of her own. "It's all about food for this one." She lapped it up with that huge tongue. Troy wiped his hand on a napkin and looked at Mercy. "We'll find the mother."

"Alive?"

"There was no sign of foul play." He chomped away at his cheeseburger in the same reasonable and resolute manner in which he appeared to approach everything else.

"Except for the corpse and explosives."

"Alleged explosives."

"So you think it's all a big coincidence?" She refused to believe that, even it was a possibility. And his believing it angered her. She could feel her face redden. The telltale curse of the redhead. It wasn't that she was more emotional than other people, it was just that those emotions played out in pink right on her face. She bowed her head away from the game warden, toward Elvis, letting her hair fall across her brow. She lowered her hand, and the shepherd dropped down at her feet, earning another deep-fried treat.

Susie Bear plopped back down as well. Troy frowned at Mercy but handed his dog another fry anyway.

"That's enough," he told her. "I happen to like fries."

"I can't help it if your dog knows an alpha when she sees one."

"Very funny," he said with a laugh, and set about systematically destroying the rest of his burger and fries.

She focused on her food and they ate in silence under the watchful eyes of their four-legged friends.

"I don't believe in coincidence," Troy said finally.

"Neither do I." Mercy tapped the surface of the table with her index finger. "Someone took good care of that baby."

"Yeah, right up until they left her in the woods to die." His voice was calm but there was a note of disgust there that cheered her.

"Maybe."

"Hail Mary pass theory again?" Troy turned his attention to his milkshake.

"Maybe they didn't leave her to die but to be found."

He stopped midslurp. "By you?"

"By somebody." She thought about it. "It is a holiday week. Maybe they figured someone was bound to come by sooner or later."

"Seems risky. The Lye Brook Wilderness is not nearly as popular as the national forest it borders. Why not pick a more well-traveled route?"

"I don't know." She took a bite of her burger. "But some of us hike there regularly anyway. Maybe they knew that."

The warden considered this. "No evidence of a struggle."

"And they left diapers and bottles and formula and wipes—everything she'd need, at least in the short term."

"Yeah."

"Elvis and I have hiked up to those falls nearly every morning since spring. We leave at dawn and take the same route, more or less. We don't usually see many people on the way up because it's so early. But we glimpse more people later on the way down. Sometimes with babies. Not often. But it does happen from time to time."

"Just because you don't see them doesn't mean they don't see you. Especially if they're off-trail." He seemed to be warming to her theory.

"True enough."

"We've got the baby clothes and the carrier. Maybe that will give us something."

"What about baby footprints?"

"There's really no database," he said. "But we can check the birth records from around six months ago, when the doc says she was probably born."

"I could take her," she said. "I mean, instead of her going to Child Protective Services." Which was ridiculous, since she didn't know that much about babies.

He eyed her with surprise. "That's not really how it works. But I suspect you know that."

"I did keep this baby alive until you came along."

"You saved her life," he said. "No question about that. And maybe her mother was counting on that."

They both fell silent at that.

Finally Mercy spoke. "If her mother left her there for me and Elvis to find, then she must be in trouble."

"Which leads us right back to the bones and bombs."

"But you said there were no bombs."

"I said they didn't find any explosives."

"But they did find something."

"You never give up, do you?" Troy looked at her with a mix of admiration and annoyance.

She didn't say anything. Just waited him out.

"I couldn't tell you at the crime scene. Too many people around." He paused. "I probably shouldn't be telling you now."

"But you will." She leaned toward him. "You know you want to."

He stiffened, and she laughed. To his credit, he laughed, too. "They found traces of PETN, a chemical compound often found—"

"Often found in explosives," Mercy interrupted. "Yeah, I know."

More important, Elvis knew. As a sniffer dog, he was trained to find weapons and to detect a number of explosives odors. When he alerted to a scent, that scent was typically gunmetal; detonating cord; smokeless powder; dynamite; nitroglycerin; TNT; RDX, a chemical compound often found in military-grade explosives; TATP, used in peroxide-based explosives; and PETN.

PETN stood for pentaerythritol tetranitrate, a powerful explosive similar in structure to nitroglycerin and used by everyone from miners and the military to terrorists.

"Of course." Troy looked over at Elvis. "That explains why he found the PETN. But it doesn't explain why he found the bones."

"Susie Bear found the bones."

"But Elvis was there, too." He frowned. "Is he trained to find cadavers?"

"Not exactly. That is, I don't know," she said. Like all military working dogs, Elvis was trained as a patrol dog, to guard checkpoints and gates, detect intruders, secure bases, apprehend suspects, and attack on command. But beyond that, most military working dogs were specialists; they were trained to sniff out drugs or cadavers or explosives. For Elvis, it was all about explosives. At least that's what Martinez told her.

Troy stood up, gathered up the litter of his meal, and dropped it all into the trash can that flanked the picnic table. Turning back to face her, he placed his large hands on the table and leaned in toward her. "What does that mean, exactly?"

Elvis promptly sat up and growled. Susie Bear reacted, too, lumbering to her feet and facing off with the Belgian shepherd as if to say, *Dude, what's up.*

"It means that I don't know." Mercy stood up, too, and steadied the shepherd with a pat on his head. "Not for sure."

Troy leaned back, straightening his spine and standing up. He looked like cops looked when you lied to them. Unimpressed.

"What kind of dog handler are you?"

CHAPTER EIGHT

I'M NOT A DOG HANDLER," Mercy said.

"But you said you were an MP." He looked confused now. "And that checked out."

She sat back down, silent. Elvis stayed on his feet. So did Susie Bear. "I've got work to do."

"Please sit. Let me explain." She gave the hand signal for *down* again, and both dogs obliged. Troy did not.

Mercy would have to tell him everything, like it or not. She didn't want the warden to lose confidence in her. Or Elvis.

He glanced at his watch. "You've got five minutes." He sat back down and folded his hands on the table.

"Thank you."

Troy waited. The dogs waited. All three pairs of brown eyes on her now.

Mercy looked past them all, out over Lillian's potager garden. "I was an MP stationed in Afghanistan. The only female MP at the base. So in addition to the usual convoy duty, I also conducted searches of female suspects and helped train female Afghanis for law enforcement."

"And Elvis?"

"He was one of the sniffer dogs attached to our unit. Martinez was his handler."

At the sound of his handler's name, Elvis sat back up again, ears up. Troy noticed, and Mercy noticed his noticing.

"Sergeant Juan Miguel Pedro Martinez," she said. "From Las Vegas, by way of the Mezquital Valley in Mexico."

"What happened to the sergeant?" Troy's voice was quiet and respectful.

"He died in action." She reached down and placed her hand on Elvis's fine head. "One year ago tomorrow."

"I'm sorry."

"His team was en route to a village that intel told us had been infiltrated by the enemy," she said. "I went along to search the women. We got ambushed on the way and needed to move to a more defensible position. Our only way out was under fire, through a couple of miles of poppy fields. In Afghanistan, poppy fields were usually rife with homemade explosives—crude but deadly."

"Not good. I did a tour in Afghanistan. Plenty of poppy fields."

"So you know," she said. "Elvis guided us through the fields to a stronger location, where we at least had a chance. But then word came down that we'd stumbled into a nest of high-value targets. We needed to take them out in an ambush of our own. As soon as we breached the perimeter of the compound, we came under fire. We fired back as we raided the compound, with Elvis going into the largest of the structures and alerting to an IED immediately. This allowed us to secure the building and move on to the others. Elvis kept on working and alerted to an underground arsenal with dozens of AK-47 assault rifles, multiple pressure plates, and nearly a hundred pounds of explosives."

"Elvis did good."

"He did. Martinez was so proud of him." Her hand was still on the shepherd's handsome head. The feel of his silky fur on her palm steadied her. "The explosives team took over then, and he and Elvis left the building to help conduct an outdoor search of the compound. A sniper took him out. They dragged him to safety, but there was only so much the medics could do. They had to get him and the rest of our injured out of there. Elvis helped the team establish a safe zone where the helicopter bound for the hospital unit could land."

Mercy hesitated, and removed her hand from the shepherd's head with a final scratch of his ears. She folded her arms around herself, suddenly cold. "They got him out of there, but it was too late. He died on the operating table."

"And then you and the dog came home." There was a question in his voice.

"I was sent home to recuperate from my own injury." At the look on Troy's face, she was quick to reassure him. "I'm fine."

"And Elvis?"

"He was never really the same again. They sent him back to the defense contractor, but I'd promised Martinez I'd take care of him myself. So I bullied them until they let me have him."

"His family didn't want the dog?"

"He was born here. But his parents were not. They worked in Las Vegas in the hotels. Undocumented workers. When they lost their jobs, they had to go back to Mexico. They're still there."

"You were obviously very close. I'm so sorry for your loss."

"We weren't supposed to be together. Non-fraternization policy, you know."

The game warden nodded.

"So we kept our feelings to ourselves." Mercy willed away the unshed tears gathering in the corners of her eyes. "As long as we were deployed together."

Elvis moved his nose onto her lap. Mercy turned away from Troy. She cupped Elvis's dark muzzle in her hands and looked into the dog's deep brown eyes. "We were going to be married as soon as our assignments changed. He put in for a transfer to train dog handlers at Lackland. He was so good with the dogs and the handlers, it was just a matter of time before they sent him to Texas. He insisted we wait until we could do it right."

Mercy released the shepherd and looked up at Troy. "And now he's dead. Nothing right about that."

"I'm sorry," he said again.

"So I'm no dog handler." She stood up abruptly. "Elvis is stuck with me, and I'm learning as fast as I can."

"That explains all the training." Troy came to his feet and reached over to pat Elvis's head. "It's not easy to take on a dog like this, who's already bonded so tightly with his handler. He's a lucky dog."

"It's the least I could do. But I've had help. My grandmother, of course. And I've been working with him one on one, the way Martinez used to."

"That's great. Do you do agility training with him?"

"Not beyond the usual obstacles on the trail. You know, jumping over logs, streams, whatever's in the way."

"You might want to try Two Swords K-9 Training. Jake over there works with a lot of dogs like Elvis. Susie Bear loves it."

Mercy knew that agility training had been part of the Malinois's training at Lackland. "I'll think about it."

"We'd be happy to take you guys over there anytime."

"Thanks. He might like that."

Susie Bear barked as if she knew what they were saying—and maybe she did, or maybe she just wanted more fries. They both laughed. Mercy divvied up the rest of her french fries between the two dogs and ditched her own mess into the trash bin while Troy checked his messages.

"Time to go," he said, his face hard with an emotion she couldn't quite name. But whatever it was, it wasn't good.

"What's wrong?"

"The baby's gone."

CHAPTER NINE

THE CHILDREN'S WING OF THE NORTHSHIRE MEDICAL CENTER was on the third floor. Troy and Mercy stood in a small office decorated with the same bright and cheerful jungle murals as the rest of the ward, interviewing head pediatric nurse Anne Dougherty about Baby Doe's disappearance. He'd warned Mercy to let him handle the questioning, and she'd complied, more or less.

But so far they'd gotten nowhere. No one knew anything or saw anything.

Troy was frustrated, but he hoped it didn't show on his face as clearly as it did on Mercy's. Even her freckles looked angry now, dark dots against pale skin flushed with impatience.

"There's a security code to get into the ward," she was saying to the nurse, although it sounded more like an accusation. "How could anyone get in?"

He cleared his throat, a signal to Mercy to back off.

"Yes," said Anne. "There is a security code. But one of our seriously ill patients took a turn for the worse, and we had to admit several young people injured in that big accident on Route 313. Much more coming and going than usual. Whoever took her must have slipped in then."

Troy nodded. "I heard about that."

"Terrible." Anne folded her hands into the pockets of her scrubs. "We were focused on getting everyone in and evaluated and treated as quickly as possible."

"Understood," he said. Anne was an implacable middle-aged woman with kind eyes and a firm manner clearly designed to deal with young patients and their worried parents. Mercy may not have been Baby Doe's mother, but she sure acted like she was. Troy wondered how someone so tough on the outside and yet so soft on the inside ever survived combat. But she had.

"Have we spoken to everyone on duty?" He stepped forward, taking back control of the interview. Mercy stayed where she was.

"Everyone but Mary Hodges," said Anne. "She left her shift early to go on vacation. Before we knew that the baby was gone."

"Where?" asked Troy and Mercy in unison.

So much for letting him run his own interview, he thought.

Anne checked her watch. "She's on the Long Trail somewhere between here and Canada by now."

"We'll want to talk to her as soon as we can." He wrote down Hodges's cell phone number as Anne dictated it. "Let's see the room where the baby was staying."

"Of course." Anne led them out of her office and down a long hall lined with patient rooms on one side and offices on the other. All the doors were painted bright colors, reminding him of the poster of front doors in Dublin that hung framed over the table in his grandmother Maeve's kitchen. She was his only Irish relation in a sea of Yankee forbearers who dated back to pre-Revolutionary days—and she never let him forget it.

The baby's room held a single white metal adjustable crib and the usual medical paraphernalia, overseen by a tower of tan and orange giraffes nibbling at the leaves of green acacia trees painted on the walls. A cheerful room, despite the hospital smell and the disheartening fact that its occupants were always sick children.

The crib was empty and unmade.

"Everything here looks like hospital issue," he said.

"Yes," confirmed Anne.

"What happened to the backpack carrier?" asked Mercy. "And the baby's clothes? The teethers?"

"We keep the patient's personal belongings in here." Anne opened the small closet at the side of the bed. "Nothing here. Whoever took the baby must have taken the baby's things as well."

"Sounds like a domestic snatch," said Troy. "So she's probably physically safe, at least."

"We've got to find her," said Mercy.

"We will," he said. "Starting with an AMBER Alert."

MERCY WAS NOT happy when Troy sent them home. Nothing she could say could talk him out of it. He kept telling her to get a good night's sleep and they'd touch base in the morning. Which she knew was cop code for "You're just a civilian, let us pros handle it." She didn't expect to hear from him any time soon. So she'd have to carry on herself, with Elvis as her right-hand canine.

The search for whoever had left the baby in the woods had turned up nothing, and odds were whoever had the baby now was long gone from southern Vermont. But she still had to try.

She turned the Jeep into the long drive that led up to the old log cabin on the hill. The small house—originally a hunting camp—sat on fifty acres of forest land fronted by a stream that ran along the back of the barn. She'd bought the property when she came home from Afghanistan, drawn to its Lincoln Log charm and desolate isolation in equal measure. Here she hid out with Elvis and an assortment of noisy birds, aggressive squirrels, wild turkeys, hungry deer, and the occasional black bear for company. And she liked it that way.

The wild turkeys were the ones most likely to overrun the property. Several fearless fowl cluttered the drive now, unafraid of the vehicle and its passengers. Even Elvis didn't scare these guys. He'd befriended the tough birds on that first day the cabin was theirs, somehow knowing they were here first and belonged here. But he did not extend that same courtesy to the other little critters on the property, which scrambled whenever the Belgian shepherd showed up.

She angled the Jeep around the turkeys and pulled up to the side of the cabin, parking by the old stone wall that separated the front yard from the driveway. She grabbed their packs and trudged to the back of the vehicle, opening the hatchback for a very animated Elvis. The dog leapt out and streaked straight for the front door. He seemed as happy to be home as she was. It had been a long day, and they were both tired.

She followed him through the weathered rose arbor and up the worn granite path through the garden that led to the wide south-facing front porch, where you could sit in one of the rocking chairs and watch the sun rise over the mountains to the east at dawn and set over the mountains to the west at dusk. When she'd first come back from Afghanistan, she'd spent a lot of time rocking on this porch, staring out at the mountains. Her only enhancement to that splendid view was a flagpole and an American flag, which flew day in and out at half mast in honor of her fallen comrades.

She paused for a quick salute. "Martinez."

Mercy always saluted when coming and going to the house—her way of including him in her life here.

It was not the life they planned, and it was not the house they planned to live that life in.

They were going to get a little ranch out on the south Texas plains and raise dogs and kids and roses. He loved roses.

Her parents would not be pleased. Both her mom and her dad had abandoned their own rural upbringing for the city life, going to law school and then setting up their own law firm together in Boston. The family firm, which she was expected to join after her older brother, Nick, bailed for medical school. Apparently becoming a doctor earned him a free pass—but the pressure was on her to fill his slot.

She never wanted to do that. She'd only ever been interested in two things: literature and law enforcement. Neither of these passions impressed her parents. So when she dropped out of Boston College, she'd joined up right away, before her parents could guilt her out of it.

Then she met Martinez. She loved him as widely and deeply as she did poetry and police work. When she lost him, she lost two of her three anchors. She was no longer a lover, no longer a soldier. She was a caretaker to a dog who'd rather be somewhere else, with someone else, just as she would, each a constant reminder to the other of all they'd lost. She had nothing but the cold consolation of words to comfort her. Even Shakespeare came up short now.

Her parents saw her fiancé's death as an opening, and resumed their campaign to bring her back to Boston to finish college and go on to law school. So far she'd resisted, but sometimes she wondered if it just might be easier to follow the path they'd already laid out for her rather than try to blaze a new one on her own.

But then, she wasn't really alone.

Elvis sat patiently at the door, ears perked, waiting for her. He seemed to understand this ritual of hers, this halting at the flag that always ended in recollection and recrimination. She plodded up the porch steps to his side, unlocking the door and shouldering her way in, dropping their packs onto the oak hall tree that served as her mudroom, and kicked off her boots.

"Come on in," she said.

The Malinois bounded in and went to fetch his bowl. He knew it was suppertime. The cabin's wide windows were full of late-afternoon shadows; the light was fading away as it did so stealthily in the long days of summer. A northwest wind shuddered through the tall white pines and sugar maples that dominated the woods surrounding the house. With the approach of sunset came the slow quieting of the forest. Not that it was ever very noisy here.

The growing silence unsettled Mercy. She locked the door behind her, something she rarely bothered to do. After all, she had Elvis, and he was trained to take down intruders. She shook off her unease and padded to the kitchen, where the dog waited, his dinner bowl between his front paws.

She grabbed a peanut butter chew treat from the cookie jar and tossed it his way.

"This should keep you busy for a while."

He caught it easily, wagged his black-tipped tail in thanks, and retreated to his bed. Which was really Mercy's couch. A deluxe dog bed made of orthopedic foam and covered in soft quilted cotton occupied a corner of the kitchen, but Elvis never slept there. It had become the repository of all his toys, including his Kong, the red rubber chew toy he adored above all things. For sleeping, the dog preferred her long sofa, with its soft butter-colored leather upholstery, preferably nested in the quilts she kept folded at each end. A maroon one for her, a teal one for him.

She'd grown up in a house where animals were not allowed on the furniture, ever, but Martinez told her, "Elvis and I share everything. When I eat, he eats. When I sleep, he sleeps." She had laughed at that—until she found herself envying the dog's sleeping arrangements. She rarely got to spend the night with Martinez.

When she moved in here, she'd brought her great-grandmother's cherry four-poster bed that they'd intended to share sans shepherd. But she couldn't bear to sleep there alone. So she usually slept on the couch with Elvis. He had his side and she had hers.

The dog destroyed the peanut butter chew treat, a process that took an average of four and a half minutes. Mercy left him there on the sofa chomping away. She took a long, hot shower, scrubbing away the dirt and sweat of the day and washing her hair. Wrapping her wet head in a towel, she rubbed her limbs down with coconut oil and slipped into her favorite moose-print flannel pajamas.

She went back to the couch, but Elvis wasn't there. She looked around the great room and over into the kitchen, but no dog.

He hadn't had supper yet, so he should be at her feet, bowl in his mouth, reminding her to feed him. The fact that he wasn't meant that he was stressed out.

Mercy knew how he felt—and where she'd find him. She went to the far side of the cabin, past her bedroom and the guest bedroom to the small workout room that had once been a screened-in porch. She'd furnished it with a heavy bag and weights, but the reason she and Elvis loved it was the yoga mat and the candles and the soft music. It was here to this warm womb of peace and quiet that they came when the stress of the outside world threatened to overwhelm them. And when the nightmares came—her dark visions of fury and firepower and his frightened puppy yelps signaling his bad dreams—marring their sleep.

The shepherd was there, curled up on the orange mat, his head resting on a long bolster pillow. He looked up at her as if to say, *What took you so long?*

She lit a candle, sweetening the air with lavender and sage, and turned on her playlist, a mix of Gregorian chant and *kirtan,* its East Indian complement. She settled cross-legged on the mat, and Elvis scooted over to her, dropping his fine head in her lap. She closed her eyes as he did.

As the haunting intonations enveloped them, she breathed in and out, stroking the shepherd's dark muzzle and scratching the sweet spot between his triangular ears. She could hear his quick panting slow and deepen as her own breathing slowed and deepened, and their respective inhalations and exhalations fell into a synchronized rhythm.

They sat together like this for a long time, until Elvis nudged her hands with a cold, wet nose. A signal that he was feeling better and ready for dinner. Funny how he was always quicker than she to know when they needed to sit and breathe, and when they were ready to move on.

She followed him as he padded into the kitchen and retrieved his dinner bowl. She poured herself a glass of Big Barn Red and made herself a roast beef and Vermont cheddar on Gérard's sourdough slathered with mustard and loaded with maple sweet pickles. Lillian Jenkins would be proud, she thought. When she wasn't running the Vermonter or the Friends of the Library or the historical society, Lillian was president of the Vermont Locavore Association and on the board of the Vermont Fresh Network. God forbid anything produced outside the borders of the Green Mountains should pass through a true Vermonter's lips.

Elvis would pass on the pickles, but he was as fond of Vermont cheddar as the next Belgian shepherd. And he wasn't a snob about it like some of his countrymen might be.

Slicing the sandwich in perfect halves, she removed the pickles from his side, placed it in his bowl, and laid the bowl on the coffee table before him. He had very good table manners, and not just for a dog. His sergeant had seen to that. Better than most of the guys she'd served with.

Elvis watched her as she carried her wine and her half of the sandwich to her side of the couch with her maroon quilt. He'd already arranged the teal one to his liking on his side.

"Bon appétit!" She lifted her glass to him, and he devoured his dinner on cue.

Mercy nibbled at her sandwich, but she still wasn't hungry. She gave the rest to Elvis. He gobbled it down, then stretched out on his side of the sofa. Within minutes he was asleep. She knew that she should sleep, too. But her head was crowded with the mysteries of the day: the missing baby, the unknown corpse, the buried explosives—or lack thereof. And Troy Warner, the lifeguard who grew up to be a game warden.

She grabbed her glass of wine and went out to the front porch, settling into her grandfather's rocker, facing west, and staring up at the darkening sky. She watched the stars blink into view, keeping the young moon company. Here in the dusk in her garden, surrounded by forest, she breathed in the scent of roses and lavender and pines and reminded herself to notice how beautiful it was here and how lucky she was to be home when so many others were not.

Even if it was lonely sometimes.

She finished her wine and put her glass down on the porch floor. Then she closed her eyes and leaned her head back against the chair, rocking slowly, slowly, slowly, until she dozed off.

THE SCREECHING OF a barred owl jolted her awake. Darkness had fallen—and out here on the edge of the forest the darkness was complete. A total void. Mercy shivered. And not just because it had grown cold. She felt uneasy, and she wasn't quite sure why.

Time to put in floodlights, she thought.

She took her wineglass and went back inside, where Elvis raised his head from the couch to acknowledge her presence and then went right back to snoring. She paced around the room, trying to reclaim her serene self.

Ordinarily just being here in this place calmed her. With its warm pine walls and thick beams and wide-planked floors, this cabin was her cocoon. She hadn't done much to the place, other than move her books out of storage and onto the floor-to-ceiling bookshelves that she built by hand with the help of her carpenter cousin, Ed. He said at the time that he didn't see how anybody would want to read so many books, much less want to keep them all, but he helped her build the shelves just the same. And it was Ed who came up with the idea of installing a library ladder so she could climb her way to the top shelves. The bookshelves competed for attention with the soaring twenty-foot ceilings and enormous flagstone fireplace—and they won. She knew he took as much pride in those bookcases as she did, because since she moved in most of the few visitors she'd had were prospective clients brought in by Ed to see for themselves what great work he could do for them should they be wise enough to hire him.

But even her wall of books failed to steady her now.

Mercy went to her bedroom. She pulled out the top right-hand drawer in the highboy and removed her service weapon. She hadn't fired the Beretta since she left the army. But she had a sense she might need it now.

The click of Elvis's paws on the pine floors turned her around. "No worries, boy, we just want to be prepared. Come what may."

He knew what a gun was. He knew what guns could do.

"It's okay," she told him. "You've had a big day, going back to work. And now this."

She scratched that sweet spot between his ears with her free hand. "Good job, good dog."

That's what Martinez always used to say after they returned from a mission outside the wire. He'd say it with a smile, and he swore that Elvis would smile in return. An acknowledgment between two peers of a job well done. But she thought he was dead wrong. Dogs didn't smile, they just curled their lips in a weird way once in a while, and people anthropomorphized that into a smile.

"Good job, good dog," she said again.

Elvis smiled at her.

Mercy laughed out loud. Wherever Martinez was now, he was laughing, too.

The dog followed her back to the living room, and they dove under their respective quilts on their respective sides of the sofa. She slipped the Beretta under one of the pillows. Elvis inched over to her side and placed his well-shaped head on her ankles.

Mercy knew she would sleep better now, with a dog on her feet and a gun under her head.

CHAPTER TEN

Troy spent a couple of hours at the regional office in town filling out paperwork and filing reports. He put out an AMBER Alert on the Baby Doe, using the pictures Mercy Carr had taken of her on her cell phone.

Susie Bear slept at his feet, spread out on the portable rollout pad he kept in his truck for long nights on the job. Troy could use some shut-eye himself, and planned on heading home for a nap before the inevitable 2:00 a.m. calls for drunk ATVers and lost campers started coming in. He whistled for the slumbering dog to wake up. Together they packed up their stuff—she carried her collapsible water bowl in her mouth, he carried everything else, including the laptop—and trudged to the truck. He'd finish up his reports and research at home when he got the chance.

They were about half a mile down Route 7A when a call came in from Dispatch.

"Old Man Horgan's gone wandering again," said Delphine. "Local PD's asked for your help."

Walter Horgan was an eighty-eight-year-old widower who lived on his own at home. Every day since his wife, Eileen, died eight years before, he left the white Victorian farmhouse with the blue gingerbread trim that he'd shared with her for sixty-one years of marriage and walked down West Road to the Northshire Cemetery on Main Street to visit her grave. The journey was just short of a mile each way, long enough to fulfill his physical need for a healthy constitutional every morning, and his emotional need to touch base with the woman he'd loved so much for so long. Everyone in Northshire knew Mr. Horgan and kept on eye on him as he made his way down the street, cane tapping the marble sidewalk in a staccato that announced his progress—until that turn onto Main Street crossed Route 7A and the sidewalk ended, forcing him to skirt the woods for several hundred yards.

During daylight hours this trek was manageable enough, but lately Walter had taken to roaming the cemetery after dark. Woods surrounded much of the twenty-acre park, and the worry was that he'd wander off track and get disoriented or dehydrated or worse.

"When'd he go missing?"

"His daughter says he never answered the phone tonight."

They knew the daughter Isobel, who lived up in Burlington now and checked in on her father by phone every night before he went to bed.

"And George?"

George from Meals on Wheels dropped by around seven o'clock each evening to give Walter his dinner.

"George says he wasn't there. And you know how much he loves Chef Pinette's meals."

Walter, a retired restaurant owner, would tell anyone who would listen how much better the food was since Pinette, a graduate of the Culinary Institute of America, had come on board.

"It's after nine now, so he's been gone at least two hours. What's the Point Last Seen?"

"As far as we know, PLS was his house, where his next-door neighbor saw him get the mail around three p.m. He was wearing his usual button-down blue shirt, khakis, and his favorite Agway cap."

"Okay. We're on it."

Susie Bear could find a lost old man faster than anyone else. Local law enforcement knew it, and often when a situation like this arose they turned to Troy and his dog, especially when they were preoccupied with tourists on busy holiday weeks like this one.

"You've already put in a full day," said Delphine. "And you'll be out again come midnight."

"It's on the way home," he told her, and hung up before she could point out that wasn't exactly true. But close enough.

He'd never turn down an opportunity to help find a lost individual, especially an elderly person. Nights like this were the reason he'd joined the service. His great aunt Renée had lived with his family when he was a kid. A retired botanist and devoted bird-watcher, she'd taken him on long nature walks, teaching him the names of the fauna and flora of her beloved Green Mountains. But as Alzheimer's set in, she grew confused on her daily walks with Troy, and he would guide her home. One autumn night she slipped out of the house and into the forest that flanked their backyard. His bedroom was next to hers on the second floor, and he never forgave himself for not hearing her shuffle past his open door and down the stairs.

The next morning his mother discovered she was gone. A search was organized; villagers and law enforcement alike went looking for her. They searched all day in the woods by his house. The fall of darkness and the threat of a nor'easter cut the effort short, and everyone came home.

Everyone except the game warden, a tough outdoorsman named Frenchie Robicheaux, and his dog Bella, a sweet yellow Labrador. They ventured deeper into the wilderness and found Aunt Renée hiding in an abandoned blind more than two miles in. She was dehydrated and hypothermic, but alive.

Frenchie and Bella saved her from the forest, but they couldn't save her from the disease that robbed her of her woodland wisdom. She died of Alzheimer's eight years later. But Troy never forgot the kindness and fierceness of the warden and his dog, and decided then and there he'd follow in their footsteps.

He parked the truck at the entrance of the Northshire Cemetery, between the two tall stone angels that stood sentinel at the gate. He let Susie Bear out, slung his pack onto his back, secured his headlamp, and switched on his flashlight.

The moon was just a silver sliver in the dark now, and the stars stood out against the night sky. They passed under the solid gaze of the seraphim and into the graveyard proper, as dark and pretty as a park of the dead should be.

Northshire dated back to 1791, the final resting place for Revolutionary War heroes, poets and politicians and philanthropists, teachers and farmers and generations of Warners, including his Aunt Renée.

The headstones shone pale and ghostly in the weak glow of the crescent moon. No place lonelier than a cemetery. They said cemeteries were peaceful, but when Troy wanted peace, he went to the woods. He knew his late aunt probably felt the same way, but hoped she'd found some eternal rest in the Warner mausoleum here on the grounds.

Susie Bear started down the southerly path toward the family plot, and he whistled to call her back.

"Not tonight, girl. Tonight we're going this way."

He led the dog down another gravel path that cut a circuitous route through the cemetery toward its eastern boundary to the headstone that read: *Eileen Gibbs Horgan, May 3, 1932 to November 25, 2010, Beloved Wife and Mother.*

And librarian, he thought. Mrs. Horgan had run the local library for decades, and encouraged everyone in town to read. Troy was never much of a reader, but when she found out he wanted to be a game warden when he grew up, she'd introduced him to Ralph Waldo Emerson and Henry David Thoreau, Emily Dickinson and Robert Frost, even John Irving. All the literary kings of New England, who understood the pull of the moon, the lure of the woods, and the solace of solitude. He missed Mrs. Horgan, and he wouldn't let anything happen to her husband on his watch.

The cemetery was empty as far as he could see. At least empty of living humans. Most of the villagers were either downtown dining and drinking or safe at home watching HBO. They weren't out visiting their dead.

Susie Bear was trained to find anything with a human scent. Troy figured the bones buried here would not distract her, because she was trained for tracking and trailing and search and rescue, looking for people who were still alive. People who were out of place, and smelled of confusion and fear. People like Mr. Horgan.

But the clever dog had done a little cadaver training as well, although she hadn't been on any official cadaver searches yet. Unless he counted today and the bones they found in the Lye Brook Wilderness. Which maybe he should.

"Search," he said, snapping on his headlamp.

The congenial beast bound through the grounds, past the faded granite stones, with no regard for the carefully tended paths or the bright flags decorating the graves of veterans of all wars, foreign and domestic. She was headed straight for the woods.

Troy jogged after the big black dog, lost to him in the dark, his head-lamp bouncing with every stride, flashing a jagged trail as he tried to keep her dark form in sight. He plunged into the woods after the disap-pearing mutt, shining the flashlight along the forest floor as well. He could hear her thrashing through the brush and struggled to catch up to her.

Now that the sun had long set, the temperature had dropped sharply—down to the forties—and Old Man Horgan would be cold. He remembered his aunt and pushed on, toward the crashing racket that was Susie Bear on the run.

The clamor stopped suddenly, and Troy knew she'd found him. Like a good search-and-rescue canine, Susie Bear knew better than to rush the lost and confused. She would run back to Troy and lead him to Mr. Horgan. Flashlight in hand, he tracked the dog along the visible trail she'd blazed through the trees and thickets, hoping to meet her halfway.

But she was faster than he was. The Newfie mutt leapt toward him, barked once, and then turned sharply, fur flying, and headed into a small clearing. He followed her and found her sitting there, her great paws forward, facing a huge fallen log lying at the base of a copse of white pine. Her long plume of a tail fluttered fiercely in anticipation of her reward for a job well done.

Mr. Horgan was nowhere to be seen.

Troy wasn't worried. Many elderly people would hide from the noise and commotion made by their rescuers, unaware that in the process they were hampering the very effort that could save them. If Susie Bear indicated that somebody was here, somebody was here. Somewhere.

He swung the flashlight around the clearing in a slow clockwise curve, lighting every inch of the small opening in the forest. *Nothing.*

He skirted the large log. Susie Bear's tail thumped wildly.

Getting hotter, he thought.

The far side of the log was hollowed out. He shined the beam of the flashlight into the cavity, and there he found the old man, folded into the close space, knees tight against his face. *Bingo.*

"Mr. Horgan," he said gently. "It's me, Warden Troy Warner. I'm your ride."

Susie Bear leapt over the log and slid to a dead stop right at Troy's heels. He slipped her a treat from his pocket for a job well done.

Walter Horgan leaned toward them. His hat was askew and exhaustion scored the deep lines that marked his long face, but his gray eyes were clear.

"That your animal?"

"Yes, sir." He reached down to help him up, grabbing his liver-spotted hands with his larger, stronger ones.

"Ready?"

"Yep."

He pulled his late librarian's husband to his feet.

"She's a big one." Mr. Horgan patted the dog's broad head, and in appreciation the dog licked his thin wrist with a thick tongue. "What's her name?"

"Susie Bear."

Mr. Horgan smiled. "Suits her."

The old man shrugged off Troy's assistance and made his way to the warden's truck, tapping his cane as he went, the big shaggy dog at his elbow. He sat tall in the front passenger seat. Susie Bear's head lolled between the two men as she leaned in from the cab. Troy glanced at the old man as he drove and wished there were more that he could do for him.

"I want to go home," Mr. Horgan said.

"I promised your daughter I'd take you to the emergency room."

The old man groaned. "No need."

"Just to get you checked out. Isobel is on her way there now. She'll take you home as soon the doctors say you're good to go."

Troy drove into the ER porte cochere at the hospital and helped Mr. Horgan into the waiting room.

"Take care of yourself," he told the old man as the nurse called him in to see the physician.

"You, too."

Troy grinned a goodbye and left. He climbed into his truck, scratched Susie Bear between her ears, and drove home to the fire tower on the Battenkill River just west of Winhall.

The fire tower dated back to the fifties. Obsolete in the era of satellites, the forty-seven-foot-high tower—basically an open fifteen-by-fifteen-foot room on stilts—had been scheduled for destruction when he bought it. He refashioned it into a three-story home by enclosing the lower portion of the tower and keeping the original lookout at the top intact. The ground floor housed the kitchen and the bathroom; his living space, which doubled as a bedroom, was on the second floor. He did most of the work himself, with the help of his dad and his brother Tyler, both carpenters. The living space may have been small, but the view was as big as the great outdoors.

He loved this place, and so did Susie Bear—even though at first she wasn't crazy about the stairs. He opened the red door—the only painted surface in the all-wood structure—and the dog rushed past him into the kitchen, stopping for a sloppy drink at her water bowl, and lumbered up the steep wooden stairs that flanked the far wall to the next level. She was as eager to hit the sheets as Troy was.

And he was right behind her.

But first he climbed a final flight of stairs to the top of the fire tower. He opened the sliding glass door and stepped onto the deck. He came out here often. To drink in the spectacular view, he told himself, but it was more than that. Sure, the outlook provided a 360-degree vista of the surrounding area, a splendor of forest and river and sky. Night or day, the effect was the same. Gazing out from his fire tower always reassured him that life was bigger than his own problems. Even after his wife ran off with that flatlander from Florida.

Tonight, the jagged tapestry of treetops against the sweep of stars and a pale sickle moon moved him more than he could say. Coming home to an empty house—empty of his wife—hurt him, especially in the beginning. He'd thought of her leaving him as the beginning of the end of his marriage. Although in truth the end had begun long ago. He'd been afraid of losing her since high school.

Meeting Mercy Carr today had reminded him of that.

Troy looked up and found the North Star. He stared at the bright star for a long time before going back inside and down the stairs. Pulling the Murphy bed down out of the wall seemed like too much trouble, so he crashed on the sectional with his dog, still in his uniform, and dozed off to the comforting sound of canine snoring.

FRIDAY
JULY 2

CHAPTER ELEVEN

Troy got about four hours' sleep before the first call came in: drunken revelers shooting off fireworks at the Northshire campground. All consumer fireworks other than sparklers were illegal in Vermont. People intent on celebrating the Fourth the old-fashioned way drove over to New Hampshire, stocked up on the explosive devices, and then sneaked them back into the Green Mountain State. Law enforcement didn't do that much to stop this smuggling activity; the priority was policing the roadways for drunk drivers.

Game wardens had to worry about drunk drivers, too. ATVers and boaters, mostly, speeding and crashing and hurting themselves and/or others in the process. But complaints for late-night fireworks disturbing the peace also came in, especially in the campgrounds, where rival groups would snipe at each other over all manner of issues, from extremely loud music to excessive marijuana smoke.

By the time Troy got there, the fireworks show was over and the complainants had gone to bed. The folks setting off the fireworks told the game warden that they didn't have any more. But a domestic dispute at the campgrounds earlier that evening had prompted an inebriated husband to take off on his ATV, and he hadn't been seen since. Troy and Susie Bear spent hours tracking the guy down, charging him with a DUI, and getting him back to the campgrounds in one piece to face his unhappy wife.

He may be lonely sometimes, but Troy was glad he didn't have to go home to an unhappy woman anymore. Dogs were so much easier than people.

The sun was coming up when they got back to the fire tower.

Another couple of hours on the couch, and he'd be ready to tackle that dead body and that missing baby.

More sleep was not to be. Long holiday weekends meant long hours on patrol. Troy got a text from Captain Thrasher. Time to get back to work. He showered quickly, put on a clean uniform, and headed out for the office with Susie Bear.

"Okay, girl," he said. "Are you ready for Eggs Over Easy?"

The big dog barked and he laughed. This tiny breakfast place in the corner of an old building on Main Street was her favorite—and his, too. He called in their favorite order—triple servings of venison blueberry sausage, wild turkey hash, cornbread, and coffee—and barreled down the road toward town.

Main Street was pretty quiet at this hour of the morning, and that meant no long line of customers waiting yet at the tiny café, which technically didn't open for half an hour, at seven, and was crazy busy by nine o'clock until they closed their doors in the early afternoon. But the cute if notoriously cranky hostess, Monique, had a crush on the captain, and all Troy had to do was say he was dropping by to pick up breakfast for Thrasher and she'd meet him right on the sidewalk outside the restaurant, food and drink packed and ready to go. By the time he pulled up to the restaurant, the slender brunette was there in a short yellow cotton dress, smiling and holding up his takeout like Vanna White changing letters on *Wheel of Fortune*.

"Now you be sure to tell the captain hello for me," she said as she leaned into the open window of the truck and exchanged meal for money.

"Will do," said Troy.

Monique patted Susie Bear before retreating. "And next time, bring him by for a real sit-down."

"Yes, ma'am." Troy smiled at her. She must have known that she was one of a long line of women waiting for the captain. But then, she was used to long lines.

CAPTAIN FLOYD THRASHER stood in the reception area and waved Troy into the small office. He scratched Susie Bear's shaggy head and led the way to the conference room, which doubled as the operations room. They were the only people there today, which was the way Troy liked it, when he had to be in the office at all. Most of his time was spent in the field. One of the many reasons he loved this job.

Thrasher, on the other hand, seemed completely at home in every environment. A former Marine with the punctilious bearing of an officer and the gravelly voice of a blues baritone, he was the most self-possessed man Troy had ever known. He seemed much taller than his five-ten frame, due to his super-erect carriage and salt-and-pepper buzz cut. His eyes were the kind of blue-green that could melt a woman's heart or nail a grown man to the floor with just a look. Of French, English, and African-American ancestry, he was movie-star handsome, at least by Vermont standards, and only grew more so with age.

Troy knew his extraordinary good looks were a sore subject for his superior officer, which made him the object of much teasing by fellow law enforcement—but only the dimmest of them dared to call him Pretty Boy Floyd to his face.

Troy was not dim. All he said when he and Susie Bear greeted the captain at the office was "Monique says hello," and handed Thrasher his coffee.

The captain grunted an unintelligible response. When his beloved wife, Carol, died a year ago of cancer, the ladies of southern Vermont had gathered around him in folds of sympathy, delivering condolences and casseroles in equal measure. He ignored them all, and shared the casseroles with Troy, whose own wife had also departed—for Orlando, with the orthopedist—in a show of solidarity and support. They continued to eat meals together, even as many of the women (Monique aside) grew discouraged and the free food dwindled.

That often meant takeout, like today's breakfast. Thrasher waited while he parceled out the sausage and hash and cornbread among the three of them: boss, junior officer, and dog. Dog got the lion's share.

They ate in a companionable silence, the only sound the slurping of coffee by the men and the scarfing of the sausage by the dog. Troy appreciated the fact that while the captain could speak eloquently and effectively on virtually any subject, he was not a big talker here at work. Troy never felt obliged to shoot the shit with him, the way he sometimes did with his other colleagues.

"Dr. Darling has narrowed the time of death of the victim in the woods to about three years, give or take a couple of months." Thrasher tossed the remains of his breakfast into the trash can under his desk. "Still no ID."

"I can check the missing persons files from that time and see what comes up."

"Do it." The captain rose to his feet. "But make it fast. It's really not our problem. And the unlicensed fishermen and drunk ATVers and pirate rafters will be waking up soon, and you'll need to get back in the field."

"Yes, sir." Troy knew that the captain didn't like the idea of people dying in their woods any more than he did. Whether by accidental death or murder didn't matter. They wanted to make it right, for the victims and their families. Even if the state police objected.

"You've got an hour," the captain said. "I'll be in my office."

Troy logged onto the computer in the operations room and began the sometimes laborious process of checking the crime records and missing persons reports filed around the time of the victim's death. Fortunately only three adult males had been reported missing during the specified time period: Gary Bowles, a forty-five-year-old unemployed truck driver from Pownal; Jack Hess, a thirty-seven-year-old science teacher from Dorset; and Wayne Herbert, a thirty-two-year-old unemployed machinist from Rutland County. Troy dug deeper, combing the databases for more information on the three missing men.

"Interesting," he told Susie Bear, who sprawled at his feet, her large head a dead weight on the toes of his boots. As it turned out, there was a story behind each of the missing individuals. Bowles turned out to be on a bender in Portsmouth, and spent a couple of nights in jail before taking off and showing up months later in Glastonbury. Hess ran off with his sister-in-law and sent his brother a postcard from Cabo featuring the happy couple on the beach. The wife eventually came home and reconciled with the brother, but the family didn't like talking about it, and delayed informing the authorities. Hess never returned to Vermont. As far as anyone knew, he was still in Mexico.

Missing persons reports were often incomplete and inaccurate, if not forgotten altogether. Most were canceled, because the missing person showed up, sooner rather than later, the victim of nothing more than a misunderstanding. Or they were runaway teenagers or dementia patients or kids abducted by their noncustodial parents.

Others were people who simply disappeared of their own free will. People who wanted to leave their old lives behind forever, for better or worse.

But then there were the victims of foul play. Like their victim.

Wayne Herbert, the last guy on the list, had never been heard from again. He was about the right age and disappeared at around the right time. He was known to be an avid hunter, and was suspected of poaching time and time again, but the game warden's predecessors had never been able to catch him in the act.

Still, given the forty thousand known remains and God knows how many more unknown scattered across the woods and fields and meadows of this country, the bones of their victim could belong to anyone. But Troy had a feeling about this Wayne Herbert. At least it was a place to start.

He printed out the case files, missing persons report, and photos of the victim and the belt buckle, and then whistled for the dog. She padded along behind him as he knocked on the captain's door and filled him in on Wayne Herbert.

"Oh, yes, the Herberts," said Thrasher. "Quite the family. Drinking, disturbing the peace, poaching."

They both hated poachers. Game wardens were pledged to protect wildlife—and poaching was one of the premier crimes against wildlife.

"Sneaky, though."

"Yeah. We've only caught them at it once. Before your time. The Herbert boys were baiting bear with doughnuts. Out of season." Thrasher smiled, showing his teeth. He had the look of a falcon, ready to swoop. "Anonymous tip. All three boys paid steep fines. And spent some time in jail."

Baiting bears was illegal. Even leaving dog food outside where it could attract bears was asking for trouble. And bear hunting was very restricted: only one bear per year was allowed each licensed hunter. Violations cost poachers plenty. Fines began at $1,000, and jail time could add up to months behind bars. The tough regulations worked, though, and the warden service knew it. The population of black bears had doubled over the past twenty years. That meant six thousand bears roaming the state looking for food when they weren't hibernating. Fierce temptation for the likes of the Herberts.

Troy smiled back.

"It's true we haven't heard much from Wayne in a while, not since his mother reported him missing. But I'm surprised that he might be our vic," said Thrasher. "I always thought he hightailed it into Canada to get away from her."

The widow Herbert had moved to Vermont with her grown sons from Maine after her husband died. Which was why Troy didn't know them from school. But he did know that since he'd joined up, the Herberts had been suspected of running dogfights, not that they'd caught them at it yet. "Queen of the Pit Bulls."

"Exactly. But we've never been able to prove anything."

"We will." The only thing Troy hated more than poaching was dogfighting. He found himself clenching his fists at the very thought of it.

Thrasher grinned. "Give her my regards."

Troy wasn't sure what he meant. It sounded like the captain wanted him to check out the Herberts on his own. The state police wouldn't like that.

The game wardens of Vermont Fish and Wildlife were supposed to stick to, well, fish and wildlife. Everything else—even search and rescue—technically fell under the jurisdiction of the Vermont State Police. Oh, the staties could call the game wardens in to help when they thought they needed them. But too often they didn't.

That arrogance had cost a hiker his life a few years back. When the young man failed to return from an early evening walk in the woods, his family reported him missing. The staties failed to notify even their own search-and-rescue unit in a timely manner—and the teenager died during the night.

Thrasher was convinced that his game wardens, who knew the woods better than anyone, could have saved him—*would* have saved him—if they'd only known. He was right—and everyone knew it. The staties were quicker to include game wardens in searches now, but that did not satisfy the captain. He didn't trust them to handle what went wrong in his woods. Neither did Troy.

"I guess you'd better see about that anonymous tip," said Thrasher.

Troy nodded in understanding. "Those Herberts are bear baiting again."

"Indeed." The captain paused. "Watch your back. And your dog."

"Yes, sir."

"And then get on to the fishing license checks."

WAYNE HERBERT'S MOTHER, Florence "Flo" Herbert, lived with her two younger sons north of the Lye Brook Wilderness in a double-wide manufactured home on twenty acres two miles off a hilly dirt road that angled off another hilly dirt road that angled off another hilly dirt road in southwestern Rutland County. Troy and Susie Bear bounced along in the truck, circumventing the bumpy backroads so typical of the state. Two-thirds of the roads in Vermont were un-paved—a whopping 8,600 miles—a nightmare in mud season but by this time of the year they were at least dry, if rutted.

Not that this could stop a game warden, for whom impassable ter-rain was often a given. The worse the road, the bigger the challenge. The Herberts' road was a challenge.

Eventually the rough drive petered out at a six-foot-high chain-link fence, which surrounded the vinyl-sided manufactured home and its outbuildings on about a square acre of the family's land. They got out of the truck. Susie Bear stood at his side, alert, tail wagging, snout up—ready to work.

Red and white *Private Property/No Trespassing* signs were posted every dozen feet along this rusted barricade. A new lock hung on the big gate fronting the road entering the compound, but the smaller lock on the slim, people-wide gate was busted. Troy let himself in through that gate, Susie Bear on his heels.

All was quiet at the house. It was after nine o'clock now; maybe the night-hunting Herberts were sleeping in. The yard—calling it a yard was a compliment—was cluttered with junk, an old broken-down wooden rowboat, a torn trampoline, a rusted swing set, and an as-sortment of snowmobile, ATV, and car parts. To the left of the Her-bert home stood a chicken coop, chickens long gone, and to the right a metal toolshed, its door hanging loose and clanging in the strong wind that swept through the pines surrounding the property. The only bright notes on the compound were the twin blue Dodge Ram trucks and a two-story steel prefab barn. Considering everything in the yard, Troy had to wonder what they kept in the barn.

A murder of crows sailed over them toward the trees. Sure sign of a carcass somewhere nearby.

"There goes the captain's anonymous tip," he said to Susie Bear, who was poised to follow them. "Sorry, girl. Not yet."

The makeshift porch, built of overturned split logs, held uneven piles of firewood. The path to the front door was strewn with timber in various stages of harvesting.

They had picked their way about halfway through the wreckage to the house when the front door swung open and two enormous snow-white pit bulls charged out, hurtling toward them.

CHAPTER TWELVE

TRUCK!" TROY YELLED AT SUSIE BEAR. The pit bulls stumbled among the junk in the yard, slowing down long enough for him and his dog to retreat behind the fence. He slammed the gate shut just as the beasts flew at him. Pit bulls were great athletes. The warden knew one Schutzhund-trained pit bull named Buck who could jump a ten-foot fence, no problem. He wondered how high these two could jump.

A sharp whistle stopped the dogs cold. They barreled back to the house, disappearing inside. Troy hightailed it back to his vehicle, and he and Susie Bear took cover. He needed to calm the situation down before the Herbert boys did something even more stupid than setting their dogs on him. At least until he could explain why he was here. He pulled the megaphone from the back of the cab just as the first rock cracked his passenger headlight. Too late, he thought, looking up at the open window from where he believed the rock had come.

"Down," he ordered his dog, who was prancing by the rear of the truck, keen to take on the attack twins, who were howling like the hellhounds they were. She dropped to all fours, but gave him a nose up that clearly communicated her disapproval. He pointed under the vehicle, and she reluctantly squirmed under its bed.

"Mrs. Herbert, this is Game Warden Troy Warner." He kept his voice cool and calm and deep, and that sureness echoed through the megaphone. "I am here to talk to you about your son Wayne."

A sudden movement at the window. Troy glimpsed what looked like a slingshot appear and disappear. Another stone flew through the air. He ducked back behind the vehicle, but this one was aimed not at him, but at the shed across the yard. The rock pierced the broken metal door, and it fell off with a clatter.

Guys like the Herbert brothers grew up slinging rocks at whatever moved. Troy sighed. He could call for backup, but that could take a while, and he didn't relish the word going out over the radio that he was under threat of a slingshot. He'd never hear the end of it. He could always leave, but skulking off in defeat was rarely a satisfactory option.

"Tell your boys to put away those slingshots before I lose my patience and arrest them for assault," he warned. "Do you want to know what happened to your firstborn or not?" Troy knew that people couldn't help but favor their eldest child, at least that had been his experience. His parents had always favored his older brother, Tyler, without apology.

The barking and the rock slinging stopped.

Troy waited.

The front door opened again and a small, wiry little woman in her mid-fifties stepped out. She was wearing camouflage cargo pants and an army-green short-sleeved T-shirt. Her gunmetal-gray hair was chopped off right at her chin, and rattlesnake tattoos roiled up her sinewy arms.

Maybe he should have called for backup, after all.

On her heels followed two enormous young men, the Herbert brothers, he assumed, each with a slingshot sticking out of a back jean pocket.

Definitely should have called for backup.

Their father must have been a giant with seriously dominant genes.

But even as the square-built boys with arms the size of their mother's thighs flanked her like two old-growth oaks, she was the one who commanded Troy's attention. Mama's monsters were just the window dressing, as were the pit bulls. She was the one in charge. She was the grieving mother of Wayne Herbert.

"Come on in," she called to him in a thick smoker's voice. "We don't bite."

"Yes, ma'am." Troy allowed himself a small smile. "I'm going to bring in some documentation with me for your review." He opened the truck door and retrieved his folder. "Don't hurt my dog."

He snapped his fingers and Susie Bear crawled out from under the truck. He pointed to the backseat and she whined. She didn't like being left behind, especially when there were bad dogs and flying rocks around. But she did as she was told, lumbering into the truck with a theatrical shake of her shaggy head.

"Stay," he said. "Good girl."

He closed the door quietly and strode through the yard, careful not to trip on any of the scrap, scattered debris, or downed limbs.

Mrs. Herbert stepped forward at his approach and shook the hand he offered her with a grip worthy of a wrestler.

"Mrs. Herbert," Troy said formally.

"Warden." She nodded to the young behemoths behind her. "My boys, Louis and Paul."

Troy shook her boys' hands as well, each the size of hams.

"Come on in." She waved a serpent arm at him and marched through the front door into the living room.

He trailed after her, taking his time to note the position of the dogs and the sons and the slingshots.

The dogs ran to greet Mrs. Herbert, snarling at him in passing. The sons took up residence in two matching supersized recliners the color of dried blood. Troy didn't trust the dogs or the sons.

Delphine had two pit bulls, Lucy and Ethel, sweet-as-pie lap dogs who proved that this was an often wrongly maligned breed. But when raised by people like Mrs. Herbert, he didn't trust them. And since she'd raised the boys, too, he'd keep an eye on them as well.

"Down," she ordered, and the pit bulls fell back, tucking their stiff curved tails and circling onto two old brown corduroy sofa cushions in the farthest corner of the darkly paneled room.

Mrs. Herbert sat on the large faux-leather couch that sat between the recliners. It was the same oxblood color as the rest of the furniture. The space was surprisingly neat given the state of the yard just outside. The only ornaments adorning the walls—apart from the big flat-screen TV—were impressively antlered buck and moose heads. The other decoration of note was a black-skirted round table that sat under a wide window looking out onto the unsightly lawn. The table served as a shrine to the lost son.

Troy stepped over to the table to take a closer look. A sentimental tableau telling the story of a young man's life: smiling baby pictures, surly middle school portraits, photographs of Wayne as a full-grown man—longer and leaner than his brothers, but with the same short sandy brown hair and brown eyes—posing with his mother, his brothers, his dogs, and his guns. There were other artifacts as well: hockey and football trophies, Red Sox and Bruins ticket stubs, a child's Bible and First Communion medal, an old compass, and an expired hunting license.

"He's a good boy, my Wayne." Mrs. Herbert joined him at the shrine.

"Yes, ma'am."

"Why did you come here?" Her voice betrayed her fear, and her dogs growled. "You're just a fish cop. What could you know about Wayne?"

"Please sit down." Troy ushered her back to the sofa. "The remains of an adult male have been found in the Lye Brook Wilderness."

"And you think it might be my Wayne."

"We're trying to determine the identity of the deceased at this time." Troy paused.

"So you're not sure." She slowly sank onto the couch.

"No, ma'am, but he died around the same time that your son disappeared three years ago."

"That could be just coincidence." Mrs. Herbert lifted her chin. She straightened on her seat, her pale lips a thin hard line.

"Maybe," he said gently. This was the worst part of his job. The part he hated. The part that made him feel completely inadequate. The part that broke his heart. Thrasher always said that if love didn't break your heart, life as a warden would. This was what he meant. "But preliminary forensics indicate that when the victim died, he was about the same size and age of your son."

"Victim?"

"The deceased was the victim of foul play."

"How?" The woman closed her eyes against the news she'd hoped never to hear.

"The victim died of a gunshot wound."

Her eyes snapped open. "How, exactly?"

He sighed. "A bullet to the brain. He wouldn't have suffered."

"People always say that," she said. "How can that possibly be true?"

Troy plowed on. "There was evidence that the victim suffered a broken femur earlier in his life."

Mrs. Herbert gripped her hands together as if in prayer. A very tense prayer. "Which leg?"

"The left," he said.

She looked down, away from him. "Wayne broke his left leg playing hockey when he was ten years old. He had a bad fall, going for the puck. He was in a cast for two months."

"I'd like to show you a picture of an object found among the remains." Troy pulled the photograph of the pewter belt buckle from his folder and held it out in front of her.

A sharp intake of breath, and Mrs. Herbert sagged, her body crumpling into middle age right before the game warden's eyes. All that pent-up energy, spent. All that tension that gave her the look of a coiled spring, released. She seemed ten years older. And ten years sadder.

Her sons, who had remained apart and silent, came and sat beside her then on the sofa, one on each side, each opening one of her clenched palms and cradling it in his huge paw.

"He was very proud of that buckle," she said, her voice ragged and hoarse. "Said it was specially made by a master jeweler. Can't recall his name. But Wayne told me the buckle was one of the last ones he made before he retired and went back to Ireland."

Troy drew a pen and notebook from his pocket. "And when was that?"

"Three, four years ago. Maybe five. I don't know." She frowned. "What about the belt?"

"Belt?" There had been no belt found at the scene, at least as far as Troy knew.

"Wayne said a buckle that fine deserved a good belt," she said. "So he went down to the Mad River Valley Crafts Fair and got one made out of bison leather. Hand-tooled by Clive Barton. Remember, boys?"

Her sons nodded.

Barton was a familiar figure among Vermont artisans, known for his leatherwork.

"I'd never seen anything like it. Told him it was a complete waste of money." Mrs. Herbert blinked back tears.

Troy waited. Paul and Louis waited.

"When can we bring our boy home?" she asked, her voice thick with resignation.

"It could be a while."

"I've been waiting a long time."

"I understand. We'll need to confirm that the remains are Wayne's." Troy paused, considering the evidence so far: the timing, the bones, the broken femur, the pewter belt buckle. The odds were that the victim was indeed Wayne Herbert. "Compare dental records, conduct DNA testing."

"The police asked me for his dental records and his hairbrush for DNA samples when he went missing. In case . . ." She trailed off.

"Good. That should help facilitate things."

"I never thought they'd really need them."

Troy realized that she'd never believed that her son was dead. Like Thrasher, she thought he'd simply up and left. "Where did you think your son had gone?"

She sighed. "I don't know. Canada, maybe. Or someplace warm. Mexico." She pulled her palms free of her sons' fists and raked her nicotine-stained fingers through her thick gray hair. "He was always talking about making a fresh start. Ever since that slut Francie Godette ran away to Ohio."

"Francie?"

"His 'fiancée.'" Mrs. Herbert made quote marks around the word *fiancée*. "At least until her parents found out. The Godettes thought she was too good for my boy. The father's in insurance. Like that's so special. So he encouraged her to hook up with this actuary from Akron." She let out a little snort. "Who runs away to Ohio?"

Troy wasn't sure what to say to that. He'd never been to Ohio. Not that it would matter. What he'd seen of the world when he was in the military was enough to convince him that Vermont was the place for him. When he and Madeline moved home after he left the service a couple of years ago, he was happy to be back in Northshire. He'd never seriously considered living anywhere else.

The Francie Godette outburst seemed to exhaust her. Mrs. Herbert closed her eyes again. Her sons looked at each other, then at Troy. He was wearing out his welcome. But there were still a few things he'd like to ask the family about.

As if she'd read his mind, she opened her eyes, now dark with sorrow. "What else do you need to know?"

"Did your son have any enemies?"

"Everyone loved Wayne," she said.

Everyone except for Francie Godette, the game warden thought.

Paul and Louis didn't say anything, deferring to their mother, but he could see by the way they glanced at each other over her head that they knew more about their brother's activities than their mother did. Or at least more than she was willing to acknowledge. But they might not say anything in front of her. Unless pressured.

Troy addressed the sons. "So, guys, can you think of anyone who might want to hurt your brother?"

"Everyone loved Wayne," she repeated.

"Not everyone, Ma," said Paul.

"The tree huggers hated him," said Louis, obviously emboldened by his brother's remark. "And the Godettes."

"Tree huggers?"

"You know, those losers always talking about saving the trees," said Paul.

"And the bears," said Louis.

"And the moose," said Mrs. Herbert.

"And the fish," said Paul.

"Morons." She rolled her eyes. "They're all about 'reducing their footprint' and living 'off the grid.' Just a fancy way of saying *poor.*"

"That Adam dude hated Wayne," said Paul.

"Adam?"

"I don't know his last name," said Louis. "But he's the worst of them. Always sneaking around in the woods, looking for trouble."

Mrs. Herbert shook her head. "They don't like outdoorsmen like Wayne. But they're basically harmless."

Troy knew that to people like the Herberts, *outdoorsman* was code for *poacher.*

"Wayne had been in trouble with the law from time to time," he said. "Poaching, drug dealing, gambling."

"No one ever proved anything." She glared at him. "My Wayne was a good boy."

"And the dogfights." He glanced over at the pit bulls, who still lay on their cushions in the corner, alert and seemingly ready to pounce.

"Ridiculous accusation," she said. "Wayne would never hurt a dog. Any dog. He loved dogs. We are a dog family."

Right, thought Troy, and tried another tack. "The remains were found in the Lye Brook Wilderness. Did Wayne go there the day he disappeared?"

"He went out early with the dogs. Said he might do some fishing."

"Not hunting?"

"Now, Warden, you know very well Wayne went missing in June." Mrs. Herbert regarded him slyly. "Off season."

"He'd been accused of hunting off-season before."

"Those charges were dropped."

"All three of your boys pled no contest to bear baiting."

She shrugged. "As I was saying, Wayne was out in the woods with Baron and Bruiser. When the dogs came home the next morning without him, I got worried. I called the police, but you lot never found him. So I figured he didn't want to be found."

"I see."

"Wayne knew the woods. He knew how to take care of himself." Mrs. Herbert shrank back against the back of the couch, and her sons leaned over her in a tunnel of protection. "My Wayne was a good boy."

Revisionist history, thought Troy. A common enough phenomenon among the bereaved. A closing of the ranks. Time to go.

"Thank you for your time." He picked up his file. "I'm so sorry for your loss." An unsatisfactory thing to say, and he knew it. But nothing else worked any better.

"You'll find him, then." It was an order, not a request. "The man who killed my Wayne. You'll find him."

He nodded. "If you think of anything else . . ." he said, looking directly at Paul and Louis.

They said nothing but stood up, then shifted on their feet, and sat back down again, the couch sagging under their weight. Troy would have to find another time to talk to them.

He left the three of them there, the surviving brothers flanking their mother, her shuttered face as solid and impenetrable as stone, her grief coursing through her tattooed arms to hands once again swallowed by her sons' huge paws.

"I'll let myself out."

The pit bulls watched him leave. No one on the sofa moved, a closed circle of sorrow.

As soon he shut the door quietly behind him, the keening began. Mrs. Herbert's terrible wails followed him all the way to the truck, and echoed in his ears long after he'd turned down the rutted dirt road and driven away.

CHAPTER THIRTEEN

MERCY WOKE TO FIND HERSELF STILL ON the couch. She'd slept late, hours past her usual rise-and-shine routine. Elvis, still lying on her feet, raised his elegant head and looked at her, dark eyes bright, eager to start the day. Martinez's dog was always eager to start the day.

"Coffee first." She groaned and dragged herself upright, wondering when she would stop thinking of him as Martinez's dog. If she ever would. Especially before breakfast.

The shepherd padded over to the kitchen ahead of her, waltzing on his feet as she filled the pot with water and ground the medium-roast organic Vermont Coffee Company beans. He knew the drill.

As soon as she finished her prep and switched on the brewer, Elvis soared for the back door, landing in a dead stop as gracefully as an Olympic gymnast, long nose level with the knob. Mercy laughed as she slipped on her Wellies and let the dog out.

She stepped onto the wide deck that ran along the back of the cabin. The sun shone brightly in a cloudless blue sky. The unnamed anxiety that had plagued her yesterday was gone, replaced by the dull pain of prolonged sorrow. Today was the anniversary of her fiancé's death. She'd mourn later, she thought, after breakfast. After she found that missing baby.

Usually she'd pull a few weeds in the fenced herb and vegetable garden she'd inherited from the previous owners, raised beds that stood between the cabin and the old red barn, while she waited for the dog to do his business in the yard. But rather than head for the deep end of the lawn, where the woods met the grass, Elvis shot toward the barn, barking all the way.

Mercy scrambled after him. She wished she'd brought along her Beretta, but she'd left it under her pillow. She considered going back into the house to fetch it, but the Belgian shepherd was already scratching at the double wagon doors on the gable end of the barn.

Mercy ignored him, spotting the footprints left by sneakers she guessed to be about a size 9 in the mud leading to the small door to the left of the big wagon doors.

"Quiet," she ordered.

He stopped midbark, trotting over to her, tail up. Ready to work. Noiselessly she opened the door, the shepherd at her side. Together they crept across the threshing floor, Elvis drawn by scent and Mercy drawn by the stamped hay. There were three makeshift horse stalls along the right side of the building and a tack room in the far corner. All signs and smells, apparently, pointed to the tack room, but she checked each stall anyway. *Empty.*

Not surprising, since no horses had been kept here for decades, at least as far as she knew. She'd always wanted a pony as a child, and Martinez had promised her a quarter horse when they moved to Texas, but that dream had died right along with him.

Slowly she and the dog approached the opening of the tack room. The only sound was the skittering of the mice as they disappeared into the nooks and crannies of the old barn they called home. All she could smell was the fading sweet, musty odor of old hay. But she knew the Malinois could smell intruders on the other side of the jamb by the way he stood, every muscle tense, his carriage proud, his desire to cross that threshold so strong his tawny fur seemed to ripple along his spine.

She flattened against the wall and whipped her head around in a quick surveillance of the room. *Empty.*

Except for a pile of horse blankets along the wall. Just sizable enough to cover something big or someone small.

"Okay," she said quietly. "Go."

Elvis barreled through the tack room, halting at the stack of stable covers. He turned back to Mercy and wagged his tail.

Friend not foe, she thought, and quickly strode across the space and tugged the sheets away from the wall.

Baby Doe looked up at her and smiled, even as the teenage girl holding her hid her face.

"Peekaboo," said Mercy.

The baby laughed and the girl lifted her face. She was about eighteen, slim and fair and scared. She looked ready to bolt, but Mercy and Elvis blocked her way.

"Are you her mother?"

The girl nodded.

Mercy fought the urge to lambaste the girl for leaving the baby in the woods. "Would you like a cup of tea?"

The girl nodded again.

"Come on inside, then." She held out her hand.

The girl looked at the dog, who pounded his tail on the barn floor and licked Baby Doe's tiny little bare foot. The infant giggled again and twinkled her toes.

Mercy grinned. "Elvis loves babies."

THE GIRL'S NAME was Amy Walker. She was very hungry, and once Mercy served up her famous blueberry multigrain pancakes, very chatty. In a stream-of-consciousness, nonlinear kind of way.

"I named her Helena, after the character in *A Midsummer's Night Dream*." Amy cut a piece of pancake for her little girl, whom she held on her lap with one hand while she forked food into first her baby's mouth, then her own. "That's Shakespeare."

"Yes." Mercy pushed the Corse Maple Farm syrup a little closer to Amy. "It's a beautiful name, for a beautiful baby."

"Yeah." Amy swapped her fork for the jug of syrup. "Dad took us to the Corse Farm sugarhouse when I was little." She drenched the diminishing stack in the sweet dark amber liquid. "It was so much fun. Even Mom said she had a good time." She swirled her index finger in the syrup and lifted it to the baby's little pink lips. Helena tested it carefully with her tongue, beamed, and then licked the rest off as enthusiastically as a puppy. "You love it, don't you, baby girl?" Amy beamed back at her, showing deep dimples in a heart-shaped face framed by choppily cut light brown hair. "I knew you'd love it.

"I mean, who doesn't like Vermont maple syrup?" Amy addressed Mercy now. "It's what we're known for, right?"

"Right."

The young mother looked even younger than her eighteen years when she smiled. At least she claimed to be eighteen, as of Valentine's

Day, her favorite day of the year, until Helena was born on Thanksgiving. Now Amy liked Thanksgiving best.

Mercy doubted she had made that up. Or anything else. Only an accomplished liar could talk so much and so fast and so randomly about whatever seemingly popped into her head and make it up as she went along all at the same time.

Or maybe all teenagers were like that. Martinez had five young siblings, and he called them all little mercenaries. Mercy knew that she should contact the police, or at least Troy, but she wasn't ready to turn over this young mother and child to the authorities quite yet. She justified her procrastination by telling herself that she wanted to make sure the pair got a good home-cooked meal before they left her. God knew when they'd get another.

"Where are your parents now?"

Amy frowned. "Dad died when I was ten years old."

"I'm so sorry."

"He was the best, you know, the best." Her dark blue eyes filled with tears. "I still miss him every day."

The baby, sensing her mother's distress, started to wail. Elvis leapt from his spot on the couch, skirting the table to check on Helena.

"More tea?"

Amy sniffed. "Sure."

Mercy filled her cup with more Earl Grey from the Old English Rose bone-china teapot her grandmother had given her as a housewarming present when she moved into the cabin. "My grandmother says tea fixes everything."

"Grandma Peg—she's my mother's mother—used to say that, too." Amy bounced her crying baby on her knee, and the little one settled right down. "But it couldn't fix my mother."

Mercy didn't know what to say to that. But she also knew that the less she said, the better. Silence was the best weapon in any interrogation. Er, *interview,* she corrected herself. She was a civilian now, conversing with other civilians.

And civilians liked to talk. Especially this one.

"Hmmmn," she said finally, accommodating but noncommittal.

"I think she'll take a nap now." Amy stood up, pulling the baby to her chest.

She was very good with her, thought Mercy. Amy was a good mother. So why did she leave her alone in the woods? This was the question she needed answering. Before she called the police. Before she called Troy. "Why don't you set her up on the sofa while I wash up?"

"I should help you." Amy bit her lip.

"Not necessary. I'm sure that you are both exhausted." She cleared the table and loaded the dishwasher, one eye on Amy, who wandered around the great room snuggling Helena on her left side, close to her heart.

She was quiet until the little girl fell asleep. The young mother spread a quilt on Mercy's side of the leather couch and laid the baby down, positioning pillows around her to keep her from rolling off. Elvis curled up on his side, his dark eyes always on the infant.

Amy backed away softly as Helena dozed. Drawn to the bookcases, she fingered the spines of the many leather-bound copies of the Bard's plays. Mercy watched as the girl pulled down a cheap paperback copy of *Othello* and studied it.

"I guess you like Shakespeare."

"Yes, I studied him in college."

Amy opened the book and started reading, somewhere in the middle, as far as Mercy could see. After a couple of minutes, the girl seemed to sense Mercy watching her, and looked up.

"I thought you were a soldier." She put down *Othello*, still open as if not to lose her place, and pointed to the photograph of a smiling Mercy and Martinez in uniform in Afghanistan that stood on the end table.

"I was." She smiled. "Soldiers like Shakespeare, too, you know. He wrote a lot about the military."

"Is that why you like his plays so much?"

"Partly. But mostly I like him because he makes me feel better about being human."

Amy stared at her. "Okay."

Time to change the subject, Mercy thought. "Some scholars believe that Shakespeare may have been a soldier himself."

"My stepfather was in Desert Storm. He hates Shakespeare."

"Maybe he's the exception that proves the rule."

"He's a jerk." Amy shrugged and tapped the silver frame with her fingers. "You look happy in this picture." She regarded her carefully, as if searching for that same happiness in her face now.

She wouldn't find it, thought Mercy.

"Is that your boyfriend?"

She nodded. "My fiancé."

"Cute. He looks like a good guy."

"He was." Mercy glanced away, looking past the girl to the window and the woods beyond. "He died."

"I'm so sorry." Amy sighed. "The good guys are always dying on you. Like my dad. And your fiancé."

Mercy was relieved when the teenager turned back to the wall of books.

"*Actors on Shakespeare, Will in the World, The Language of Shakespeare, Hamlet's Advice to the Players . . .*" Amy read off the names of several titles. "I didn't know there were so many books about him."

"Thousands and thousands," said Mercy. "This only represents a small sampling."

"Wow. We had some at the school library. But nothing like this."

Amy tapped the spine of a slim paperback of *A Midsummer's Night Dream.*

"We did this one junior year," she said. "In Mrs. Berentz's English lit class. I played Helena."

"I bet you were good." Mercy could see her in the role of the devoted, thoughtful romantic desperately in love with the indifferent Demetrius.

"I was. Mrs. Berentz said so." Amy smiled. "She liked me. She said I was 'college material.'" These last two words punctuated by her slender fingers twisted into imaginary quotes marks. "Like that was ever going to happen."

"It's not too late." Mercy climbed up the library ladder and retrieved a stunning limited edition of the Bard's most beloved comedy, beautifully illustrated by W. Heath Robinson.

"I never graduated. Quit when I got pregnant senior year." Amy paused. "But it's cool. I'm a mama now."

Mercy bit her tongue to keep from asking who—and where—the father was. She climbed back down and handed the girl the book. "I think you'll like this one."

Amy held the old volume carefully and slowly flipped through the pages. "These illustrations are so pretty."

"Yes." The book was one of her prized possessions. At least it was back when she still cared about possessions.

"I still think it's weird," said Amy. "A soldier who likes Shakespeare."

"You sound like my parents." Mercy grinned. "They wanted me to be a lawyer, like them."

"Boring."

"You have no idea." She laughed at that, then sobered. "But speaking of mothers, would you like to call yours? You can use my phone."

"No, thanks."

For the first time, the girl looked scared.

CHAPTER FOURTEEN

A RE YOU ALL RIGHT?"
     The baby fussed a little, and Amy picked her up. "You can't tell my mother I was here."

"Okay."

"Or my stepfather." She shot to her feet, Helena in her arms. "Especially him."

The bitterness in her voice told Mercy everything she needed to know. "Okay."

"Promise." She bounced the startled baby against her chest. Up and down. Up and down. Up and down.

"I promise." Mercy fought the urge to reach for the child. "I'm sorry. I didn't mean to upset you."

Amy wound down the bouncing to a slow swaying. Helena giggled.

Time to take the plunge, Mercy thought. "What about the father?" she asked gently.

"No." The girl's voice was firm.

"Not a good guy?"

Amy shut the old book and returned it to the shelf. "He's not a bad guy. I mean, I love him. And he loves Helena." She shook her head. "But he's all stage-five clinger now."

"How's that?"

"It started out fine." She settled onto the sofa, holding Helena on her lap. "Adam is an artist. Real creative. Real smart. A genius, you know?" She paused. "You should see the sculptures he makes. Out of stones and salvage and wood. Recycled art, it's called."

"Art trouvé," said Mercy.

"Yeah. Of course he only uses reclaimed wood. He loves trees."

Mercy sat on the arm of the couch. "Trees?"

"He's totally into saving the woods. One tree at a time." Amy smiled. "That's what he says. We put up posters, held rallies, planted trees. Disease-resistant elm trees. To save the forest."

"That sounds like good work."

"It was." Amy's smile faded. "But after Helena was born, Adam wanted to do more. He said we had to live off the grid."

"Off the grid?"

"Way off the grid. Deep into nowhere. He wouldn't let us leave. We were practically prisoners."

"Stage-five clinger."

"Yeah." Amy kissed the top of her baby's head. "It's *so* not fair. He gets all jealous when he's the one with all the crazy exes."

"What do you mean?"

"Groupies. They're the worst."

"Adam has groupies?"

"Art lovers, he said." Amy rolled her eyes. "Always hanging around, throwing themselves at him, trying to sleep with him. Like some of his genius will rub off on them." She leaned in toward Mercy, cradling Helena's small head with her palm. "When I first met Adam, he was such a *ho*. But then we got together, and he stopped hooking up with them. They weren't too happy about it. They all hated me."

"That must have been hard."

"Yeah. But eventually they all went away. I was glad at first, because I wanted him all to myself. He was so sweet, you know?"

Mercy nodded. She did know.

"But then we had Helena, and he changed. It started getting really weird. I just had to get us out of there." She leaned back and rocked the child in her arms.

"Is that why you left the baby in the woods?" Mercy held her breath, hoping for an answer that she—and Child Protective Services—could accept.

"I thought we could slip away from Adam on our bird-watching walk. Lately that's the only time he lets us out of the compound. He says walks are good for the baby. We stay off-trail, mostly in the blowdown area, where hikers don't usually go. He likes hiding from everybody."

She looked at Mercy. "But we see you and Elvis every morning. Like clockwork."

"Really? I never realized . . ." Some trained investigator she was.

"We keep out of sight, so you probably never saw us." Amy laughed. "But Elvis finds us off-trail and comes and says hello. He likes the baby."

Mercy smiled. "Yes, he does." She suspected the shepherd was better than she was at practically everything. "How did you get away from Adam?"

"Sometimes he gets all inspired with some plans for his art and tells us to go back to the compound on our own. He's very secretive about his work. Doesn't like anybody to see it before it's finished. I figured the next time that happened, and he told us to go back without him, we would just not go back, you know? Head for Route 7 instead. Hitchhike." Amy hesitated.

"But something went wrong."

"Max came with us."

"Max?"

"He's Adam's best friend. An artist like him, only creepier." Amy frowned.

"You don't like him."

"He makes me nervous."

"Why is that?"

"I don't think he likes me very much. Or Helena. He's not good with babies." Amy nuzzled her daughter, who was dozing off again. "He calls us a distraction."

"Back to what happened in the woods," Mercy said gently.

"Oh yeah." Amy looked at her. "Adam told me to take the baby and go back to the camp. I headed off that way with Helena, but then double-backed and started for Route 7. I heard Max and Adam fighting. Max was yelling something about me and the baby. I got scared and cut through the blowdown to get away from them. Away from Max. I heard someone behind me, and I figured it was him. I saw Elvis on the other side of the blowdown and knew Helena would be safe with him. So I put her down in the clearing and ran the other way."

"I see."

"I didn't know what else to do."

"It sounds like you did the right thing." That was all Mercy needed to know. Now she could text Troy and tell him Amy was here, and that the baby was safe.

Elvis sat up, ears perked. He bolted for the front door, in a frenzy of barking.

"What's wrong?" The young mother shrunk back against the bookcases, shielding her little girl's head with her pale hands.

"Stay here." Mercy went to the front window and saw a forest-green truck making its way up the long drive to the cabin.

"Who is it?" Amy was right behind her, bouncing little Helena on her hip.

"Troy Warner."

"Who's he?"

"The game warden."

"Adam says all cops are bad news." Amy backed up away from the window, out of sight. "Especially game wardens. Adam says no one has the right to police the woods."

That was an argument Mercy had no time to refute. "We should tell Warner that Helena is safe."

"Don't let him in. Please." Amy went back to the couch with the baby and pulled the quilts up around them, as if to hide.

Mercy followed her. Elvis stood his ground at the threshold, noisy as ever.

"There's an AMBER Alert out on the baby. You could get in big trouble if we don't talk to him. I could get in big trouble."

"I don't know."

"I know Troy Warner. He's a good guy. With a good dog." Mercy snapped her fingers. "Quiet, Elvis."

The shepherd kept on barking and she could hear Susie Bear barking back as the truck approached the house.

"You don't have to answer the door."

"He knows we're home. He's not going to just give up and leave." Her Jeep was parked outside and she knew the game warden could hear Elvis, so he would figure that she was here, too, somewhere. He'd just wait them out. It's what she would do.

"Send him away."

"We can trust him, you'll see."

Amy frowned. "Whatever."

CHAPTER FIFTEEN

T ROY PULLED THE TRUCK UP next to the red Jeep. On his way to Stratton Pond, he'd stopped by the office and told the captain about his encounter with the Herberts. Well, everything but the slingshots. He'd face the humiliation of that busted headlight later, when he wrote up his formal report.

"So Wayne Herbert might well be our victim, after all," said Thrasher. "Of course we'll have to wait for DNA analysis to confirm. Good work."

"Thank you, sir."

"The AMBER Alert has attracted a couple of good leads," said Thrasher. "A Canadian bird-watcher named Rufus Flanigan reported seeing a teenage girl hiking in the woods with an infant who looked a lot like the missing baby girl. He claimed to have seen the two—whom he assumed were mother and child—walking through the forest many times over the past few weeks. Another witness, Mabel Hennessy from Burlington, gave a young female hitchhiker and a baby fitting the description a ride out of town from a gas station not far from the hospital to about a mile north of a convenience store in East Dorset."

"That's on my way."

"Right." Thrasher paused. "Your new girlfriend lives right near there."

"Sir?"

"Mercy Carr."

The captain believed that the best game wardens were happily married game wardens and he was always quick to encourage Troy to forget about his estranged wife and move on. But he couldn't seriously be suggesting that Troy get involved with Mercy Carr.

"She's, uh, a little young, sir," he said, remembering that summer long ago.

Thrasher raised an eyebrow. "How so?"

"When I was in high school, she was just a kid."

"High school is over. And she's all grown-up now. As you are meant to be."

Troy wondered if high school was ever really over. Especially when you lived in the same small town all your life. As he had, apart from his time in the military—another community with long memories.

"She's a decorated war veteran. With a real dog."

"Sir?"

"You know, a real dog. Not one of those pip-squeaks some women carry around in their purse."

"True. That Malinois is a real dog."

"And from that dopey look on your face, I figure she must be pretty easy on the eyes."

Troy could feel his face redden even as he tried for a poker face.

"Courage, beauty, real dog." The captain laughed as he ticked off Mercy's fine qualities. "What more could a man want?"

Troy didn't answer what he hoped was another one of his boss's rhetorical questions. The captain was fond of rhetorical questions.

Thrasher checked his watch. "The morning's nearly gone. Better get on to East Dorset now. Start with Mercy Carr."

"I'll check her out."

"Good for you."

Of course that's not what he meant at all. But then, Thrasher knew that.

Which is how he found himself here with Susie Bear at the Mercy Carr residence. The well maintained if rustic cabin sat on a sweet piece of property in the middle of a sunny clearing that nestled up against the forest. To its right was a big barn. He could hear the rushing of a stream somewhere nearby—and the yowling of Elvis inside the house.

They strode up the stone path through the front yard, a generously landscaped garden planted in deer-resistant perennials—lavender, heather, and rosemary, daisies and black-eyed Susans, bee balm and butterfly weed and coneflowers—that reminded him of his grand-mother Maeve's garden. Susie Bear sailed past him to the generous front porch that ran the width of the cabin, barking in return.

In the middle of the flower beds in midsummer bloom stood a tall pole flying the American flag at half mast. He stopped in front of it and saluted.

"I'm coming," he told the impatient dog waiting for him, black tail whomping away in anticipation. But before he could knock on the bright orange door, it opened. Just by a couple of inches, revealing two noses—one pale and small and freckled, the other long and furry and black and wet. Elvis pushed by his leg to greet Susie Bear snout to snout. He doubted Mercy Carr would like him to follow suit.

"Hi," she said.

"Good morning. I'm sorry if I woke you." Although she looked wide awake to him.

"Can you give me just a minute?"

"Sure."

Mercy disappeared behind the door, but Elvis shot out onto the porch before it closed behind her. The shepherd greeted Susie Bear with a snort and a butt sniff. She returned the compliment. The dogs played like old friends, ducking and rolling and chasing each other. They exchanged short yelps and then raced off together for the barn, Susie Bear in the lead. She started to bark, her trademark "I've found something, now where's my treat?" howl that always heralded a good find. Elvis joined in, aggressive intruder–alert mode kicking in, barking like the world was coming to an end.

Troy looked at the closed door in front of him, shrugged, and jogged after the dogs, wondering what had them so fired up. Maybe there was a baby hiding in the barn.

He skidded to a stop just as Susie Bear began to paw at the handle on the side door of the barn. A simple wooden latch she'd figure out in no time. If she didn't destroy it first.

"Down!" he ordered.

Susie Bear shook her pumpkin head at him, but she did drop back away from the door. She did not stop barking. Neither did Elvis.

He heard footfalls behind him and turned to see Mercy running toward him. She was wearing black yoga pants and an army T-shirt. Her pale skin shone and her blue eyes regarded him with interest. She looked as bright and cheerful as one of her daisies. Until she frowned at him.

"What are you doing down here?" She seemed confused.

"What's in the barn?"

"WE NEED TO talk. Come on up to the house."

"What's in the barn?" Troy repeated. "The dogs are alerting like crazy."

"There's nothing in there." She shrugged. "Tools, hay, snowmobile, firewood, the usual."

Nothing that his dog would consider worthy of a treat.

"Horses?" Susie Bear loved horses.

"No, but there are a few stalls and a tack room." She spoke loudly to be heard over the bellowing. Between the two dogs, it sounded like a kennel on fire. "Let's go back up to the house. I need to show you something."

"I'm going into that barn." He didn't know why she was trying to keep him out of there.

"Fine." Mercy sighed and opened the side door. "But it's a waste of time."

Susie Bear shot into the barn, Elvis on her heels. The Newfie mutt barreled through the middle of the large, two-story space, ignoring the scattering of mice. She was definitely onto something worthy of a treat.

Mercy hung back as he marched after the dogs into the tack room. Susie Bear lay on the hay-strewn floor, her nose within an inch of a pink baby blanket.

"Good girl." Troy pulled a peanut butter and honey doggie treat from his inside jacket pocket—Susie Bear's favorite reward, saved for her best finds—and tossed it to her. He gave Elvis one, too.

He turned to Mercy. "We had some movement on the AMBER Alert. A girl was seen with a baby matching the description of our Baby Doe. We think she hitched a ride with a woman named Mabel Hennessy, who reportedly dropped them off just west of here." He held out the blanket. "What's the meaning of this?"

"I've been trying to tell you, but you're not listening."

She gave him a look he'd seen before, on his estranged wife Madeline's face, the look that always preceded his surrender. But Mercy

Carr was not his wife and this was professional, not personal. Surrender was not an option.

"'What we've got here is failure to communicate,'" he quoted.

"Cool Hand Luke." She smiled. "So you're listening now."

"I'm listening now." At least she got the reference, which was more than he could say for Madeline.

Mercy looked down at the dogs. "I found the baby and her mother in the barn this morning. Well, Elvis found them." She raised her head and looked him straight in the eye. "I was going to call you right after I got them something to eat."

"Right."

"They were hungry and exhausted." Mercy leaned toward him.

He ignored this entreaty. "When was this?"

"About twenty, thirty minutes ago."

"And now?"

"They're in the house. I was going to let you in, I was just reassuring her that you were, you know, good people. But when I came back to the door you were down here."

"Let's go." He whistled for Susie Bear and headed out of the barn. Mercy and Elvis kept up with them.

"Look, she's just a kid. A scared kid."

"Maybe." Troy kept walking. "But she did leave her baby alone in the woods."

"She had a good reason. She loves that child. You'll see."

She let them all into the cabin. Once inside, he stepped aside and allowed her to lead him into the great room, a towering space with a Vermont stone fireplace and the most impressive wall of books he'd ever seen outside of a library. Mrs. Horgan would have approved.

The living room was separated from the open-style kitchen by an antique oak dining table and chairs. Beyond was an island topped with reclaimed wood and three steel bar stools.

But no baby. And no mother.

"She was right here, right here with the baby, I swear." Mercy looked around the room. "Amy," she called. "Come on out, everything's fine."

They searched the rest of the small house—an exceedingly neat master bedroom in blue and white, a small yellow guest room furnished with two twin iron beds, a spotless all-white bathroom, and an odd workout room equipped with only a heavy bag and boxing gloves, a yoga mat and meditation pillow, and a small altar with candles and Buddhas and family photos. Mercy Carr, he was beginning to realize, was a complicated woman. And, as the captain said, all grown-up now.

"I think it's safe to say that they're not in the house," she said.

"I got that." Troy spotted a copy of *A Midsummer's Night Dream* on the table. A yellow scrap of paper stuck out of its pages.

"Amy likes Shakespeare."

He retrieved the paper by the upper right corner with the tips of his fingers. The note read, "Thanks for breakfast," in a loopy handwriting. He handed it to Mercy.

"So she's gone." She shook her head. "I thought I was getting somewhere with her. She was confiding in me. I guess she just panicked when you pulled up. She's afraid of law enforcement."

They walked back to the great room. Rain was falling now, and the skies were gray outside the big windows that ran along the back of the cabin.

"I'm sorry. I was going to text you."

"When?"

"Right before you showed up. Really."

"Look, I understand," Troy said. "But you interfered with an on-going investigation and failed to report on an AMBER Alert."

"I said I was sorry."

"This is not your investigation. You're a civilian now."

"And you're a game warden. It's not your investigation, either."

"We're working with the sheriff and the state police on this."

"I shouldn't have said that. I apologize." Her face flushed so deeply that he couldn't help but believe her.

"Apology accepted." She wasn't the first person to point that out to him and she wouldn't be the last.

"I thought I could help her. She needs help." She told him about the child's possessive father and Amy's abusive stepfather.

"We've only got her word for that," he said.

"She's telling the truth."

"How can you be so sure?"

"I was a cop, too. I've got the same built-in bullshit detector you do."

"Susie Bear and I will find her. We'll start with the woods."

"We'll come with you."

"You've done quite enough for one day." Troy's cell phone beeped. A text from Thrasher: *Missing boater on Stratton Pond.* "I've got to go."

"What are you going to do? Amy and Helena are in trouble."

"Do you think the baby is safe with her?"

"Yes. She's a good mother. The question is, are the two of them safe from the boyfriend? Or the stepfather?"

"We can't help her unless she files a complaint." Troy texted the captain back, and told him they were on their way.

"But if she comes in, what will Child Protective Services do? Amy's only eighteen. A kid with a baby."

"She's an adult in the eyes of the law. And we don't know for sure who the custodial parent is." Troy knew that CPS was overworked and understaffed and that if Amy Walker was indeed the custodial parent, odds were that she would not be charged with kidnapping. She could possibly be charged with child endangerment. But even if he reported it now, CPS wouldn't get to her case for weeks. Certainly it wouldn't happen over the long holiday weekend.

"Yes, but she's got nowhere to go. She doesn't want to go home. And she doesn't want to go back to the baby's father, either." Mercy gave him a pleading look that only the strongest man would be able to resist. "Don't call CPS. I can find her."

Troy hesitated. By law he had twenty-four hours to report suspicion of child endangerment to the proper authorities. So technically he would not be breaking the law if he waited a few hours.

"Please."

"I'll think about it." He whistled for Susie Bear and she leaped to his side. He hurried out of the cabin with the dog and went straight to his truck. He could hear Mercy and Elvis on their heels.

"Goodbye," she yelled after him.

Troy waved his hand without looking back. He hustled Susie Bear into the Ford F-150, slamming the door in his haste. They had a missing boater to find and a murder to solve.

And the day had barely begun.

CHAPTER SIXTEEN

"THAT WENT WELL," MERCY SAID TO ELVIS as they stood together on the porch and watched them drive away.

She could see that the encounter with Amy and little Helena had affected her. She felt energized; the same buzz that coursed through her when she was on duty reverberated through her now. Today the mountains and the woods and the sky spoke to her, not calling her to escape but calling her to act.

Elvis felt this sense of mission, too; she could see that in the way he nudged her with his cold nose, bullying her to get moving. She felt useful for the first time since Martinez died.

This is what it felt like to engage with the world, to care what happened next, and to whom. This was dangerous. But this was living.

The Malinois cocked his dark triangular ears.

"I know, you're right. We'd better go find them before they get into any more trouble."

Within five minutes Mercy had restocked her pack and they were on the move. The rainfall had stopped as quickly as it had begun, making tracking Amy and the baby pretty easy. She found broken twigs, disturbed debris, and footprints in the mud leading into the forest. The light morning shower made the work easier for Elvis, too, because cool, moist air kept the scent closer to the ground.

They traced the young mother and child northwest through the woods to the county road. There the trail ended abruptly.

"Probably hitched another ride," she told the dog. She wondered if the game warden had called off the AMBER Alert yet. If not, another witness might come forward, as Mabel Hennessy had done.

Meanwhile, there was another place to look.

"Home." She trudged back through the wet forest, Elvis bounding ahead. When they arrived at the cabin, she settled on her end of the couch and booted up her laptop. The shepherd curled up on his side and dozed off while she Googled "Amy Walker." What came up confirmed much of what the teenager had told her. She'd been a student at Northshire Regional High School and a member of the drama club, and stills of her in costume as Helena in a production of *A Midsummer's Night Dream* appeared on the school's website. A short video clip of the scene in which Helena delivers her famous monologue revealed Amy as a surprisingly good actress. The baby's birth announcement was reported in the *Northshire Review-Journal,* but there was no mention of the father. And Karen Walker, Amy's mother, had posted several photographs of both her daughter and her granddaughter on her Facebook page.

"Bingo." She researched the mother online and found that she lived with her husband, Donald Jonas Walker, in the middle of nowhere northwest of Sunderland. She knew that her mother's house wouldn't be Amy's first choice, but if she felt that she had nowhere else to go . . . it was worth a shot.

Mercy snapped her computer shut. "Wake up, soldier."

At the sound of her voice, the dog awoke.

"Time for a ride."

Elvis jumped from the sofa and trotted over to her pack. He carried it back to her, dropped it in her lap, and waited patiently while she pulled on her boots.

She smiled. He was happy to be back at work. And she was, too.

THE WALKERS' RESIDENCE was even more dilapidated and depressing than Mercy had expected. There was an old rusted green Dodge truck on blocks and nothing but weeds and dead leaves and dirt where the front yard should be. The old tin-roofed farmhouse had seen better days; its gray paint was peeling and its windows were boarded up as often as not. The front porch sagged under the weight of years of wear and tear, neglect, and three abandoned sofas.

But what struck her the most were the cats. She sat in the Jeep, momentarily stunned by the spectacle of dozens of tabbies, torties, and calicos peeking out from under the house, cuddling on the couches, lounging on the steps and the railings, and crowding every inch of the planked floor. Elvis danced on the passenger seat beside her, desperate to leap into the fray of felines.

She peered through the gloom, looking for more of them. There had to be more of them.

But other than the cats on the porch, the place seemed deserted.

"Stay," she told the shepherd, who pushed at her hand on the steering wheel with a cold nose as if to say, *Come on. Let me go.*

"Stay," she repeated firmly, but she left the hatchback open so she could call for him if she needed him. And to see if he could really resist the siren call of all those cats.

Mercy stepped carefully around the kitties, few of whom bothered to move. Many seemed lethargic; she hoped that the listlessness was not due to hunger or disease but that was probably a faint hope at best. She would call the animal rescue folks when she got home. But first she needed to talk to Karen and Donald Walker.

At the front door, she paused, then rapped sharply on the faded blue painted wood. The door creaked open.

"Hello," she called. "Mrs. Walker? Mr. Walker?" She listened for any sound of human activity inside. At first she thought they might be sleeping in, but she could hear the muted broadcast of a soccer game on television. Martinez had loved soccer like she loved baseball—and they'd spent many a long night in the desert debating the relative merits of each sport.

A black cat slipped through her legs. Her nose was smudged with red. A sudden roar from the TV signaled a goal, and the little pussy sprang off the porch and across the yard and disappeared around the Dodge. Still no sign of the Walkers or anyone else.

Mercy whistled for Elvis and heard the phlegmatic creatures screech as they scuttled away from the Malinois as he tore up to the house. To his credit, he ignored them all and halted at her hip. At her nod, they entered the house together.

The small front room was cluttered with empty Bud Light cans and old newspapers, scattered potato chips, and what was left of a half-eaten bologna and cheese sandwich. A flat-screen TV played the game she'd heard, a repeat of Arsenal playing Manchester City, in Manchester, home team leading 2 to 1, much to the screaming crowd's delight. Martinez loved Manchester City, almost as much as he loved Club America and the Houston Dynamo.

Under the dingy window that looked out on the yard sat a ragtag version of the velveteen love seat that graced the parlor in her parents' stately brownstone in Boston.

The love seat appeared to be the only tidy spot in the room. Even the cats weren't sitting on it.

In the middle of the room about three feet away from the television loomed a torn black faux-leather recliner, its back tilted toward Mercy. She could see a pale hairy hand spilling off to one side of the chair's right arm.

"Mr. Walker?" she asked as she circled the recliner to get a better look.

Splayed in the seat was a thick-bellied middle-aged man with white spindly legs sticking out of knee-length Hawaiian-print shorts and a white wifebeater shirt that partially revealed a colorful tattoo wrapping around his left bicep and disappearing over his shoulder. He had a broad, jowly face and dyed jet-black hair that came to a widow's peak high on his forehead.

But the most striking thing about him was the Buck hunting knife that stuck out of his chest, right under his left nipple, the fatal bulls-eye of a dark red blood blotch that stained his T-shirt with death.

CHAPTER SEVENTEEN

THE MAN WAS DEAD. Mercy knew that just by looking; she'd had enough experience to know death when she saw it. She didn't have to feel for a pulse, but she did anyway. She assumed that he was Donald Jonas Walker, Amy's stepfather. There was nothing she could do for him now.

She didn't think he'd been dead very long, so she and Elvis were careful as they checked the remaining rooms of the house—a small cramped combination kitchen/dining area, a master bedroom, a smaller bedroom, and one large if outdated bathroom with a claw-foot bathtub—but there was no one around. They checked the back of the house, too, but there was nothing out there but a weed-choked strip of concrete barely keeping the woods at bay.

Nothing to do but contact the authorities. She texted Troy about the murder, and he texted her back right away to say that he was out in the field and that she should call the police and let them handle it. Understandable, since he was a game warden, after all, not a homicide detective. And that's what this situation called for. He may have already overstepped his boundaries, and if he had that was probably her fault. But she could only feel so bad about that, because she had done what she thought she needed to do, for the baby's sake.

She called 911, and while she waited for the authorities, she snapped photographs of the scene with her cell phone while Elvis amused himself in the yard raising dirt and chasing cats. He was going to need a bath when they got home.

When she heard the sirens, she whistled for the shepherd, and he trotted up to her, nose in the air. His way of bragging. That's when she realized that he had something in his mouth. "Drop it," she said.

But he didn't drop it; instead he waited and when she finally held out her open palm in frustration, he opened his mug and let a purple pacifier fall into it.

She stared at the baby binky. A car door slammed outside. Mercy slipped the pacifier into one of her cargo pockets and by the time footfalls sounded on the porch, she and Elvis were standing quietly in the front room.

The young deputy who walked in the front door had *rookie* written all over him. His name was Josh Becker and this was obviously his first violent death. He shook her hand, petted Elvis, and secured the crime scene—all by the book with a careful, if nervous, thoroughness.

Then he excused himself politely to throw up behind the house. She could hear the sounds of his retching outside. She knew how the first time felt—an assault on all your senses, most notably your sense of smell and your sense of humanity.

She waited patiently for him to pull himself together and get on with it. After a couple of minutes, she could hear him call in the Major Crime Unit before rejoining her inside.

"Detective Kai Harrington, the Crime Scene Search Team, and Dr. Darling will be here shortly," he told her. "I'll take your statement, but he'll want to talk to you, too."

"Fine." She smiled at him, hoping to put him at ease.

Becker still looked green, whether from the aftereffects of murder or the thought of Harrington, she wasn't sure. He took her name and address and phone number, and asked her what happened. She told him, and she answered all his questions truthfully. Which was easy, because he was not a skilled investigator. At least not yet. She didn't say anything about the pacifier.

Before he could drill down more deeply, she was saved by the arrival of the medical examiner. The ever-cheerful Dr. Darling gave her a big smile. "I didn't expect to see you again so soon."

Mercy smiled back. "An unexpected pleasure."

"Indeed." The doctor leaned in conspiratorially. "We've got to stop meeting like this. Harrington won't like it."

"Detective Harrington didn't come to the other crime scene."

"He likes them fresh." Dr. Darling laughed as she began her examination of the dead man.

"What?"

"No glory in a cold case." The medical examiner winked.

"I see."

"Kai will be here for this one." Dr. Darling stared past Mercy at something behind her. "Speak of the devil."

"Doc." Detective Harrington nodded at the medical examiner. He was tall and dark and slickly handsome and he carried himself like he knew it in his way-beyond-his-pay-grade custom-tailored gray suit.

He introduced himself to her with a quick firm handshake and a frank once-over that infuriated her.

"I understand you discovered the body."

"Yes. I dropped by to see Mrs. Walker."

"And you just let yourself in?"

"The door was open. Nobody answered me when I called out. I knew something wasn't right."

"So you went in to check it out. Alone."

"I had Elvis with me."

"Elvis?"

"My dog." She felt Elvis stiffen at her side as he stared down the detective.

"Right." Harrington stepped back under the shepherd's glare. "I understand that this is your second crime scene in as many days."

"Just lucky, I guess." Mercy smiled back at him, her equilibrium restored, thanks to Elvis. She wasn't going to let this guy get away with anything.

Dr. Darling laughed.

Harrington shot her a dirty look, but the perky medical examiner remained as imperturbable as ever. Mercy decided that she really liked this woman, who could obviously hold her own in the testosterone-driven world of law enforcement. She knew firsthand how hard that could be.

"What can you tell us about the deceased?"

"Nothing, really. I assume it's Donald Walker. But I never met the man, so I can't make a positive ID for you."

"You say you were here to see Mrs. Walker." The detective checked his notes. "That would be Karen Walker?"

"Yes."

"We're trying to locate her. Do you have any idea where she might be?"

"No." She stopped at the sound of a ruckus on the porch. A distraught woman burst into the room, poor Becker hot on her heels.

"I'm sorry, sir, she just barged right by me," said Becker.

"Don? What's happened?" The plump blonde rushed into the room, right smack into Detective Harrington, who held her away from him with long strong arms. Her resemblance to Amy Walker was striking: the daughter's same heart-shaped face and narrow build burdened and bloated with age in the mother.

"Where's my husband?" Her voice was shrill now.

"Karen Walker?" asked the detective in a growly voice that managed to be intimidating and ingratiating at the same time. He turned a practiced look of compassion on the hysterical woman, and all the energy fueling her distress emptied out of her.

Mercy marveled at the man, whom she knew would have the poor widow weeping on his shoulder and spilling all her secrets in short order.

"Let's talk on the porch," he said quietly to Mrs. Walker, and ushered her out of the house, looking back over his shoulder to tell Becker to take Mercy's statement.

"I already did," said Becker.

"Then do it again."

Becker stared at the detective's back as he disappeared outside with Mrs. Walker, murmuring his condolences. Then he remembered her. "I'm sorry, but . . ."

"It's fine," she said, and walked him patiently through her discovery of the body one more time. When she'd finished and it was obvious the rookie had no clue what to do next, she took him aside. "Look, you have all my information. If you need anything else, you know where to find me."

"You can't leave yet."

"I'm just in the way here." Mercy waved a hand at the team working the scene behind them. "And my dog is tired." Elvis had dozed off, not so much because he was tired but because there was little else to do now that all of the cats had abandoned the porch and the crime scene techs had arrived. She suspected that the kitties were all hiding under the house, away from the commotion.

Through the front room window she could see Detective Harrington leaning against the porch railing, talking to Mrs. Walker, who sat on one of the sagging sofas, her back to the house. If he had known how many mangy cats had slept on that railing, she thought, he'd never do that. She wished she could hear what they were saying.

"Let her go." Dr. Darling was standing now, backing up from the victim. "Not much more to do here."

Becker relented, and Mercy mouthed a thank-you to the medical examiner. She whistled for Elvis, who took his sweet time getting to his feet. "Come on," she said, and took the long way around the house to the Jeep, hoping to eavesdrop on the detective. But all she heard was an angry Karen Walker.

"Amy hated him," she was telling Harrington. "If anyone killed my Donald, she did."

Mercy stopped to listen, hoping to hear more. Elvis heeled. She patted her pocket to reassure herself that the binky was still there.

"Ms. Carr," yelled the detective, calling her out. "Don't leave town."

Not trusting herself to turn and face them, she held up a hand and wiggled her fingers in reply. Without a backward glance, she strode toward the Jeep.

Elvis beat her there. He stretched himself out along the passenger door, his long nose pointed at the front tire.

"You are full of surprises today." Mercy squatted down by the dog. "What have you found now?"

She peered under the vehicle. A thin, straggly tiger-striped cat with a white chin and white paws was curled under the wheel.

"It's just a cat," she told him. "This place is crawling with them." She turned back to the sleeping tabby. "Come on, kitty. Time to go."

The cat slept on. At least she thought it was sleeping.

"I can hear it breathing."

Elvis pushed at the cat's belly with his nose.

"She'll move," she told him. "Don't worry about it." She opened the door and slammed it, thinking that was sure to startle the cat into action.

But the little feline only meowed faintly, winding herself more tightly into a furry ball.

"She must be sick." She gathered the poor thing into her arms, intending to take it back to the house.

Elvis whined his disapproval.

"They're probably all sick. I'm going to call animal rescue as soon as we get home," she told him. "They'll come get this one and all the others, too."

The Belgian shepherd whimpered again. The cat lifted her tiny head and licked Mercy's hand with a scratchy pink tongue.

"Oh, all right." She didn't need a cat. She had her hands full with Elvis.

With a sigh, she deposited the too-quiet kitty on the floor in the back. "Now let's go, boy, it's way past lunchtime."

His dark eyes brightened at the word *lunch*, and he jumped in, settling on the backseat to keep watch over his new charge. He stayed in that same position, still as stone, while Mercy drove them all home.

When she pulled into the long drive that led up to the cabin, Elvis alerted. She let him out of the Jeep, and he barged up the path to the cabin, barking so wildly that there was only one explanation Mercy could think of: someone was in the house.

CHAPTER EIGHTEEN

MERCY CALLED ELVIS BACK TO HER. "Quiet," she said, and together they approached the front door, she sidling carefully along the side of the building and over the porch railing, and Elvis leaping alongside of her. She waved Elvis down into a sit and flattened herself against the outside wall. Peeking inside the window, she caught sight of a tall figure in dark clothes wearing gloves and a ski mask. He—she felt sure it was a man—was running through the great room.

She hesitated, not wanting to go in there. Especially unarmed and maybe outgunned. Elvis nudged her hand with his nose. He wanted to go after the guy. She held back, but the dog was braver than she was. He broke away and raced for the front door. She scrambled after him and threw open the door. Elvis tore after the intruder in a blur of fur and fury.

Mercy dashed after the shepherd into the cabin and tripped, plunging to the floor, her fall softened by a pile of coats and boots and backpacks cluttering the entryway. They'd been pulled right off the hall tree. Elvis circled back to make sure she was all right. She hauled herself to her feet and stepped over the objects strewn across the floor. Somebody—presumably this guy—had tossed the place, her closets emptied, her drawers dumped, her bookshelves cleared.

She heard the back door slam and hurried its way, Elvis bounding ahead of her. He scratched at the wood furiously, barking wildly, until she let him out. He sped across the lawn just as the man in the ski mask slipped into the woods. The shepherd was within yards of overtaking the prowler when a shot rang out. Elvis yelped.

"Down!" shouted Mercy, her command voice echoing across the

lawn. She dropped to the ground herself and crawled to cover behind one of the large rhododendrons that ran along the side of the backyard. She saw the dog fall to his haunches, halfway hidden by a small fat spruce. She prayed he'd stay there. "Down!"

Another shot, this one wild and wide of both Elvis and Mercy. But it spooked the shepherd nonetheless, and he hauled himself to his feet and hightailed it for the barn. He disappeared around the far end of the tall structure.

Out of her sight—and the shooter's. She listened and waited and listened and waited some more. This was the hardest part, waiting and listening for the bullet or the explosive or the missile that was going to kill you—and deciding whether to advance or retreat. Elvis had chosen retreat. Even though he was trained to wait for that order, Mercy was glad that he was out of harm's way. She couldn't let anything happen to him.

No more bullets whistling toward their targets now. Just the sound of the man crashing through the brush and withdrawing into the shelter of the forest. Mercy desperately wanted to follow him, but she would have to wait to kick his ass. *The dog comes first.* Martinez was whispering into her ear now. *The dog comes first. Revenge will wait.*

As soon as she dared, Mercy ran for the barn. She circled the building quickly. But the shepherd was nowhere to be seen. Both doors were closed, so he must have found another way in. Old barns like this one—dating back at least a hundred years—had plenty of loose or missing boards that might provide him easy access. Failing that, he could always simply tunnel through to the other side if he were motivated enough to do so. His paws were shovels of the best kind; he could dig his way through anything.

The shots must have triggered his canine PTSD. Otherwise the überdisciplined dog would never have abandoned the field during a mission. Even if they were in Vermont, not Afghanistan. She circled the barn a second time, more slowly, looking for tracks. On the north side of the structure, she found his large paw prints and trampled grass by a gap in the wood just large enough for a Belgian Malinois to wriggle through.

She jogged around to the side door and let herself in, shutting the door behind her and calling for Elvis. He didn't answer, and she couldn't see him. She listened hard and finally heard his panting. His heavy breathing led her to the first empty horse stall on the left. The dog lay there, a tense ball of trembling tawny fur. He lifted his head and strained to lick his left hindquarter.

Mercy knelt down beside the distressed shepherd. "What's the matter, boy?"

He whimpered in response.

"Let me see." She gently separated the fine soft hair that ran along his backside, longer and paler than that which covered the rest of his strong, lean frame. Elvis whined, and now Mercy could see why. A bullet had grazed his haunch, at least she hoped that it was just a grazing. Elvis had licked away most of the blood, and the bleeding seemed to have stopped. She could see no evidence of a bullet. A flesh wound, but a wound all the same.

"Poor baby," she cooed, stroking the shepherd's fine head. "We've got to get you checked out." Elvis closed his eyes under her tender fingers. "Can you get up? Up?"

He lifted his heavy head, ears soft, and opened his dark eyes slowly. They were clouded with a pain Mercy hadn't seen in them since Afghanistan.

"Sorry, boy, but we've got to get you to Patience."

His tail thumped listlessly at her grandmother's name. He loved Patience.

Elvis weighed sixty-five pounds—all deadweight muscle. She could carry him, but doing so without bumping his wound might be tough. So she untangled herself carefully from the dog and retrieved a horse blanket from the tack room. Folding it lengthwise, she stretched it under Elvis's belly, pulling it together at both ends to make a kind of sling for his hips.

"Up," she said, helping the princely beast to his feet by lifting his hips off the ground with the makeshift sling. "Walk."

He moved forward easily on his front legs, obviously trusting her to serve as his hind legs, as she held his hurting backside aloft. She steered the shepherd slowly through the barn, out the side door, and across the front yard to the Jeep, where she helped him into the backseat.

The little kitten she'd rescued from the Walkers' place was still there on the floor, curled up tight as a fiddle fern. Just as well, she thought, the little tiger tabby had been safer out of sight. But Patience should probably look her over, too. She texted her grandmother to let her know they were on the way.

"Okay, you two, let's get you over the river and through the woods."

She slipped into the front seat, buckled up, and turned on some sacred music. She found it calming and she hoped Elvis did, too. His whimpering had given way to panting, but now his breathing slowed as the Jeep swelled with the sound of a didgeridoo and Tibetan singing bowls.

She kept one hand on the wheel and the other on his head as she drove down the road a couple of miles, where her grandmother lived and worked on the outskirts of Northshire, along the Battenkill River. Patience Fleury O'Sullivan was a big-animal vet, specializing in the farm animals so ubiquitous in Vermont. In a fully equipped bright yellow mobile unit that she drove all over the state, she treated horses, goats, sheep, and, of course, cows. Notably dairy cows. And the occasional moose or bear, among other wildlife, when asked.

But she also treated cats and dogs and other small animals, too, right here in the oversized Victorian farmhouse, with its attached barn that served as the hospital. Patience had converted the barn into treatment rooms and the connecting room into a reception area. The result: a state-of-the-art facility funded by her widow's pension and the sale of her late husband's dairy farm up in Lamoille County. She held on to a small parcel of land up there, deep in the timberland of the Cold Hollow Mountains, and sold the rest.

Mercy knew that her grandfather's family, the O'Sullivans, had not been happy about the sale, but Patience was determined to make a new life for herself. The life she'd planned before she met the handsome sheriff.

And she had. She'd opened her hospital—the Sterling Animal Hospital—nearly twenty years ago, when Mercy was a girl. Naming it in honor of her late husband, Sheriff Sterling O'Sullivan, himself named after the Sterling Mountain of his home county. Mercy spent her childhood summers here, helping Patience run the clinic—and she still helped out from time to time, now that she was back home in Vermont.

Her grandmother was outside waiting for them when they drove up in the Jeep. "My darling girl."

"Hi, Patience." She leaned in to give the lively gray-streaked blonde a kiss, struck as always by the energy and optimism that radiated from this woman she was lucky enough to call her grandmother.

Not that Patience would ever allow that. She insisted that everyone call her by her given name, Patience, including her children and grand-children. A useful name, she said, and one that reminded people of one of the great unsung virtues. Her family had been Quakers, and while she married an Irish Catholic and agreed to raise her children in that faith, she'd remained a Quaker all her life and named her children accordingly. Mercy knew that even her own mother, chris-tened Grace O'Sullivan, did not defy Patience on that score. Which was why her own name was Mercy.

"I'll help you carry him inside."

But when she opened the door, Elvis backed away from her, curl-ing up in a tight ball in the corner of the backseat.

"Not good," said Mercy. Usually the shepherd would leap out in a hurry, and race to greet Patience.

Her grandmother handed her a doggie treat. "Try this."

"Come here, Elvis," cooed Mercy. "Here's a treat."

The shepherd didn't even lift his head.

"I thought you said the bullet just grazed him."

"That's right. Not much more than a scratch as far as I could tell."

"Go around to the other side of the Jeep and open that door. I'll try on this side. Between the two of us, we'll get him out of there."

Mercy did as she was told, while her grandmother leaned in toward Elvis. "There's a sick cat on the floor here."

"Long story," said Mercy.

"One animal at a time." Patience laughed, and the shepherd's trian-gular ears perked up. She had a great laugh, one that inevitably lifted the spirits of all two-legged and four-legged creatures within its range. "It's okay. You don't have to be a tough guy all the time. Let's get you checked out." She held out another treat in her palm.

Elvis crawled across the seat and licked the treat right out of her hand with a gentle slap of his tongue. Her grandmother backed up slowly and he followed her, jumping out of the Jeep, even though he winced as his back legs hit the pavement.

"Your tough guy image remains intact," Patience told the shep-herd.

Together they ushered the whimpering dog inside. They laid him on the examination table in the largest of the treatment rooms. While Patience checked out the shepherd with her quick, clever hands, Mercy talked and Patience listened. She was a good listener. It was one of her great strengths as a healer and as a grandmother.

Mercy told her all about Amy and Helena, Elvis and the game warden, the bones and maybe bombs in the woods, the sick cat, dead Donald Walker, the intruder, everything.

Finally Patience spoke. "You've both been through a lot during the past thirty-six hours."

"I guess." *Nothing compared to Afghanistan,* she thought.

"Life offers us many kinds of challenges, on and off the battlefield."

Mercy nodded. Her grandmother was always full of aphoristic guidance, both oblique and direct. But somehow it didn't irritate her the way her mother's pointed advice always did.

She stroked the dog's dark silky ears while Patience administered local anesthesia and then cleaned the gash. Under the glare of the bright lights the wound appeared uglier than before, at least to Mercy.

"No stitches needed," said Patience. "Best possible outcome given the circumstances."

She looked at Mercy. "But I'd like to give him a sedative and monitor him for a while."

"Okay."

"You're awfully antsy. Are you all right?"

"Fine." She stroked the shepherd's back.

"You know it's not as bad as it looks."

"I know." Mercy knew exactly what it was like to get shot in the ass. Painful but not fatal. And more than a little embarrassing. She doubted that Elvis would be as humiliated as she'd been.

"You actually do." Patience laughed.

She laughed, too. Her grandmother was the rock in her life, and the light, too. Whenever she was with her, she felt both safe and hopeful.

"Let me remind you that you needed a couple dozen stitches, and you're fine now. He'll be fine, too."

"I know. Thanks."

"Done." Patience bandaged the injury and slipped the shepherd a mild tranquilizer treat. She then secured a cone around his neck. "Just to keep him from licking for a while." She stripped off her gloves and flipped the switch to lower the examination table.

As soon as the table began to move, Elvis stumbled off and ran out of the room.

CHAPTER NINETEEN

Let him go," said her grandmother. "He'll sleep it off."

"Are you sure?" Mercy fought the urge to run after him.

"He's going to be fine."

"Okay."

"Promise." Patience squeezed her shoulder. "Now what about that cat?"

"I'll go get her." She went out to the Jeep and gathered the kitten in her arms and carried it into the hospital. She could feel its tiny ribs right under the matted fur.

"Poor little thing." Patience took the skinny bag of bones from her.

"I know. And there are a lot more where she came from." She described the abomination of abused cats at the Walker place.

"I'll let the animal rescue folks know." Patience sighed. "We'll organize an evacuation."

"Good."

"This one is a cutie. What's her name?"

Mercy shrugged. "I don't know."

"She'll need a name."

"Okay."

"You're distracted. And it's not this tiger tabby you're worried about." Patience led the way to one of the smaller treatment rooms. "It's the prowler. You're itching to go after him."

"Yeah." Mercy shifted on her feet and looked away from her grandmother's sharp blue eyes.

"Without backup." Patience examined the cat, from ears to tail. The kitty just stood there, body trembling, tail twitching, whiskers twiddling.

Mercy's grandfather never waited for backup either. It had killed him in the end.

"Everyone's working overtime. The holiday."

"Call Troy Warner."

"He's a game warden," she said, a little too loudly. "He's busy writing up drunk boaters."

The cat quaked at her tone.

"You're scaring her."

"Sorry." She nuzzled the frightened kitty and lowered her voice. "So sorry, kitty."

"You know better than that."

Mercy wasn't sure if her grandmother was talking about the cat or the warden. Either way she was probably right. She usually was.

Patience straightened up. "Probably nothing wrong with this little girl that a little love and food and a couple hundred bucks' worth of shots and meds can't fix."

"Great. Just add it to my bill."

"I'll take it out of your inheritance, per usual." Patience grinned at her, then frowned. "Troy Warner is a good man with a good dog."

High praise for her grandmother.

"You sound like you know him well."

"I'm his vet."

"You're everyone's vet."

"He adopted Susie Bear, you know."

"Nice dog," Mercy said evenly.

"*Great* dog," said Patience. "She was a rescue from Alabama. Left to die in the woods down there. Half starved, full of parasites, missing teeth, evidence of a cracked skull somewhere along the line . . . she was a mess when they brought her up here. I'd bet money somebody hit her in the head with a shovel. Or a baseball bat."

"That's terrible." Mercy shook her head. "She seems fine now."

"Thanks to that handsome young man. Hold the kitten."

She held the timid creature—still shaking like a leaf—and sweet-talked her while Patience injected the little cat with a slew of vaccines. "I'll have to keep her here for a couple of days until those parasites are cleared up. And get her spayed."

"Whatever she needs. You know best."

"Remember that." Her grandmother retrieved a cat carrier and slipped the kitty inside. "I'm afraid it's quarantine for you, little one." She waved Mercy ahead of her. "Let's take her into the kitchen with us for a cup of tea. She needs food and water anyway."

"I should get going."

"You need to eat something before you head off after an armed robber."

Mercy knew there was no point in arguing with her. Patience had an infuriatingly gracious way of making you feel like an unreasonable boor if you disagreed with her. "Can we check on Elvis on the way?"

"Sure."

They found him curled under the long window seat in the living room, hiding from the world. He was already dozing off, his light snores the bass to the sweet purring of the half a dozen cats—all rescues—stretched out on the plump velvet cushion lining the window seat right above him.

"As you can see," said Patience, "he's fine. That sedative will last him awhile."

Mercy was relieved to see that he was breathing easily and sleeping normally. She'd promised Martinez she'd take good care of him, and here she'd gone and gotten him shot. She would never forgive herself if anything happened to him on her watch.

"Feeling guilty?"

She didn't answer, but she didn't have to. Her grandmother had been reading her mind since she was three years old. Maybe longer.

They walked through the reception and through the French doors that separated the clinic from the kitchen in the house proper. Not that there was much difference, apart from the medical equipment. The house was decorated in the same clear and bright Zen palette as the hospital. Patience believed in the healing power of color, and every room was painted according to the desired effect—calming blues and greens for surgery and treatment rooms, soothing violets and purples for recovery and post-op rooms, cheerful oranges and yellows for the reception area and the kitchen. Music played in the background, an eclectic if melodious mix of mellow reggae and soft rock and harmonious Gregorian chants and *kirtan*. Patience insisted the music encouraged positive behaviors in dogs and cited the studies to prove it when Mercy expressed any skepticism. Which she never did anymore, now that she knew from her own time on the mat with Elvis that it worked.

The kitchen was her favorite room in the house. Her grandmother loved to cook, and she'd modeled her chef's kitchen after the ones she'd visited in the south of France. A large, welcoming space dominated by a big island topped with white marble, the room reminded her of a Van Gogh painting come to life. The deep yellow walls nearly glowed in the natural light that poured in from the big windows and French doors leading out onto the porch that wrapped all the way around the house. Gleaming copper pots and pans hung from the ceiling and colorful pottery from Provence brightened the open shelves. And there on the long pine table, just where she hoped to see it, was a freshly baked carrot cake.

"Put her down in the corner." Patience handed her the cat carrier.

She placed it on a Windsor chair by the baker's rack, then pulled up a stool at the island and watched while her grandmother turned on the electric teapot and then filled two cerulean blue bowls, one with water and the other with kitty kibble.

Mercy placed the bowls in the carrier with the kitten, who wasted no time in availing herself of what might be her first real meal in way too long.

"You cut the cake and I'll pour the tea," Patience said.

Time for a chat, thought Mercy. Tea and cake was how her grandmother always began delicate conversations. Not that there was ever anything delicate about her direct approach.

"And how are you?" Patience handed her a bright orange mug filled with spicy chai.

"Fine." She sipped. "Tastes as good as it smells."

"Fine? Really?"

"Why wouldn't I be? I'm in your kitchen eating your cake." She slipped a generous bite into her mouth. "Good cake."

"Let's see." Patience counted down on her capable fingers. "You found and lost a baby, then you found and lost her teenage mother, you discovered a corpse and maybe explosives, your house got tossed by an armed intruder, your dog got shot . . . have I missed anything?"

"When you put it that way . . ."

"And you met a man." Her grandmother snapped her fingers. "I knew I forgot something."

"What?" Mercy laughed. "Who?"

"Troy."

"Seriously?"

"You could do worse."

"Not my type."

"If I remember correctly, you were pretty sweet on Troy when you were younger."

"I was fourteen," Mercy said, her mouth full of cake.

Her grandmother continued as if she hadn't heard. "After he saved that copy of *Romeo and Juliet* from the Landry boy, you proclaimed it your favorite play."

"It was always my favorite play when I was a kid."

"You slept with it under your pillow."

Mercy rolled her eyes. "At the risk of repeating myself, I was fourteen years old. It was just a schoolgirl crush on an older man."

"Older man?" Patience scoffed.

"He was a senior," repeated Mercy. "I was just starting high school."

"You're a big girl now. Troy is only, what, four years older than you are. That's nothing." Mercy's grandfather had been twenty years her grandmother's senior.

"He seems older."

"You both seem older than your years. Due to your shared military experience, no doubt."

"Maybe." Certainly she felt older than most of the people she met her own age.

"Four years. You wouldn't even need a Plan B."

Mercy knew she was talking about her grandfather again. Patience had often told her that while she'd loved every minute of their time together, good and bad, they always figured that given their age difference, she'd need a Plan B.

As it turned out, it happened far sooner than they'd thought it might. The life of a cop is always on the line—and thanks to an arrest gone wrong, Patience ended up the widow of a man cut down in his prime, rather than an old man doddering around the house while she played nursemaid. She would have done it, and done it happily, but the last thing he'd told her before he went into surgery to repair the gunshot wounds that killed him was "Live your life, Patience." Her grandmother was fond of repeating this advice whenever possible.

"Live your life, Mercy."

And there it was. She tried another tack. "Troy Warner is married to the most beautiful girl in the county."

Patience refilled her cup from the teapot. "She ran off with a doctor from Orlando."

Mercy nearly choked. "Seriously? When?"

"Christmas before last." Patience sighed. "They moved back home after he left the service, and within six months she'd hooked up with this orthopedist. It hit him hard."

"I bet."

"It was inevitable," Patience said.

"Maybe."

"That lightweight was never right for him."

Calling someone a lightweight was the worst thing her grandmother could say about anyone. It meant that she believed that you were not up to the hard work and hard choices of real life.

"A match made with a lightweight is a match made in hell," continued Patience.

Mercy had heard this theory before. Notably when her first love, a wrestler she'd met her freshman year of college, was expelled for steroid use and tried to take her down with him. Patience had warned her against him when they'd visited her over Thanksgiving break. If only her grandmother had met Martinez. She would have liked him. He was made of strong stuff. She suspected Troy Warner was as well.

"And the game warden is no lightweight." Mercy smiled at Patience.

"He's a good man with a good dog."

"So you've said."

"Have some more carrot cake."

Mercy cut herself another piece. She knew there was a lecture coming on—and her grandmother believed that a spoonful of carrot cake helped the medicine go down.

"I've been a widow now for nearly twenty years." Her grandmother leaned in. "I'm not lonely, mind you, but we women do have needs."

"Patience."

"I'm serious. That's why I have Claude."

Claude Renault was an animal surgeon from Quebec, a congenial man who had kept her grandmother company for several years now. Mercy was sure he'd like to have a more permanent place in Patience's life, but he wasn't the first man to amuse her and Mercy suspected that he may not be the last. That said, she liked the guy, and sometimes she felt bad for him.

"Don't look at me that way. I got married, I raised my children, and now I can play. With Claude."

"He died. I buried him."

"I know, sweetheart." Patience reached for her hand and squeezed it. "But maybe you need a Plan B, after all. Just as I did."

"I'm not as brave as you are."

"Nonsense. You're braver than I'll ever be. And you're young. You need to get married, have a family. You owe it to yourself."

"I can't do that now."

"Maybe not. But you will. You must."

That was enough grandmotherly advice for one day. Mercy pulled her hand away gently. "I have to go."

"I know. You want to catch your masked man."

"He's long gone by now."

"But you won't rest until you know that for sure."

"I should sit with Elvis."

"It's not like he's going to die," Patience said gently. "Promise."

She hesitated.

"Go on. Elvis will be fine. I'll take good care of the wonder dog."

Her grandmother had been married to a cop for years; she knew the drill. Which was more than Mercy could say for her parents.

She smiled her thanks. Patience held out her hands, and Mercy obliged her with a hug. Her grandmother gathered her in her arms, just as she had done when she was a little girl. There were few things on earth more comforting than this kitchen, this carrot cake, this woman hugging her.

They walked out to her Jeep together.

"Take your gun," Patience said. "And name the cat."

CHAPTER TWENTY

As soon as she got home, Mercy slipped her Beretta into her belt, grabbed a light pack, and went out to track the intruder. She followed his boot prints easily across the lawn to the tree line. She looked for shell casings but didn't find anything, and didn't really expect to. This guy knew what he was doing. And he knew better than to leave shell casings behind.

She continued through the bramble into the forest. The damp leaves and mud and debris readily revealed the man's trail. Too easily.

She realized that he hadn't cared if she could track him or not. He must have known he could get away. She pushed on through a long thicket and around a small patch of bog, coming to a thick line of spruce. Swatting pine needles away from her face, she shouldered through the close crowd of trees. On the other side of the copse was an ATV trail. The prowler's prints ended there, on the flank of the trail, where disturbed ground indicated that a large weighted object had recently occupied the spot. He must have come by ATV, parked it here while he tossed her house, then raced back to his machine and disappeared down the trail. Leaving behind nothing but tread marks in a tangle of tread marks left by the heavy traffic of the holiday.

She could hear the roar of several all-terrain vehicles speeding along; their numbers would grow as the day went on. ATVers were nothing if not notorious for riding on private property without permission, driving while under the influence, riding unlicensed vehicles, and more.

Most of the land out here was owned by a flatlander from Boston, an investment banker named Daniel Feinberg who'd bought a big estate named Nemeton that included a large tract of timberland. They say he'd bought the land to preserve it from logging, and had mostly done just that, apart from weekend parties in the summer and skiing parties in the winter. Guilt money, many Vermonters called it, but Mercy didn't mind as long as the forest benefited. She was sure Feinberg would not welcome trespassing ATVers any more than he welcomed poachers on his land. Still. Absentee owners often led to trouble, sooner or later.

Nothing more she could do here, for Feinberg or for herself. At least not today. It was late afternoon now and she was tired. Long day. Long two days.

She trudged back through the woods, missing Elvis. She'd grown more attached to him that she'd thought possible. Truth was, she used to envy him. Just a little, anyway. Her fiancé had loved that dog, and in some ways was closer to him than he was to her. She'd been a bit jealous. Ridiculous. She'd share Martinez with a kennel full of dogs if only she could have him back just for one walk in these woods.

Back at the cabin she began the thankless and time-consuming job of cleanup. She reshelved books, replaced pillows, restocked her desk, repacked clothes in drawers and closets. She swept up the debris of her emptied pantry and kitchen cabinets and bathroom vanity.

A mess, to be sure, but nothing seemed to be missing. What she most valued—her books and her pictures—were mostly no worse for the violation. But the bastard—for that was how she thought of the intruder now—had broken the frame of the photograph of her and Martinez. The one Amy said she looked so happy in. She did look happy, her face alive with a luminosity that occurred only when her freckles and her pale skin aligned in rare moments of true contentment. She wondered if she'd ever be that happy again. She wondered if that happy woman was lost to her forever. Trapped in the past with all her memories.

The glass had shattered and the silver frame was bent beyond repair. Carrying the mess to the kitchen, she dumped the glass and the frame into the trash. Carefully she brushed the picture free of shards with a paper towel. She'd need a new frame, but for now she simply hung the photo on her fridge with a magnet. She stared at the man she loved, eye to eye now, squarely facing him. He looked happy, too, but as always his handsome features were animated with a life force that went beyond happiness. He was a man who believed in passion— in body, mind, and spirit. *Time to get with the program,* he seemed to be saying, *get moving, get on with your life.* She loved to look at the photo-graph, even when it hurt. But at this eye-to-eye level, it suddenly seemed like a rebuke. She turned the picture over and placed it back on the fridge. Nothing but an empty white space now, dated with a time stamp long expired.

It was nearly suppertime and she was hungry and thirsty. What she needed was dinner and a glass of wine. Not necessarily in that order. Mercy poured herself some Big Barn Red and pulled a frozen lamb shepherd's pie from the Northshire Union Store out of the freezer. She popped it in the oven. The new owners of the two-hundred-year-old store had added frozen gourmet to-go dinners to their menu that Mercy—and Elvis—loved. When she didn't feel like cooking, which was admittedly most of the time, she simply opened her freezer, stocked with homemade lumberjack vegetable soup, chicken pot pies, mac and cheese, and her hands-down favorite, lamb shepherd's pie. Whenever Patience complained that she wasn't eating enough, she just invoked the sacred name of the Northshire Union Store.

While the frozen dinner heated up in the oven, Mercy curled up on the couch and sipped her wine and thought about Elvis's close call. She closed her eyes, and tried to breathe through the fear that she'd failed him and Martinez. Just as she'd been breathing through her grief for the past year. Never mind step by step—breath by breath was how she'd made it this far.

She kept on breathing, and eventually her inhalations and exhalations allowed her to surrender to her exhaustion. Mercy dozed off, finally, dreaming of masked men and crying babies and lost lovers.

THE OVEN TIMER was chiming and the doorbell was ringing and her wine was perched precariously at the edge of the coffee table when she awoke with a start, the name of her lost soldier on her lips.

"Coming!" She stumbled as she scrambled off the sofa, and caught the nearly empty glass just before it stained her lap with the last of the Big Barn Red. Jogging for the front door, she checked the peephole. There on her front porch stood her grandmother and Elvis, on his feet if a little groggy. And more than a little perturbed at the unwieldy protective cone around his handsome neck.

"Elvis!" Careful to avoid the cone and the bandage on his butt, she body-hugged the dog, burying her head in his soft, shiny coat. Whether he was more embarrassed by the cone or the hug, she wasn't sure.

"He's fine." Patience pushed her way into the cabin.

Elvis shook Mercy off. She stepped aside and watched as they passed by, wondering if the shepherd held her responsible for his injury. He trotted breezily behind her grandmother, as if he were returning from a holiday picnic rather than the animal hospital. Despite the cone, which he obviously considered an affront to his dignity. He turned to look back at her with those dark eyes, as if to say, *Come on, Carr. Move it!* Just like his sergeant would have done.

She traipsed after them into the kitchen. Her grandmother snapped off the timer and peeked into the oven. She retrieved the shepherd's pie, which bubbled around the edges but was still frozen in the middle.

"You're supposed to defrost it first."

She shrugged. "I just secure the perimeter and eat around it."

Patience laughed. "At least it's Northshire Union. You could do worse."

"Elvis likes it."

"I bet he does."

Mercy got down on her hands and knees so she could get a good look at him. She whistled and he trotted over to her, dropping into his favorite Sphinx position. She leaned forward, headfirst, into the cone. Now they were nose to nose. His was cold and wet, and now hers was, too. She laughed.

"Good boy," she said, her voice high with praise.

He licked her face, a soppy sign of affection he'd always reserved for Martinez alone. She let him lick her cheeks again and again before finally pushing him away, still laughing. "Okay. Enough."

Patience grinned as she sorted through her bag for a tissue and handed it to her. "Wipe away that slobber."

Anything anyone ever needed was in her grandmother's battered wine-colored leather backpack, a worn and weathered antique she'd had as long as Mercy could remember. She was, in some ways, the Mary Poppins of Vermont. And like a rabbit from a hat, she always pulled from it whatever the moment required: Band-Aids, ointment, coins, keys, paper money, pen and paper, apples, chocolate Kisses, pet treats, and more.

Patience pulled a doggie biscuit from the pack and slipped it to Elvis. "Go to your bed now and rest."

He chomped the bacon chew happily and retreated to his side of the sofa.

"Eat," her grandmother ordered, handing Mercy an empty dish. She poured herself a glass of wine and refilled Mercy's as well. "His anxiety seems to have abated. Of course the meds help."

"That's good news." Mercy spooned some of the shepherd's pie onto the blue plate. She wondered how he'd be when they wore off. He'd had a very stressful day. "How long does he have to wear the cone?"

"Until he's completely healed or until he destroys it. Whichever comes first." Patience sighed. "I know he hates it. They all do. But a dog like this one . . . if there's a way to get it off, he'll find it. And he'll probably drive you crazy until he does. Just try to keep him away from that wound."

"Will do." Mercy sipped more wine. "How's the kitty?"

"She's fine. Still no name?"

"Not yet."

"Maybe tomorrow's cat rescue will inspire you. The crime scene has been processed, so the Cat Ladies have gotten the clear to go over to the Walker place in the morning." Her grandmother gave her an expectant look.

"I don't know. Elvis needs to rest." The Cat Ladies was a rescue group funded by the estate of a local heiress who'd left her big farmhouse as part of the bequest. The eighteenth-century Northshire saltbox served as home base for the foundation—and home to more than a hundred felines at any given time, waiting for forever friends to adopt them. Mercy liked the Cat Ladies, and she knew she should help, but she wanted to look for Amy and the baby.

"He'll be fine." Patience raised her eyebrows. "Let me remind you that like it or not you are now a civilian. You need to stay out of this investigation."

"I know." Mercy looked down at her food, away from her grandmother's scrutiny.

Patience sighed. "But if you need a legitimate reason to revisit the crime scene, this would be it."

"Well, when you put it that way . . . count me in." Mercy raised her head and grinned at her grandmother. "Always glad to help."

"I thought so. I'll be keeping an eye on you both."

"No doubt."

Patience paused, and Mercy knew she was watching to make sure she was actually eating.

"I'm eating, I'm eating."

Her grandmother nodded, and speared a bite of her own from the edge of the pie and popped it into her mouth. "This is good." She leaned toward her. "Now tell me the rest of it. What happened to your masked man?"

Mercy recounted her unsuccessful trek through the Feinberg property to the ATV trail and the cleanup effort after her return to her trashed cabin.

"I don't get it," Patience said. "Why do you think he tossed the place? What was he looking for?"

"Nothing that I can tell. At least so far."

"Weird."

"I have the feeling that I'm missing something."

"It's really not your problem."

"It's my house. My dog. My life."

"I know." Patience sighed and served herself some pie. "Want to talk it through? I used to do that with your grandfather. He always said it helped."

"Okay." Mercy washed down the last of her pie with a gulp of wine and retrieved her cell phone, flipping through the photos of the murder crime scene for her grandmother. Including the close-ups of the victim, Donald Jonas Walker.

"Lovely guy. No wonder the poor child ran away."

"Yeah." Once again Mercy examined the middle-aged man with the seedy, spotty beard and the pale bloodshot eyes—open even in death, as if he'd been surprised by his violent passing, as he'd undoubtedly been—and the bloodstained, dingy white wifebeater shirt that bore the rust-red marks of the knife wound that killed him.

There were several pictures of the victim, from different angles. In one of the photos, the tattoo that inked his upper left arm was more visible than in the others. Something familiar about it drew her attention.

The art was crudely drawn, but the faded black-and-white images clearly revealed a pine tree against the mountains, bundles of grain, and a stick-figure cow.

"What is it?"

"This tattoo." Mercy enlarged the image on her phone and handed it to her grandmother. "What does it remind you of?"

"It looks like the Vermont coat of arms."

CHAPTER TWENTY-ONE

Patience pointed to the poorly printed word *Vermont* and the state motto, "Freedom and Unity," that ran along the bottom of the tattoo. She drew her finger upward. "But are these crossed rifles? That's not right. They're supposed to be evergreen branches."

"You're a real Vermonter," said Mercy. "This adaptation is the same image that appears on the belt buckle we found."

"With the bones."

"Yes."

"So the two deaths may be connected."

"Looks like it."

"You knew it." Patience beamed at her. "Clever girl."

"But I don't know what it means."

"Your grandfather used to say that the best clues raise as many questions as they answer."

"He got that right."

"You'll figure it out. You're your grandfather all over again." She gave her back the phone. "Aren't you going to tell Troy?"

"I want to check a few things first."

"Of course you do." Patience pushed her stool away from the bar and stood up. "You have work to do. I'll let myself out."

"What about Elvis?"

"I'll be back tomorrow. You won't be going anywhere tonight."

Mercy hesitated. "Probably not."

"Don't. Because if you do, he'll want to go with you. And while he's not badly hurt physically, emotionally he could use a rest. So could you."

"If I do go out, he'll stay right here on the couch."

Patience shook her head. "No, he won't. Would he stay put if it were Martinez?"

"No."

"What he needs more than anything is you." Her grandmother gave the dozing dog a pat. "You're his Martinez now."

"We'll stay right here tonight."

"Uh-huh." Patience kissed her forehead. "If you do anything stupid, take him with you."

"Yes, ma'am."

Her grandmother laughed and headed for the front door. When she heard it slam behind her, Mercy poured herself another glass of wine and moved to her side of the couch. Careful not to disturb Elvis, she sat down cross-legged, balancing her laptop on her knees, and logged on to research the various symbols of Vermont. Some of the information confirmed what she already knew: the scene depicted on both the belt buckle and Donald's tattoo was very much like that on the coat of arms, which dated back to the time of the Vermont Republic, when Vermont was an independent state, before joining the United States in 1791.

That explained the motto, thought Mercy. But not the rifles that replaced the evergreen branches on both the belt buckle and the tattoo.

She kept on Googling and hit on several articles on the Vermont Republic's latter-day imitations. The so-called Second Vermont Republic was one of the most active secession movements in the country, its members dedicated to the reestablishment of an independent Vermont. Detractors of the cause called these "Vermont Firsters" everything from anarchists to racists to ecowarriors, depending on their respective associations and affiliations.

A man called Adam Wolfe was mentioned briefly in one of the pieces, and a search on his name revealed a couple of profiles of the self-proclaimed Vermont Firster, an artist activist dedicated to "saving the authentic Vermont."

Amy's Adam.

She couldn't wait to tell Troy.

This was the guy the young mother had talked about, the father of Helena. He certainly looked the part of the wild creator, with his wire-rimmed glasses and shoulder-length brown hair and full, unkempt beard. She didn't see much of him in Helena, who far more resembled her mother, and she was unfairly glad of it.

One essay in an academic journal expounded on the relationship between art and politics, and featured Wolfe and his sculptures, a series of big and bold abstract bronzes that the author—one Candace Winters, PhD, professor at Bennington College—said explored the political nature of the cosmos.

Did politics and art and the cosmos equal explosives? Mercy wasn't sure, so she figured she'd just have to track this woman down and find out.

Elvis twitched in his sleep, paws moving as if he were running. He yipped and yapped as if he were a pup in pain—sounds he never made when awake. A nightmare.

Mercy cuddled up to the shivering shepherd. "Just a bad dream," she said, stroking his back. "You're okay, big guy. We're okay."

She couldn't leave Elvis. Not like this.

It was up to Troy. She texted him, filling him in on all that she'd discovered about Wolfe, Donald Walker, Wayne Herbert, and Dr. Winters. She left out the part about the intruder and Elvis; she didn't want him playing her rescuer. She could take care of herself.

She told him they'd have to follow up, and he told her he was out on patrols, but that he'd pass it all along to Thrasher. She asked about Amy and Helena, but there was no news there.

She hoped Troy and Thrasher could do what she could not.

Because her grandmother was right: she had a dog who needed her. She would stay right here on the sofa, watching over her poor suffering shepherd, and hoping that Amy and Helena were safe and on their way back to her.

Mercy pulled up the quilts around her. Her mind raced with random thoughts and images and associations just out of reach, but she knew she should at least try to get a good night's rest. Her grandmother and her animal rescue friends were morning people. Early morning people. She reached for her wineglass. If deep breathing didn't help her sleep, more Big Barn Red might.

Her Beretta was still under her pillow. In case the masked man returned for whatever he was looking for—and had obviously failed to find.

CHAPTER TWENTY-TWO

Troy was sweaty, tired, and wet. Susie Bear sat beside him in the truck as they drove home for a shower and a change of clothes. And a nap, time permitting, before his late-night shift. The big dog thumped her thick plume of a tail to the beat of Spoon and "Can I Sit Next to You."

They'd spent hours checking fishing and boating licenses, and chasing down those driving under the influence, failing to provide life vests on board, and exceeding the catch limit. One drunken boater had thrown a wild punch at Troy, stumbling right into the water in the process. Susie Bear leapt in after him, but the guy was so inebriated that he thought she was a real bear and panicked, kicking and splashing so desperately that Troy had to go after him himself. That's how he got so wet.

He was really looking forward to a hot shower and a cold beer. But by the time they got home and he cleaned up and fed Susie Bear and popped the tab on a Heady Topper, there was a text waiting for him from Thrasher telling him to call him. He answered on the first ring.

"We followed up on that information your girlfriend sent you." Thrasher waited for his reaction, but Troy had no intention of giving him the satisfaction.

"Sir."

"We ran Adam Wolfe by the local PD and the Feds," said Thrasher. "They say he's in Quebec."

"Quebec?"

"Hobnobbing with the secessionists up there."

"What about his activities down here?"

"They suspected him of setting fire to a couple of logging trucks, but they couldn't prove anything. They did cite him for putting in art installations on private property without permission."

"Art installations?"

"Apparently he's a sculptor. Pretty good one, at least until he gave up doing bronzes for big money and switched to creating works of natural materials for free."

"Am I supposed to know what that means?"

"Look it up."

"So no one's going to move on this."

"He's in Quebec."

"Right."

"We've got our hands full with the holiday. Stay out of it."

"Right." He knew how territorial law enforcement could be. But he didn't see how he could stay out of it as long as Mercy wouldn't stay out of it. And she was nothing if not stubborn.

All he could do was try to discourage her somehow. Because as long as she was in it, he was in it, too. No matter how much everyone tried to warn him off.

"You like her." Thrasher laughed.

Troy ignored that. "Sir."

Thrasher was still laughing when he hung up.

THIS TIME MERCY let him in right away. She seemed surprised to see him. Her blues eyes were sleepy and she held a glass of red wine in her long fingers.

"I'm sorry to disturb you," Troy said, sounding stiff even to himself.

"No problem." She scratched Susie Bear between her shaggy ears, then stood aside to let the black dog rumble in to say hello to Elvis, who lay forlornly on the couch, obviously embarrassed by his condition.

"The Cone of Humiliation," he told Mercy. "What happened?"

She told him about the intruder.

"This is the first I've heard of this." He was not happy.

"I didn't report it."

"Why not?"

"He's long gone."

"For now." There she goes again, he thought. Her own private army of one. Two, if you counted the dog. Troy always counted the dog. He suspected she did, too. "He could be connected to this investigation. We should at least dust for prints."

"He wore gloves. He knew what he was doing."

"You don't think he's left any evidence behind."

"No, and I don't think anything is missing. Besides, Elvis is my first priority."

"Understood." Troy looked over at Elvis, seemingly content to hang with Susie Bear, cone and all.

"Patience says he's fine. Just a little rattled."

"If she says so, then it must be true. She's the best."

"Yes, she is." Mercy looked at Susie Bear. "She told me all about your rescuing this big girl. She said she'd been badly abused down South."

"Yeah. But with your grandmother's help, she recovered."

"That's not how Patience tells it. She says you saved Susie Bear."

"She would." Troy looked over at the Newfie mutt, who raised her heavy head at the sound of her name. "She was very scared and subdued. So timid she'd shake whenever I came near her. But over time she learned to trust me." He grinned. "Now she's the happiest dog in the world."

"You must have worked with her a lot."

"I did. Lots of classes over at Two Swords." Troy smiled at her. "And of course your grandmother's good influence."

"You just missed her." She smiled back at him.

And he could see her grandmother in that smile. "Did she leave any carrot cake behind?"

"I'm afraid not." She laughed. "But I have some shepherd's pie left if you're hungry."

Troy hesitated.

"Come on. We'll never eat it all." She headed for the kitchen. "Want a glass of wine? Or are you a beer guy?"

"Whatever's easiest."

"So you're a beer guy."

He followed her and expected Susie Bear to follow suit. She loved kitchens for all the obvious reasons, but she stayed behind with her friend Elvis as a show of support. Between the two of them, there was not a free full inch left to spare on the sofa. Troy wondered if Mercy allowed Elvis on the furniture all the time or if this was a special circumstance due to his injury.

The shepherd looked pretty comfortable there so Troy suspected that he'd taken his usual seat. Either way it was too late. The dogs had the couch now and they weren't going to give it up.

The kitchen opened right onto the living room, separated by a long pine dining table and an island topped with what appeared to be an old barn door, which also served as a bar.

"I've got Heady Topper and Battenkill Ale."

He had to admit that the woman had good taste where it mattered: dogs and beer.

"The Heady, please."

She pulled a cold one from the fridge and handed it to him.

"Thanks." Even better, she knew that real Vermonters drank this beer right from the can.

While he popped the tab, she scooped up a large heaping of shepherd's pie onto a blue plate and put it in the microwave to heat up. He drank his beer and watched her move around the counter, cutting thick slices of pumpernickel and serving it in a basket along with a small pot of homemade butter.

"Animal Farm Butter," she said, grinning as she handed him a knife and fork wrapped in a bright yellow cloth napkin. "Patience takes care of their cows."

"Sweet." Troy smiled as he smeared the golden butter on the dark brown bread. "Thanks."

She nodded and placed the now hot shepherd's pie before him.

He ate and she talked, briefing him on the break-in.

"He didn't take anything, at least that I can tell."

"So you have no idea what he was after."

"No."

"But when you interrupted his search, he ran."

"And then fired."

Troy could see the concern in her eyes. "Maybe he was afraid of Elvis."

Mercy nodded, but didn't say anything.

He followed her glance back across the room where the dogs slept nose to nose on the sofa, the cone sheltering their heads. "I'm glad he's okay."

"Patience says he's more wounded emotionally than physically."

Troy considered this. "Jake's really good with working dogs."

She didn't say anything, so he plunged on.

"Working dogs need to work," he said.

"Elvis is retired." Her voice was firm.

"With all due respect, he didn't act very retired today. And neither did you."

"I know." Mercy sighed.

He heard a world of hurt in that sigh. "I'll be happy to take you over to Two Swords any time."

"Thanks. I'll think about it." She went to the fridge and got him another beer. When she came back to the table, she wore a determined look that told him she was about to change the subject.

"I took some photos and did some checking." She showed him the cell phone pictures of the deceased Donald Walker and the research she found online.

"Good work," he said. The truth was, he really was impressed. She must have been a good MP. He told her what Thrasher had given him on Adam Wolfe.

"I'd like to talk to this Dr. Winters."

"I don't know about that. Way out of our jurisdiction."

"Law enforcement is not going to do anything. They're all busy with the fireworks and parades and drunk and disorderlies."

"Not true," he said. "Now that it looks like there could be a connection between the cold case and Walker, Harrington's going to be all over this."

"If you mean Detective Kai Harrington, I met him at the crime scene today. Dr. Darling told me he was ambitious."

"You have no idea." Troy sighed. "Captain Thrasher told me to stay out of it—and that was before we knew the cases might be related."

"But this professor is our best lead to Wolfe and these Vermont Firsters," she said, sipping her wine. "Who knows what they're up to."

"It's Harrington's turf." He drained his beer. "Look, Harrington hates the captain. He doesn't need much of an excuse to make his professional life miserable. Or mine, for that matter."

"Why?"

"Thrasher fought hard to move Search and Rescue from the Vermont State Police to Fish and Wildlife."

"The hiker who died in the woods because the staties sat on it," she said. "I remember that case. My grandmother upset a lot of my grandfather's cop friends by siding with the game wardens."

"It didn't work, but Harrington still holds a grudge against the captain. And the captain still thinks Harrington puts ambition before saving lives."

"I get that. But it doesn't change anything. We've still got a missing mother and baby, bones in the woods, and a dead Donald Walker. Not to mention evidence of explosives and an armed intruder."

"I know."

"And the one common denominator is Adam Wolfe."

"Who's in Quebec."

"Maybe." She leaned in across the table toward him and tapped his chest lightly with her wineglass. "Maybe not. What do you think?"

"I don't know what I think."

"But Dr. Winters might know where he is." She put her glass on the table and stood up. "Can I get you anything?"

"No, thanks." He sighed again, and finished the last of his beer. "That was great."

"My pleasure." She started to clear the table, and in her precise movements he saw the determination that drove even her smallest actions. She wasn't going to give up.

"You're going to go see her whether I go with you or not," he said.

Mercy put the dishes in the sink, then turned to face him. She squared her shoulders and planted her fists on her hips. "He shot my dog."

There was really no arguing with that.

"Okay." He wiped his mouth with the cloth napkin. "But I do all the talking."

"Understood," said Mercy, all business now. "It would be good to confirm that Wolfe is in Canada. Failing that, maybe Dr. Winters can tell us who his associates are."

"We're on second shift tonight. So we'll be by in the morning."

Mercy frowned. "I promised I'd help Patience rescue the cats."

"Cats?"

"At the Walker place. Dozens of them. Half starved and sick."

"Why am I not surprised." If what Amy said was true about her mother and stepfather, they probably didn't treat their animals any better than they treated their kids.

"Exactly."

"The Cat Ladies?"

"Yeah."

Troy grinned. "Susie Bear loves the Cat Ladies."

Mercy glanced over at the dogs dozing happily on her couch. "Elvis, too."

"Okay, I'll text you when we come off patrol."

He whistled softly and the Newfie slowly shambled to her feet. Elvis, obviously still feeling some effects of sedation, didn't move. Mercy walked them to the door and stepped out onto the front porch with them.

"See you tomorrow."

"Good night," she said.

He could feel those blue eyes watching him as he and Susie Bear climbed into the truck and drove off. He took the driveway slowly, keeping an eye on her in the rearview mirror as she stood there bathed in the halo of the front porch light. They were nearly to the county road before he saw her go back inside. The porch light shut off, and the cabin was dark again.

Troy thought a trip to Bennington was probably a wild goose chase. But he wasn't going to let her go off on her own again. Dead bodies turned up whenever she and Elvis ventured out alone.

Besides, Patience would never forgive him if he let anything happen to either one of them.

As long as Harrington didn't find out.

SATURDAY
JULY 3

CHAPTER TWENTY-THREE

THE NEXT MORNING, PATIENCE LED the way in her fully equipped mobile clinic, a bright yellow oversized commercial van that Mercy had christened the Nana Banana. She and Elvis followed her grandmother in the Jeep, whose cargo section was stacked with cat carriers. She was glad they were getting a fairly early start, as this promised to be a hot and humid day, at least by Vermont standards. Her Yankee tolerance for heat had never been high, and the furnace that was the Afghan desert-of-death had not improved it. At least here she could pray for rain—and it might actually rain.

Patience pulled the van right up to the Walker residence; Mercy parked her Jeep alongside the drive behind a line of other vehicles.

"Stay," she told Elvis, who whimpered in protest but remained seated nonetheless, his dark eyes focused beyond the windshield on the activity in the yard. He was nearly back to normal, apart from the bandage on his backside and the cone around his neck. Still, he needed his rest, and there was nothing restful about a cat rescue.

She patted him carefully on the head and grabbed the stack of carriers from the back. Leaving the hatchback door up so he'd get plenty of air, she strode up to join Patience, now sporting a raffia sun hat with a wide brim. She was talking to Denise Boudreaux, the Northshire Animal Control officer, and Doris and Maureen, the Cat Ladies. The tiny silver-haired sisters had inherited the Cat House estate from their great-aunt Clara, the Grand Cat Lady herself, who'd left her sizable fortune to "cats in need."

A dozen volunteers busied themselves unpacking cat carriers, setting up card tables with supplies, and passing out protective gear. Mercy recognized many of them from former rescue ops: firefighters and their families as well as Friends of the Library, Northshire Garden Club members, and the local VFW.

The Walker homestead itself seemed deserted. The yard was still mostly dirt and weeds and clutter and cats. The Crime Scene techs had come and gone. Mercy wondered where Karen Walker was, and hoped that it wasn't anywhere near Amy and Helena.

"Hello, Mercy," said Doris, the elder and more gregarious of the sisters. "Thank you for coming."

"We thank you," added Maureen. The sisters were so united in their cause that they often finished each other's sentences and spoke almost exclusively in the plural.

Doris lowered her voice to a stage whisper. "We understand you found him."

"The body," clarified Maureen.

Mercy nodded. "I did. But I'm not at liberty to speak about it."

"We understand," said Doris. But Maureen looked very disappointed to hear it.

"At least not yet," Mercy added, and Maureen beamed at her.

"Hoarders?" asked Doris.

"No. The place is messy, but I don't think it's toxic."

"Hoarders are the worst," said Maureen.

"So we won't have to wear the HAZMAT suits," said Doris. "That's something."

"The forensics team chased all the cats outside so they could examine the crime scene. So they should all be out here."

"We think most of them stay outside, at least during the day. At night they sleep in the house," said Doris.

"Or under it," said Maureen.

"They'd have to," said Patience. "Otherwise the coyotes would get them."

"Or eagles," said Doris. "Hawks."

"Owls," said Maureen.

"That's why we didn't want to waste any time getting out here." Officer Boudreaux spoke for the first time.

"Let's get started." Doris called the volunteers over. "Most of you know the drill. You use the treats to lure the cats into the carriers."

"One per carrier," said Maureen. "We don't want to overfeed them."

"Most of the cats will be like the one Mercy brought home," said

Patience. "Full of fleas and ticks and parasites. They'll need food and water and debugging and deworming and lots of shots, but ultimately they'll survive."

"You stole one of the cats?" Another stage whisper from Doris.

"Yeah."

"I didn't hear that," said Officer Boudreaux.

"Elvis made me do it." Mercy knew that while the county had the authority to remove the animals, ownership remained with the Walkers until the criminal charges of neglect and abuse were proven, and ownership of the cats was revoked and could then be transferred to adoptive pet parents. So technically she did steal the cat.

Doris high-fived her sister, and together they turned to high-five Mercy. She was sure Officer Boudreaux was rolling her eyes behind her mirrored sunglasses.

"Sorry, Officer."

"Call me Denise," she said, with a smile that transformed her severe look.

Doris addressed the volunteers again. "The ones too sick to be seduced by the treats need to go straight to the doc in the van."

They passed around fanny packs full of treats, and Mercy secured one around her waist. Like everyone else, she wore long sleeves and long pants tucked into high boots to protect against fleas and ticks.

"Let's see those gloves," said Patience.

Mercy and the rest of the volunteers dutifully slipped on the gauntleted rabies gloves, which were lined with Kevlar and layers of thick leather designed to protect against scratches and bites. She held up her own gauntleted arms for inspection, and everyone else followed suit.

"You need a proper hat," her grandmother told her, pulling the straw boater she was wearing right off her head and plopping it on Mercy's head. "I've got another one in the van."

"Pair up and get started," said Doris.

Mercy's partner was Jade Wilkinson, a seventeen-year-old from Boston spending the summer with her grandparents. She was tall and skinny and ungainly and not much younger than Amy. Mercy again hoped that wherever Amy was, she and her baby were safe.

"Where do we start?" asked Jade, as the volunteers fanned out across the yard. "They're everywhere."

"Let's aim for the porch."

Jade removed one of her gloves and started snapping pictures with her phone.

"You have to wear the gloves."

Jade ignored her.

Mercy could see that she'd be doing most of the work, if only because she was the only one wearing both gloves. "Listen, why don't I catch the cats, and you snap their photos as we go. That way we'll have a record of each one."

"Cool. I'll post them on Snapchat, too."

"Okay. I guess we can use all the publicity we can get." Mercy leaned her stack of cardboard carriers against the trunk of an elm tree and plucked up the first one. Opening the top, she pulled a treat from her fanny pack and tossed it into the carrier. She placed it carefully down on the ground next to a very skinny black cat. She thought the poor thing was asleep, but as soon as she stepped away, the creature opened its eyes—a haunting yellow-green—and uncurled itself in a long stretch. She could see its ribs.

In a flash of movement that startled her, the black kitty leaped into the carrier and pounced on the treat.

Jade, quick as the cat, clicked a photo. "We'll call this one Loki."

"Next," said Mercy, and put down another treat-loaded carrier.

The challenge was to catch only one cat at a time. The healthier ones were anxious for those treats, and willing to fight over them if necessary. The more infirm of the kitties did not have the strength to jump. Those Mercy simply lifted up and placed in the carriers herself, and Jade delivered them to Patience in the van.

Together they caught a dozen cats: two tiger tabbies, two blacks, two oranges, three calicos, and three torbies. Jade named each as she snapped its photo: Blaze, Vapor, Steel, Storm, Bizarro, Remy, Parker, Micro, Mystique, Shade, Odin, and the original Loki.

"How do you come up with the names so fast?"

"Superheroes and villains." Jade rolled her eyes. "Duh."

"Of course." She'd remember that when she named her little kitty at home. If there were any superhero names left.

"Look!" Jade pointed to an old sleeping bag tucked under an upside-down wheelbarrow on the south side of the porch, where a torbie tabby was nursing four kittens. The kittens came in a rainbow of colors: one gray, two gingers, and a calico.

Mercy knelt down and regarded the mother cat, who looked up at her with big green eyes. Startled, the kittens started mewing, letting go of their mother's teats and crawling around up and over each other. Not easy, given their youth—they couldn't have been more than two weeks old—and their stubby little legs.

"OMG, they're Munchkins!"

Munchkins were the dachshunds of cats; due to a gene mutation, their legs were far shorter than the average cat's legs. Mercy knew these were a controversial kind of cat, and that some organizations in the cat world had refused to recognize the breed. "Who's going to adopt these poor little things?"

Jade was videotaping the kittens as they scrambled around their mother. "Seriously? Munchkins are, like, huge. I guess you haven't seen the cat videos."

"Uh, no." Cat videos really weren't her thing. But she did stream a lot of performances of Shakespeare's plays from around the world. Somehow she doubted that would impress Jade.

"Paris Hilton has one named Shorty."

Mercy had only a vague idea who Paris Hilton was.

"Can you believe it? Such a lame name."

"I have to agree with you there." She smiled at the teenager. "Now put your gloves on and help me round up these little guys." Mercy scooped up the mama cat in her leather-clad hands and planted her in the carrier, closing and opening the top in turn as Jade plucked the kittens up one by one and placed them in with their mother. When the last mewling baby was safely gathered, she secured the top one last time. "Well done!"

Jade stripped off her gloves and retrieved her cell from her jeans pocket. "I'm going to post the video online right away."

She grinned. "Don't you have to name them first?"

"We'll call the mother Gamora. And the kittens Star-Lord, Groot, Rocket, and Nebula."

"Wow, that was fast. I should never have doubted you."

"*Guardians of the Galaxy.*" Jade gave her a look that said unless Mercy had been living in a cave she should get that reference.

"Right." Mercy laughed. "I've actually seen that movie. It was funny."

"Duh."

"Let's take the Guardians to Patience." Mercy picked up the carrier, and together they walked back to the mobile vet clinic.

The yard was relatively cat-free now, the neglected animals curled up in their carriers—the docile ones sleeping and the aggressive ones screeching and scratching at the walls. A cacophony of cats, thought Mercy.

The volunteers were packing up and leaving, their cars loaded with cats, headed for the Cat House, where a couple of Patience's fellow vets were on standby.

"I guess we're about done here." Jade sounded disappointed. "Back to boring."

Mercy watched as the teenager slouched back to her grandparents, texting all the while. She was struck again by how young Jade was, how unprepared she'd be to have a child, how unprepared young Amy must have been when she had Helena. And yet she appeared to be a good mother, given how healthy and happy Helena was. Mercy wondered how that worked, if the hormonal changes helped make a mother no matter how old she was. Like Gamora and her kitties. Like all the teenage mothers she'd seen overseas and the millions, maybe billions, of teenage girls who'd been having babies for thousands of years.

Maybe motherhood was like war: You either rose to the challenge or you didn't. And hoped that no one died before you figured out what to do and how to do it. She thought about her grandmother telling her that she owed it to herself to marry and have a family someday.

Someday was a long way off.

CHAPTER TWENTY-FOUR

B Y THE TIME TROY AND SUSIE BEAR got to the Walker place, there were no cats or Cat Ladies to be seen. But he did see Mercy with her grandmother and Officer Boudreaux.

"Got 'em all?" Troy looked around the Walker homestead, imagining how the desolate place must have looked overflowing with cats. At least they would have given it some life. Now it was just another crime scene, marked by violent death.

"We were just going to have Elvis search for any stragglers," said Mercy, who managed to look good covered from head to toe even in this heat. He remembered his mother saying that women didn't sweat, they glowed, and Mercy might just be the first evidence he'd found that proved this. She wore a straw beach hat, and her face was flushed with a fine mist. She was glowing, all right.

"Will the cone slow him down?" He smiled at her. "I'm sure Susie Bear would be happy to help."

"Troy!" The veterinarian gave him a quick hug. She, too, wore a straw hat. Which explained why Mercy had swapped her baseball cap for the straw number. He could just imagine her grandmother insisting on it.

"You can take his cone off," she told Mercy, "but just for the search. When it's over, it goes right back on."

"He'll love that." Mercy snapped off the cone, and the shepherd shimmied with delight.

"Hey, Warner." Denise Boudreaux nodded smartly at Troy, saving her enthusiasm for Susie Bear, who greeted her with unreserved joy.

"Hey, Boudreaux." He'd worked with the Northshire Animal Control officer many times, repatriating black bears and capturing rabies-infected raccoons and rescuing injured bald eagles. He admired her competence, as well as her ability to be tough and compassionate at the same time. Both qualities were required for law enforcement of any kind, but most people erred in one direction or the other. The ones who erred on the side of compassion often didn't last—and the ones who erred on the side of tough often went on to give the rest of them a bad name.

"I guess we all know each other," said Mercy.

Seeing grandmother and granddaughter together for the first time side by side, he was struck by a resemblance he had not expected. Mercy had her legendary grandfather's coloring—redhead rather than blond—but she had inherited her grandmother's fine features and blue eyes. She was taller by several inches, but the long legs and athletic build were the same. Good genes, he thought.

"How many cats did you get?" he asked.

"Thirty-three," said Patience. "Most of them should make it."

"That's great." Troy knew that it didn't always work out that way.

"Let's wrap this up," said Denise, as Susie Bear ran over to greet Patience.

"Sure." Mercy turned to Elvis, who'd been prancing in place, desperate to be released so he could give his canine friend a proper welcome.

"Search," said Troy and Mercy in unison.

At the sound of the call to work, both dogs bounded off, happy to be together on the job again.

"Yin and yang," said Patience.

At what must have been the blank look on Troy's face, she added, "Male and female energies. Opposite, and yet complementary."

"Right." He loved the vet, but when she went all woo-woo on him, he tuned out.

"Exactly," said Denise, grinning at him.

"Excuse us," Troy said, as Mercy took off after the dogs.

"Certainly," said Patience, who couldn't resist winking at him as soon as her granddaughter's back was turned.

"I saw that," said Denise.

Troy raised his hands in defeat and followed Mercy.

The dogs scoured the perimeter, stopping along the way, trying to sniff out any wayward kitties. While the trees and the scrub and the

earth did a good job of filtering out the worst of the bad cat smells—
at least from the human nose's point of view—he thought the foul
feline odors might be overwhelming to the dogs' more sensitive snouts.
Of course, what smelled terrible to him might smell just great to them,
or at least interesting. For their sake he hoped so.

"You think they can find anything?"

"Every dog loves the opportunity to corner a cat. Even the ones who
like cats."

"Like Elvis and Susie Bear."

"They make a good team," said Mercy.

"Yep." Troy agreed with her there.

As if on cue the dogs ran to the porch and stuck their snouts under
the loose boards, barking.

"I'll check under the house," said Denise. Armed with a flashlight
and long tongs designed to capture feral cats safely by the neck, the
animal control officer slipped the tool underneath the porch.

"Find anything?"

"Score!" Denise pulled out a frightened and feeble torbie and handed
her to Mercy, who placed her into a carrier and closed it up.

Elvis yelped and circled around the house, Susie Bear lumbering
right after him, apparently all yin to his yang. Or maybe it was the
other way round.

Mercy and Troy trailed along after them. The backyard wasn't really
a yard at all, but rather a cracked and gutted narrow slab of concrete
flanked by the forest. Nothing much there but a rusted old Weber grill
and two broken green plastic lawn chairs.

The shepherd loped across the run-down patio and around the far
end of the Walker home. Susie Bear crisscrossed the concrete slab in
a more leisurely fashion, nose quivering, as if to say, *What's your hurry,
dude.* Then she disappeared around the corner.

Troy heard her bark. "She's alerting to something."

They sprinted around the house and found the dogs sniffing around
at the edge of a pile of broken flowerpots. Susie Bear barked again and
Elvis dropped to his haunches.

"What you got there, guys?" Mercy squatted down and peered between two of the largest shards of terra-cotta planters, which topped
uneven stacks of old pottery. She put her gloves back on and pulled
the pieces away.

"Careful." Troy knew how sharp broken shards could be; he had the scars on his hands to prove it. She ignored him, but then he suspected that she ignored most caution against dangers large and small when she was focused on achieving a positive outcome—meaning the mission is won and no one gets hurt. It was a recklessness he could appreciate.

"There's a cat in here."

Troy pulled on his own gloves and helped her remove enough of the clutter to reveal a ginger kitty hidden among the fractured earthenware.

Mercy reached down to pick it up, but the sly little thing leapt past her long fingers.

Troy dropped to his knees and opened his arms just in time to catch it in his hands like an errant football. "Gotcha!"

"Good save," she said, laughing.

And like a fool he grinned in pleasure for having amused her. He held out the orange kitten so she could get a better look at him.

"Another Munchkin."

Susie Bear and Elvis gave the little guy a good snuffling, as the kitty meowed wildly and waved his short legs around as if he were dancing on air.

"He's a lively thing." Patience appeared with a carrier in hand. "You forgot this, and by the sound of that mewling you're going to need it."

Mercy opened the top and tossed a treat from her fanny pack inside. Troy put the kitty inside and it scrambled to collect the prize.

"We need Jade to name it." Mercy told him how the teenager who was helping her named the cats after comic book characters. Closing the kitty in, she handed the carrier back to Patience.

Troy looked back down into the pile of pottery. "There's more stuff here."

"I'm not surprised," said Patience. "They call Munchkins magpies, because they love shiny new objects. They steal pretty things and hide them."

Mercy laughed. "Quite the stockpile."

"Gambit," said Troy. But he could tell that neither woman got the reference.

"Remy LeBeau," said Denise, walking toward them. "The Cajun mutant thief from *X-Men*."

Mercy shook her head.

"You know," said Denise. "Wolverine."

"Hugh Jackman," said Mercy.

"With blades for fingers," said Patience. "I remember now."

"Perfect," said Mercy. "Jade would approve."

"We'll take Gambit back," said Denise. "Unless there's anything else."

"Sure," Troy said, but he didn't move. Neither did Mercy.

"Are you two coming?" asked Patience.

"Not yet." Mercy looked at Troy. "I'd like to go through Gambit's stash first."

"Technically this is a crime scene," he reminded her.

"All the more reason to check it out. Maybe the crime scene techs missed something."

"I didn't hear that," said Denise.

"Will we see you back at the Cat House?" asked Patience.

"Maybe later," said Mercy, handing the straw hat back to her grand-mother.

"Uh-huh." The vet wrapped an arm around Denise's shoulder. "I guess it's just you and me and the Cajun mutant thief, then."

"Don't you kids stay out too late," yelled the animal control officer over her shoulder as she and Patience walked away with the magpie Munchkin.

"She can't be any older than you are."

"Pay no attention to them." Mercy pulled off her other rabies glove. "Got any more of those plastic gloves? God knows what's on these by now."

Troy pulled a couple of pairs from his pocket, gave her one, and swapped out his own rabies gloves for plastic ones. The woman was nothing if not thorough.

He stood there with a dog on either side of him as she picked through the jumble of stolen goods.

"Do you think that Gambit stole it all, or did they all contribute to the, uh, kitty?" Troy was thinking about what Patience said about the breed's criminal tendencies.

Mercy rolled her eyes at his bad pun. He couldn't help it, he loved puns, the worse, the better.

"Could be plenty of sticky paws here," she said. "A den of thieves."

"And not just the cats. Whatever Donald Walker was up to, it got him killed."

Mercy opened her fist and he spotted a couple of mismatched earrings. "There's more where that came from."

Troy opened the only evidence bag he had on him and Mercy dropped in the earrings. "Hold this, while I go get some more bags." He jogged around the Walker house to his truck, Elvis and Susie Bear accompanying him, just for the fun of it. Denise and Patience were gone; his truck and Mercy's Jeep were the only vehicles left. As he gathered up some more bags and headed back with the dogs to Mercy, he thought about what Harrington would say about their removing evidence from the scene. If you could call it evidence. Probably not much, but then Harrington didn't think much of anything Troy did outside of Fish and Wildlife.

Besides, he doubted anything a cat dragged in could bear much relevance to the case. But he kept that to himself as he held out the open bags for Mercy as she dropped the found items inside: a couple of thin silver bracelets, four old keys, a brass shell casing, two gold barrettes, a number of silver screws of various lengths and thicknesses, a plain gold wedding ring, and a few necklaces, one gold one with a small cross, one silver, and two cheap shiny pairs of beads that reminded Troy of the Mardi Gras beads that hung around the rearview mirror in Thrasher's truck. The captain had worked search and rescue in New Orleans after Katrina.

They bagged everything.

"This is the last one." Mercy held up a delicate if dirty silver chain with a silver pendant. "It's a mountain range, with pines." She pointed to the image on the pendant.

"Like the Vermont coat of arms."

"Not exactly. But definitely inspired by a landscape like ours." She squinted at the piece. "And close enough in style that it could have been made by the same jewelry designer. Maybe."

"Coincidence or tied to the belt buckles?"

"I don't believe in coincidence," they said at the same time.

CHAPTER TWENTY-FIVE

S HE SMILED AT HIM. "It looks handmade, which means that there may be a maker's mark."

"I'm assuming you don't mean the bourbon."

"No. The best jewelers stamp their work."

"The belt buckles didn't have a mark."

"No," said Mercy. "But they were definitely handmade. Maybe whoever made them didn't want to be associated with the Vermont Firsters." She snapped a couple of photos of the pendant with her cell phone, front and back.

"I'll have them take a good look when they clean them up."

"Better safe than sorry. Maybe when I get home I can blow these up and get a better look myself."

"You don't have to do everything yourself, you know."

"I know." Mercy frowned. "You're going to be in trouble for removing evidence. Harrington won't like it."

"But I didn't do anything." He grinned at her as she handed him the pendant. He dropped it into another evidence bag. "You found the Munchkin and removed the kitty's favorite things, as part of an animal rescue."

"Having first received permission from local authorities." She grinned back at him.

"Unfortunately, the cat's stash was found right after the Northshire Animal Control officer left the scene."

"Unfortunately."

"Okay, let me take in this evidence. And then we'll go see Dr. Winters, as promised."

They headed back around the house, dogs running ahead.

"Maybe we should stop off on the way somewhere and feed and water the dogs," he said, as Susie Bear and Elvis sat by their respective vehicles, thick tongues hanging out. "I think they could both use a drink and a snack."

"Me, too. I know you've got to get back on patrol eventually, but if you've got the time I wouldn't mind a quick pit stop myself."

"How about Hound Dawgs? It's on the way."

Susie Bear barked her approval and Mercy laughed. "Sounds good."

THIRTY MINUTES LATER they were feasting on the best hot dogs in Northshire in the abandoned lot where the popular food truck was stationed every summer. Plain dogs and water for Susie Bear and Elvis, loaded chili dogs and vanilla cream sodas for Troy and Mercy.

"This is summer food at its best," said Mercy, washing down the last of the bun with a slurp of soda.

"Yep." Troy admired her appetite. Madeline would never have indulged in a Hound Dawg; she was a fussy eater who lived on kale and grilled chicken and insisted that no self-respecting female could survive on the meat-and-potato diets that men preferred. There was nothing fussy about Mercy, and yet she was still feminine. Maybe the captain was right, and he'd let Madeline define his idea of the ideal woman for too long. Maybe that's what comes of marrying the high school girl of your dreams. Maybe you grow up, and everything changes.

"Want anything else?" asked Mercy. "My treat."

Elvis and Susie Bear raised their heads at her question, their own frankfurters long devoured. She laughed, a big belly laugh like her grandmother's. "I wasn't talking to you, dogs."

"I'm good," Troy said. And he was.

Mercy snapped the cone back on Elvis, much to his distaste. He barked his disapproval, and shook his head so hard Troy thought he might harm himself.

"Knock it off," she said in that command voice of hers. Elvis stopped in midshake. She laughed, and he licked her hand.

"Good dog," said Troy.

"Was there any doubt?"

They piled back into their respective vehicles and drove to the police station, where he dropped off the evidence bags for Harrington.

Luckily the detective was not there, and he could just hand it off to a uniform and bolt. He'd still have to tell Thrasher about it, and that would undoubtedly earn him another warning about the consequences of stepping on Harrington's toes.

He came out of the building, gave Mercy a thumbs-up, and climbed into the Ford F-150.

"Onward," he said to Susie Bear, and she thumped her plumed tail in agreement.

They took both dogs and both vehicles, in case Troy got called in to work, which was very likely. He could sleep next week.

He and Susie Bear led the way, careful to keep Mercy and Elvis in his rearview mirror. Thirty minutes later down Route 7, he turned the truck into a quiet old neighborhood not far from downtown Bennington. Nineteenth-century houses lined the wide street under a canopy of oak and maple trees.

The professor lived in the most imposing of these Victorian piles, an enormous painted lady done in dark purples, reds, and blues. The kind of house that had both intrigued and intimidated him as a kid. His aunt Edith had lived in a place like this, and she'd been as finicky and foreboding as her hulk of a house. He wondered if Dr. Winters was anything like his aunt. If so, this might prove an unpleasant and unsuccessful interview. He parked across the street and waited for Mercy and Elvis to pull up behind him. Susie Bear whimpered when he told her to stay put and stepped out of the truck without her. Mercy followed suit, and Troy figured Elvis wasn't any happier about being left behind than Susie Bear was.

"Creepy house," she said.

"Yeah." He didn't tell her about his aunt Edith.

They walked up a long stone path made of granite and up a half-dozen steps onto the wraparound porch, crowded with dark wicker furniture and planters overgrown with succulents.

"That's one angry gargoyle." She pointed to the big brass knocker on the door.

"Go ahead," said Troy.

Mercy raised her strawberry-blond eyebrows at him and he grinned. She banged the brass knocker, then stepped back, allowing him to take the lead. So far, so good.

The small woman who answered the door didn't look like a gargoyle or his aunt Edith. At first glance she seemed every bit the mousy professor, with her messy brown hair, pale skin, and gray eyes huge behind her nerdy black glasses. But her lips shone with red lipstick, and her prim white blouse and navy pants fit so snugly it was obvious she was not wearing anything underneath them. Overall, the effect was as subtle as it was devastating. He could only imagine how she held her students spellbound as she expounded on whatever it was she expounded on in her classes at Bennington.

"And you are?" Dr. Winters slipped her thick glasses down her thin nose and peered up at him with those myopic eyes.

"Warden Troy Warner."

"A man in uniform." She ran those expressive eyes over him once more before turning her attention to Mercy. He could feel his companion stiffen behind him. She stepped forward, and suddenly he felt like a moose caught between two she-wolves.

"This is Corporal Mercy Carr," he said.

"Not in uniform," said the professor.

"We're here to talk about Adam Wolfe," said Mercy.

"Oh, Adam." Dr. Winters walked away from them, down a wide marble-tiled hall that served as the very formal entry to the very formal house. She stopped and turned, her long tousled hair falling around her pale face, framing her red mouth. "Come on."

He caught Mercy rolling her eyes behind the professor's back as they followed her into what his aunt Edith would have called her parlor. Heavily curtained mullioned windows ran the length of the room, which was decorated within an inch of its life with antique furniture and cupboards cluttered with knickknacks against walls papered in peacock feathers. At least he thought they were peacock feathers. All historically accurate—he knew enough to know the reason these old houses were so awful was because they were historically accurate— but not a single place to sit that looked the least bit comfortable. Aunt Edith would have loved it.

There was nothing of his aunt in the way Dr. Winters curled up in a love seat as neatly as a cat. "What's Adam done now?"

"We understand that he's active in the Vermont First movement."

The professor laughed. Laughed just like Madeline. A tinkling sound that raised the hair on the back of his neck.

"Adam is an artist, not an activist." She dismissed the thought with a flutter of her small hands. "No matter what he says."

"You seemed to take him seriously enough when you wrote that article about him in the arts and politics journal," said Mercy.

Dr. Winters smiled. "When it comes to politics, Adam is a poseur. But when it comes to art, he's the real deal." She pointed to the only modern note in the room other than electricity, a two-foot bronze sculpture that sat on an ornately carved stand in the corner under a recessed spotlight. The striking piece was of a vaguely female form, all curves and whirls and hollows, all strength and softness and shine.

"That's his work?" Troy had to admit the guy had talent.

"It's lovely," said Mercy.

"It's brilliant," corrected the professor. "That piece is one of the last of his series of bronze nudes."

"He sold the rest?" asked Troy. "He must be very successful, then."

"He would have been." Dr. Winters shook her head. "He sold a couple of the pieces and kept the remainder of the series of bronzes in a locked warehouse close to his studio. Thieves broke in and stole them all." She sighed. "I comfort myself with the thought that they're locked away somewhere in some sheik's private art collection for the amusement of his harem."

"But that's not what happened," he said.

"No one really knows, but the suspicion is that the pieces were sold for scrap." She unwound her lithe body slowly. "Such a waste. Criminal."

"You were the model," said Mercy with a small smile.

"Yes." Dr. Winters licked her red-stained lips. "I'm grateful that in recognition of my contribution as his muse he gifted me with my first choice of the series. This one is my favorite, and it's safe here with me."

"No more modeling, then?" asked Mercy.

"Alas, no. Adam abandoned his work in metals to create natural sculptures."

"Which means what, exactly?" Troy never had looked it up.

"He gathers material he finds in nature—stones, sticks, feathers, bones—and creates sculptures there on site, integrating the art into the natural landscape."

"In the woods?" He was trying to picture this art, and failing.

"Woods, fields, bogs, streams, wherever."

"How can it last?"

"It's not meant to last. It's meant to be ephemeral. Like life."

"Like a sand painting?" asked Mercy.

"Adam does not create work only to have it blown away with the first strong wind. He designs it to last as long as possible, with the understanding that Mother Nature will have the last word."

Troy wanted to steer the conversation back to the matter at hand: Adam Wolfe's recent illegal activities and current whereabouts. "He's been accused of setting fire to logging trucks, trespassing, and creating his art on private property. Among other things."

"Absurd." The professor slid over to the sculpture. "Adam only wants to preserve the gallery that houses his art now."

"The woods?" asked Mercy.

"Exactly. He wants to save the trees." She ran her slender fingers along the curves of the artwork, which modeled her own. "It's called *Candy*."

"So you were close."

"We were more than close." The professor backed away from the sculpture and regarded Mercy in that feline way some women had of challenging other women. "We met at a party, and then we went to the south of France together."

"The south of France," repeated Troy.

"The French understand love. Or at least lovers." She smiled at them. "I spend every summer there. With a lover."

He didn't know what to say to that.

"It's July," said Mercy. "You're late."

"It's un-American to leave before the Fourth of July," the professor said, her eyes still on Troy. "I'm leaving for Provence on Tuesday. And I have an extra ticket."

He heard Mercy stifle a laugh. "Back to Adam Wolfe."

"Of course." She crossed her hands over her heart and sighed. "It was *très merveilleux* while it lasted." She turned to Mercy. "You know how it is. Or at least I hope you do."

Mercy nodded curtly, but he could see the sadness that suddenly clouded her eyes.

"These things run their course, don't they?" Dr. Winters smiled, whether in sympathy or spite he wasn't quite sure.

"I had other interests," she continued. "And tramping around in the wilderness . . . let's just say that's not my natural habitat." She curled back up on the love seat, perfectly framed by the peacock feathers—he was sure now—on the wall. "Adam became a hermit of sorts, living out in the woods, creating his art, growing more distraught over the loss of his natural space. Vermont's loss of wilderness. We lost touch. The last I heard he was in Canada."

"Lots of secessionists up there," he said.

"Lots of wilderness, too." She raised a pale eyebrow at him. "You said your name was Warner."

"Yes, ma'am." He could guess where this was going.

"As in Seth Warner."

"Yes, ma'am." Seth Warner was a captain in the Green Mountain Boys, the militia group active in the formation of the Vermont Republic. He later served as a colonel in the Continental Army during the Revolutionary War, lauded for his leadership during the capture of Fort Crown Point, the Battle of Longueuil, the siege of Quebec, the retreat from Canada, and the battles of Hubbardton and Bennington.

Troy's famous ancestor—at least famous among Vermonters and American history buffs—was a subject he usually tried to avoid.

"Then you should understand. 'Freedom and Unity.'"

"The Vermont motto."

"Then you do understand."

Troy did not bother to correct her. "Is there anything else you can tell us about his whereabouts?"

"I'm afraid not."

He handed her a card. "If you think of anything . . ."

"You know where I live." She smiled at him.

"Yes, ma'am."

"You never told me what this was about."

"Adam Wolfe is wanted in connection with a possible murder," said Mercy.

Dr. Winters laughed. That tinkling sound again. "Impossible."

They left her there in the parlor, tinkling still. Troy felt a surge of relief as he stepped out of that woman's hothouse into the cool shade of the oaks and maples.

"Wow." Mercy inhaled deeply and exhaled slowly.

"Some house," he said.

"Some woman," she said. "'Love is all truth, Lust full of forged lies.'"

"What do you mean?"

"I mean that I didn't believe a word of it. Except the part about her being the model for that sculpture."

"Why would she lie?"

She shook her head. "You don't know much about women, do you?"

Troy shrugged. "Maybe not." He checked his phone for messages. "I've got to get back to my patrols."

"Understood."

They crossed the street to their vehicles.

"Thanks for doing this," she said.

"I'm not sure what we've accomplished here."

"We've learned that everyone wants us to believe that Wolfe is in Canada."

"You think the Feds and local PD are lying?"

"I think they're mistaken."

"Unlikely."

"Amy says he's here."

Troy shook his head. "He's long gone. And so is she."

"You don't really think she killed her stepfather." Mercy shook her head. "Her mother is not to be believed."

"Agreed," he said. "But Amy remains a person of interest."

"So you are looking for her."

"Yes. But she's probably in Canada by now. With him."

"She was serious about leaving him." Mercy shook her head again, a flurry of loose curls. "I've met her. I can't believe she's capable of killing anyone."

"Amy is not capable of murder, Wolfe is not capable of murder, none of our suspects is capable of murder, and yet two men are dead."

Troy walked Mercy to her Jeep. Elvis was sitting up, cone in place, leaning against the window, alert as ever.

"You should go home. Get some rest."

"Sure," she said. "But first I'm going to get me and Elvis a creemee. Do you want to join us?"

"Thanks, but we've got to get back."

"Suit yourself."

He could feel her bright blue eyes on his back as he jumped in the truck, scratched Susie Bear's ears, and took off down the road. He watched her in the rearview mirror as long as he could, then tried to put her and her dog and the Vermont Firsters out of his mind.

Back to his real job.

CHAPTER TWENTY-SIX

MERCY WAITED UNTIL TROY'S TRUCK had disappeared from view. Then she drove around the block, coming back to the street where the professor lived and parking out of her sight several houses away behind a blue Land Rover. She bided her time feeding Elvis treats and sipping bottled water. She was used to waiting. The army taught you patience if nothing else. A patient soldier was a smart soldier.

Elvis was a smart soldier, too. Martinez had seen to that. The high-energy shepherd could stay perfectly still, quiet, and alert, as long as needed. Even when wearing the Cone of Humiliation, as Troy had called it. She smiled and patted the dog's head, scratching that sweet spot between his ears.

"I don't think it will be too long," she told him. "That's a woman in a hurry."

But not too much of a hurry. Nearly two hours passed before the heavy oak door with the angry gargoyle knocker opened and Dr. Winters came out, now dressed in cargo pants, hiking boots, and a white T-shirt. She had tied a beige cardigan around her shoulders and a camouflage-colored fanny pack around her hips.

Mercy watched as the woman drove off in a forest-green SUV. Her Vermont vanity license plate read *DR ART.*

"Let's see where Dr. Art goes," she told Elvis. "Ten bucks says she takes us right to Adam Wolfe."

When the professor was a couple of blocks away, Mercy began to follow her. The streets were relatively quiet; there weren't many vehicles on the road. It was late afternoon now; most everyone who was going anywhere on this holiday weekend was already there. When she could stay a car or two behind she did, but when she couldn't, she fell back, slowing down to avoid detection.

"I think we're in for a long ride," she predicted, as Dr. Winters headed onto Route 7 going north. She was right, not that Elvis argued the point. He was always content to let her drive.

Nearly an hour later, the SUV exited Route 7 and navigated a number of increasingly remote and rugged roads. Mercy pursued her at a discreet distance, thankful for the many highs and lows and twists and turns of these roads, which afforded her red Jeep some much-needed cover. Surveillance was a critical skill for a cop, military or otherwise. She excelled at it; she liked the role of observer, especially when she herself was unobserved. People behaved differently when no one was looking—usually for the worse than for the better, but not always. She wondered how the professor would behave, but she didn't hold out much hope that it would be for the better.

The SUV jostled down an old logging road. Mercy drove carefully, maneuvering the Jeep to minimize the bumping for Elvis's sake. Although he seemed fine, apart from the cone, which he obviously hated even more after his taste of freedom, shaking his head vigorously from time to time in an effort to remove it.

Her cell phone had stopped working several miles back. If she was going to keep this up, she'd need a vehicle with satellite GPS, she thought. Not that she was going to keep on surveilling people. This was just for Amy and Helena. A one-off. She was done with police work.

The SUV came to a sudden stop. She stopped, too. They were the only vehicles on this road, and odds were that would not change. She had to be even more careful now. The risk of exposure was high.

Elvis whined and tossed his head, and the cone shuddered.

"You are so smart." Mercy held the cone steady with one hand and the steering wheel with the other. "You know I'm going after her, don't you, and that you won't be coming along."

The professor did not get out of her car, but again began to bump along the logging road, which grew narrower and rougher as it led deeper into the spruce-fir forest.

The more slowly Dr. Winters went, the greater the risk of Mercy being spotted. She let the SUV go on ahead and the Jeep fall back. If the woman drove any more slowly, she'd have to pull over and pursue Dr. Winters on foot.

Elvis was agitated now, banging the cone against the side of the passenger door.

"Settle down," she ordered.

He ignored her, bashing the cone harder. He began to bark.

"Quiet."

The stubborn shepherd bellowed.

"Look, she's getting away. I've got to go now."

Elvis continued to whip his head around, more wildly still.

"Okay, okay." She unsnapped her seat belt. "You're going to go hurt yourself if you keep this up."

Patience had warned her that he'd resist the cone, and that it should stay on until he was healed or he destroyed it. At this rate it wouldn't be long before he achieved the latter. She didn't have the time to deliberate, so she made a decision. She released him from the cone and hoped she wouldn't regret it. Elvis shook his handsome head, his dark eyes shining with triumph.

"Show-off." She tried not to laugh as she parked the Jeep as far over to the side of the road as she could in a little clearing behind a thin copse of young birch. Not the perfect camouflage, but better than nothing.

"Let's go," she said sternly, slipping her pack onto her back and pushing the door open for him. He leapt along the road, which was little more than a pitted path at this point, overjoyed to be free of impediments and on the job again.

She jogged after him, her eyes on his bandaged backside. He seemed completely normal, suffering no ill effects that she could tell. Whether that was from a lack of pain or an excess of pride she wasn't sure. Just like Martinez.

The SUV was out of sight, but she could still hear it caroming farther and farther into the wilderness. The sun hung lower in the sky now, an orange blaze on its slow descent toward a summer sunset. Only a few hours of daylight left. Mercy let out a low whistle and Elvis bounded back to her.

They kept to the tree line, veering off into the woods when the road straightened and they were in danger of being seen. The sound of the SUV was their guide, competing with the pounding of woodpeckers and the rustling of squirrels and the distant cries of loons. The logging road wove in and out of the national forest proper, skirting private property. *No Trespassing* signs appeared from time to time, marking areas forbidden to strangers.

The hardwoods forest was thick with pine, maples, beech, and birch, but as they climbed pockets of spruce and fir appeared, eventually to give way to the softwoods forest of the higher elevations. She navigated the thickets of hobblebush, beaked hazelnut, and shadbush, admiring the mountain azalea even as she avoided the stinging wood nettle.

This was obviously a road little used by loggers in recent times. There were only a few sets of tire treads, made by ATVs mostly, along with the professor's own SUV and the odd truck. Mercy knew that squatters were scattered throughout these woods in abandoned camps and makeshift shelters and hand-built cabins. They were an eclectic bunch: seasonal farmers and marijuana growers, hermits and the homeless, survivalists and cultists.

Vermont had its share of crazies like everywhere else. As Patience liked to say, "Where there's woods, there's wacky." Mercy wondered what kind of wacky Dr. Winters was leading them toward. She suspected that it was Adam Wolfe's compound or art colony or whatever it was.

The professor drove so slowly that they were in danger of catching up to her. The so-called road was little more than a wide ditch now. Mercy and Elvis trudged along a parallel path close to the trail's edge, but when the SUV finally came to a full stop before a clumsily fenced encampment, they ducked deeper into the forest. The barbwire rolls that comprised the barrier were standard-issue military-grade perimeter controls, three-foot-wide cylinders of sharp points designed to discourage intruders—hastily constructed but effective enough to dissuade most interlopers.

The compound itself was a glorified squatters colony of three ten-foot-by-ten-foot tent cabins on raised logs and a long, thirty-foot-by-fifteen-foot Quonset hut, all cuddled together in a clearing shaped like a baseball diamond. A large commercial-grade truck about the size of a rental moving van was parked in front, its back door rolled up to accommodate a ramp. Mercy couldn't see what was inside, apart from a vague sense of folded boxes and tarps.

She watched as a tall man in dark running pants and a dark T-shirt approached the SUV and talked to Dr. Winters across the fence. She couldn't hear them very well—they were too far away and the rush of a nearby stream made it even harder to discern what they were saying—but from the looks of his face and her gesticulations, he was not happy to see her. She thought she heard the professor call him Max as her voice raised in protest over something he said. Eventually he shook his shaved head, stomping over to open the gate and letting Dr. Winters drive inside. He guided her over to park by the side of the tent cabin nearest the gate, providing a clean entry and exit in and out, presumably for the truck. Mercy couldn't see any other vehicles, at least not from this vantage point.

The man offered the professor a hand to help her out of the SUV, but she shook him off, jumping down to the ground as gracefully as a lynx. She strode off to the tent cabin in the middle without a second glance at the guy she'd called Max.

Mercy wanted to get a closer look. She held a finger to her lips, signaling silence to Elvis, and quietly made her way with the dog around the colony, following the barbedwire fence. The woods were very dense and layered here. The forest floor was thick with branches and brambles and slick with pine needles and moss. Elvis stepped through the chaos carefully, and she followed in his wake. He alerted, whether to the tall man or to Dr. Winters or to whatever was in that truck, Mercy wasn't sure. The shepherd's black triangular ears perked up and he pushed as close to the barbwire as he could get. So close that she worried he'd nick his nose. But he sank into his classic Sphinx pose, his snout still intact.

She turned her attention back to the tall man. There was something familiar about the way the he held his shoulders but she couldn't say for sure whether he was the masked man she'd seen running from her house or not. As she studied him, he raised his head and looked their way. She didn't think he saw them, but she wasn't taking any chances.

"Come on," she whispered to Elvis. Together they melted back into the forest, and proceeded around the perimeter of the clearing from the safe perspective of at least twenty feet deep under the leafy cover of maples and beeches and birches.

If the entrance to the compound was home plate, then the tent cabin where Dr. Winters had gone was about second base. They were somewhere between first and second base when they came upon an art installation. The work was so cleverly woven into the natural landscape that Mercy nearly missed it.

Elvis found it first. About thirty feet away from the barbwire perimeter, secreted among the logs of a small blowdown area, was a stone structure seemingly suspended between two granite outcroppings. The arch was made of river rock, smooth granite stones chiseled into rough bricks and seemingly held into place by gravity alone.

She stepped up to the sculpture to take a closer look. She was afraid to touch it, for fear that it might fall down. But she knew that it most likely would not; the stones were packed tightly and meticulously, and the structure appeared sturdy enough. The artfully shaped crescent seemed to grow right out of the boulders that served as its abutments. Along its archivolt, the length of smaller stones that ran underneath the main arch, there were faint, fairly shallow markings that looked like Greek letters. Her Greek was terrible, and her Latin only marginally better. She snapped cell photos of the arch, including close-ups of the lettering.

A dry riverbed of rocks ran underneath the arch. When Mercy squatted down to examine the stone current, she realized that this, too, was part of the sculpture. The spirals of stone were too perfect to be natural. Fractal patterns of swirls echoed the curve of the arch overhead and the Greek lettering on the granite blocks themselves.

More photos. She wasn't sure of the significance of this art installation, if any, but better safe than sorry. The materials and settings of the two art pieces she had seen today—the bronze sculpture in Dr. Winters's parlor and this natural sculpture here in the woods—were very different, but she could see the hand of the same artist at work in each piece. The feminine curves and hollows and whorls of the bronze were echoed here in this piece, enhanced and expanded and enlightened in the wilderness.

Adam Wolfe, thought Mercy. She wondered who might be the model for this work—the ebullient Amy Walker as Madonna or the sexy professor Dr. Winters as nerd goddess or maybe simply Mother Nature herself.

Elvis did not alert to the sculpture, after finding it. He backed up a couple of yards and kept looking toward the compound, inching toward the barbwire fence, his eyes on the truck and the tall man loading it.

She snapped her fingers softly and he trotted over to the art installation. He showed little interest in the formation.

Sometimes a sculpture is just a sculpture, thought Mercy. She tried to use her phone to text Troy, but of course she got no signal. On the other side of the installation Elvis sniffed at a hiking trail that led through the woods. Mercy figured that the trail must lead back through the northwestern corner of the forest. She thought they'd stumbled upon it on one of their hikes last fall, but she wasn't sure. Elvis would know. He never forgot a trail.

Wherever it led she was glad to see it; if the way back around the compound and out to the Jeep was blocked and they needed to escape quickly, they'd need an alternate route. And here it was.

"Good job," she whispered to Elvis.

She heard a snap behind her. The shepherd growled, a guttural utterance from deep within his chest guaranteed to frighten most anyone, whether they liked dogs or not.

She spun around. A man of medium height and weight stepped forward. A bird-watcher, if the birding binoculars around his neck and the field bag slung over his shoulder and the vented safari hat on his head were any indication. He wore a gray and blue plaid flannel shirt and khaki trousers and scuffed-up hiking boots. He was about thirty-five years old, with tired hazel eyes and short brown hair.

"It's a little late in the day for birding, isn't it?" Mercy noted that as far as she could tell he had no night-vision gear with him, so if he said anything about nocturnal viewing she'd figure he was lying.

"I was hoping for a close-up glimpse of a bouquet of black-throated warblers," said the bird-watcher. "They come here to breed in the summertime." He cocked his hatted head. "If you listen carefully, you can hear their *zoo-zee, zoo-zee* song."

She listened, and followed the lazy, buzzy birdsong to a sapling, where she spotted an open nest woven of bark strips and lined with pine needles. A little gray bird perched inside, while its brighter blue mate darted among the leaves, looking for dinner.

"Beautiful, aren't they?"

"Yes."

"They're making a comeback, at least for now. If they don't cut down all their wintering grounds in the Caribbean, we'll see them here every summer."

Elvis growled again.

Enough about birds, thought Mercy.

"What do you know about that compound?" Her voice held a command in it, and the bird-watcher looked startled.

"Rufus Flanigan," he said, putting out his hand with caution, one anxious eye on the dog.

"Mercy Carr," she said and shook his hand.

"Are you a police officer? You act like a police officer."

She didn't say anything. Just let him ramble on as Elvis snarled at him.

"I was on my way home. Then I saw the girl and her baby again. You know, the one in the AMBER Alert. I reported seeing them yesterday."

She nodded. "Were they all right?"

"They were in the company of a man who looked, I don't know, sketchy. The girl seemed unhappy about it."

"Where are they now?"

"I think they're in one of the tent cabins, the one over on the far side of the compound. I was going to hike out and call for help, and then I saw you. And your dog."

"I don't think she's here because she wants to be."

"Me, either. I see the mother with her baby on my hikes. I've never approached them, I like to mind my own business in the hope that other people will mind theirs." He smiled slightly. "But when the AMBER Alert went out, I thought I should come forward. I never believed that she'd ever hurt her baby. They always looked so happy together. I was just worried that they might be in trouble. And then I see them with this creepy guy." He waved his hands, big rough mitts that attracted Elvis's attention. Noting the dog's interest, he quickly stuck them in his pockets, out of sight if not out of range.

Mercy smiled back at him as a counterpunch to the shepherd's fierce muzzle. "Look, I'm retired law enforcement. We sometimes assist . . ." She trailed off and let him make whatever assumptions might prove valuable to her. "Hike out of here and get help. Call this number." She fished Troy's card out of her back pocket and handed it to the guy, who managed to look impressed and intimidated at the same time. Probably thanks to Elvis, who still appeared ready to pounce on him at any moment. "Tell Warden Warner what you told me. He'll know what to do."

"What are you going to do?"

"We'll see."

He glanced toward the compound. "Be careful."

"I've got Elvis."

"Okay." He backed up. "I'll take this trail. It leads back around through the Lye Brook Wilderness and hooks up with the Long Trail. I'll call as soon as I can get a signal."

He turned to go. She wasn't sure what she thought of him, and it was clear Elvis didn't much like him. But there was no one else around to help them.

"He's all we got," she told the dog as they watched him hike away down the path. She hoped she could trust him.

The woods swallowed up the bird-watcher and the trail completely within fifty yards. All that was left of him was the call of the black-throated warblers.

He was long gone by the time Mercy realized he'd never said anything about the art installation. He must have seen it before. If this was Wolfe's art colony—or whatever—he may have followed Amy and Helena back here. Maybe he was a stalker. Or maybe he was as scared of Elvis as he appeared to be, and art was the last thing on his mind.

Together she and the shepherd continued to circle the compound. She was looking for a break in the fence. She needed to get through that barbwire, one way or another, so she could find Amy and the baby. Or at least a spot far enough away from the tent cabins and the Quonset hut and out of the line of sight that she could snip the razor-sharp wire and wiggle through unharmed.

She patted the cargo pocket on her right hip, reassuring herself that her trusty knife was still there as always. The Swiss Champ version that her grandmother preferred boasted a whopping thirty-three functions, including a wire cutter.

She found no breach in the fence, which was to be expected. No one bothers to put up a barbwire barrier in the forest unless they are serious about keeping people in and critters out. Bear, moose, deer, even the occasional bobcat roamed these woods, along with the smaller but equally tough mammals like pine martens and mink.

They stayed hidden in the forest about a dozen feet within the perimeter of the compound. They didn't see anyone, other than the man who accompanied Dr. Winters to the tent cabin in the middle. He was back loading the truck with cardboard boxes. Elvis still didn't like the guy, but he kept quiet. Whoever else was in the clearing—the professor, Amy and Helena, the elusive Adam Wolfe—was apparently in a tent cabin.

Mercy and Elvis were directly behind the middle cabin now. The one into which the professor had disappeared and from which she had yet to emerge. The shepherd shadowed her as instructed, although all his prancing and dancing indicated that he was as itching to get into that colony as she was.

It was slow going. The forest floor was cluttered with vegetation and downed branches and loose stones, and the trees towered so closely together over them that moving silently was especially tricky. Dusk was falling now and soon the forest would be cloaked in darkness. They wouldn't have too much time left in the light for exploration. She had a flashlight but using it would announce their presence like a beacon.

Fifteen minutes later, they came around to the back of the last of the tent cabins, round about third base of the baseball diamond–shaped compound. They were still about a dozen feet away from the barbwire fence. She sneaked up toward the barrier. Elvis dropped to his haunches, scooting beside her, alerting and crawling at the same time.

She didn't see anyone; even the man loading the truck was gone. Or at least out of sight. The truck was still there, its cargo now secured behind the closed roll-up door.

She could sense the shepherd's agitation and he could sense hers. She could feel their respective anxieties fueling each other, and that was no good. She stopped to breathe, slowly inhaling and exhaling, and stroking Elvis's fine head and neck the way she did on the mat. Calming them both down.

"Good boy," she whispered. "Stay." She didn't know what was waiting on the other side of that fence. So he needed to stay put.

Mercy opened her knife and pulled out the wire-cutting tool. Carefully she snipped through the wire, avoiding the slashing points. She was about halfway through the triple rolls of metal, when Elvis perked up and started pawing at the ground, ready to dig his way under the fence if she couldn't slice through it fast enough.

Then she heard it, too. The faint cry of an infant. *Helena.*

"Stay," she ordered the dog in her deepest alpha voice and hurried to cut through the remainder of the wires. Once it was cut, she pulled the fence apart cautiously. As soon as she'd managed a foot-wide opening, Elvis slipped past her and into the compound proper, bounding toward the sound of the crying baby.

"Come," she commanded. But the shepherd ignored her. He'd never have disobeyed his sergeant this way, she thought, cursing as she scrambled in through the barbwire after him. She stood up, ready to follow the dog. The snap of a twig behind her stopped her cold. She heard Elvis snarl just as she sensed someone behind her and the blow to come. She couldn't let anything happen to him again. "No, Elvis!" She needed him to be safe. "Go home. Home to Patience!"

The last sounds that registered in her brain were those of a dog barking and a baby crying and a shot firing. Or was it a truck backfiring? She didn't know. Her brain wouldn't work. She stood there, somehow suspended in time, while the inside of her head exploded.

"Patience," she said again, but her voice was just a squeak, and she went down.

CHAPTER TWENTY-SEVEN

Troy and Susie Bear stopped by the office on Main Street in Northshire on the way back out on patrol. Thrasher was there, with reports from the Major Crime Unit on the murder of Donald Jonas Walker. He was perfectly turned out as always, his uniform pressed and boots shined, despite the long days on the job this time of year. His boss hadn't had any more sleep than he'd had, but where Troy knew he'd need a shower and a shave and a change of clothes to look presentable, Thrasher looked every inch the prepared and alert professional.

They stood in the back of the warden service office by the whiteboard, which bore a map of the area marked with the locations of the victims and sightings of Amy and the baby, as well as photos and facts pertaining to the case. They went over what they knew so far about the Walker murder and the Bones case, as they were calling it unofficially.

"Two dead men, three years apart, both found with representations of the Vermont coat of arms."

"Adaptations of the coat of arms," corrected Troy, who regretted the correction as soon as the words were out of his mouth.

"Adaptations of the coat of arms," repeated Thrasher good-naturedly. He was petting the shaggy dog's floppy ears, his blue-green eyes on Troy. "A belt buckle and some ink. Pretty thin."

"Don't forget the pendant."

The captain raised an eyebrow. "Hidden by a cat."

"A cat with a clue."

Thrasher rolled his eyes. "They found twenty thousand dollars in cash hidden in the recliner where Walker was sitting when he died. Now that's a motive."

Troy whistled. "That's a lot of money for a guy living in a crap house full of cats."

"His wife claims he won it playing bingo." The captain smiled as Susie Bear rolled over, exposing her belly for a sweet rub. He squatted down to humor her with a good tummy scratching. Her big black tail thumped away on the wide oak-planked floor as he dragged his fingers through the long black fur that graced her rumbling stomach. "I think she's hungry. Let's go get pizza."

"Bingo?" Troy laughed. "Definitely time for pizza."

Pizza was one of the Newfie mutt's favorite words, along with *lunch, supper, treat, play, walk,* and *search*. She shuffled to her feet, and led the way out of the office and down the street to Pizza Bob's Wood Fired Pie Company. Pizza Bob's was the best place in town for pizza, and not only because it was the only one with outside seating that accommodated the dog. It wasn't much to look at, outside or inside, but the massive one-of-a-kind pizza oven decoratively painted with graffiti art made up for it. Susie Bear's favorite kind of pie was the Howl: hand-tossed with pepperoni, sausage, bacon, meatballs, and ham. With a large bowl of water on the side.

Troy and Thrasher shared an extra-large with the dog and passed on the water in favor of the fresh root beer on tap.

"So who wins twenty grand at bingo?"

"According to Karen Walker, her husband went to the American Legion in Middlebury every Wednesday," said Thrasher. "Says they have a three-thousand-dollar pot at their bingo."

"Seriously?"

"That part could be true. Big bucks in bingo."

"Yeah, but, that doesn't mean Walker came by the money that way."

"Easy enough to check out," said Thrasher. "The staties are on it. Bet you a Howl pie it won't."

"No, thanks." Troy had a long history of losing pizza bets to the captain. Which was only fair, since his dog ate most of the pie anyway. But he wasn't biting this time.

"The wife says it's hers now, wherever it came from."

Troy gave Susie Bear another slice of her favorite pie. She waited politely for him to do so, then devoured it in three rapid chomps. "She also says her daughter killed him."

"No love lost there."

Troy remembered how Mercy Carr had put it: *She's not to be believed.*

"Maybe not. But she's denied any abuse on his part. Or hers." Thrasher reached for another slice with greasy fingers.

"She would."

"Maybe. They've issued a warrant for Amy Walker's arrest."

"Based on the mother's word?"

Thrasher drained his mug of root beer. "And the baby's abandonment and subsequent disappearance."

"Mercy Carr believes that Amy is the victim, not the perp."

"And you?" The captain's voice held an edge Troy had learned to respect.

"I don't know." He proceeded with caution. "But I do believe that the two deaths are connected to the explosives the dog alerted to."

"Maybe."

"Elvis is a military working dog. You know how well trained they are." Susie Bear perked up at the sound of the Belgian shepherd's name and took her eyes off the remainder of the pizza to regard Troy with interest. He shook his head and tossed her another piece to make up for her canine buddy's absence.

"Could have just been fireworks."

"Mercy says he had the best nose in Afghanistan."

"Well, if Mercy says so . . ."

Troy could feel himself flush. He thought the captain was teasing him, but he was never quite sure. The man's deadpan delivery always threw him off. "What I mean is, she's not the kind of woman who exaggerates. Sir."

Thrasher grinned. "Point taken."

"And she's done some solid police work. Given us some solid leads."

"Yes, but she's still a civilian. Let's not forget that."

"She was an MP."

"Exactly. She *was* an MP."

Troy wasn't making a strong enough case. He tried another tack. "What about the Vermont Firsters?"

"Cranks. But harmless."

"So say the staties." Troy told the captain about the intruder who tossed Mercy's house and shot at Elvis. And their visit to see the professor. Better he should tell him himself rather than risk his finding out some other way.

"I'm glad the dog is all right." Thrasher lifted his hands and frowned, whether at his greasy fingers or his warden's confession, Troy wasn't sure. "Any idea what the guy was after?"

"No, sir."

"Let's hope it wasn't the baby."

"Yes, sir."

Thrasher wiped his hands carefully with the substantial stack of paper napkins Pizza Bob knew the fastidious captain would require, and always made sure to provide. "What did you think of Dr. Winters?"

"She's an interesting woman."

"She's a piece of work. Or so I've heard."

Troy wonder how and what he'd heard, firsthand, secondhand, or up close and personal. The captain knew more about people, places, and things in Vermont than anyone he'd ever met. Including the state databases.

"Doesn't mean she's guilty," continued Thrasher. "And she confirmed that Wolfe was in Canada."

"That's what she said," he admitted.

"But you didn't believe her."

"Mercy Carr didn't believe her."

Thrasher's blue-green eyes were smiling now. "And you did."

"I don't know."

"You never did know much about women."

It was Troy's turn to frown. "That's what she said."

Thrasher laughed. And every woman at Pizza Bob's turned to look at him. He rarely laughed out loud, but when he did, he did so with a strong laugh that raised the roof and the blood pressure of every female in the room. "Smart girl."

Pizza Bob dropped by the table with the check, and the captain paid it over Troy's protests.

"At least take what's left."

"And deprive this outstanding canine of a late-night snack?" Thrasher shook his head and handed him the box with the leftover pizza. "Look, I know you like the girl and her dog. But stay out of it."

"Yes, sir." He took the box, holding it high and away from Susie Bear as they walked back down to the office.

"I mean it," said Thrasher. "A body in our wilderness is one thing. You found it on our beat, and that gave you some small justification for keeping your hand in even after we turned it over to Harrington. But you didn't find Donald Walker dead in the woods. There's no way you can interfere with that investigation, whether the two murders are connected or not. He won't stand for it. You know what he's like."

"Yes, sir."

"Let the Major Crime Unit handle it," said Thrasher. "You've got patrols."

TROY AND SUSIE Bear spent half the night tracking down drunk boaters and issuing citations for speeding and writing tickets for expired fishing licenses. But at least he stayed mostly dry this time. By the time they got home to the fire tower it was after eleven, and they were both exhausted. He more than she, since the dog had an unfailing ability to nap practically anywhere—on the dock, on the boat, in the truck, wherever. Although she was always quick to rise in the event of suspicious activity, if he needed her. Or if there were kids or food around. She loved all kids and all food, not necessarily in that order.

He took a quick shower, pulled down the Murphy bed, and tumbled into it. Susie Bear ate the rest of the pizza and then joined him, taking up more than her fair share of the queen-size mattress.

By midnight the phone was ringing. He reached for his cell, and to his surprise it wasn't Thrasher or Mercy Carr calling.

It was Patience O'Sullivan.

CHAPTER TWENTY-EIGHT

FIFTEEN MINUTES LATER he and the Newfie mutt were at the Sterling Animal Hospital in the vet's brightly colored kitchen rich with the smell of freshly brewed Speeder & Earl's Adirondack Blend coffee. Patience poured him a cup while she told him what had happened.

"Elvis showed up at my back door. Dirty and dehydrated and completely stressed out."

Susie Bear sniffed her canine friend all over, deliberately and devotedly, from tail to nose. Finally she licked his dark snout, apparently convinced that he was all right. Then she banked up next to him, placing her large noggin along the curve of his curlicue tail.

Troy drank his coffee with one hand and petted the shepherd's fine head with the other. "He seems okay."

"He's fine now. Watered and fed and somewhat rested."

"You took off his cone?"

"No, I didn't. He didn't have it on. No sign of it anywhere, either."

"And his injury?"

"I changed the bandage and dressed the wound. Pretty clean despite the rest of him, which was a mess."

"Ticks?"

"A scourge. That hard-core flea-and-tick collar and the vaccine and meds help. I put him on antibiotics for anaplasmosis just in case."

"Where's Mercy?"

"She's not answering her cell or her landline. I drove over there and she's not at home. The Jeep's not there, either. No sign of forced entry. That's when I called you." Patience's voice was steady but her hand shook slightly as she sipped her coffee.

At the sound of Mercy's name, Elvis sat up and whined. Susie Bear followed suit in a show of canine solidarity.

"She likes him," said Patience, with a smile. "And why shouldn't she? He's a handsome devil."

Troy hoped that she was talking about the dogs. At least he told himself that he hoped she was talking about the dogs.

"She was going after the intruder."

He shook his head. "I left her at the professor's house. She was on her way home."

"Was she?"

"My fault." Troy felt stupid, and worse, incompetent. "She asked me if we wanted to join them for a creemee."

"And you declined."

"Patrols."

"Uh-huh." Patience looked at him. The same look her grand-daughter had given him when she told him he didn't know anything about women. "Elvis knows where she is."

"I'll get Thrasher to put a trace on her cell." Troy texted his boss, then stood up. Susie Bear scrambled to her feet. "Don't worry. We'll find her."

"What about Elvis?"

Troy looked down at the dog, resting quietly. "He should probably stay here."

"But you'll need him. Mercy will need him."

"If you're sure . . . I don't want to be responsible for anything happening to her dog."

"I don't, either. But I'm not sure you could stop him. He came here to me for a reason."

"I'm not sure what you mean."

"Mercy sent him here. Otherwise he would never have left her."

As if to prove her right, the shepherd leapt to his feet. He danced around Troy, barking and nudging his hands with his nose. "Okay, okay."

With both dogs ready to roll, he snapped on the tracking leads Patience provided. Elvis pulled at the leash and bounded for the back door.

"That's where I found him. He came from there," she said, pointing at the forest that edged her property down the hill past the outbuildings.

Thrasher called him back with the results of the trace on Mercy's phone. "Signal ends at the northwest end of the national forest. I'll text you the coordinates."

"Thank you, sir."

"I'm afraid you're on your own," said Thrasher. "Everyone's either in the field or down in Bennington."

"Understood."

"Probably a wild goose chase." Thrasher paused.

"She'd never leave the dog." As soon as he said it, he realized that it was not just an argument, it was the truth. Patience said the dog would never leave her, but it was just as true that she would never leave the dog. He was going to find her, one way or another.

"If you need backup, it may take a while." The captain sounded worried.

"What else is new?"

"Be careful."

"I'll be fine. These are my woods."

TIME TO GO. Elvis balked when they headed for the front door, but the vet helped steer him out to Troy's truck. The shepherd still didn't seem convinced. Troy opened the door to the backseat of the cab, and Susie Bear leaped in. But Elvis did not follow.

Patience smiled. "Smart. This way they won't fight over the front seat. Which is mine."

"You need to stay here."

"I'm coming along." She helped persuade the Belgian shepherd into the back with Susie Bear. He was not happy about it.

"Stay," ordered Patience, and the dog settled down.

She opened the passenger door, but Troy reached out to block her way.

"You need to stay here," he repeated. "In case she calls or comes home."

The vet glared at him, but he knew she would stay behind, because he was right, whether she liked it or not. The dogs yowled.

No one was happy with him.

"Find my girl." It was an order, not a request.

"Yes, ma'am."

"She can take care of herself—but something's happened. She needs help or she wouldn't have sent Elvis." She slammed the door shut, then walked around to the driver's side and handed him a pack. "Extra water, food, and first aid. For them." She wrapped a big piece of carrot cake in a cloth napkin and handed it to him. "For you."

Elvis barked his displeasure as Troy pulled out of the animal hospital parking lot and onto Main Street.

Susie Bear nudged Elvis with her nose, as if to say, *Chill, he knows what he's doing.*

Not that he was very sure he did. Thrasher was right. He had no idea where Mercy Carr was or what she was doing. Only that she'd disappeared and left her dog on his own in the woods.

But he drove on anyway. Seven miles up Route 7, Troy pulled into a dirt road, the first of many unpaved roads that led to the co-ordinates that the captain had given him. They were deep in the forest that made up three-quarters of the state of Vermont. Forest rich in flora and fauna and secrets, both natural and man-made. He wondered what hidden dangers Mercy might have encountered in these dark woods—bear or bobcat or worse. This was not new territory for her; she knew the perils of the wild as well as the pitfalls of the battlefield. She knew what beasts were capable of, human and otherwise.

He found himself hoping that she was armed. As a retired MP she could carry in the state of Vermont, provided she'd followed regulation to the letter. Which he'd bet she did. She seemed like a by-the-book cop—in a good way. Which meant until she wasn't. Just like him.

As he approached the coordinates, Troy slowed down. He stopped the vehicle just long enough to make sure the twenty-foot tracking leads on both dogs were secure. He didn't want either one of them running off in the dark and leaving him behind. He trusted Susie Bear to obey his commands, but Elvis didn't seem to answer consistently to anyone. From what he'd seen, the shepherd did what Mercy told him to do when he felt like it and ignored her the rest of the time. Troy suspected the only person Elvis had ever obeyed without question was his sergeant. The man Mercy loved. Obviously a brave man, good with dogs, but then he had gone and gotten himself killed. And now two fine soldiers—Mercy and Elvis—still mourned him.

Troy parked the truck at the precise point indicated by the coordinates, on an old, deeply rutted logging road. He knew this part of the wilderness; he'd tracked some squatters who were night hunting and deer baiting in this general vicinity last autumn. It was possible that Mercy could have run afoul of them, never the kind of guys you'd want to run into anywhere, much less here. But any number of undesirables could be lying in wait around here.

He slipped his headlamp, red light shining, around his head. He slid on his pack, armed and ready, the dog leads tight in one hand, his flashlight in the other. He let Elvis and Susie Bear out, and they bounded down the road, Elvis in front, straining at the leash. Troy jogged to keep up, careful not to trip in the ruts.

A mile down the trail they came upon Mercy's Jeep, partially hidden behind some trees in a clearing that flanked the rough road. Its tires were all flat, thanks to long cuts obviously made by a knife. Troy held up the flashlight and peered inside the locked vehicle; everything seemed normal apart from the absence of its operator and the slashed tires.

The Malinois ignored the Jeep and danced at the end of the leash, pressing onward and nearly toppling him.

"Stay," he ordered, and to his surprise the athletic dog stayed. But he whined and whimpered his impatience to get on with the chase.

Satisfied that there was nothing more the disabled vehicle could tell them, Troy examined the area around it and saw where Mercy and Elvis had tracked someone, sticking close to the tree line. Her Jeep's tread marks stopped where it was parked, but another set—belonging to an SUV or sport truck by the looks of them—continued down the potholed road deeper into the forest, north toward Peru Peak.

"Go on," he told the dogs. "Search."

Elvis leapt for the tracks she had left behind, and Troy and Susie Bear charged after him. He thought about Mercy, out here all alone but for the beasts of the woods and the dark of the night and whoever slashed her tires.

He had a bad feeling. He picked up his pace. Elvis felt his increase in speed and ran faster, faster, faster. Susie Bear lumbered along, the steady metronome between the wired shepherd and his own anxious self.

Troy hoped they weren't too late.

CHAPTER TWENTY-NINE

Mercy's head hurt. She was cold and wet and lying on the forest floor. She found herself within the compound, a couple of feet from where she'd cut through the barbwire fence. Her Red Sox cap was still clamped over her curls. She raised her hands and tentatively touched the back of her skull, and felt around with her fingers. No blood, just a whopper of a bump on her head.

She knew she had to try to stay awake, but moving was hardly an option. Every time she tried to stand up, her head swam and her knees buckled. The third time she called it quits, and crawled on her hands and knees over to a beech tree, fighting down the bile that rose in her throat every step of the way. She rolled over onto her butt and sat in front of the tree, leaning against the thick trunk for support, her legs splayed in front of her, breathing heavily.

It was quite dark. The silence was deafening, the only sounds the white-noise rush of a nearby brook and the occasional hoot of a barred owl or the yodel of a coyote. She listened for the rumble of a car along Route 7, which you could sometimes hear by day, even when deep in the forest. But not tonight.

It hurt to hold her head up. It hurt to listen. She held her throbbing head in her hands. She was thankful for the barbwire, which at least kept the largest of the mammals out of her way. But the bugs were out in force. She straightened her back and raised her head. She swatted and slapped at the pests that beset her in the dark as she pulled water from her pack and sipped, eyes closed while she waited for the nausea to pass and the sun to rise.

There was no sign of activity in the compound. All was quiet. And the darkness was so complete that she could not even make out the shapes of the tent cabins. Or maybe it was simply that her crown ached so badly that whenever she opened her eyes, she could hardly see what was in front of her, light or no light. Her phone and her gun were gone, but her pack remained.

She had a flashlight in her pack. If she could only rouse herself enough to get it out.

The temptation to give in to sleep—or was it unconsciousness?—was overwhelming. She needed to stay awake. She did what she used to do when she needed to breathe through boredom and pain on a long march at boot camp in Fort Leonard Wood: she quoted Shakespeare. Her favorite soliloquies, the ones she knew by heart, rotating among her favorites. Hamlet's *To be or not to be.* Henry V's St. Crispin's Day speech. Portia's *quality of mercy* speech. Othello's *It is the cause.*

But here, in the dark, as she hunkered down against the tree trunk, her skull drummed to the beat of *Richard II*:

> . . . And nothing can we call our own but death
> And that small model of the barren earth
> Which serves as paste and cover to our bones.
> For God's sake, let us sit upon the ground
> And tell sad stories of the death of kings;
> How some have been deposed; some slain in war,
> Some haunted by the ghosts they have deposed . . .

She mouthed the words over and over again, for what seemed like hours and hours. *And tell sad stories of the death of kings. And tell sad stories of the death of kings.*

The time passed slowly, quickly, stood absolutely still, then rushed by again. She didn't move. Finally, she felt well enough to open her pack and retrieve the flashlight. She turned it on, and the bright blaze of light blinded her. Her head blazed, too. She shut her eyes again, and waited until the throbbing subsided. Then opened them slowly, shading her brow against the light, pleased to see that she could now discern objects in the gloom. She waved the flashlight at the darkness, and images appeared. Trees and tarps and abandoned tent cabins.

No vehicles. No people. No Elvis.

She hoped that meant that he had gotten away and gone home to

Patience. That's what she'd told him to do. But she had no confidence that he'd listened to her.

When his sergeant was dying, Elvis had tried to protect him against all comers, covering his body with his own and snarling and snapping those powerful jaws at anyone who came close, his fellow soldiers included. Mercy, too. Martinez knew they might hurt Elvis if he attacked them as they tried to help him, so he whispered, "Home. Mercy." And the dog backed off, going to Mercy, as he was told to do.

She and Elvis stayed with him until the medics arrived. They watched as the medics worked on him. Loaded him up and flew him away to the field hospital, where he died on the operating table. Far away from Mercy. Far away from Elvis. She doubted the dog had ever forgiven her. Certainly she had not forgiven herself.

A rustling at her feet. A flapping over her head. A cawing in her ears. Slowly, deliberately, painfully, she rotated her head toward the commotion and shined the light on its source. As her battered brain cleared and her focus sharpened, she spotted the body.

A man, she thought. A dead man. Prone. With a Buck hunting knife in his chest, buried right up to the hilt. The same type of blade she'd seen piercing Donald Jonas Walker's chest.

This was getting to be a bad habit, Mercy thought. Still unsure that she could stand upright, she crept over to the corpse, waving her arms at the critters feeding on what was the newly deceased form of the bird-watcher Rufus Flanigan.

He hadn't been there long, at least his corpse hadn't been, or the scavengers—beetles, squirrels, crows—would have gotten to more of him. Fortunately, the same barbwire fence that had partially protected her had kept the larger carrion feeders—bears, moose, coyotes—at bay.

He was definitely dead. Stabbed through the heart with precision. Just like Walker.

And just like Walker, there was nothing she could do for him now, except try to keep the worst of the night eaters from converging on his corpse. By daylight all of the carrion feeders would be out in force.

She struggled to her feet, lurched toward a slim birch, and held on tight while she steadied herself. She felt faint, and it wasn't due to the dead body. She was used to dead bodies. This light-headedness was the concussion working on her. She inhaled and exhaled six times, and six times she silently chanted, *And tell sad stories of the death of kings.*

The bird-watcher was no king, but it was a sad story anyway. She covered his mottled face with his safari hat, and his torso with her hoodie, in a mostly ineffective effort to keep away the scavengers. She drew her pack up on her shoulders and trudged over to the tent cabins, lighting her way with the flashlight. They were standard campground structures, simply framed with canvas walls and roofs and wooden floors and flimsy doors no one had bothered to lock. The first two were empty. Nothing but discarded water bottles and piles of old newspapers and stacks of fliers urging the people of Northshire to save the trees on one side and join the town's Fourth of July festivities on the other. Tree huggers should have taken better care of their own environment, she thought. But then maybe saving trees was not what these people were really about. Either way, they'd left in a hurry, and they'd left a mess.

She stuffed one of the fliers in a back pocket; maybe she could find out who printed them and that would lead to something. Or not.

In the third cabin, the one where Flanigan claimed she could find Amy and the baby, she found a baby bottle among the plastic litter left behind. So she and Helena had been here. But where were they now?

There was no sign of the man loading the truck or the professor or Adam Wolfe. The place was deserted. No sign of Elvis, either, which came as a relief.

The only secured dwelling appeared to be the Quonset hut, which was locked up tight, a brand-new padlock in its wide roll-up door. She pulled out her knife, grateful that whoever tried to crush her skull did not pocket it, and found its thinnest tool. Holding the flashlight between her thighs so she could see what she was doing, she slipped the tool into the lock mechanism. Another trick Martinez had taught her during the long hours of downtime between missions. He loved puzzles and riddles and locks of all kinds, the way she loved Shakespeare's scripts and sonnets and soliloquies.

It was all about manual dexterity and misdirection, he said. The secrets of magicians and thieves. He told her a story once about a young monk who decided to leave the monastery and go out into the world on a pilgrimage. He came to a roaring river too wide and wild to cross. Across the choppy currents he spotted a wise old priest. "How do I get to the other side?" he asked, shouting to be heard over the rushing water. "You are on the other side," the old priest yelled back.

I'm on the other side of the river now, she thought. Mercy wiggled the tool to trip the lock. The concentration required set her head to throbbing again, and she shut her eyes briefly against the pain. Then she steeled herself, opened her eyes, and pulled the shackle out of the body of the lock. She snapped the tool back into the knife and returned it to her pocket, along with the padlock. She rolled up the door far enough so that she could step inside.

The large space was mostly empty, at least at the first wave of the flashlight. The lack of windows gave the place a murkiness that retreated only briefly even in the glare of the beam. The gloom eased the strain on her eyes, and she was grateful for that. She shuffled around the edge of the hut, looking for something, anything, that might indicate what had been here.

At the back of the long steel building, a line of steel trunks hugged the wall, so similar in color to the wall itself that they nearly blended right in. As if they were meant to go unnoticed.

These trunks were secured with padlocks much like the one on the roll-up door. The same silver-metal mechanisms, just as easy to open. Nothing here but a lot of packing material—foam sheeting, bubble wrap, rolling tubes, brown paper, folded cardboard boxes—and a few scraps of metal and a couple of granite pebbles and a short length of what looked like clothesline. Barely an inch long, but she knew det cord when she saw it. Maybe that was all the explosives they'd ever find. But it was enough to prove Elvis right.

She thought about slipping it into her pocket, too, but technically this was a crime scene so she decided against it. She could already be in enough trouble for tampering with evidence. She could always blame it on the concussion.

She replaced all the padlocks on the trunks as well as the one on the Quonset door. Time to think about getting out of here. The question was, which way would be the safer route? She wasn't up for any sort of confrontation, with man or beast.

The fastest route would be the way she came. The tire tracks of both the SUV and the truck led out of the compound and down the same old logging road that the professor had used to get here and that Mercy had used to follow her. She hoped her Jeep was still there so she could drive it back to her cabin. Assuming she could make it to the Jeep without passing out again. Her head was still throbbing and the dizziness persisted. But if she didn't rush it she thought she might be able to do it.

First she needed to check a couple of things, starting with Elvis. She walked back to where she'd been attacked, and where the bird-watcher was still dead. Her jacket had not much deterred the scavengers, and their nibbling was more than she could bear. She stomped her feet at the rodents and snapped her hoodie like a locker-room towel to shoo away the birds. The beasties scattered—even the beetles—at least for the moment.

The effort exhausted her, and she stumbled, falling hard on her butt, which hurt her head so meanly she bit her lip and tasted blood. She pulled some water from her pack and took a long drink. Something she should have done earlier to fight dehydration. The concussion was confusing her thinking. Confusion was the enemy.

She went through her pack, and found a granola bar and a bag of yogurt-covered raisins. She ate it all and washed it down with more water. Feeling better, she dragged herself to her feet and went in search of signs of Elvis, canvassing the area where she'd snipped open the barbwire fence. It was clear that the dog had gone back that way, but someone had pulled the fence back together. She was relieved that she could find no traces of fur or blood on the razor-sharp points, which meant he'd made it out of the compound before whoever had come along and righted the barrier.

Mercy reopened the fence, and tracked Elvis back through the bushes and past the art installation to the trail the bird-watcher had told her about. The one she hoped Elvis would remember from their autumn hike. The trail had been used by humans and animals alike, and she struggled to distinguish traces of Elvis in the jumble of old and new footprints and paw prints. But it was still too dark to see much, even with the flashlight, and just looking at the ground made her head swim with pain.

She caught her breath and made her way back through the barbwire, pulling it closed behind her, to the corpse in the compound. She squatted down so she could examine him again, more thoroughly this time. He was wearing the same khaki trousers and gray and blue plaid flannel shirt he'd been wearing when she'd met him. His birding binoculars still hung around his lifeless neck. Nothing unusual, apart from the knife in his chest.

Using a long stick she found on the ground, she removed her hoodie from his body. As she pulled it away, the victim's shirttails parted, revealing his belt. He was wearing a brown leather belt with a pewter belt buckle. She leaned in for a closer look. It was the same belt buckle with the same gun-toting adaptation of the Vermont coat of arms that was found with Walker's bones. Not your average bird-watcher, after all.

So who was this guy, really? Mercy searched his pockets and found his wallet, thirty bucks in cash, a burner phone, a Canadian passport in the name of Rufus Flanigan, and a flier like the one she'd found in the tent cabin.

Mercy sighed. According to Troy, the Feds and the staties agreed that Adam Wolfe had gone to Canada to work with secessionists in Quebec. And here was this bird-watching, Vermont First belt buckle–wearing corpse from across the northern border. Surely not a coincidence. She thought about what that might mean, but her skull was drumming again. She'd love to just lie down and go to sleep, but she knew that was a bad idea. She needed to get home.

She waved away more bugs and birds and rodents. She was facing a catch-22: either she messed with the crime scene or the critters did. She'd have to leave the body, and she'd have to leave it where and as it was, to the delight of the forest creatures, until law enforcement could secure the crime scene.

Her phone was gone, not that she'd get a signal up here anyway. More important, her gun was gone. Most important, Amy and the baby were gone. She couldn't help but think they were in trouble, given they were most likely keeping company with a murderer, whether they knew it or not. She had to find them. But first she needed to get out of here, before whoever killed this guy and knocked her out came back to finish the job.

Securing the crime scene was a joke, given the scavengers all about, but she retrieved the duct tape from her pack and roped off the area anyway—hoping to keep out people if not creatures. She started the long hike back to her Jeep, going through the gate at the front of the compound, which they hadn't bothered to lock in their hurry to leave. An odd oversight, given the fact that they'd remembered to lock up the empty Quonset hut and the mostly empty trunks it housed.

She worried over what that meant, but it hurt her head too much. So she focused on moving down the trail, staying close to the tree line. She thought about Elvis. As long as he wasn't hurt—and there was no sign at the scene that he was—he could have made it back to Patience all right. If any dog could make it back, he could.

But he was stronger than she was. She was not so sure she could even make it back to the Jeep without passing out. She proceeded slowly, and every hundred yards or so she paused, leaning against a tree to beat back the dizziness. Whispering the sad stories of kings. Waiting for the fog to clear.

She'd gone about a quarter mile when she heard sounds of movement up ahead. She ducked behind some pines along the road and switched off the flashlight. The quick action rattled her brain, and she closed her eyes, sinking down to the ground on her knees. She felt the darkness spinning in on her again.

Her own sad story.

CHAPTER THIRTY

IN HER DREAM—OR WAS IT DELIRIUM?—she was rolling, rolling, rolling on the forest floor, a dead soldier unfurled from a Stars and Stripes shroud. She came to a stop on her back, face-up, blind to the light. The darkness was a living, breathing, pulsating thing, and it enveloped her. Shuttered her brain. Swallowed her whole. Sucked the soul right out of her. And left the remains to the feeders.

A SLAP OF cold and wet hit her chin. She opened her eyes to a blur of tawny fur and a sweet dark muzzle nuzzling her face. *Elvis.*

She threw her arms around him and hugged him hard. He seemed as happy to see her as she was to see him, licking her nose and cheeks and ears thoroughly.

Troy was right behind him, a headlamp bathing her in red light.

"How did you find me?"

"Patience sent us." He held a flashlight with one hand and held back Susie Bear with the other. The Newfie mutt strained at her lead, looking like she'd like to get in a lick or two of her own. He told her to sit, and she did so reluctantly, scooting close to Mercy until her shaggy butt was right up to hers. Elvis sat, too, and they both regarded her as if to say, *Do something useful.*

"Is Elvis okay?"

"He's fine, your grandmother says so. But what about you?" Troy squatted down to get a good look at her. His flashlight hurt her eyes, and she blinked. "Sorry."

"I'm good. Just don't like the light."

Troy touched the bill of her baseball cap softly. "What happened to your head?"

"Someone hit me from behind. Knocked me out. But I'm good now." Which was at least mostly true. She was feeling much better now that the canine cavalry had arrived.

"I'm taking a look," he said in a heavy voice that told her there was no point arguing with him. He slowly removed the Red Sox cap, careful not to hurt her. Still, that gentle movement brought tears to her eyes. She shut them, quick.

"Sorry." He brushed away her hair gently with his fingers and examined her skull. "Some bump you got there."

Mercy remembered to breathe. "I'm fine."

"No blood that I can see." He pulled an ice pack out of his first aid pack. "Here. That should help. At least until we can get you home and shave your head."

"Don't even think about it." She opened her eyes and smiled at him. The cold felt so good against her sore skull she almost cried with relief. Her nausea subsided and she was able to think more clearly.

"Did you see who hit you?"

"No. They came up behind me. I didn't hear them until right before the blow. Too late." She told Troy about the baby wailing and Elvis running toward the cries.

He frowned. "You should have waited for backup."

"They're all gone now," she said. "But there's something I need to show you."

"Of course there is."

She started to rise, and fell against him.

"Whoa." Troy caught her and helped her up, his strong forearms supporting her as she wobbled to her feet, one hand still clutching the ice pack to her head.

"I'm good."

"Take it easy."

"You really have to see this." She led him and the dogs back down the old logging road to the compound. Both Elvis and Susie Bear danced around, tails flying, eager to search, but as instructed they accompanied Mercy and Troy as they walked over to where the dead body lay.

The game warden shook his head. "What is it with you and the woods?"

She chose to ignore that remark. "Rufus Flanigan. Stabbed just like Don Walker."

"The bird-watcher who called in on the AMBER Alert?" He seemed surprised.

"If that's what he really is." She pointed her flashlight at the belt buckle. "Same as the one we found buried with the bones."

"And the tattoo."

"Yes."

"I'd better get this called in." Troy looked around. "It'll be a while until the techs can get here. Will you be okay while I secure the scene?"

"I'm fine. I can shine the flashlight for you."

Troy looked doubtful but she knew he would choose to believe her so that he could do what needed to be done for the investigation.

She watched him go through the vic's wallet just as she had done. He snapped photos with his phone and secured the crime scene with quiet efficiency. She did feel better, but then she had Elvis and Susie Bear on either side of her, bolstering her up, the furry ballast she needed to maintain her balance. Troy shooed away the scavengers, more effectively than she had done, and covered the corpse with a plastic tarp from his pack. He roped off the scene with duct tape, then turned to her.

"Anything else you'd like to show me?"

"The rest of the compound. I took a look around, but I wasn't too steady on my feet. I might have missed something."

"You?" Troy laughed. "Impossible."

She flushed.

"I need to examine the area anyway," he said. "And I'm sure between the two of them, our sniffer dogs will find whatever can be found. Even if we miss something in the dark, odds are they won't."

She stepped forward to lead the way and tripped over a branch. Troy caught her again, and though she tried to wave him off, he insisted on helping her.

"Just hang on to my arm," he ordered. "You don't need another bump on that head."

"Yes, sir," she said lightly.

"You are one stubborn soldier." But he didn't let go and she didn't shake him off this time.

She hobbled through the compound on his arm, shining the flashlight and pointing out the areas of greatest interest like some woodlands tour guide. She felt ridiculous but tried not to let her pride hamper the investigation.

They let the dogs go, and they bounded ahead, following their respective noses. She and Troy made their way around the encampment, and in and out of the first two tent cabins. As they explored, she briefed him on the activity she'd witnessed before she'd been knocked out.

Susie Bear loped around with her usual good cheer, covering the ground within the fence from end to end. Elvis circled the compound in his own aggressive fashion, stopping at several spots, including where the truck had been parked and loaded. He headed for the Quonset hut and sat on alert at the door, while his Newfie companion settled in front of the third tent cabin, the one which had housed Amy and the baby.

Mercy and Troy checked out the tent cabin first. They congratulated Susie Bear on finding the baby bottle, slipped her a treat, then joined the shepherd at the Quonset hut. The shaggy black dog sat next to the elegant Malinois, two energetic canines on alert.

The door was shut, the padlock in place.

"This is where the steel trunks are?" he asked.

Oops. She hoped that was a rhetorical question. Maybe he wouldn't connect the dots.

"It's locked," he said.

Uh-oh. She didn't know whether to lie and say the lock wasn't there earlier when she went in or to come clean. She wasn't sure it was a good idea to let a game warden know she went around picking locks at crime scenes. Even one who seemed to be on the side of truth and justice.

"There weren't any locks on the tent cabin doors," Troy went on. "There must be a reason they locked this one."

Mercy pulled away from him, whistling for Elvis. She watched as the sleek shepherd raced toward her.

"What do you think?" He regarded her with amusement.

"Huh?" She had a feeling that playing dumb with him wouldn't work. You couldn't fool a good cop, and even though he spent most of his time in the woods Troy Warner was still a good cop.

"You picked the lock, didn't you?"

She felt her face flush, but she met his look head-on. She was a good cop, too. Or at least she had been once upon a time. "Maybe."

"Two working dogs have alerted to this building." He grinned.

"That's probable cause. Let's see you in action." He held up the flashlight for her.

Mercy picked the lock quickly and handed him the open padlock.

"Outstanding," he said.

She stepped aside and the dogs barreled into the steel building, heading straight for the trunks that lined the rear wall. Troy nodded toward the locks that protected them and she picked those, too. She showed Troy the packing material and metal shavings and the pebbles and the short piece of det cord.

"Is that our explosives alert?" He looked at Elvis, who sat at attention at her side.

"It must be."

"It's not much."

"They could have more with them."

"Or they could have used it to take down trees to clear the area. Loggers use it out here all the time. Or maybe it's all that's left from Wolfe's days blowing up logging trucks."

"Maybe."

"I need to get to a place where my sat phone will work."

"One more thing."

"What?"

"I found something in the woods, just outside the perimeter."

"Okay, let's see it."

Mercy led the game warden and the dogs to the snipped section of the barbwire fence and drew it apart.

"I guess that's how you got in," said Troy with a smile.

Through the opening they all went, trailing her as she trudged to the art installation in the trees, spotlighted now in the bright beams of both flashlights.

"What is it?"

"It's one of those natural sculptures that Dr. Winters told us about. You know, the art that Adam Wolfe was making instead of the bronzes of her."

"Okay." Troy ran his hand along the arch made of stones, then stepped back to view the entire piece again, from the dry riverbed of fractal rock patterns to the crown of the arch itself. "I like it. It's kind of ingenious, the way it melts into the landscape."

"I know."

"But what's this got to do with anything?"

"I'm not sure," Mercy said. "But I feel like we're missing something."

"We've got three dead bodies and a disappearing mother and child and the possibility of explosives. I'd say we're missing about everything so far."

She showed him the Greek lettering. "I hope your Greek is better than mine."

"It's not."

"It must mean something."

"I'm sure it does, but probably only within the context of the artwork itself."

"Maybe," she said.

"What else could it mean?"

"I don't know. But I think this piece is trying to tell us something."

Troy looked at her. "I think you got hit in the head and need medical attention."

"I'm fine."

"Mercy." He took her arm gently. "We need to go. Now."

"Okay." She knew he was right. Not about seeing a doctor but about getting back. "What about Amy and Helena? I'm worried about them. If the vic was right, they're in real trouble."

"We're doing everything we can to find them."

"Okay." Still, she wanted to get out of here so she could look for them herself. "But they need to know that Amy is trying to save her baby, not abandon her."

"Understood. Do you think you can make it back to my truck?"

"I can drive myself."

"Not a good idea." Troy frowned. "Besides, someone slashed your tires. You're not going anywhere in that Jeep for a while."

"Seriously?" In her frustration Mercy shook her head, then winced. Her skull still ached when she moved too fast.

"You need to get that injury checked out. I'll arrange a tow for you as soon the crime scene techs have come and gone."

The man didn't miss a trick.

"I'm fine, really."

"Let's let Patience be the judge of that." He smiled at her.

Smart-ass, she thought. Invoking her grandmother's name was not playing fair.

But she smiled back at him anyway.

They put the dogs on their leads and left the compound through the entry gate, setting off down the logging road. Mercy insisted on proceeding on her own steam, without the game warden to lean on. He shrugged and kept on walking, but she knew he was moderating his speed on her behalf.

She was grateful to him for that.

"This case is getting crazier by the minute," she said, hoping to engage Troy and distract herself from the pain.

"I know."

"So many pieces to the puzzle."

"That's assuming it's just one puzzle."

"It's got to be connected," Mercy said, wincing as she stumbled over a large root. "Think about it. In the past couple of days, Amy ran away with the baby from a Vermont Firster's compound and three guys with Vermont Firster sympathies turn up dead."

"True, but that doesn't explain the twenty grand we found in Walker's recliner or the guy who broke into your house."

"And shot Elvis."

"And shot Elvis," he repeated.

The shepherd barked as if he were protesting the very bullet that grazed him. Maybe he was.

"And what's Dr. Winters got to do with it?" Mercy asked.

"Maybe she's a Vermont Firster, too."

She laughed. "The only Vermonter she's putting first is herself."

"Thrasher would agree with you. He says she's a piece of work."

"Amy says her boyfriend has a lot of groupies. I guess she could be one of them."

"She did call him a genius."

"Yes, but she doesn't really fit the groupie profile."

"Which is?"

"You know, adoring young women who'll follow rock stars anywhere." Mercy rolled her eyes, and even that small facial movement hurt her head.

"Sounds more like Amy."

"Yeah. And look where that got her." Mercy sighed. "God, I hope she and Helena are all right."

"From what you say, she's pretty sensible for a teenager." Troy slowed down some more and took her arm. This time she let him. "She's probably just lying low somewhere with the baby."

"I hope you're right."

"I agree that Dr. Winters is not a groupie," said Troy, bringing the subject back to the professor in a sweet if obvious ploy to ease her mind.

"I bet she has her own groupies." Mercy smiled at him. "Impressionable young college students hanging on her every word . . . while they wonder if she's wearing any underwear."

Troy colored, and she laughed. "She's the kind of woman who collects men."

"The south of France."

"Exactly."

"Which brings us back to the Vermont Firsters," said Troy. "What a weird group."

"We've got the activist and artist Adam Wolfe, the lowlife Donald Walker with the tattoo, and the belt-buckle guys."

"The body in the woods aka Wayne Herbert, and the bird-watcher from Canada."

"Right," said Mercy. "And that guy Max, who was at the compound. And who might be the guy who broke into my house."

Troy raised an eyebrow.

"I can't say for sure," she admitted. "Amy says Max is Adam's best friend. She's scared of him." Mercy was getting tired, and her head pounded with every step. Elvis stayed close by her side, nudging her hand with his nose as they plodded along.

"So far, the compound is the common denominator." Troy still held her arm, helping her over the roughest patches of the trail. "Not much farther now."

"I'm fine," she said, even though she wasn't. "The compound is where Elvis alerted and we found the det cord."

"Wolfe has been in trouble for blowing up logging trucks. Maybe he's planning on blowing up more."

"That doesn't explain Max or the truck or its unknown contents. Contents that Elvis alerted to. We need to figure out where that truck was going."

"And why."

"It can't be a coincidence that all this has happened in the past few days."

"Things do appear to be coming to a head."

They reached her Jeep just as she was sure she couldn't take another step. She sighed at the actual sight of her slashed tires and leaned against the hood to rest for a moment. Troy excused himself to call Thrasher.

She waited, brooding over the evidence they'd found so far: the explosives, the truck, the timing.

The timing.

Timing was everything.

Make use of time, let not advantage slip.

CHAPTER THIRTY-ONE

S HE PULLED THE "SAVE THE TREES" flier from her pocket, the
one she'd found at the compound. She scanned the Northshire
Fourth of July activities listed on its B-side: fun run, parade, concert,
fireworks, and so forth. By the time Troy got off the phone with
Thrasher, she knew what they had to do.

"I keep thinking about the timing of all this. Maybe there's a reason it's coming to a head right now."

"What do you mean?"

"Maybe it's staring us right in the face, and we've been too blind to
see it." She handed the flier to him. "The Fourth of July. Independence Day. The perfect time for the Vermont Firsters to make their
move."

Troy nodded. "I can see that."

The dogs danced at their side, ready to move on. Mercy ignored
them. "It's got to be the parade. Lots of hotshots will be there, including the senator."

"I thought the senator was going to be down in Bennington for the
Fourth, with all the real big shots."

"I guess he's making a pit stop in Northshire first."

"If the senator's going to be there, they've already got people in place
for the parade. They know what they're doing." He turned those warm
brown eyes on her. "Besides, you need to go to the hospital."

"I'm fine."

"Sure you are. That's why you're so eager to go the last mile here
to my truck."

Mercy stood up straight. "I was just taking a little breather while
you talked to your boss."

"Right."

"Let's get going. The sooner we get back, the sooner we can check on the prep for the parade." She barreled down the trail, trying not to let her fatigue show. Elvis and Susie Bear ran past her to take the lead.

"It's mostly speculation, you know." Troy strode beside her. "But I'll let Thrasher know."

"You need us," she told Troy. "I'm the only person who's seen Amy and that guy Max. And you're going to need all the bomb-sniffing dogs you can get."

"Even I'm not really supposed to be there," said Troy. "It's the local PD and staties' show. The Feds could be there, too."

"The parade is open to the public. Elvis and I are the public. We're going, even if we have to steal my grandmother's car to get there."

They argued all the way back to Troy's truck. She was determined to wear him down, concussion or no concussion. "I know that Amy and Helena are in trouble."

"Not your problem. None of this is your problem. You've done enough. Time to let the professionals take over."

She knew what he was thinking: she was just another civilian now. But she couldn't accept that. Not as long as Amy and Helena were unaccounted for.

"You nearly got yourself and your dog killed. I don't understand why you are doing this." He leaned in toward her. "What aren't you telling me?"

Mercy backed away and climbed into the passenger seat. She closed her eyes and listened to the comforting sound of the dogs scrambling into the backseat, followed by the slam of that door and then another as Troy took his rightful place behind the wheel. But he did not turn on the engine.

"Tell me," he said.

He was more perceptive than she thought. She sighed. What's more, she knew he was right. She was holding back. And she knew that he would wait her out. Because that's what she would do.

She might as well tell him everything. "We were doing a house-to-house in a small village several miles outside the wire. We'd built a school there, the first in decades. The Taliban torched it. The teacher—just a teenager herself—and her baby had gone missing the morning of the fire." She stopped, unable to go on, her head pounding.

"I take it back. You don't have to tell me," Troy said gently.

She opened her eyes. "It's okay. You should know. Maybe then you'll understand. Maybe then I'll understand."

"Okay." He took her hand in his and squeezed it gently. "Go on."

"We searched every house in the village. Nothing. We finally found the teacher in an abandoned field, bound and gagged and beaten, her baby left to die beside her. But they were both alive. Just barely, but alive. The mother was scared for her little girl. I told her everything would be all right. We got them to the hospital as quickly as we could, and I stayed with them as long as I could. I held her hand, like you're holding mine." She looked down at his large hand covering hers. "She begged me to stay, but I finally had to go. Another mission outside the wire."

"You did what you had to do."

"By the time I got back, it was too late. The little girl was dying, and the mother was so upset they had to sedate her to save her. I held the baby for her, and she died in my arms. The mother survived, but a week after she left the hospital, she hanged herself."

They fell into silence for a moment.

"It's the ones with kids that haunt you." Troy looked past her, at something only he could see. "We had a little girl go missing a couple of years ago. Wandered away from her family's campsite at Grout Pond. Her parents were frantic. Seemed like nice people, an accountant and his wife from New Hampshire. We pulled out all the stops—grid search, sniffer dogs, dredging—and forty-eight hours later we found her, drowned, in the lake."

Mercy felt feverish, whether from his sad story or her sad story or the blow to her head, she wasn't sure. "That's terrible."

Troy looked at her, his jaw tight. "Dr. Darling did the autopsy. The little girl—her name was Madison—had drowned, but the doc's examination revealed a number of broken bones as well as old and fresh bruises. She'd been systematically abused her whole life." He hesitated. "By her own mother."

"Lord." No wonder Troy didn't trust Amy. "What about the father?"

"The father was clueless—or at least claimed to be. He got off, and she was institutionalized."

Shades of Lady Macbeth. *I have given suck and know* . . . Aloud Mercy said, "I'm so sorry."

They sat there quietly in his truck, the darkness of the forest all around them, each lost in their own unhappy thoughts. The dogs settled down in the back, curling up together like spooning lovers, ready to doze off until called into action again.

Mercy squeezed Troy's fingers and pulled her hand away. "Maybe you're right, and nothing's going to happen at the parade, and this is all overkill. But better that than something terrible happening and knowing we could've stopped it. Or at least tried."

"Okay." Troy turned the key in the ignition and the Ford F-150 roared to life, the headlights beaming a bright light into the tree line. "The parade isn't until noon. It's nearly three now. We all need to get some rest. Then, if Patience agrees that you can go, I will drive you there myself."

SUNDAY:
INDEPENDENCE DAY
JULY 4

CHAPTER THIRTY-TWO

MERCY AND ELVIS ENDED UP spending the night at Patience's house. Mercy had refused to go to the hospital, and Patience had finally agreed to that, provided they stayed right where she could keep an eye on them.

She felt guilty the next morning as she watched Patience pour coffee into her mug. Her grandmother looked much older today than she had yesterday. Purple circles darkened her eyes and her smile lines had deepened into sharp worry lines—and Mercy knew that was down to worry about her and Elvis. She was happy for the distraction when, true to his word, Troy showed up with Susie Bear for breakfast.

"How's her head?" Troy asked Patience between bites of bacon and eggs and biscuits.

"Contusion, certainly. Concussed, most likely." Her grandmother passed the wildflower honey to Troy.

"I'm fine," said Mercy.

Troy raised his eyebrows at Patience.

Her grandmother did not look at Mercy as she addressed him. "Her pupils are not dilated. Pulse rate and blood pressure are normal."

"I'm fine."

"Do you think she's really up to this?"

"I think she should get a CT scan just to be safe and, failing that, at least get some rest today." Patience offered him another biscuit. "But she's as stubborn as her grandfather."

"I'm sitting right here, guys," Mercy said.

They both ignored her.

"What about Elvis?" asked Troy.

"His wound is healing well." Patience glanced down at the shepherd, who sat with Susie Bear at her feet. Both dogs were waiting for another slice of Dakin Farm cob-smoked bacon. "How much he'll like crowds and parades right now is another story. But he certainly performed well last night. I'd say he's on the mend on all fronts."

Mercy wasn't so sure. Afghanistan cast a long shadow. Elvis might never be the same again. Any more than she would be.

"I reported the det cord you found," Troy said to Mercy. "Thrasher passed the word, and everyone's on alert. They can handle it."

"We're good to go," insisted Mercy.

"If the senator's there, Harrington will be, too. The captain says he likes the limelight."

Mercy nodded. "Dr. Darling told me as much."

"Thrasher warned me to steer clear."

"Understood." Mercy grinned at Troy. "But he's not the boss of me."

Patience sighed. "There's really no stopping her."

"Okay, but you keep a low profile." Troy slathered a last bite of biscuit with honey. He popped it into his mouth.

"Deal."

Mercy and Troy both looked at her grandmother.

"Oh, all right." Patience frowned. "But when you get back, you go in for that CT scan."

"Promise."

SHE AND TROY and the dogs piled into his truck for the short ride to the village. Most of the Fourth of July festivities were held in the original town center, which dated from the 1700s, only about a hundred years older than the rest of Northshire. *Historic* was a relative term in the state of Vermont.

Many of the buildings and houses throughout the village were vintage, with even the most recent additions having witnessed at least one centennial. Even the modern enterprises—gas stations, outlet stores, supermarkets—were housed in Victorian-era structures that might have been remodeled on the inside to accommodate modern conveniences but on the outside looked just like they might have done centuries before. Mercy was one of those woodchucks who never wanted that to change, no matter how many flatlanders invaded Vermont.

Main Street had few stoplights, relying mostly on its rotaries at each end of town to slow things down. Today most of the road was closed to traffic for the parade.

"The crowd is bigger than I expected," said Mercy.

Long before they reached the old downtown district, they encountered throngs of people as well as roadblocks detouring them around the parade route.

"Usually triple the population in summer," said Troy, maneuvering his vehicle expertly around the barricades and parking on a side street just beyond the historic yellow courthouse with its green shutters and handsome cupola. "Maybe more, since they're rededicating the Fountain of the Muses on the village green tomorrow."

"I'd forgotten all about that," said Mercy. The Fountain of the Muses was a lovely Beaux-Arts fountain featuring the three original Muses of Greek myth: Melete, the Muse of meditation; Mneme, the Muse of memory; and Aoide, the Muse of song. It was said that these three were the qualities one needed to master the poetic arts at the Greek temple at Mount Helicon. At least that was what the town librarian, Mrs. Horgan, always used to tell her when she was a girl.

Every child in Northshire knew these Muses. The fountain was a gift to the village by the famed sculptor Flora Blodgett, a local artist made good. She'd studied with Augustus Saint-Gaudens at the illustrious Cornish Art Colony upstate in Windsor before the Great War, and was known for her graceful sculptures of goddesses and angels as well as ordinary women and children.

A century of harsh weather had taken its toll on the grand centerpiece of the common. Its zinc components had begun to break down, destabilizing the structure. It had been decades since cascades of water had flowed through the fountain. But tomorrow, on the final day of this long holiday weekend, a year after it had been dismantled and shipped off to South Carolina for restoration, the Fountain of the Muses would return to its rightful place in Northshire, in all its former glory. Art and architecture aficionados from the world over were here for the rededication and party on the green to follow.

"More people, more crowd cover," said Troy.

"Makes it even harder to find them. Good thing we have the dogs."

She slipped the body armor onto Elvis while Troy prepped Susie Bear. Mercy was worried about the shepherd; this was the first time he'd worn the protective gear since Afghanistan. He seemed okay, standing still if alert while she snapped on his lead. He licked her hand and then danced against the door until she let him out of the truck and onto the sidewalk. He knew he was here to work.

"Put this on." Troy handed her a covert vest.

Mercy didn't argue with him. Technically she was a civilian—an unarmed civilian now that someone had stolen her Beretta. "Stay," she told Elvis and hunkered down in the cab to take off her T-shirt. She put the vest on over her cami and then slipped her T-shirt back on. Tight fit, and she knew she'd be overheated in no time—but thankfully the warmth of a Vermont summer could never compete with the brutal heat of the desert in Afghanistan.

"Ready," she told Troy.

"The 5K Fun Run is nearly over." He pointed to the middle of Main Street, which was blocked off from all motor vehicle traffic and flanked with crushes of men, women, kids, and pets. A couple of stout stragglers dressed in red, white, and blue running clothes and matching painted faces slowly melting in the sun jogged down the middle of the road. "That means the parade will be underway shortly."

"Right." She held Elvis's lead firmly. Both he and Susie Bear were excited, tails wagging and paws prancing, as they waited for instructions. She hoped that the shepherd's high-energy level reflected his anticipation of a fine reward for a job well done—and not anxiety triggered by the distractions and the noise and the people.

Troy led them through the crowd on foot, weaving around bystanders and camp chairs and strollers and puppies to the starting point on the parade route. Most everyone smiled at the working dogs, waving their Stars and Stripes flags in greeting—except for one nervous guy on stilts dressed like Uncle Sam who gave the Belgian shepherd and the Newfie retriever a wide berth. Scores of floats and antique automobiles and school marching bands and Morgan horses and motorcyclists and veteran groups were lined up in the street, waiting for the spectacle to commence.

"The logical mark is the grandstand," Troy said over his shoulder. "That's where the bigshots will be."

"You mean the politicians?"

"Yeah. If the Vermont Firsters are up to something, then they'll target the pols."

They stood behind a stone barricade that kept traffic on a side street

from turning onto Main Street. The Northshire High School marching band at the front of the parade line struck up a blaring rendition
of "Yankee Doodle Dandy," signaling the kickoff of the next stage of
the Fourth of July festivities.

The long procession snaked forward along Main Street.

"Let's split up," said Troy. "I'll take that side of the route, you take
this one. Keep me in sight if you can. Text me if you see anything."
He gave her a hard look. "Don't try anything on your own. And keep
that dog of yours under control."

He waited for her to say something, but she didn't. No point in making promises she might not keep.

Troy shrugged and trotted away, Susie Bear at his hip. Mercy stood
with Elvis and watched them go, then turned her attention to their
side of the street. She had Patience's phone in her pocket, so she could
contact Troy if necessary. But she missed her Beretta. She wanted her
gun back.

Elvis pulled at the lead, whining. The Malinois seemed rattled;
maybe she was inadvertently communicating her worry over the absence of her weapon right down the leash to him. She needed to keep
a handle on her own emotions if she expected him to perform well in
this chaotic environment.

"We're here to work." She leaned over and scratched his dark triangular ears, then straightened up and scanned the crowd. "Search,
Elvis."

CHAPTER THIRTY-THREE

MERCY HAD NO IDEA WHAT ELVIS WOULD DO or how he would do it. Even as a human with limited olfactory skills, she was overwhelmed by the smells on the street. Every shop and restaurant had flung open its doors, and Carl's Texas BBQ and Yankee Candles and Donna's Donuts mixed with sun and sweat and smoke and a million other odors she couldn't identify. She only hoped that Elvis could.

The shepherd launched ahead, and they were off. She spotted Troy and his big dog making their own way through the crowd on their side, the poster boy for law enforcement and his picture-perfect cheerful canine sidekick. She wondered if Vermont had a game warden calendar, and smiled at that thought.

A young mother with a baby caught her eye. Fair-haired, but too short. Not Amy. Not Helena. Like a sniffer dog, she was alerting to every sighting of an infant, seeing Amy and Helena in every young mother with a baby. She also scrutinized every tall man and every curvy brunette and every wild-haired hippie, thinking she might be looking at the tall man called Max or the elusive professor Dr. Winters or the activist artist Adam Wolfe.

Ceremonial cannons fired on the common and Elvis stopped short. Mercy nearly fell over him, bumping an oblivious teenager bent over her phone. The girl flipped her off and the shepherd growled. Mercy drew him away from the scowling teen, who shrunk back and kept on texting without a beat.

The dog was nervous. She didn't want him to bolt, especially in such a busy place. The drummers in another marching band banged out the rhythm to John Philip Sousa's "The Army Goes Rolling Along" just a couple of feet away, and both Mercy and Elvis winced, she at the memory of Martinez and he at the bursts of percussion.

She held the dog back until the band had passed and the drumbeats dimmed. While she waited, hands cupping the dog's sensitive ears, she took note of all of the law enforcement and military personnel. State police, local PD, the local sheriff and deputies, the National Guard. Working dogs, too; so far she'd seen a black Labrador retriever and a Belgian Malinois like Elvis, unmistakable in their black vests with the bright yellow K-9 Unit lettering. Maybe they didn't need her or Elvis, after all. Maybe she should just take him home, where he would be safe. Then she remembered the intruder, who'd shot her dog right outside the house. No, she was right to stay, and to keep Elvis with her. They needed to catch these guys, whoever they were, and put them away. That's when they'd be safe. And maybe Amy and Helena would be safe then, too.

A cortege of well-dressed riders on spectacular Morgan horses trotted by, to the delight of everyone, except for Elvis, who first regarded them with suspicion, then ignored them. The crowds grew thicker on both sides of Main Street as they approached the grandstand, where the local and state dignitaries were sitting. Mercy recognized the senator, the mayor, the governor, and at least one congressman, along with their respective families. Harrington was there, too, in another one of his expensive suits, chatting up the mayor. And Lillian Jenkins, who was probably running this whole show.

Apparently the village had attracted more luminaries than usual on this Independence Day. At least that's how it seemed to her. She never remembered there being so many people at the parade, but then it had been a few years since she'd been here for the July Fourth holiday. Still, the long-awaited unveiling of the Fountain of the Muses must have something to do with it, she thought. Either that or her home state was on the verge of becoming as overrun with flatlanders as the crankier native Vermonters had warned against all her life.

Calmer now, Elvis plowed on, tail high, and Mercy held on and navigated the throngs of happy and energetic July Fourth revelers as best she could. She tried to keep Troy and Susie Bear in sight but she lost them as they disappeared into the swell of good citizens celebrating the birth of their democracy in good old Yankee style.

The clock on the two-hundred-year-old Congregational church struck noon, and the twelve peals of its bells rang out over the din of the parade. The sun was hot overhead, and she was sweating. The bulletproof vest rubbed stiffly against her damp skin. She'd have blisters tomorrow.

Across the road on the village green a small group of Revolutionary soldiers fired their muskets. She was worried about Elvis's reaction, but he didn't seem to notice. She did. Each shot was a blow to her concentration.

She pulled her Red Sox cap out of her pocket and slipped it carefully over her hair, wilder than ever in this humidity. She was grateful to Elvis for doing his job without drama. To his credit and her pride, the shepherd remained poised and focused on his search, despite the bedlam all around him. She wished his sergeant could see him now. She wished he were here with them now. She wished she could get past this wishing. *What's gone and what's past help should be past grief . . .*

They kept moving. No sign of the tall man or the professor or Amy and the baby. They were directly in front of the grandstand now, and the dignitaries gathered there. The law enforcement presence here was even more noticeable, lots of local and state cops, Feds, and even Secret Service protecting them and the public. Thrasher must have believed there was a credible threat, she thought, if the Secret Service were here. Usually they didn't protect senators, unless there was a specific threat or if they were running for president.

She saw a couple more working dogs on the job as well. All on the lookout for the unattended backpack or suspicious person or the smell of det cord.

Or a sniper. She knew all too well that there was always the possibility of a sniper, but the greater risk today was explosives. That's what Elvis had alerted to. And Troy agreed with her. Mercy knew that with such a concerted effort, the authorities had the immediate area covered. Or at least she hoped they did.

She surveyed the scene again from every direction. The easiest way anyone could get close enough to the grandstand to endanger one of the dignitaries without detection would be on a float. She sent Troy a text saying that she and Elvis were going back to where the floats were lined up. She knew that law enforcement had probably run their sniffer dogs through that area earlier, but now their efforts should be focused on the grandstand. There were only so many trained bomb-sniffing dogs, and their noses could get tired after a few hours. They couldn't be everywhere all the time.

Elvis did not protest when she turned around and indicated that she wanted to move back toward the beginning of the parade route.

"Search," she told him again, looking herself for anything out of the ordinary, focusing on the floats themselves. The theme of this year's parade was "Arts in America," a nod to the return of the Fountain of the Muses to the village green. There was a Grandma Moses float and a Vermont folk art float and a monuments of Vermont float and even a dairy-arts float, complete with sculptures of cows carved from butter. She wondered how long they'd last in this heat. How long she'd last.

Next in line was the Vermont Republic float, festooned with a living diorama of the coat of arms complete with a tall pine tree and sheaths of grain and even a cardboard cow against a green mountain backdrop. And the Green Mountain Boys band, featuring a girl singer and two beefy male fiddlers dressed like Minutemen accompanying her on the "Ballad of the Green Mountain Boys."

> We owe no allegiance, we bow to no throne,
> Our ruler is law and the law is our own;
> Our leaders themselves are our own fellow-men,
> Who can handle the sword and the scythe and the pen
> Hurrah for Vermont! For the land that we till
> Must have sons to defend her from valley and hill
> Our vow is recorded—our banner unfurled,
> In the name of Vermont we defy all the world!
> Then cheer, cheer, the green mountaineer,
> then cheer, cheer, the green mountaineer

As she listened to that last verse of the song she'd learned in grade school, she realized that this float could hold the key to these murders. She sent a text to Troy, telling him about the float and her suspicions. She looked at Elvis, but the dog did not alert. She hustled the shepherd through the crowd along the parade route, following the Green Mountain Boys.

"Search, boy, search!"

Again the bomb-sniffing dog did not alert. In fact, he paid more attention to the unsteady Uncle Sam on stilts. Mercy was so sure that he would find something of interest on that float, so sure that she had been right.

But nothing happened. What was wrong with this dog?

Elvis zoomed on, intent on his search, indifferent to the band and the Vermont Republic float on which they continued to play, now a vigorous rendition of "Moonlight in Vermont." Much of the crowd tried to sing, or at least hum, along, but the beloved tune was notoriously hard to sing well. The girl singer was botching it, too, which didn't help the crowd's sing-along or Mercy's mood.

She must have been wrong. Maybe her skills as a criminal investigator were as lost to her as Martinez was. Maybe she should have listened to her parents and become a lawyer, after all.

Her head ached, her vest was hot and scratchy, her confidence lagged. She stopped in front of the Ben & Jerry's storefront, where a cute girl about Amy's age with dark curly hair and a diamond stud in her nose was handing out free samples of Cherry Garcia and Chunky Monkey ice cream. She chose the Cherry Garcia for Elvis and the Chunky Monkey for herself. "Nice dog," said the girl, whose name tag read *Taylor.*

In a rare moment of kindness to strangers, Elvis allowed Taylor to pet him, no doubt inspired by the promise of more ice cream to come. His strategy worked, and he downed another free sample compliments of his new favorite human while Mercy collected herself. The Ben & Jerry's sugar rush helped, and she thanked Taylor before pulling Elvis away from his friendly supplier of Cherry Garcia. She turned away from the scoop shop to view the parade.

A guy dressed like a Minuteman broke through the crowd on Troy's side of the street and ran alongside the Vermont Republic float, jumping onto the back as the float continued to move down the street.

"Better late than never!" he yelled. The crowd laughed, and clapped for the intrepid latecomer.

There was something familiar about this Minuteman. His militia tricorn hat hid most of his face, but he was tall and moved gracefully, as had the intruder who ransacked her cabin. He carried a musket; a hunting cartridge, a haversack, and a fife case were slung over his shoulder. A canteen was belted to his hip.

Why a musket *and* a musical instrument? Mercy wondered. The assumption was that if he were going to join the Vermont Republic float, he was a member of the band. She took a harder look at his hunting cartridge and haversack. Both seemed out of place. Something was off with this guy, she thought, even as he pulled out the fife and began to play.

Elvis didn't like him, either. The Belgian shepherd's ears perked up and he pulled at the lead. They circumvented the people waiting patiently for free ice cream and pushed past several rows of parade-goers to get to the curb. They jogged by the Friends of the Library, marching en masse, pushing their metal book carts decorated with art posters ahead of them. She spotted Old Man Horgan among them, widower of the late town librarian Mrs. Horgan. He sported a cane and a vague look of confusion on his face, but otherwise he seemed all right, with an earnest young librarian and Matisse's *Woman Reading With Peaches* for support.

She didn't stop to say hello but smiled at him as Elvis pulled away from her, gaining on the Vermont Republic float, which was running about two blocks ahead of them. A posse of farmers steering bright green and yellow John Deere tractors, a contingent of sharp cadets clad in navy and white uniforms from a military school upstate, and the Old Vermont Fife and Drum Corps were the marchers separating them from the float.

No sign of Troy or Susie Bear yet. She hoped he'd gotten her text. The game warden had warned her against going it alone but she would have to if he didn't show up soon. The Belgian shepherd shot through the tractors and the cadets, and Mercy struggled to keep up with him. She stumbled, dropping the leash. A cadet helped her to her feet, and she raced up past the fife and drum corps to join Elvis.

"Elvis!" Mercy panted and kept on running. She was almost there.

But the Malinois didn't even slow down. He caught up to the Vermont Republic float, keeping pace alongside it.

And then Elvis soared.

CHAPTER THIRTY-FOUR

MERCY SAW THE SLEEK SHEPHERD SAIL after the moving target that was the Minuteman on the Vermont Republic float. He landed lightly on all four paws, barking like the hound of Hades.

The girl singer stopped singing. The fiddlers stopped fiddling. The music stopped and the girl screamed and the tall man turned. He dropped his haversack and hunting cartridge to the floor of the float, and raised his musket against the dog.

"No!" Mercy pumped her legs and her arms and lunged for the float. The flatbed hit her at the hip. She pulled herself up onto the platform, and still on all fours, threw herself forward towards the Minuteman's legs, aiming to trip him. She stared up at the tall man as she clamped her fingers around his ankles. He tried to escape her grip, and his hat fell off, exposing his shaved head. She recognized him at once as the man Dr. Winters had called Max.

He pounded the musket butt on the floor of the float, just missing her hands with the first blow. Mercy let go and rolled away before the musket struck again.

"Get him," she ordered.

Elvis tackled the guy, chomping down on his wrist as he'd been trained to do. Max cursed, dropping the rifle and wobbling toward the edge of the float, trying to shake off the dog and get away. But the ferocious shepherd hung on, forcing his perp to the floor.

Mercy kicked the musket away from Max, sending it flying right off of the float. The girl singer kept on screaming. The two fiddle players moved in to help Max, but thought better of it as Susie Bear bounded onto the float. She was barking, too, a low guttural bellowing Mercy had not heard before and that impressed her with its fierce-

ness. It worked on the fiddle players, too, who backed off from the
fight, edging to the far end of the float and leaving their friend to the
dogs.

Troy heaved himself onto the float after his Newfie mutt, nodding
at Mercy as he cornered the fiddlers.

"Don't move, boys," he said. "You can't outrun her. She's faster and
meaner than she looks. Stay right where you are or you'll end up like
your friend here."

Mercy saw Max struggling to sneak a cell phone from his pocket
with his left hand. He got it out about halfway when she twisted his
wrist, hard, and snatched the device from him. She didn't know if
he was using it as a detonator or not but she certainly wasn't taking
any chances.

"I've notified Thrasher," Troy told her. "Backup is on the way."

The float rumbled on past the grandstand. No one seemed to notice that the Green Mountain Boys weren't playing anymore, maybe
because everyone was much more interested in the pretty girls riding
in the vintage Cadillacs in front of them. Behind them, the cadets
marched on and the tractors chugged along and the Old Vermont Fife
and Drum Corps struck up "The Star-Spangled Banner."

Mercy kept her eye on Max and Elvis as two pairs of police officers
flanked the float at the front and rear, walking alongside and instruct-
ing the driver to make a right at the next intersection. They removed
the barriers that flanked Main Street, diverted the onlookers, and then
guided the float onto a side street, replacing the barriers as soon as it
was clear of the crowd. All with an admirable minimum of fuss.

She called off Elvis and he sat by her, ears up, as the police officers
arrested the tall man, who identified himself as Max Skinner from
Provo, Utah.

"I don't know what you're talking about," he was telling the cops.
"I'm an artist."

She heard him ask for a lawyer as they took him off to the station.

Troy and Susie Bear joined Mercy and Elvis, and together they left
the float, giving the bomb squad the room they needed to clear the
vehicle.

They sat on a fence fronting a Victorian charmer housing a real estate office and watched as the rest of the band were escorted away for
questioning. The dogs sat at their feet.

"The fiddlers are Paul and Louis Herbert," Troy told her. "Wayne Herbert's little brothers."

"They're wearing the same belt buckles as the one we found with the bones."

"Yeah. You'd think they would have mentioned that when I talked to them. I wonder what their mother, Flo, will have to say about that."

"Who's the girl?"

"Sarah Lavery, a sous chef from Bennington. Not sure what she's got to do with this yet."

Together they watched as the bomb squad checked out the float, and found no evidence of explosives. Or of anything else criminal. The hunting cartridge that Skinner had carried was empty. The knapsack held a tambourine. And the canteen was filled with water.

"I don't understand it," said Mercy. "Elvis is a bomb-sniffing dog. He's trained to alert to explosives. That's what he does."

"They didn't find anything."

"He alerted to PETN in the woods. Your own people confirmed that."

"Yes, but not this time," said Troy. "Maybe it was Skinner himself. If he was your intruder, Elvis may have alerted to him."

"I know he alerted to something."

"They would have found it." Troy leaned in toward her. "You know Elvis has been all over the place lately. I knew a dog handler who used to say that his sniffer dog loved granola bars and would alert to them everywhere they went."

"Elvis does not alert to granola." She tossed her head, not caring that it still hurt like hell whenever she did that. "Look, can we go now?"

"You'll have to make a statement."

Mercy knew they were missing something. She was missing something. Time to go home with Elvis and have a good think, as her grandmother liked to say. And maybe some of her carrot cake.

"I really don't feel up to hanging around the station for hours." She touched her crown gently to underscore her meaning. "And it looks like rain."

"Of course." Troy stood up. "Stupid of me. You should be home in bed. Or whatever Patience thinks you should do. I'll explain to the captain."

"I don't want to get you in trouble with Thrasher." Mercy stood, too, and stared up at the storm clouds that had suddenly darkened the sky. "Or Harrington."

"Don't worry about it." He offered her his arm and she took it. The dogs followed them as he led her along the side streets, avoiding the crowds, to his truck. He was so solicitous of her that she almost felt guilty.

"I am sorry," she said. "This is not what I thought would happen."

"I know." Troy ushered them all into his vehicle just as the downpour began.

"I was so sure." Mercy couldn't understand how she could be so wrong. About the parade. About Elvis. About herself.

"You may have been wrong about the parade, but you aren't wrong about the case."

"You don't have to say that." She appreciated his good intentions, but the more understanding he was, the worse she felt.

"Something *is* going on here." He switched the windshield wipers on high and pulled out onto the road, proceeding carefully as people rushed to their cars to get out of the rain. "We've got the dead bodies to prove it."

"And a missing mother and child."

"Yeah," he said, maneuvering the big truck through the traffic that crowded the slick streets. Visibility was poor, even with the lampposts. "Still no word on them." He looked over at her with concern. "But the evidence team did clean up that pendant. I'll text you the images."

"Okay." She knew he was just trying to make her feel better. Not that it was working. "If I don't figure it out soon, Amy and Helena may be the next . . ." She stopped. She couldn't say it out loud.

"It's not all on you. We'll figure it out."

"What about Harrington?"

"You let me worry about Harrington."

They fell silent. Mercy stared at the rain slashing at the windows. "It just doesn't add up," she said finally. "Yet."

Troy smiled. "You're like a dog with a bone."

"I'm sorry."

"Don't apologize," he said, keeping his eyes on the road. Now that they were out of town, it was slow going as the deluge continued. "All the best cops are."

She wasn't a cop anymore and he knew it. But she appreciated the sentiment. She smiled back at him, then leaned her head back against the headrest and closed her eyes.

"Are you all right?"

"It's been a long day.

"And night," said Troy.

"I just want to go home."

"Not to your grandmother's?"

"Home."

"She won't like that."

"Home."

Elvis barked.

Troy laughed. "Home it is."

If there was one thing Mercy hated, it was going home in defeat. But retreat was not always defeat.

So she'd retreat . . . for now.

CHAPTER THIRTY-FIVE

MERCY TEXTED HER GRANDMOTHER, and by the time Troy dropped them off at the cabin, Patience was waiting for her at the dining table. As the storm raged on, Patience listened to her sad story of humiliation and defeat at the Northshire Fourth of July "Arts of America" Parade with generous offerings of sympathy and red velvet cake. The dark red sheet cake was iced in white cream cheese frosting and decorated with blueberries and sliced strawberries to look like the American flag. Lovely and delicious and perfectly suited to the holiday. The next best thing to carrot cake.

"What are you going to do now?"

"I don't know."

"The proper answer would be 'CT scan.'"

"Not in this weather."

"They say the storm will be long gone by morning. It's just going to last long enough to postpone all the fireworks until tomorrow night."

"I'll go tomorrow. Promise."

"The swelling is down, and your vitals are good, but I'm still going to hold you to that. Better safe than sorry."

"I feel good. Really. My pride may be hurting but my head is fine."

Her grandmother watched her wolf down her painstakingly created dessert with those bright blue eyes. "Certainly your appetite is healthy enough. But you still need your rest."

Mercy glanced over at Elvis, who was curled up on his side of the couch, snoring lightly, content after the good vet's ministrations and an early dinner of steak and hash browns. "Elvis would obviously like the rest of the day off."

"Why don't you join him in a nap?"

She popped a blueberry into her mouth. "I won't be able to sleep. Amy and Helena are out there somewhere."

"The police will find them."

"But maybe not in time. Harrington doesn't think Amy's in trouble, he thinks she killed Walker."

"Then you'll find them."

Mercy wished she could channel her grandmother's confidence in her. "My mind keeps circling back to some fleeting something just out of reach. The key to this whole business."

Her grandmother poured her another glass of milk. "Drink up. You need your calcium."

"And vitamin D." Mercy grinned. She'd heard this before. "I got plenty of vitamin D at the parade this morning. A useless exercise, other than that."

"Not really. Your grandfather used to say that eliminating possible solutions was as important as nailing the right one."

Having finished off the cake on her own plate, Mercy plucked another blueberry off the sheet cake. "I eliminated one solution in high style today. Grandpa Red would be proud."

Patience slapped her hand away from the cake playfully. "And now which are left to investigate?"

Mercy stared at her. She reached for her borrowed phone. "Troy said he was going to text me the photos of the pendant we found at the crime scene."

"The magpie Munchkin."

"Exactly. We think maybe the jeweler who made the belt buckles made this, too."

"Why don't you take a look while I clean up. But try not to think too hard. Give that pretty little red head of yours a break."

"Thanks." Mercy abandoned the table for the couch, giving the dozing Elvis a sweet scratch between the ears before settling on her side with the phone and her laptop. She pulled up the photos and looked at the maker's mark on the pendant. She read off the letters and numbers that ran along the perimeter of the back of the piece: POM 925, followed by an image of a calla lily:

"What did you find?" Her grandmother stood behind her, looking over her shoulder.

She pointed to the symbols. "*POM* should be the designer's initials; 925 means it's sterling silver, that is, 92.5 percent pure silver. And the calla lily is probably the designer's logo."

"And you know this how?"

"Mom." Mercy's mother knew all there was to know about the finer things in life.

"Of course." Patience laughed. "Who would believe that I would raise such a fashion plate?"

"I need to track down this artist." The initials and the calla lily held the secret to the jeweler's identity. Just as a jeweler's stamp should.

"Of course you do. But don't spend too long on that computer. Not good for your head."

"Uh-huh."

"I'm going to give you half an hour, and then it's lights out."

"Okay." She didn't have much time. She waited until Patience had gone back into the kitchen, then texted Troy. He told her that Flo Herbert claimed the artist who made the buckles had retired to Ireland, and the police were trying to trace the maker's mark. Then he told her to get some rest and signed off. Back to his patrols, no doubt.

Ireland, thought Mercy. Ireland of the Easter Rising, the famous rebellion that kicked off the Irish revolutionary period during Easter week in 1926. Calla lilies, long the symbol of Easter, had become one of the symbols of a free Irish Republic as well.

She grabbed her laptop and went to work—Googling Irish jewelry designers in Vermont, mountain-range silver pendants and 925 pine-tree necklaces, and the initials *POM* and calla lily logos. After dozens of searches and fifty-one websites she found a pendant on eBay just like the one the Munchkin found, designed by one Patrick O'Malley.

"Time's up," said Patience, looming over her.

Mercy jumped, and her head throbbed. Maybe her grandmother was right. She shut her laptop. "You startled me."

"You need to go to bed so I can go home."

"You're leaving?" She wanted her grandmother to stay. Elvis lifted his head and looked at Patience. He wanted her to stay, too. Everyone always wanted Patience Fleury O'Sullivan to stay.

"I've got to get back to the sick kitties."

"How are they doing?"

"So far, so good. But I need to get back."

"What about tomorrow? Will you need help?"

"Thanks, but I've already arranged for help." Patience waved her arms in the air. "I'm going out," she said grandly.

"Going out where?"

"The reception. I wasn't going to go, but since the cats are doing well, and you are feeling better . . ."

"What reception?"

"I've wrangled an invite to the poshest affair this town has seen in years. They'll be unveiling the restored Fountain of the Muses on the village green tomorrow at noon. Half of southern Vermont will be there."

"I thought that was open to the public."

"It is. But before the unveiling there's a very la-di-da event at the Northshire Historical Society and Museum. The society is hosting an art exhibit dedicated to the Muse, in honor of the return of the fountain. Your neighbor Daniel Feinberg is the grand master."

"Really? I didn't take him for the committee type." Not that she knew that much about the billionaire whose land cozied up to her own minimal acreage. She'd only seen him a couple of times, by happenstance, on hikes in the wilderness. His wilderness, mostly.

"He's not. But he's a serious art collector and has been very generous to the museum. He underwrote the restoration of the fountain. And he's donating the famous Grandma Moses painting of our village green to the museum. You know the one."

"Yes." Everyone in Northshire knew the one. The acclaimed primitive artist had painted the village green—with the Fountain of the Muses center stage—in the spring of 1954, and called it, simply, *Northshire*. The Bennington Museum down south housed the largest collection of Grandma Moses paintings in the world, and had been angling to acquire the piece for decades. But the owner had held on to the painting and refused to sell. "How'd he pull that off?"

"Billionaires have their ways, I suppose," said Patience. "He wields increasing influence here."

"Why is that?" Vermonters were notoriously disinclined to hand over any authority to outsiders, however well positioned. "I thought they hated guys like him."

"They do, and they hated him, too, at first, especially when he built that enormous place out there in the woods."

"Nemeton."

"Right. Something to do with ancient Celts and druids and sacred groves. At least that's what Lillian Jenkins says."

"If anyone would know, it's Lillian." Mercy grinned. "Is she on his side?"

"Now she is. Feinberg made his mea culpas by buying up as much acreage as he can, in order to preserve it," said Patience. "Saved it from the lumber companies."

"Tree hugger."

"Of the richest kind," said Patience. "That buys him enormous support among a growing segment of our population."

Vermont was changing, as more and more flatlanders moved in and started getting involved in local politics, often to the dismay of the native woodchucks. In some communities, the newcomers had formed majorities on planning commissions and the like, allowing for such long-outlawed travesties as overly large signage. That hadn't happened in Northshire, at least not yet. On the plus side, many of the flatlanders were as keen to leave the wilderness alone as they were to tamper with historically strict village zoning laws.

"Good for him, I think."

"The first viewing is tomorrow morning," her grandmother went on, "and they're having a fancy reception to celebrate. Anyone who's anyone in the New England art world will be there. I'm surprised you haven't heard about it."

"You know I'm not big on the news." She avoided all manner of media, since as far as she was concerned no news was good news.

"You really need to rejoin the human race sometime soon." Her grandmother turned to go.

Mercy remembered the flier that had led her to the parade—and disaster. She'd posted it on the fridge to remind her of her hubris, right next to the facedown photo of Martinez.

She got up and snatched it off the fridge, and carried it back to the couch. She consulted it now, looking at the activities for the day after the Fourth, which she'd ignored in her obsession with the parade. In typical no-frills Yankee fashion, the only mention of the gala was a brief listing in the schedule of events:

Sunday, July 4
10 a.m. *5K Fun Run ($20 registration fee)*
Noon *Fourth of July "Arts in America Parade" (free to the public)*
10 a.m. to 5 p.m. *Sidewalk Sale*
7 p.m. *Fourth of July Concert and Talent Show (free to the public)*
9 p.m. *Fireworks! (free to the public)*★
★*In the event of rain, fireworks will be held Monday, July 5*

Monday, July 5
10 a.m. *Northshire Historical Society and Museum Reception*
(limited tickets available, contact society for more information)
Noon *The Unveiling of the Fountain of the Muses (free to the public)*
Noon to 5 p.m. *Art Fete on the Green (music, food, face painting, arts & crafts fair, open to the public)*

Her grandmother tapped the reception entry on the page. "That's it."

"Are you going to get all dolled up?" asked Mercy, using her grandmother's favorite expression for dressing up.

Patience laughed. "It is a semiformal affair. Of course, this is Vermont, so the fashion bar should be pretty low. Still, one should make an effort."

Mercy wondered what that effort might look like. She tried to remember the last time she'd seen her grandmother out of her usual uniform of pants and top—wool in winter, linen in summer—with a white

veterinarian's jacket and sensible shoes. And, as required, the appropriate outerwear, like yesterday's raffia sun hat.

"You'll want to hold your own with the beautiful people," Mercy
said, thinking that if all the artists in Vermont were there, Dr. Winters and Adam Wolfe could be, too. Or at least some of their friends
and colleagues. "Do you think you could wrangle me an invitation?"

"Are you serious?"

"I was thinking I might want to go. You know, something to do.
To rejoin the human race."

Her grandmother wasn't fooled. "You hate functions like this."

"I'm very supportive of the arts."

"Sure you are."

"I am in theory; you know that. Maybe I should put that into
practice."

Patience sniffed. "What about the CT scan?"

"I could go right after the reception."

"Your parents will be there."

Mercy sighed. "Let me guess. They're Feinberg's attorneys." Time
for another piece of cake. She'd need more fortification if she was going
to see her mother.

"Yep."

"So the Commonwealth of Massachusetts isn't big enough for
them?"

"They're just a couple of his attorneys. The man must employ an
army of them."

"I bet." Leave it to her parents to represent the man who was buying up the state. They never missed an opportunity to grow the family
business.

"Of course you should get that CT scan. Or at least stay home and
rest. Stay out of the heat." Her grandmother smiled at her, a smile of
collusion. "But I do happen to have an extra ticket. It was supposed
to be for Claude, but he's stuck in Quebec with a very sick stallion."

"How did you score two invitations?"

"Friends in high places." Patience walked back to the breakfast
bar. "My reward for neutering Ralph, the mayor's philandering
dachshund."

Mercy laughed. "Of course."

"Maybe your handsome game warden will be there."

"I doubt it. He's on patrol. I imagine that he's happier in the woods after this morning." Poor Troy. No cake to comfort him.

"Wouldn't you be happier in the woods, too?"

"I couldn't let you go all alone. I'll be your plus one."

"I can think of a million reasons why you wouldn't want to go—and only one why you would. You think you might learn something. You're going as a spy."

Mercy demurred, but her grandmother laughed her off. "At least this way I can keep an eye on you. So make yourself presentable. Do us all a favor and wear something your mother would like." She kissed her cheek. "*Do* you have anything your mother would like?"

"Sure." Mercy gave her a quick hug. "I have shopping bags full of clothes from Nordstrom and Macy's and Lord & Taylor that she chose for me herself."

"Perfect." Patience waved goodbye as she headed for the front door. "I'll pick you up tomorrow morning at nine-thirty sharp. We don't want to be late for your mother." She turned just before she closed the door behind her and yelled, "Don't eat all that cake in one sitting!"

CHAPTER THIRTY-SIX

AFTER TAKING MERCY AND HER DOG HOME, Troy went out on patrol for a few hours, then headed back to the office, hoping for the chance to talk to the captain about the disaster at the parade before Detective Harrington did.

But he was too late. His superior officer texted him and told him to meet him at the police station. Harrington's turf.

"Rotten luck," he told Susie Bear, who responded by spraying him with water as she shook off the rain. She'd been doing this off and on for half an hour now, and was still quite damp, thanks to her thick double-layered coat, which took forever to dry.

Troy was drenched, too. He wouldn't have minded, given the heat, but going to see Harrington and Thrasher sopping wet was not ideal. He ran his fingers through his hair and mopped his face with a towel before using it on Susie Bear's big mug.

"Let's get this over with," he said to her as he parked the truck in the lot behind the station. Together they went in to face the music, which he imagined that on this Independence Day would be John Philip Sousa. Or maybe the Green Mountain Boys band.

He laughed at his own dumb joke.

"What's so funny, Warner?" Harrington appeared at the door of his office, an imposing presence in a light gray custom-tailored suit that cost twice his monthly salary. Harrington was perfectly dry.

"Nothing, sir." Troy fought the urge to wipe away the moisture pooling on his brow from his hairline.

"Nothing funny about that colossal screwup this morning."

"No, sir."

"We have you and your girlfriend to thank for that." Harrington raised his voice and the clatter of the office quieted as everyone around them strained to hear Troy's dressing-down.

"She's not my girlfriend." Troy hesitated. "Sir."

"Detective Harrington." Captain Thrasher strode toward them. "Let's take this inside, shall we?" He shook Harrington's arm and drew him into the office.

"Come on." The captain spoke to him very quietly, never a good sign. The angrier he was, the richer his baritone.

"Leave that dog outside," said Harrington, perching himself on the edge of his large desk to underscore the fact that he was the one in charge.

"Stay," Troy told Susie Bear, who gave him a baleful look as Thrasher closed the door on her.

"Warden Warner, that was some stunt you and that woman pulled this morning. I've spent all afternoon doing damage control—with the Feds and the pols and the media."

"Sorry, sir." Troy tightened his lips against the grin that threatened to overtake him at the thought of Harrington at the mercy of the media.

"I hate doing damage control." Harrington pulled a yellow silk square from his breast pocket, refolded it neatly, and replaced it.

"Sorry, sir," repeated Troy.

"That Mercy Carr is trouble, Warner. Damned attractive, but trouble."

"She's a decorated war veteran." Troy willed himself not to throw the punch his clenched fist was thirsting for. He moved his hand behind his back, out of sight. "Sir."

"That explains it. They all see IEDs everywhere."

Troy started to protest, but a look from Thrasher silenced him.

"Look, if you want to sleep with her, sleep with her," said Harrington, his voice now a booming stage whisper. "But stay away from her while you're on the job."

"Sir."

"And while we're on the subject of your job, let me remind you that your job is not homicide. Homicide is my job. Your job is fish and game." Harrington said this last bit with such contempt Troy felt sure that if he didn't hit him, Thrasher would.

But he was wrong.

"Warden Warner is needed out on patrol right away," said Thrasher. "This storm is bound to hit hard."

"Patrols." Harrington nodded. "That's where you belong, Warner. For the foreseeable future."

Troy looked Harrington in the eye. He saw resolve there. He answered it with a resolve of his own. "Sir."

"Women are women and work is work," said Harrington. "Don't shit where you eat. Every damned fool knows that."

Troy bounced on his toes. The captain placed his hand on his shoulder, and guided him out of Harrington's office and through the station and outside into the torrent. Susie Bear followed on his heels.

They ducked into a bus stop shelter, out of the worst of it as the rain pounded the roof and the wind rattled the glass-paneled walls.

"Breathe, son."

Troy exhaled, and steadied his temper. "Yes, sir."

"That debacle at the parade was the final straw. He wants your badge."

"Can he do that?" Troy watched the water stream down the sides of the shelter. He loved his job. If he weren't a game warden, he wouldn't know what to do with himself.

"He's got powerful friends."

"So do you."

"True." Thrasher rocked back and forth on his heels. "But that may not always be enough. No more stepping on his toes. Make yourself scarce for a while."

"Patrols."

"Yes. Meanwhile I'll do what I can to keep a lid on him."

"Thank you, sir."

Together they stood in silence as the wind blew and the thunder clapped and the lightning streaked across the darkened sky.

"I like patrols," said Troy.

Thrasher smiled. "Just as well."

MONDAY

JULY 5

CHAPTER THIRTY-SEVEN

THE NEXT MORNING MERCY LAID out the gifts her mother had given her since she'd come back from Afghanistan: at least a dozen outfits, due to her insistence that her only daughter needed an entire new wardrobe now that she was a civilian again and would be applying to law schools in big cities soon, preferably in Boston or New York. Her mother was not at all discouraged when Mercy went instead to Vermont and lived off her small pension and modest life savings until she could figure out what to do next; she believed that sooner or later her daughter would come to her senses and get a life. The life her mother had always wanted for her.

Martinez had also left an insurance policy, naming Mercy as beneficiary. But much of the small payout had gone to saving Elvis, and the remainder she'd earmarked for his siblings' education later down the road. His Social Security benefits went to his mother in Mexico, and helped support the large family he'd left behind.

Her mother knew all this, and had told her more than once that the best thing she could do for his family was to become a lawyer and make a lot of money. Mercy hated this argument, if only because it did hold some merit. How could she help his family hiding out here in the woods? Couldn't she help them more if she had a good job?

Understanding her daughter so well, her mother had not given up. Mercy figured that she never would. Martinez always called her stubborn, but he'd never met Grace O'Sullivan Carr.

The gifts were mostly work clothes, what her mother like to call "power suits," featuring tailored jackets, two paired with pants and three paired with skirts, all in various shades of gray, from dove to charcoal. For "after hours" wear, she'd curated no fewer than four little black dresses. Her mother was very big on little black dresses. Nothing Mercy would actually be comfortable wearing, as they'd all show either too much leg or too much décolletage.

One shopping bag left. Mercy prayed for something normal, at least as normal as her mother could buy. She pulled out a navy jumpsuit made of light cotton jersey, with wide palazzo-style pants and a cold-shouldered top.

She grinned. She could definitely move in this, without showing too much skin. Even better, the pants had deep pockets, and she could add the Chanel fanny pack—a little quilted black purse on a leather and gold chain belt—at her waist. Plenty of room to carry a cell phone, her Swiss Army knife, and whatever else she might need. For once she was grateful for her mother's obsession with pricey accessories, though she shuddered to think what this outfit, all told, had actually cost.

At one time, she'd considered selling all this stuff on eBay and giving the proceeds to the Martinez family college fund, but she just couldn't do it. She loved her mother, even though she rarely agreed with her on anything, from career to clothes. She couldn't give her gifts away, and risk hurting her feelings any more than she already had, simply by living her own life her own way.

Mercy showered, smoothed ointment over the tender skin chafed from the bulletproof vest, and slipped on the jumpsuit. She secured the Chanel purse belt around her waist, and added the gold hoop earrings her parents had given her on her eighteenth birthday and low-heeled gold sandals that she could run in if needed.

The worst thing about dressing like a girl was that you weren't free to run, at least not very fast and not for very long. A girl never knew when she'd need to run like hell. Mercy liked to be prepared for that eventuality. She always laughed when she saw female cops on TV chasing down a suspect in four-inch heels. Like that was ever going to happen.

A glance in the mirror told her that she should add a little blush and mascara and lip gloss. She did not cover up her freckles with foundation, as her mother always advised her to do. Enough was enough.

Her hair. The only thing her mother hated more than her freckles was her hair. But there was no containing it in this humidity—and she doubted her mother would approve of her wearing her Red Sox cap with this ensemble.

She ran some styling mousse though her damp frizz and crunched the curls with her fingers. Au naturel would have to suffice, whether her mother liked it or not.

PATIENCE WHISTLED WHEN she saw Mercy.

"You look pretty good yourself," she said, admiring her grandmother's turquoise silk tunic, which she wore with black silk pants and silver ballet slippers. Dozens of thin silver bracelets jingled on her wrists.

"Too bad your game warden is on patrol," said Patience.

"He's not my game warden," she said.

"Oh, but he could be." Her grandmother winked at her. "Especially if he saw you right now."

"Come on, let's go."

Elvis jumped up.

"Sorry, boy." Mercy patted his head. "You're staying home."

The shepherd whined his disapproval, looking to his favorite vet for support. But she shook her head at him. Defeated, he went back to his side of the sofa.

"Guard," Mercy told him and locked the door behind her as she followed Patience to her "fun" car, the little red Mustang convertible that spent most of the year in the garage. Except for beautiful sunny days like this—yesterday's storm a mucky memory—in summer and early autumn, that brief shining interlude between mud and snow.

"Your mother will be pleased," Patience said as she peeled down the drive and out to Route 7A. When unencumbered by four-legged passengers, she liked to drive fast.

"I live to serve," said Mercy, holding on to her seat.

"She loves you."

"I know."

"Be nice," her grandmother admonished her as she shifted into high gear.

"I'm always nice."

"You're always polite. Polite is not the same as nice. Not when it comes to your mother. Or any mother, for that matter."

They fell silent. Mercy closed her eyes and leaned her head back, letting the wind rush over her face as they sped down the road, sure to make it to the village in record time.

THE NORTHSHIRE HISTORICAL Society and Museum sat on the western edge of the village green. The large white building was built in 1825 in the Greek Revival style, with a long front porch supported by graceful fluted white columns that ran the full length of the façade. The gracious lady was festooned with red, white, and blue bunting in celebration of the Fourth, and a long banner topped the porch roof, proclaiming the "Arts of America Exhibition."

Two police officers in dress uniforms flanked the double-door entry. A teenage girl decked out like she was going to her junior-senior prom checked the invitation list, while another uniform checked all the parcels and purses. Backpacks were not allowed.

Security was tight, thought Mercy, at least at the door. Inside, she could see an eclectic assortment of creatively attired artists and academics, well-heeled patrons, and local politicians and businesspeople in power suits, mixing and mingling and overindulging in the champagne passed around on silver trays by waitpeople in black and white formal wear.

Lillian Jenkins, chairperson of the society's Arts in America Committee, stood just inside the entrance, at the head of the reception line. The restaurateur had abandoned her Vermonter Drive-In apron for a dazzling sparkly gold dress that befitted Northshire's queen of the meet-and-greet. The little woman looked just like the firecracker she was.

Lillian embraced her and her grandmother in turn.

"You look very pretty," she said. "Did you bring that handsome Troy Warner with you?"

"Uh, no."

"I think they're having a thing," said Lillian to her grandmother.

"We're not having a thing," said Mercy.

Lillian ignored her. "At least I hope they are."

"We're just friends."

"I thought you were smarter than that." Lillian frowned.

"They don't come any smarter," said Patience.

Lillian beamed. "I knew it."

Mercy capitulated. "He's on patrol."

"Then you'll have to settle for his yummy captain." Lillian waved her golden arm across the room at Captain Thrasher, a fairy godmother casting a spell. "Isn't he something?"

The captain was resplendent in his dress uniform, with its tailored scarlet jacket and distinctive black trim and black leather belt, complete with gun holster and gear holders. Sort of a macho version of her own Chanel fanny pack, thought Mercy, and smiled.

Then the captain shifted on his feet, and she saw that he was talking to her parents.

"Chin up," said Patience as they nodded goodbye to Lillian and moved on down the line.

"Let's get this over with." She didn't know what was worse, having to make small talk with her parents or having to make small talk with Thrasher. Given how disappointed they all were with her right now for various reasons, neither was a prospect she relished.

Her grandmother took her arm in solidarity and marched her over to the distinguished couple and the dashing captain.

"Darling, how wonderful to see you," said her mother, offering her a cheek.

"Hi, Mom." Mercy kissed her cheek dutifully.

"Let me look at you." She grabbed her by the shoulders and stepped back to inspect her. "Wonderful. I knew that color would flatter you."

Her mother was a slim pale blonde impeccably dressed in one of her perfect little black dresses, the compleat rich man's wife, no hint of the canny lawyer on display now. Her father stood beside her, a tall, stooped man who looked more like a professor than the adroit attorney that he was. Mercy was struck as always by how harmless they seemed when encountered outside the courtroom, just your average middle-aged American marrieds of means whose benign appearance completely hid the sharks that lurked beneath the surface.

"I'm surprised to see you here," said her father. "In that getup."

"That is not a getup, that is Ralph Lauren," said her mother. "She looks lovely."

"You do look lovely, Mercy," her father said. "It makes a nice change from fatigues."

"Pay no attention," Patience said to Captain Thrasher, who was watching them all very intently with those extraordinary eyes. "We appreciate those in uniform."

"This is my daughter, Mercy Carr," her father told the captain. "And my mother-in-law, Patience O'Sullivan."

"I know the captain," said her grandmother. "He's the fine human to a magnificent Maine coon cat named Crispus."

Mercy smiled as she shook the man's hand. Crispus Attucks, a former slave, was the first casualty of the American Revolution, killed during the Boston Massacre in 1770.

"She knows everyone," Mercy's father said.

"At least everyone with a pet," her mother added.

While her family sparred, she waited for the captain to fire a shot of his own. He may look the charmer, but she knew from Troy that he was a tough and demanding officer of the law. In his own way, his exterior was as misleading as that of her parents. She could only imagine what else they might have in common.

"I had an extra ticket," said Patience, turning her attention to the captain again. "And Mercy was delighted to come along as my plus one."

She smiled a warning at her grandmother not to overdo it. Thrasher could not have been pleased about the ruckus she'd caused at the taxpayers' expense at the parade yesterday. Troy was probably paying the price for it right now, in extra patrols or paperwork. She wondered what price the captain would have her pay for her part in the fiasco.

"May I steal your granddaughter for a moment? I'd like to show her something."

Before Patience could protest, the captain touched Mercy's shoulder and guided her over to a finely rendered pen-and-ink drawing of Shakespeare's Dark Lady by an up-and-coming young artist from Burlington. She hoped there was no hidden meaning in that.

"We have a mutual friend," he said.

"Yes." She waited to see what he would say next.

"You've distracted him," he said. "And not in a good way." He smiled slightly.

"I'm sorry." So much for hidden meanings.

"Are you?" He frowned. "You keep turning up at our crime scenes. And now you seem to see criminal activity wherever you go."

"Elvis was alerted to something, sir."

"The dog." Thrasher crossed his arms in front of his imposing, scarlet-clad chest. "You and your dog caused the service some considerable embarrassment."

"I am sorry about that. But three people are dead. A young mother and her baby are missing. And that man Max Skinner is involved somehow. I think he's the man who broke into my house."

"Understood. But you can't prove any of the allegations you've levied against him. He and the Herbert brothers have been released for lack of evidence."

"That was a mistake. Sir."

"Calling out the bomb squad is an expensive proposition for a false alarm."

"Better a false alarm than an unfortunate outcome." She paused. "And what about Dr. Winters?"

"Dead end, according to Harrington."

Mercy frowned.

"Harrington is not happy," said Thrasher, lowering his voice. "And when Harrington is not happy, our mutual friend is at risk."

"I understand." Now she knew why Troy Warner preferred being alone in the woods with Susie Bear on patrol. "I wouldn't want to hurt our mutual friend in any way."

"Good." Thrasher pursed his lips. "I know that you served with distinction in Afghanistan, and I appreciate that. But you are a civilian now."

"Yes, sir." She caught sight of her mother coming toward her and for once was glad of it. "I must get back to my family." She turned her back on him and went to join her mother.

"Let's take a look at the exhibition, shall we?" Her mother squeezed her arm. "There are some people I'd love for you to meet."

Which Mercy knew was momspeak for "Have I got a man for you!" Or as she had come to think of it, another bad first date waiting to happen. But if the alternative was another warning from Thrasher, she'd sooner make the rounds with her overzealous mother.

CHAPTER THIRTY-EIGHT

T HE GALA WAS NOW IN FULL SWING. People wandered from room to room of the graceful mansion, taking in the art that represented the best of the Green Mountain state.

The prized Grandma Moses painting stood on an easel, covered with a midnight-blue silk cloth, in the middle of the Grand Gallery, a huge space with twelve-foot ceilings, an imposing white marble fireplace, and ornately patterned inlaid hardwood floors.

The covered masterpiece was the featured centerpiece of the room, set off by swags of red velvet rope strung between brass posts and guarded by two uniformed police officers. With the viewing an hour away, partygoers were focused on drinking champagne and eating hors d'oeuvre and networking, networking, networking. Mercy's idea of hell.

But she had a job to do.

While her mother trotted her around to meet the various potential sons-in-law *in situ*—a tax attorney, an intellectual property attorney, a mergers and acquisitions attorney—Mercy smiled sweetly at the perfectly nice young men and surreptitiously checked out the museum's artwork and the security measures in place to protect that art. She spotted motion sensors in the corners, and video cameras hanging from the ceiling, providing full coverage of the galleries.

In addition to the uniforms, plainclothes cops roamed from gallery to gallery. She also noticed some private-security types in black suits and earphones slipping in and out of the building. Maybe they were the billionaire Feinberg's guys.

Patience rescued her just as her mother was introducing her to a personal-injury attorney, whom she knew could not be her parents' first choice. That was probably why her mother did not resist all that much when her grandmother pulled her aside.

"They must be getting desperate," she whispered to Patience.

"They just want you to be happy."

"They have no idea who I am." Her parents had not initially approved of Martinez, a soldier from Las Vegas with Mexican illegals for parents whose career goals began and ended with the military K-9 dog training school in Texas, *of all places*. Which is how her mother referred to anywhere outside the Northeast. While they eventually came around, and were truly sympathetic and supportive when he died, Mercy never could quite forget their initial reaction.

"It's nearly time for the viewing of *Northshire*," her grandmother said. "Come on."

Everyone started gravitating toward the roped-off area in the Grand Gallery, clustering in a crescent in front of the easel.

She held back while her grandmother and her parents edged forward with the rest of the partygoers. Daniel Feinberg and the mayor stepped up to begin their presentation. All eyes on the prize now— except for those of Mercy, who scanned the crowd, noticing the people she knew: Mr. Horgan, Lillian Jenkins, her own family members, Captain Thrasher, Pizza Bob, the owners of the Northshire Union Store, and all of the single age-appropriate lawyers known to her mother.

No Adam Wolfe. No Max Skinner. No Herbert brothers. No Dr. Candace Winters. And no Amy and Helena.

The speeches began, and Mercy tuned out. She grabbed a flute of champagne from a silver tray and downed it. What a waste of time and effort and Ralph Lauren this had been. The bubbly rushed to her head, and her skull started to pulsate. She should have known better. Sparkling wine gave her a headache even when she didn't have a concussion.

Head pounding, she went in search of a ladies' room and a cool, damp cloth. The restrooms were in the back of the building, by the kitchen, and because nearly all of the gala guests were at the viewing, for once there was no long line of women snaking out of the ladies' room door.

Mercy walked right in, and there she was, preening in front of the long mirror: Dr. Candace Winters, dressed in her signature subterraneanly sensuous style, in a tea-length powder-blue piqué dress with a white Peter Pan collar that seemed thoroughly prim and proper when seen from the front, but was completely backless, revealing a sinuous and sexy stretch of creamy skin from the nape of her neck to the base of her spine.

In comparison, Mercy felt practically puritanical in her cold-shouldered jumpsuit.

"Dr. Winters," she said, acknowledging her with a nod.

The professor finished applying her trademark red lipstick before she spoke. "Corporal Carr." She smiled as she slipped her lipstick tube into her matching blue clutch and turned to greet her. "I didn't know you were an art connoisseur."

"My family is very supportive of the arts."

"Ah, *those* Carrs." Dr. Winters regarded her thoughtfully with those huge gray eyes of hers, magnified through her nerdy black glasses.

Mercy changed the subject. "What do you think of the exhibit?"

The professor leaned in toward her and whispered, "It's not the best curation, is it? But it does have its moments. Have you made it to the West Gallery yet?"

She shook her head. "I don't think so."

"You won't want to miss it. Second floor, on your left."

"Sure. I'll check it out."

Dr. Winters pursed her ruby-red lips. "I hardly recognized you. You look so *presentable*." With that, she swept out of the ladies room, her bare back glistening with what Mercy swore was a subtle glitter.

What a piece of work is woman, she thought, remembering Thrasher's words and paraphrasing the Bard. She ran a paper towel under the faucet and wrung it out before patting her forehead and cheeks and collarbone. The damp cloth felt cool against her face, and the throbbing in her head subsided.

She made her way quickly back to the viewing area, where Dr. Winters had joined the crowd, which was far larger now that the speeches were winding down and the moment they'd all been waiting for approached. There must have been at least three hundred people in the gallery. Standing room only.

The mayor stepped forward to pull the ceremonial covering from the easel with a flourish, revealing the work. Painted with oils on a sheet of Masonite about two feet wide by three and a half feet long, the naïve work pictured the village green in early summer, children in their Sunday best playing around the Fountain of the Muses, their parents looking on under a canopy of trees and a blue sky. The North-shire Historical Society and Museum was there, too, along with the First Congregational Church with its classic New England spire.

The crowd oohed and ahed and surged forward. Mercy lost sight of the professor. But then she spotted her again, over by the entrance, on the arm of the mergers and acquisitions attorney her mother liked so much. They seemed quite enthralled by one another, if the way he ran his hand up and down her bare back was any indication. She wondered if he'd ever been to the south of France.

By the time she made her way through the throngs of gala guests, Dr. Winters was out the double front doors and gone. So was the attorney.

Mercy considered going after them, but given the fact that they probably had sex rather than murder on their minds, she wasn't sure what that could achieve, other than embarrassment on her part.

Besides, she had no car and no plan and Harrington was blocking her way.

CHAPTER THIRTY-NINE

M S. CARR?"
Harrington took her by surprise. She blinked. "Yes?'

"Daniel Feinberg would like a proper introduction."

Another surprise. But one she could hardly refuse, if only for her parents' sake. They did work for the man, after all. And it would be unneighborly to decline. Not to mention Harrington would not take no for an answer.

"Sure."

He grabbed her harshly by the elbow and pushed her through the crush to the billionaire, who was surrounded by a clutch of admirers. Feinberg spied them approaching, and excused himself to come and meet them halfway. She appreciated that. Maybe he wasn't as boorish as his friend Harrington.

The detective hustled her along to within a foot of Feinberg. But before he let her go, he leaned over and whispered in her ear. "Watch yourself. Because I am watching you."

She didn't say anything. Just shook the man off and smiled at the billionaire.

"Thank you, Harrington," said Feinberg in a dismissive tone and turned his attention to Mercy.

Harrington nodded at Feinberg and glared at her, before falling back into the crowd. Out of her sight. But still watching her.

"It's a pleasure to meet you, Ms. Carr," said Feinberg.

"Please call me Mercy."

"Mercy." He smiled at her, and she was struck by the aura of power that emanated from the man.

She'd seen him from afar on several occasions when she and Elvis were out hiking, and they'd exchanged waves, neighbor to neighbor. Up close, he made a strong impression, with his full head of wavy salt-and-pepper hair and dark brown eyes that went from warm to wary to warm again in a split second. He was the kind of imperious guy who could play high-stakes investment games with a poker face—and win every time.

They walked together toward the elegant staircase that led to the second floor of the museum. Two bodyguards in black suits and earpieces followed at a discreet distance. As she and Feinberg climbed to the upper galleries, one of the bodyguards roped off the steps at the bottom of the staircase. Obviously this was meant to be a private audience.

"It's nearly noon," said Feinberg, consulting his Patek Philippe watch, the only obvious sign of his wealth apart from the bespoke suit he wore. "Everyone will be going out to the village green for the return of the Fountain of the Muses."

"Don't you want to see it?"

"I've seen it. I'd rather talk to you about what you found on my land."

"Okay."

They reached the second-floor landing, and he escorted her into the West Gallery, another large graceful space with an inlaid hardwood floor. Tall windows looked out into the full-leafed bower of two-hundred-year-old maples and oaks and beeches that surrounded the museum on three sides.

This gallery was devoted primarily to sculpture. There was a modern Madonna and Child completely conjured up out of computer chips, an angel's wings crafted from the blades of kitchen knives, a nineteenth-century figurehead of an exotic raven-haired beauty that reminded Mercy of Cleopatra. "Eternity was in our lips and eyes, Bliss in our brows' bent . . ."

"Pardon?" asked Feinberg.

Mercy flushed, realizing to her embarrassment that she'd quoted *Antony and Cleopatra* out loud to herself. Good thing her mother wasn't here, or she'd be haranguing her to get out more. With those single attorneys, no doubt. "Sorry, sculpture always brings out the worst in me. Shakespeare."

"Interesting." Feinberg gave her a shrewd look. "And unexpected."

But Mercy was barely listening. She walked away from her host toward the back of the room, where a striking bronze glowed like fire in the afternoon sun that poured in from the windows.

Another one of Adam Wolfe's pieces. This sculpture was much like the one she'd seen in Dr. Winters's parlor, only far larger and yet more intricate at the same time. The massive curves seemed to fall into themselves, repeating in sensuous waves that flourished and flowed and folded and somehow reminded her of the professor's bare back.

"It's called *Confection*." Feinberg came up behind her and smiled at her obvious appreciation of the sculpture.

Mercy laughed, as much out of dismay as delight. "Of course it is. 'Oh, shame, where is thy blush?'"

"Indeed." Feinberg smiled. "Do you know Adam's work?"

"I've only recently discovered it," she said. He didn't need to know how she'd learned of the artist's sculpture. "It's beautiful."

"Yes, he's very talented." Feinberg cleared his throat. "You found a dead body at Adam's compound in the woods."

"Yes, I did." There was no point in denying it.

He nodded. "The dead man was a Canadian, they tell me. A bird-watcher from Toronto."

"Rufus Flanigan. I met him hiking the day before. He seemed all right."

"But Adam was not there."

"No. Everyone was gone, most everything was cleared out, really, except for the victim."

"So Harrington has told me." Feinberg's dark brown eyes grew wary again. "I own that land."

"Squatters?"

"No, I gave him permission to set up a studio there. I admire his work, and we share a commitment to preserving the land."

"Did you know him well?"

"As an artist, yes. As a man, that's harder to say." Feinberg gazed at the bronze *Confection*. "I met him in Quebec."

"Quebec?"

"I do a lot of business there. And at the time I was in the market for a piece by Paul-Émile Borduas. Do you know his work?"

Mercy shook her head and waited for the billionaire to enlighten her.

"One of Canada's foremost abstract painters. Leader of the *Automatistes* movement and chief author of *Le Refus global* manifesto."

"Manifesto? So he was an activist as well as an artist."

"Very antiestablishment. That's why Adam likes his work so much. He fancies himself an activist as well."

"You sound skeptical."

"Adam is a wild man, given to enthusiasms." Feinberg shrugged. "His so-called activism is one of those enthusiasms."

"He's been hanging out with a lot of Vermont Firsters."

The billionaire laughed. "He's not really a Vermont Firster. He's not even from Vermont. He's from Quebec. He left there to revitalize his career, just as his hero Borduas did back in the fifties. Borduas went to Provincetown, Adam came to Vermont. I encouraged him."

"You're his friend as well as his patron."

"We bonded over Borduas. I thought he had talent. He was doing bronzes back then."

"Like this one."

"Not quite."

Mercy grinned. "So you know Dr. Winters."

"I introduced them. When he first came here, I let him stay in my guest house for a while. I hosted a party in his honor and invited everyone in the local arts community. He met the professor, and the rest is right here before us."

"Another one of his enthusiasms."

He shrugged. "Or hers."

"They both seemed to have moved on," she conceded, remembering the attorney's fingers caressing the professor's exposed skin. "Do you know Adam's new girlfriend Amy Walker and the baby Helena?"

Feinberg nodded. "I've met them a couple of times, at the art colony. She's a sweet girl, devoted to Adam and the baby. And the baby seems well cared for, as far as I can tell. I don't go to the compound often; as you know it's not so easy to get to. Usually Adam comes to the house."

"You don't think he was keeping her there against her will?"

"That's quite a question." Feinberg looked at her sharply. "Why would you think that?"

"She told me that he'd gotten very possessive."

"I've never seen anything that would lead me to believe that. Of course, she is very young." He shook his head. "Artists live by their own rules."

"Amy and the baby are missing."

"And you want to find them."

"She came to me for help. And now she's gone."

"Understood. I'd like to know what's really going on myself."

"I thought he might be here today."

"So did I." Feinberg stared past her at the bronze. "He was supposed to be here."

"You'd think he'd want to be, with his art on display."

"He's a bit indifferent to exhibitions, even his own. Probably to the detriment of his career. But I'm surprised he'd miss this."

"When did you see him last?"

"Oh, it's been several weeks. He's off creating, and I have my own work to do."

Mercy watched Feinberg as he continued to stare at *Confection*. "You must have been disappointed when he abandoned the bronzes for natural sculpture."

"Not at all."

"Really?" Mercy looked at him, but he seemed serious.

Feinberg turned away from the bronze and looked past her to the trees beyond the windows. "Do you know what a folly is?"

"As in foolishness?"

"That's one definition."

"You're not talking about that kind of folly."

"No. I'm talking about the decorative Greek ruins built on the grounds of old estates in Britain and France. Just for the hell of it."

"What do you mean, just for the hell of it?"

"No purpose. That was the point of follies, that they served no purpose."

"No purpose but art," she said.

"Art is its own purpose." Feinberg waved his arms at the world outside the museum windows. "I commissioned Adam to create natural-sculpture follies on my land."

"He was cited for putting art installations on private property."

"I know. It was my land and my complaint. But when I realized what wonderful work he was doing, I paid the fines for him myself and commissioned the follies."

Mercy thought about that. "I think I found one not far from the compound." She smiled. "A beautifully crafted arch made of chiseled stones, with a dry riverbed running underneath. Fitted between two trees so perfectly it seemed to grow right out of the forest."

"That was his first." He smiled back, and this time his brown eyes smiled with him. "A twenty-first-century folly, illustrating the virtues of the natural world."

"Ingenious," she said.

"He's finished two of them, the one you found and another one south of the art colony, somewhere closer to my house."

Feinberg's house, as he called Nemeton, was a massive thirty-thousand-square-foot mountain lodge built out of native stone and lumber about halfway between Northshire and Stratton. The one her grandmother said had upset some of the townspeople when he built it.

"I'd love to see the other one."

"Then you'll have to find it, just like I have to do." He laughed. "He says he's working on ideas for the third, but I have no idea yet where it will be."

Mercy grinned. "Nice."

Feinberg grinned back at her. "There will be nine in total, scattered through the woods and the meadows like jewels."

"Nine," muttered Mercy. "As in a cat's nine lives. Nine circles of hell. Nine innings in a baseball game. Nine months of pregnancy. Nine Supreme Court justices. Nine Worthies." She snapped her fingers. "Nine Muses."

"You got it." Feinberg's smile faded. "If he comes back."

"That's why you thought he'd be here today. For the return of the Fountain of the Muses."

According to Greek mythology, the three original Muses—the meditation Muse, Melete; the memory Muse, Mneme; and the song

Muse, Aoide—were the ancient ones featured on the Fountain of the Muses. Over time these three became the Nine Muses—from Calliope, the Muse of epic poetry, to Urania, the Muse of astronomy—who together embodied all of the arts and inspired artists of all kinds.

"Yes," said Feinberg. "Shall we go have a look?"

CHAPTER FORTY

THE BLACK SUITS TRAILED MERCY AND FEINBERG back down the staircase to the ground floor of the museum. The galleries were empty now, the guests having retreated outside to the village green. Only the cleanup crew and the security guards and the art remained.

"Heavy security," she said as they stepped out onto the porch and the guards shut the doors behind them.

"Can't be too careful. Art theft is on the rise statewide. So we've upgraded the security measures here."

"Smart."

Feinberg nodded. "We've put in the very latest in alarms, infrared and microwave motion detection, scanners, twenty-four-hour video surveillance, staffing vetting and security, et cetera. It's been quite an education, really." They stood on either side of one of the fluted columns that supported the roof of the porch, surveying the scene in front of them. The village green looked much like it did in the *Northshire* primitive painting that so celebrated it: the First Congregational Church anchoring one end, the happy pedestrians walking the gravel pathways, young couples picnicking on the grass, vendors selling balloons and cotton candy, elderly citizens sunning on park benches, children playing by the three-tiered fountain. The only real differences being the arts-and-crafts tent that housed the artisans and their wares and the makeshift stage where a local eighties tribute band now played "Maneater."

"Grandma Moses would love it," said Mercy. "Except maybe for the Hall & Oates."

"Don't you?"

"I do. But Vermont is more than charm."

Feinberg laughed. "Agreed. That's why I like it so much."

Together they walked down the middle path of the village green for a closer look. The Fountain of the Muses was truly restored to all its former glory. Now cast in durable aluminum and painted in a striking burnished dark antique copper, the Three Muses—Melete, Mneme, and Aoide—glistened in their diaphanous gowns as they sat in contemplation of the arts, crowned by curls of water spraying forth from the mouths of cherubs.

"You've done a good thing here," she said.

"The merits of charm aside."

"Yes. But this is more than charm for charm's sake."

"Thank you. That was the intent. Besides, charm can be fun." He waved his arms, encompassing the scene. "This is fun."

Fun. One of the shrinks her mother had dragged her to after she came home from Afghanistan had once told her that his richest clients came to him for one reason: to learn to have fun. They'd spent so much time working that they had no idea how to play. Now they had money and time and no idea what to do with it. Feinberg knew how to play. He played with art.

"I imagine your own private collection is quite impressive. Not just fountains and follies."

"I've been collecting art for more than twenty-five years."

"Did you ever meet Max Skinner or the Herbert brothers?"

"I know the Herbert brothers—or at least *of* them—because my groundskeeper caught them poaching on our land a couple of years ago. We didn't press charges, but we warned them to stay off my private property."

"Hard to know sometimes where your property begins and ends."

Feinberg smiled. "If you're referring to my buying more acreage, that's true. But we allow snowmobilers and hikers to use the trails on the land, except for those that pass too close to the house. We allow hunters during the season, with permission. We've posted 'No Trespassing' signs wherever it's appropriate to do so."

Mercy nodded. "All good."

"And hunting out of season is against the law, no matter whose land you're on."

"Yes." She thought of Troy, whose dangerous job it was to catch those people hunting out of season. He certainly didn't think much of the Herbert brothers, even if they could play the fiddle. They obviously weren't the brains of whatever operation was going on here. Which may or not involve explosives at all, no matter what Elvis alerted to. Nothing had happened at the parade and nothing had happened at the art gala and nothing was happening here at the unveiling of the Fountain of the Muses. Nothing but people having fun. Just like Feinberg said. But there remained the question of the tall man. "What about Max Skinner?"

"Adam talks a lot about his buddy Max, but we've never actually met. He did arrange for me to see some of his art in Quebec. But I didn't connect with it."

"Why not?"

"I found Skinner's work too dark and disturbing. While it's true I consider my art an investment, I also have to like what I buy."

They circled the fountain, appreciating it from all angles. Feinberg's presence was beginning to attract notice, and several people came up to greet him, Harrington among them. He glared at her and she glared back.

"I'm sorry," Feinberg said, shaking her hand. "Do come to the house. I'll arrange a tour."

"I'd like that." She turned to go, then thought better of it. "Did you ever buy that Borduas?"

"It's hanging over the fireplace," Feinberg said. "You'll like it. It's called *Chinoiserie,* aka *Birches: Winter.*"

"Two names?"

"Yes. Two names, like Paul-Émile Borduas. Adam says it's the nature of duality."

"Duality," she repeated. "Opposite sides of the same coin. Like light and dark. Good and evil. Artist and activist."

Feinberg smiled. "That's one way to look at it."

She smiled back. He was a cagey one, this enigmatic neighbor of hers.

Well-wishers converged on the billionaire, under the watchful eye of Harrington and his bodyguards. Mercy waved goodbye and went in search of a snack. The green was lined with vendors: the American Legion grilling hot dogs and burgers, the Friends of the Library hosting a bake sale, the Boys and Girls Club pouring iced tea and lemonade, Animal Rescue selling fried dough.

Lured by the sweet heady scent of crispy crust and powdered sugar, she asked for a double order and smothered it in extra dustings of sugar, some of which blew onto her navy jumpsuit. She hoped her mother wasn't watching and hightailed it to a park bench partly hidden behind a tree. She scored a seat next to Mr. Horgan and offered him some of her dessert.

"Thank you, my dear." The old man tore off a piece carefully. Mercy handed him a napkin.

They sat there together quietly, watching the people pass by as they chewed on their fried dough and wiped powdered sugar from their faces.

"Eileen loved this fountain."

"I know. She used to tell us stories about the three Muses." Mercy patted his thin shoulder.

"She fought for years for the village to refurbish it. They never listened." The old man sighed. "Until this Mr. Feinberg came along."

"I'm sure she would be pleased."

"They did a good enough job, I suppose." Mr. Horgan popped the last piece of the fried dough into his mouth.

"It's beautiful."

The old man wiped his sugared hands on the napkin, then pointed it at her. "You're the Shakespeare girl."

"Yes, sir." Mercy smiled. Mrs. Horgan had given her free range in the library's Shakespeare section from a very early age. In her honor, and for her grieving husband, she recited:

O for a muse of fire that would ascend
The brightest heaven of invention!
A kingdom for a stage, princes to act,
And monarchs to behold the swelling scene!

"Nicely done." Mr. Horgan applauded. "I miss her."

"Me, too." She took the old man's wrinkled hand and squeezed it gently.

Mr. Horgan squeezed back, more strongly than she expected. "She said you were too young for the tragedies, but I told her you could handle it."

That, she didn't know. "Thank you."

"You grew up to be a soldier." He looked at her with an expression she could not quite read. "I was right."

MERCY STAYED THERE with Mr. Horgan thinking about being a soldier and fighting the good fight and finding Amy and Helena. The old man didn't say much, just sat there drinking in the sun while the world went on around him. She wondered if he'd had anything else to eat today besides that fried dough, and if George from Meals on Wheels would drop by his house later to make sure he had more than dessert for dinner.

But she didn't want to take any chances. "Would you like a burger?"

"You don't have to do that."

"No trouble. I'm going to get myself one anyway. Will you save my seat?"

"Of course."

She stood in line at the American Legion booth and ordered two burgers and Cokes, and headed back toward Mr. Horgan's bench. Out of the corner of her eye she caught sight of her mother talking to Lillian Jenkins. They were about twenty feet away, and her mother did not look happy. She had a terrible feeling the ebullient Lillian had said something that upset her. Probably about a certain game warden.

Mercy watched as her mother scanned the crowd for her. She darted for cover into the arts-and-crafts tent, where she knew she'd be safe among the vendors selling homespun cloth and home-thrown pots and homemade candles. Her mother wouldn't be caught dead buying anything in here.

She walked up and down the double aisles, glancing at the paintings and the wood carvings and the dream catchers. At the jewelry vendors she scrutinized the displays for belt buckles like the ones found on the victims, but she didn't discover anything remotely similar. She stopped in front of a "Natural Wonders" booth, which displayed a number of creations with a wildlife theme: sea-glass necklaces and moose snow globes and silk-screened T-shirts emblazoned with endangered species. Bats and butterflies, whooping cranes and condors, wolves and wolverines, whipsnakes and sea turtles and crocodiles.

Mercy thought about buying a T-shirt for her grandmother, but choosing among the endangered species would be tough. Her grandmother went to Georgia during hatching season every year to help the loggerheads, but she'd also worked at a whooping crane breeding center in Wisconsin and volunteered at a wolf sanctuary in upstate New York.

She was partial to the wolves, but maybe that was just because she had another wild Wolfe in mind.

Wolves. Wolfe. Wolf.

He's mad that trusts in the tameness of a wolf.

She ran out of the arts tent as quickly as she could without spilling the sodas. Past her mother and Lillian Jenkins. Past Feinberg and his fans. Past Harrington and his dark looks.

She slowed down just long enough to give Mr. Horgan the burgers and Cokes.

"Aren't you going to eat yours?"

"No, it's all yours. I've got to go."

"More battles to fight." The old man smiled at her.

She smiled back. "Yes, sir."

"Give 'em hell, Shakespeare girl."

CHAPTER FORTY-ONE

THERE WAS NOTHING LIKE A HOT SHOWER after long patrols in the woods and a dressing-down by Harrington. Troy sang along with the Avett Brothers on the radio as he washed away the dirt and sweat and humiliation of the past twenty-four hours. Susie Bear snored loudly to the beat from the other room. He'd have time for a quick nap himself before going back out again on patrol tonight, making sure that the fireworks people weren't supposed to have, and weren't supposed to set off, didn't get out of hand—which invariably they did. The storm last night had put a damper on the proper July Fourth fireworks, so everyone would be eager to make up for it tonight.

He was tired, but it was a good tired. He'd worn himself out on the trail, the best way he knew to work off his anger and frustration. Miles of forest later, he was feeling more in control.

He wondered what Mercy was doing to wear herself out. He knew that she must be as embarrassed as he was, but her job wasn't on the line. His was. Lesson learned.

From now on Troy would stick to what he was good at: reading the woods, patrolling the wilderness, protecting the wildlife, and enforcing the law of the land that would preserve it all for generations to come. *Fish and game,* as that smug bastard Harrington had put it.

No more parades. No more goose chases. He knew he should say no more Mercy Carr, too, but he wasn't sure he could. There was something irresistible about her.

As he shut off the water and dried himself off, he heard Susie Bear scramble to her feet and lumber to the front door, barking all the way.

He tied the towel around his waist and followed the dog. Through the wide front windows he saw a red Mustang convertible he didn't recognize parked in front of the fire tower. The kind of car you only saw in this state in the summertime, usually driven by a flatlander. But this vehicle sported Vermont license plates. The top was down but the seats were empty. So much for that nap. He cursed whoever had invaded his privacy and the convertible they rode in on.

There was a pounding on the door.

"Sit," he told Susie Bear, and she sat, tail thumping wildly. Which meant she liked whoever was on the other side of the door.

He opened it—and found Mercy and Elvis. The dogs greeted one another excitedly, then took off, chasing each other around the side of the house.

"Hi," she said.

She was all dressed up, as if she'd been to a party. He hadn't pegged her for a party girl, but then, what did he know? About women or parties.

"What are you doing here?" He was stunned to see her so decked out. She looked pretty great. Girly, even. He wondered where she'd been dressed like that. And with whom.

"Sorry for just dropping by like this, but it couldn't wait. Something amazing has happened."

"Uh-huh." She was all worked up, that was for sure. Her pale skin was so flushed with exhilaration, she was practically luminescent. Damned attractive, to quote Harrington.

"I figured it out," she said, her voice high with excitement. "Adam Wolfe and Rufus Flanigan are the same person."

Troy stared her. This might be her craziest idea yet. "What are you talking about?"

"Has his next of kin identified him?" There was a challenge in her blue eyes.

"I don't know. I'm not sure they've even had time to find his next of kin. He's not from here."

"You should run his prints."

"You'd better come in." Troy whistled for Susie Bear, and she barged into the house, Elvis on her heels. He stood aside and waved Mercy inside. For the second time in as many minutes he found himself admiring the way she filled out the jumpsuit she was wearing. Which was what he thought you called it. Not the kind of thing he ever expected to see her in, or that he expected her to look so good in. She wore it well, but it still seemed to him as if she were in costume. He thought he liked her better in her usual uniform of cargo pants and T-shirt.

"Very cool place," she said, taking in the large kitchen, which commanded most of the first floor.

"Thanks."

Mercy stood just inches away from him. So close he could count the faint freckles on her nose and breathe in the scent of lavender and lemon in her red hair.

"I think Max Skinner killed him."

"Like he blew up the parade."

The dogs alerted. Two pairs of canine ears, one triangular and one floppy, perked up.

"I know I was wrong about that," she said in a low voice. "And I'm so sorry. But this is different. I'm not wrong now."

"We've just come off patrol, and we have to go back soon." He stepped back, away from that freckled little nose and that red hair. The dogs relaxed, along with their ears.

"Please let me explain," she went on. "I can prove they're one and the same person."

Troy hesitated. If that was true, then that would be amazing. She'd been right about everything else . . . well, except for the explosives. The woman was nothing if not stubborn, but she was smart, too. "Why don't you have a seat and tell me all about it." He pointed her to a chair at the kitchen table. "From the beginning."

"Okay." But she didn't sit down.

"I was just about to make us some supper before we go out again. Are you hungry?"

Both dogs barked at the sound of one of their favorite words: *supper.*

"Why don't you feed them while I change? The Crock-Pot on the counter has Susie Bear's stew in it. You're welcome to share it with Elvis. There should be plenty."

"Smells good."

The dogs thought so, too. They each sat down on the wide pine planks of the kitchen floor as close as possible to the Crock-Pot. Susie Bear was so big that she simply laid her pumpkin head right on the counter and waited. Elvis could not quite reach that far, so he craned his neck, snout up in the air, and sniffed.

"I make it myself," he said. "Beef-stew meat, chopped carrots, celery, potatoes, vermicelli, and bouillon. Eight hours in the Crock-Pot and it's good to go."

"Lucky Susie Bear."

"If Elvis likes it, I'll give you the recipe." He headed across the room. "Dog dishes in the pantry. Help yourself to whatever you need."

He climbed the stairs to his living and sleeping quarters, and changed into a clean uniform. Just in case she wanted to see the rest of the house, he lifted the Murphy bed back into the wall, and tossed the dirty clothes into the hamper. There was nothing he could do about all the dog hair, but she had a dog, too. Of course, nothing shed like a Newfie. He'd lucked out as far as the slobbering went—Susie Bear didn't slobber nearly as much as most Newfoundlands—but the hair, *man,* the hair was everywhere. Sweeping it up was a daily battle he hadn't had the time to fight lately.

He pulled a record from his vinyl collection on the far wall. The Lumineers. If he couldn't get any sleep, at least he'd get a little "Ho Hey." He put the record on the turntable and then went back downstairs.

He found Mercy chopping up tomatoes and cucumbers for the salad she'd made. The rich smell of Mocha Joe's Hometown Blend hit him hard. Just what he needed.

"I found the box of produce from the farmers association in the fridge," she said. "I hope that's okay."

"Great. I'll make the omelets while you chop and talk. Cheddar cheese okay?"

"Sure. I'm afraid between the two of them they finished off all of the stew." She watched as he beat eggs in a bowl and poured them into a skillet.

"That's okay. I don't eat Susie Bear's stew."

"Oh." Mercy frowned. "So you cook for your dog but not for yourself?"

He laughed as he grated the cheese and added it to the eggs. "I'm not a fan of the Crock-Pot. More of a grill guy myself. I do share my meat with Susie Bear."

She nodded, and he was struck by the sadness that washed suddenly over her face, and then was gone. He flipped the omelet on a plate and placed it in front of her with a side of the salad. "Coffee?"

"Thanks."

He poured them each a cup and then sat down at the table with her. "Let's hear it. From the top."

She nodded, and in between bites she told him about the Historical Society's gala reception. "You know, where they unveiled the Grandma Moses painting."

"Lillian Jenkins," he said.

"Exactly. I went with my grandmother."

That explained the party clothes, he thought.

She told him about her conversation with Daniel Feinberg about Adam Wolfe and Paul-Émile Borduas and his comment about two names. "I think he was referring to the names of his two personas—Adam Wolfe and Rufus Flanigan."

"Kind of a stretch."

"Not really. Something about the bird-watcher had been bugging me. I knew I was missing something. And then it hit me. Wolves."

"Wolves." He had no idea where she was going with this.

"They had this arts-and-crafts tent on the town green today. There were all the usual vendors, you know, clothes and jewelry and pottery. One guy was selling silk-screened T-shirts with pictures of endangered wildlife on them."

"Like wolves."

"Exactly."

"Go on." This was getting interesting.

"Adam Wolfe. Rufus Flanigan." She grinned at him. "Is your Latin any better than your Greek?"

"Not much," he admitted. "I know that *Canis lupus familiaris* is the scientific name for dog, and *Canis lupus lupus* is the scientific name for wolf, from the Latin. Right?"

"Right."

"I still don't get it."

"*Canis lupus lupus* refers to the common wolf. But the scientific name for the red wolf is. . . ." She looked at him, like a patient teacher waiting for her favorite student to do well.

"*Canis lupus rufus.*" He didn't know what else to say. It was just bizarre enough to be true.

"I looked up the etymologies of Flanigan and Adam, too. Adam is Hebrew, and means 'red,' supposedly a reference to ruddy skin or to the red soil in the Garden of Eden from which he was made, according to the book of Genesis."

"The Bible." Troy wasn't too sure how helpful that source would be to the case.

"Yes." Undeterred, she went on. "Flanigan is Gaelic, a diminutive of *flann,* which means—"

"Let me guess," he interrupted her. "'Red.'"

"'Red' or 'ruddy,' yes." She hesitated. "So Adam Wolfe means 'red wolf' and Rufus Flanigan means 'red wolf red.'"

"There's two reds in there. Like the two lupuses. It almost makes sense."

Mercy frowned. "I supposed it could be just some crazy coincidence, but I don't think so."

"It's not crazy." He laughed. "It's brilliant. And it sounds like the kind of thing this guy would do."

"I followed it up. And it checked out." She pushed over the cell phone that Patience loaned her. "Here are the images of Adam Wolfe I found on the Internet."

He flipped through the photos of a hippie-looking long-haired dude with a full beard and mustache while he tried not to inhale his food. "Looks like a cross between Hagrid and Van Gogh."

"Yeah." She leaned across the table. "Now picture him with a short haircut like yours—no beard, no mustache, no wild mane."

Troy tried to imagine that. He pulled his own phone out, and compared the photos of the dead Rufus Flanigan and the living Adam Wolfe. "It's possible. I'll talk to Thrasher about running Flanigan's prints if they haven't already."

"Great. Thanks."

"Why would he need two identities?"

"For his two personas. Artist and activist." Mercy pointed to each likeness in turn on the phones. "The question is, which one was murdered? And why."

"When he was murdered, he was Rufus Flanigan."

"But that doesn't mean the murderer knew him only as Rufus Flanigan."

"Maybe that's the reason he was killed," said Troy between bites. "Because someone found out about his double life—and didn't like it."

"We have to find this guy Max Skinner," she said. "He was in the position to know about both Wolfe and Flanigan. I'm sure he's behind the murders and Amy and Helena's disappearance."

"You know they questioned him and let him go."

"But he's the only common link," she said. "He's connected to Wolfe and the Herbert brothers and through them, to Dr. Winters and Amy and Helena and Donald Walker."

"You could say the same thing about Amy Walker."

"You don't believe that."

"I don't know what I believe about Amy." He pushed his empty plate away and yawned. "But I know what I believe about you. You're some kind of genius, really, to figure all this out."

"Thanks." She smiled shyly at him. "By the way, I think the jeweler who made the buckles and the pendant is a guy named Patrick O'Malley. You might want to check it out." She pointed across the room to the dogs, sleeping side by side at the threshold of the front door. "I know you're exhausted, too. Go on and get some sleep. I'll clean up."

"That won't be necessary."

"It's the least I can do." She started clearing the table. "Elvis and I can let ourselves out."

"Okay." Troy yawned again. He could really use a nap before he went out again. "But I can't let you leave without showing you something first."

She followed him up the two flights of stairs, past his living and bedroom space, and up to the deck on the roof at the top of the fire tower. He slid open the sliding glass door and waved her outside.

"Wow," she said.

They walked around the perimeter of the deck, which comprised the entire footprint of the tower. The view stretched for miles down the Battenkill River and out across the meadows and forest in all directions.

He watched her as she stared out across the valley, her eyes full of unshed tears.

"This is beautiful," Mercy said. "'One touch of nature makes the whole world kin.'"

Shakespeare again. Whenever she seemed overcome with emotion, she quoted the Bard. He'd have to ask her about that sometime.

But not now. Now was too perfect.

They stood there for a few minutes, not saying anything, just drinking in the view of the land they both loved. Troy liked that she was comfortable with silence. Not that many people were, and he'd learned that the people who couldn't handle silence often couldn't handle life. Silence was good.

He yawned.

"I've kept you long enough," she said quietly.

He took her back downstairs, where she went straight to the kitchen sink.

"I'm doing the dishes," she said, in a voice that told him there was no point in trying to stop her.

He handed her the "Licensed to Grill" BBQ apron that hung on a hook by the oven, a gift from his estranged wife that he wished now he'd given away, as he had most of the other reminders of his failed marriage. But Mercy needed something to protect that fancy outfit of hers.

She took it from him. "Thanks."

"I meant it when I said you're brilliant. But you need to go home now and stay out of it. And so do I. I'll pass all this along, but it's up to Harrington and the Major Crime Unit now."

"Harrington." She frowned. "I don't like him."

"I don't like him much, either. But he is a decent detective."

"If you say so."

"It's his case. Seriously. It's not your job—and it's not mine, either. He's made it very clear that if I overstep jurisdiction again, he'll have my badge."

"Understood." She slipped on the apron, tying it behind her back. She looked far better in it than he did.

He cleared the table while she loaded the dishwasher.

"Go on up," she said. "Get some rest. Elvis and I will let ourselves out."

"Right." He hauled himself up to his couch on the second floor and fell into it. He lay there, willing himself to stay awake. Listening as she finished up, whistled for Elvis, and left the house, closing the door behind her and going out to the driveway.

Troy smiled. Hard to stay away from a woman like that. Even if she could get you fired.

He heard the car door slam and the sound of the little red convertible roaring off, and Susie Bear shambling up the stairs to join him.

She settled at the other end of the sectional, and he texted Thrasher about Rufus Flanigan's fingerprints. That was all he could do for now. Finally, finally, finally, he gave into his overwhelming urge to snore.

HE'D BARELY CLOSED his eyes when his mobile beeped. It was a text from Thrasher, asking him how he knew that the dead bird-watcher Rufus Flanigan was really Adam Wolfe, and telling him to phone right away. He sighed and placed the call.

Thrasher picked up on the first ring. "Don't tell me. Mercy Carr."

"I went out with Susie Bear on patrol as ordered, sir. When we came home between shifts, she showed up at the house with Elvis unannounced."

"She ambushed you." The captain almost sounded amused.

"She did some research and figured it out." He told him about the meaning of the two names. "But that's not all. We compared photos she found on the Internet to those I took of the dead bird-watcher, and it seemed possible that they could be the same man, so I agreed we should run the prints."

"You were supposed to stay out of it."

Troy paused. "She *was* right, sir."

"No denying she's smart as a whip." The captain chuckled. "Where is she now?"

"I told her we had to go back out on patrol, and that the Major Crime Unit would handle it. She went home."

"Make sure of that. Harrington is beside himself." The captain chuckled again, then stopped midlaugh. "It really isn't funny. I'm doing damage control, but there's a limit to my influence. Keep her—and yourself—off his radar."

"Yes, sir."

"I mean it."

"Yes, sir. Thank you, sir." He smiled as he hung up. The captain loved showing up Harrington as much as he did. And Thrasher would always save his sorry ass if he could.

But it was up to Troy to save Mercy Carr's ass.

CHAPTER FORTY-TWO

THE RED CONVERTIBLE WAS PARKED UP by Mercy's cabin. Troy hoped that meant Patience was back on site, monitoring her headstrong granddaughter.

No such luck. Mercy answered the door, and let him and Susie Bear in right away. Elvis greeted him with a short yelp and then both dogs bounded back toward the kitchen. No sign of Patience.

"I thought you were going back out on patrol." She'd changed back into her usual hiking clothes, a blue hoodie over a white T-shirt and tan cargo pants with hiking boots, her Red Sox cap covering her red hair. Not as sophisticated as the girl in the navy jumpsuit, but even more beautiful somehow.

"I thought we should check on you first." He looked around the neat kitchen, where a backpack sat on the counter, next to bottles of water and packages of beef jerky. "Where's Patience?"

"She's still in Northshire, hobnobbing with Vermont's beautiful people."

"And you're going out?"

"Just a little walk in the woods."

"Shouldn't you be resting?"

"Elvis is a little rattled. This will calm him down." She looked at him with those bright blue eyes, all innocent concern over her dog, who seemed perfectly at ease, sitting there in his Sphinx pose with Susie Bear, waiting for a beef jerky treat.

"Right." He laughed, as much out of frustration as amusement. "You are a terrible liar."

She started to protest, then laughed with him. "So I've been told."

"What are you really up to?"

"Just a little walk in the woods." She grinned. "That may take us past the compound."

"Why? We've been there, the crime scene techs have been there, whatever is there to be found has been found."

Mercy shook her head, and those red curls fell around her face. "We didn't know who the victim was then. And it was dark. I'd like to get a look in daylight. See what we're missing."

"If anything."

"If anything." She smiled at him. "But I know we're missing something."

"You never give up, do you?"

"Never give up, never surrender." She was dead serious now.

"Thrasher says I need to keep you out of this investigation." He was dead serious, too.

"I thought Thrasher was a good guy."

"He is," Troy said. "But Harrington is another story."

"Yeah." Mercy hesitated. "He's got it out for you and your boss."

"And you." Troy weighed his options. "But you were right about our victim. And we still don't know where that baby is." He was not convinced that going out to the compound again with her was a good idea, but he couldn't babysit her all afternoon, and he couldn't have her traipsing around the crime scene without him. And he and Susie Bear had to go back out on patrol anyway.

"Or her mother." Mercy reached over across the counter and touched his hand. "I promise I'll follow your lead."

Troy sighed. "We'd better get going, it's nearly four o'clock."

"Just a little walk in the woods," she said.

Just a little walk in the woods that could get me fired, thought Troy. Or solve the case.

THE CRIME SCENE techs had come and gone. They'd made pretty quick work of it, probably urged on by the desire to get back to their families for the rest of the July Fourth festivities. The woods were quiet now. The summer sun was on its long descent toward evening. There were only a few hours of daylight left, and then the last of the holiday celebrations would begin in earnest—fireworks and beer, not necessarily in that order. A recipe for disaster—and one that would undoubtedly occupy Troy's evening hours. All the more reason to get through this exercise as quickly as possible.

"Not much changed here," he said, pointing to the area where she'd found the victim, which looked much the same, apart from the obvious comings and goings of the crime scene techs and the scavengers. "We've been all over this before. And so has the forensics team."

"We need to go back to the basics," said Mercy. "Means, motive, opportunity."

"Okay," said Troy. "Let's assume for now that Max Skinner had both means and opportunity, since he was known to Wolfe and was seen here at the compound and knew the Herbert brothers, who were hunters with access to hunting knives."

"And he's from Utah, which means he's probably a hunter, too. In any event, it's realistic to assume that he could get his hands on a common hunting knife like the Buck that killed Wolfe."

"Which leaves us with motive," said Troy, "at least for the sake of this discussion."

"Envy," said Mercy. "Feinberg told me that Skinner was an artist, too. But he wasn't as successful as his friend. Wolfe tried to help him, and he approached Feinberg about buying his art, but he declined."

"So he was jealous?" Troy shook his head. "That wouldn't explain why Wolfe came to you as Rufus Flanigan, and told you where Amy and Helena were. Or why he called in the AMBER Alert in the first place."

"He must have believed that Amy and Helena were in danger," she said. "Max could have been jealous of his family as well as his art."

"Or maybe Wolfe wanted Amy and Helena back, and used the AMBER Alert to help locate them," he said. "He came to you as the bird-watcher to find out how much you knew. He told you where they were so you'd go after them, and then once you were distracted, he bonked you on the head and left you to die in the woods."

"Only, someone killed him first," she said. "Wolfe is the key to this whole thing. If we understood him better, maybe we'd understand why someone would want to kill him."

"Thrasher says the Rufus Flanigan passport is a fake; a good one, but a fake. So he definitely had something to hide. Otherwise, he wouldn't need two identities."

"The nature of duality, that's what he said, according to Feinberg," said Mercy.

"Duality?" He grinned. "Yin and yang?"

"Very funny." She laughed. "But yes, you're right. Two identities. Two homelands. Two styles of sculpture."

"Two women." He had to admit that he liked the way her mind worked, when he could follow what she saying. He liked watching her think. She stood by the barbwire fence, her hands on her hips.

"Two follies."

"Follies?"

Mercy told him about the follies and the natural sculptures that Feinberg had commissioned Wolfe to create on his land. "Maybe he wasn't trying to kill me, maybe he just hit me over the head trying to keep me away from the folly."

"Why would he do that?" She'd lost him once again.

"I don't know. But there's nothing more to be learned here. Let's go take another look at the folly."

They called for the dogs, who were chasing each other around the compound. He followed her to the section of the fence where she'd cut it, and they pulled it apart. She led the way to the folly.

"This is the first one he finished," she told Troy. She ran her index finger along the markings on the stones, which looked like this: Ερατω.

"Greek to me," he said.

She rolled her eyes at him in response. "Couldn't resist, could you?"

"Nope." He grinned at her.

"I think this is the name of a Muse," she said, serious again. "Feinberg commissioned nine follies, one for each Muse."

"But Wolfe only finished two of them. Which one is this?"

"I don't know. Feinberg didn't know, or at least he didn't say. I snapped a photo of it with my phone, intending to look it up later on the Internet when I got home, but then of course, I got hit on the head and someone stole my phone."

"Do you think that could be why?"

"I don't know. I did look up the Nine Muses, and their Greek names, to try to jog my memory. If I had to guess, I'd guess that this is Erato, Muse of erotic love."

"I wonder if that was meant for Amy or the professor." Troy took some pictures of his own of the folly.

"I'd bet on Amy. Feinberg believes that he loved her, and the baby." Mercy snapped a couple on her grandmother's phone as well. "Not that Erato seems to be helping us."

Together they went round the arched structure again, looking for something, anything, that might tell them something. They squatted down to examine the dry riverbed of stone, searching for meaning in the patterns. But the lovely whirls and swirls revealed nothing to them.

"See anything?"

"No." Mercy plopped down onto a large downed limb. "Maybe this is my folly."

"That's not true." Troy sat down next to her. "You saved the baby. You found the bones. And Don Walker. And you figured out who Rufus Flanigan really was."

"We still don't know why Elvis alerted to explosives. And Amy and the baby are still out there somewhere."

He knew that he should just send Mercy and her dog home. And get on to his patrols. But he didn't think she'd go, and he couldn't just abandon her here in the woods. "What you said before, about how knowing the victim will help us figure out the motive. Well, what do we know about him?"

"We know nothing about him was as it seemed."

"Right."

"Amy told me that he was very secretive about his art. He wouldn't let anyone see it until he was finished."

"Looks like he was secretive about everything."

"That's true. He hid his studio on the compound, and his girlfriend and his baby in a tent cabin, and his folly in the forest."

"And then there's the name thing. He didn't just pick any name for his second identity, he picked one with a hidden meaning."

"A puzzle," said Amy.

Troy looked back at the folly again. "This folly is a puzzle, too. It's constructed like a Jenga—pull out one piece and the whole thing might fall down."

"No, it wouldn't. He's far too clever for that. He's built this to last, at least as long as Mother Nature allows. That's what Dr. Winters said."

"If that's true, then conceivably you could pull out a piece."

"Now that would make a good hiding place."

They looked at each other, then jumped to their feet, jostling one another. Mercy stumbled, and Troy steadied her, catching her hips with his hands.

"You start at one end, and I'll start at the other." She went to the right-hand side of the folly's arch and started running her fingers along the edges of the granite stones. Troy went to the left-hand side and did the same. They'd nearly met in the middle when his thumb caught on the edge of the block just to the left of the keystone. He pulled the wedge of stone out.

"Look," he said. The block was not nearly as deep as the others.

"Well done." Mercy peered up into the space where the stone had been.

"What's in there?"

"See for yourself."

There, on a narrow ledge, was a small rectangular box, the kind used for gift cards. "You do the honors."

Carefully she removed it from the cavity and held the box out to him in the palm of her hand.

"Go ahead, open it."

She slipped the top off and revealed the prize: a slim blue plastic card that looked much like a credit card or a hotel key card. "Odd." She plucked it up by the corners and presented it to Troy. "What is it, exactly?"

He held it up by its edges. "I think it's a security pass card, the kind employers issue to their employees to get in and out of their offices."

"Why would he have that?"

"We didn't see anything that he'd need it for at the compound," he said. "So there must be somewhere else he used it."

"Feinberg was talking about this at the gala. He underwrote the whole thing, including comprehensive new security measures. He specifically mentioned staff vetting and security."

"Art theft is often an inside job." Troy nodded. "You look to the family first when there's a murder, and you look to the staff first when there's a theft."

"Art theft." Mercy gave him back the box. "All that packing material we found in the steel trunks could be used to pack stolen art just as well as legitimate art. Feinberg has a very valuable art collection. Wolfe knew it. He must have been planning to rob him all along. Like you said, an inside job."

"We don't even know if this key belongs to Feinberg. Besides, Wolfe is dead."

"Max must be in on it. He killed Wolfe so he wouldn't have to share the proceeds."

"Why kill him before he got the key?"

"I don't know. But that could be what he was looking for at my house. Maybe he thought Amy had it."

"That's a lot of *maybes*."

"Max knows he's on your radar now." Mercy's face flushed. "He's going to make his move soon, if he hasn't already. And today is the perfect time. Everybody's in town."

"I'll let Thrasher know about the key."

She grabbed the box from him. "Not good enough." She whistled for Elvis, and he came bounding over.

"What are you doing? That's evidence."

"Evidence you would never have found without me." She strode off down the trail that ran south through the forest, the handsome shepherd on her heels. "We're going down there," she yelled over her shoulder. "Are you guys coming or what?"

Susie Bear danced in front of him, desperate to tag along with her new friends. So much for following his lead. Troy cursed under his breath, and jogged after them.

CHAPTER FORTY-THREE

In the end, Troy talked her into going back to the compound and getting his truck. They were burning sunlight and he didn't want them wandering around the woods after dark looking for a place neither of them had ever been to before and had only a vague idea of where it was anyway.

They bounced down the logging road away from the art colony, then along the back roads until they got to a place where they could get a signal. Troy plugged Feinberg's address into his GPS and contacted Thrasher. Another twenty minutes on backroads and they came to the unmarked three-mile drive that led to Daniel Feinberg's estate.

About two miles in, a massive black iron gate crossed the road, part of a six-foot iron fence that stretched between the trees as far as they could see in either direction. According to the GPS, the road led up to Feinberg's lodge, which sat at the edge of a forested ridge looking east out over the mountains. Most of the house was hidden by trees, but a couple of stone and log turrets peeked just over the ceiling of the forest.

Troy spotted security cameras in the decorative copper caps that topped the gate posts and pointed them out to Mercy. Before he could say anything, she was out of the truck, checking out the cameras. And back in a flash.

"They've been disabled," she said, getting back into the front passenger seat. "And the intercom has been smashed in, with a hammer, by the looks of it."

"Not good. I'm calling for backup."

"The electric gate is locked," she said. "And we don't have the remote. We have to find another way in."

"We should wait for backup."

"That's what you always say."

"That's what Thrasher always says." Even if they rarely arrive in time to help, thought Troy—but did not say aloud. "And this time he's right." He put in the call.

"How long will it take?"

"Hard to say. We're pretty far off the beaten path, and Delphine says that between the fireworks in Bennington and Northshire and all the big shots who need babysitting, coming to check out a possible burglary won't be a priority."

"It will be when they tell Harrington it's Daniel Feinberg's house."

Troy grinned. "You might be right. But it could still take a while for them to get up here."

The sound of a low boom echoed down the ridge from the direction of the lodge. Elvis yelped. Susie Bear bellowed. Mercy and Troy looked at each other.

"Fireworks," Troy said. "Just the beginning."

"Or our thieves decided not to wait for the security pass," she said. "We need to go, before they get away."

"Doesn't Feinberg have staff?"

"Yeah, but it's a big place. His bodyguards are with him in Northshire. And it's a holiday, a lot of them could be off." Mercy pursed her lips. "There's a groundskeeper, too. Feinberg told me he caught the Herbert brothers poaching on his land."

"So they know Feinberg and they know Max. There could be a lot of perps up there. More reason to wait for backup."

"But there's only one road out of here," said Mercy. "And we're blocking it."

"If it is Skinner or the Herbert brothers, they know these woods. They could just disappear into the forest and head north." He could see the flush beginning at her collarbone and rising up her neck, and knew he was frustrating her again. But she needed to listen to reason. "It doesn't take that long to cut a painting out of a frame, roll it up, and carry it out on foot."

"Or on an ATV," Mercy said "Feinberg has a lot of ATV trails running all through his property. And we know Max has one."

"I'm betting the Herberts do, too."

"Which means we don't have the time to wait for backup. Besides,

Amy and Helena could be in there. Not to mention maids and cooks and—"

"Okay, okay." Troy knew she was right. He at least needed to do some reconnaissance and see what was going on up there. "I'm going in for recon, so we have a better sense of what we're up against. You stay here."

"No way," she said, stepping out of the truck.

"You're staying here with Elvis." He got out, too, grabbing his binoculars and holstering his pistol.

"I'm going with you."

"No, you aren't," Troy said in his toughest voice. He shouldered his rifle. Better safe than sorry. "Vests in the back, for you and Elvis. And a twelve-gauge shotgun. I assume you know how to use it."

"Of course."

"Okay. After we're gone, pull the truck across the road to block the gate and wait for backup. If there's any trouble, just drive like hell out of here."

"Like that's going to happen." She looked at him as if he were crazy.

"Stay out of trouble." Whether he left her here or took her with him, she wasn't going to listen to a thing he said. She was going to do what she was going to do. And he couldn't stop her. "Don't be a hero."

"Understood."

"Hold on to your dog."

"Elvis will be fine."

Maybe, Troy thought. He put on a vest and armored up Susie Bear as well. No sense in taking any stupid chances. Not without backup. "Come on, girl."

The big dog jumped out and hit the ground running. Troy heaved himself up over the fence and landed on the drive on the other side. Susie Bear raced after him, barreling over the six-foot fence, black fur rippling, plumed tail flying. She landed on her thick shaggy paws with a *bump ba dum bump.*

"Pretty impressive," said Mercy said through the fence. "I didn't know Newfoundlands could jump that high."

Troy grinned. "They can, they'd just much rather jump into water. But she'll jump anything. I think it's the retriever in her."

He waited while Mercy got in the truck and parked it just like he'd asked.

Then he and Susie Bear headed down toward the house, keeping to the tree line along the road, hidden from view as they traced the hairpin turns that wound up the hill.

Until the drive's loops ended and the woods opened up, revealing the enormous estate of Nemeton. A magnificent mountain lodge the size of a resort, made of native stone and hand-hewn logs, sat at the top of a ridge surrounded by forest, against a backdrop of mountains. Three stories high, with walls of rock supported by pillars of wood, the enormous home was a warren of decks and balconies and turrets, a billionaire's version of a kid playing with rocks and Lincoln Logs.

A grand porte cochere extended over the crescent-shaped drive that fronted the house, anchoring the entrance of the lodge. There was a white twelve-foot box truck parked there. Through his binoculars, Troy could see that the roll-up door on the back of the truck was up. Two guys dressed in black and wearing ski masks and gloves came out of the house, carrying rectangular objects wrapped in mover's blankets.

Paintings, thought Troy. Damn if the redhead wasn't right.

He kept a tight rein on Susie Bear's lead as they skirted the lodge, staying hidden in the maples as they made their way to the back of the property. Which was really the front, since this side faced a spectacular vista of the forest, the valley, and the mountains beyond. Water surrounded the estate on three sides, flowing from swimming hole to fishing pond to twin waterfalls cascading over granite boulders, and feeding a rich landscape of ferns and flowers and trees and carefully manicured topiary.

Other than the pair of masked men loading the truck, he didn't see anybody. He trained his binoculars on the colossal windows that allowed the people inside to see that view—and the people outside to view inside. He scanned all three floors, and discovered two other guys in the house, also in black and wearing ski masks and gloves.

Four in all. At least as far as he could see. He used the sat phone with no problem—no surprise given that the billionaire's home was so well situated, even in the middle of the mountains—to call Delphine at Dispatch and confirm his report about a robbery in progress at the Feinberg estate.

"You be careful," Delphine said.

"Roger that."

He turned to Susie Bear. "Stay."

He moved stealthily past the wooden bridge separating the fishing pond from the swimming hole and up to the three-car garage attached to the west side of the lodge. He wondered if the groundskeeper lived above it. If so, he didn't seem to be there now. Probably out chasing holiday trespassers off the estate, and making sure the hikers and ATVers treated Feinberg's land with respect.

He backed up against the stone wall of the garage and inched his way around to the first outside door, which was marked *Service Entrance*. It was locked, but there was a keypad there. Troy pulled the key card out of his pocket and tried it, and with a beep, the door opened.

Mercy Carr was right.

Again.

Wolfe had a key card, presumably because he was working for Feinberg. Or he simply stole it off one of the staff while he was on the property.

Troy found himself in a mud room lined with a wall of lockers, many of which were secured with padlocks, presumably for the employees. The mud room led to another door, also opened only with the key card. He edged up to peek through the small square window in the door and smiled. He'd located the chef's kitchen. He slipped into the room, gun at his side.

This should be a relatively safe place; even if the thieves had entered this way with a key card of their own, they wouldn't exit from here. As soon as they had the truck loaded, they'd leave by the front door and drive away. There was little chance of their venturing back this way; the most valuable art in the house would be found in the living and entertaining areas, and in the bedrooms. Not the kitchen.

This room led to two additional cooking spaces, a huge pantry and a walk-in freezer, and an extensive potted herb garden. He moved quietly through the rooms and into a wide hallway that connected the food prep area to the rest of the house. He spied the first empty walls in the room to his right, a huge dining room with a glass-topped table with at least two dozen chairs that could seat Troy's entire extended family for dinner. These were walls that in the home of a billionaire art collector would be hung with paintings. The pale dove-gray walls bore slightly lighter patches, faint impressions left by the artwork that had graced the space.

He heard the sound of a vehicle backfiring and tucked himself into a corner by the massive sideboard while he peered out the window. Two of the masked men were rolling down the back door of the box truck. They were getting ready to leave.

He raced back down the hallway and through the kitchens and the mud room and outside the way he came. He ran around the side of the house to the porte cochere. The truck was moving forward, out of the crescent drive and into the road. He waved his badge and yelled, "Stop! Game warden!"

Someone answered him with a shot. Troy saw the rifle extend out of the truck window, and he dove into the small copse of birches that flanked the entrance.

The truck rumbled on and he cursed. Now Mercy and her dog and his Ford F-150 were the only things between these thieves and freedom. Not a good scenario.

He darted back around the house to the edge of the property where Susie Bear was waiting for him, practically coming out of her skin. Her shiny long black coat was rustling, her sturdy muscular body shaking with energy under the body armor.

"Come on, girl," he said, and they were off, running through the trees along the edge of the forest. Not the best cover but better than nothing.

What mattered was speed. He needed to get to that gate as quickly as possible, but he couldn't outrun a truck, not even one as clumsy as a box truck.

He was going to be too late. He ran harder, and Susie Bear bound ahead of him. She didn't care about cover, she only wanted to win the race.

And they were racing.

The big Newfie mutt was not an attack dog, she was a search-and-rescue dog. But her protective instincts were strong, and while she was not trained to take perps down the way Elvis had taken down that guy on the float, she had protected Troy in tense situations in the past.

Her formidable size and guardian growl alone were usually enough to intimidate most people. But when that proved inadequate, she could knock bad guys right over with a jump and sit on their chests, immobilizing them. When he'd first rescued her, she was the biggest puppy he'd ever seen, and her enthusiasm had often laid him flat. He'd trained her to curb that enthusiasm, but when she got excited she sometimes forgot herself. And she was excited now.

She bolted down the hill, with no regard for the landscape, nimbly navigating the trees and boulders and plantings, headed right for the gate as the crow flies. Troy cursed again and sprinted after her.

The road twisted and turned as it wound its way between the lodge and the gate. The truck veered out of sight as the driveway curved west. They were safe for now, out of view, and they could conceivably catch up with the thieves by forgoing the road's hairpin turns and cutting straight down through the trees. Troy and Susie Bear plowed on through the landscape, determined to beat the thieves.

The truck came back into view, gaining on the entrance, which was just around the next bend. Only five hundred yards away. Only five hundred yards from Mercy and Elvis and his Ford F-150.

Troy wanted to disable their vehicle before it got there. He was betting that Skinner and company had the remote control, and would use it to open the gate. The electronic gate would swing in toward the truck, which meant that they'd have to stop or at least slow down near the entrance until the dual black aluminum-alloy doors opened wide enough for them to get through.

Troy holstered his pistol and pulled his rifle from the case. He positioned himself behind a boulder and whistled for Susie Bear, and she circled back to him. He needed to get her out of the line of fire.

"Down," he said.

Normally, he'd never try a stunt like this. But they'd taken a shot at him, so he could justify deadly force. And he didn't know who was in that truck. For all he knew Amy and her baby were in there. So he couldn't aim for the driver, since he couldn't predict where that bullet might end up if it bounced around the cab. Then there was the priceless art. He didn't want to damage a Picasso, for God's sake.

He could aim for the engine or the tires. The tires were the safest bet, but hitting a tire on a moving vehicle was far harder in real life than in the movies. And there was no guarantee that would stop them. But with any luck it could slow them down.

As soon as the dog plopped down behind the rock with him, he took aim and blew out the left rear tire of the white box truck. The truck swerved wildly but kept on going. Troy got off another shot just as the vehicle approached the loop of the next hairpin turn. Missed.

One of the masked men leaned out of the passenger window and fired as the truck bumped and bounced along with its lame wheel. The bullet splintered the slender trunk of a young birch tree several feet to Troy's left.

"Let's go," he told Susie Bear, and again they took the rough short-cut through the trees. He hoped Mercy had taken the shots as the warning they were and that she would heed that warning.

CHAPTER FORTY-FOUR

MERCY HEARD THE GUNFIRE AND GRABBED the shotgun. "Down," she told Elvis. The shepherd was practically imploding with energy, the fire in his belly so hot she thought he'd never settle down. But at least he didn't move. Just to be safe she turned on the ignition so she could roll his window up and hers down, to keep his head in and her gun out.

She considered her options. They could stay in Troy's truck, and she'd pull it over to the side of the road, the better to chase down the thieves as they tried to make their getaway. Or she could leave it right here in the road and take cover in the trees with Elvis, and slow them down with the shotgun if Troy's truck didn't do the trick.

There might be another way as well. She turned off the ignition and hopped out, going around back to the bed of the truck. Everybody who drove a truck—civilian or law enforcement—carried chain in the bed, and Troy Warner was no exception. She dragged the chain out and ran to the gate. She could hear the rattle and roar of the thieves' vehicle in the distance, growing louder and nearer.

Elvis banged his head against the window, yelping like a puppy, not unlike the way he yelped when he had a nightmare. "Steady, boy." She hoped he wasn't going to freak out.

He clawed savagely at the window, scratching the pane.

"Okay, okay." Worried he'd break the glass—his nails were fierce— she let him out. He barked his approval—a low guttural non-nightmare bark—and sat by her side. Waiting for instruction.

"You got what you wanted. Now stay."

Elvis watched her without comment while she quickly wrapped the chain through both sides of the gate, looping the doors together. One loop. Two loops. Three loops. And several more for good measure.

The white box truck made its final turn toward the entrance. It lurched along with an ungainly gait, and she saw that one of its tires was flat. She smiled. The game warden was a good shot.

Good for you, she thought.

Elvis gave a short bark, as if to say, *Time to get moving.*

"Agreed," she said, and together they abandoned the Ford F-150 and raced for the stand of maple and beech trees about one hundred feet from the gate. She had the shotgun and her pack and an extra box of ammo. The warden's keys were in her pocket, along with a pair of handcuffs. Wishful thinking, that.

Standing behind the thick trunk of a beech, she instructed Elvis with a wave of her hand to lie down. She was a good shot, one of the best in her graduating class of MPs at Fort Leonard Wood. But she hadn't fired a shotgun since Afghanistan and hadn't been out to the firing range for target practice since she'd come home to Vermont. Here's hoping that she could still outshoot these guys. If they were the Herbert brothers, they were experienced night hunters and poachers. Good shots.

"Steady, boy." She squatted down and gave Elvis a hug for good luck. They were both going to need it. This could prove the nearest thing to a battlefield that either of them had seen since Martinez died.

Now it was a year later and she didn't know if Elvis would go crazy again. Or if she would. She'd been leery all along about adopting him, but a promise was a promise and she'd never break the one she'd made to her fiancé as he lay dying. She brought the dog home from the defense contractor to the quiet and solitude of Vermont and tried to take good care of him. All the day hikes through Lye Brook Wilderness, all those nights sleeping side by side on the couch, all that inhaling and exhaling on the yoga mat. After six months the aggressive shepherd seemed to be settling in with her—and then this happened.

When Elvis had gotten shot at the cabin, he'd run for the barn. A sensible move, if not the correct one. But if he bolted this time she might not be able to go after him.

She could only protect Martinez's dog so much. She could only protect herself so much.

Life happened. Even in the woods. Maybe especially in the woods.

"We're a team now, Elvis. Like it or not." She took a couple of deep breaths, and Elvis licked her hand. She scratched his head before rising to her feet.

"We've got this." She pumped the shotgun. "'We few, we happy few, we band of brothers . . .'"

He looked up at her as if there were no doubt.

"You seem fine." She smiled at him. "I guess I'm the nervous one, then, huh?"

Shoulders squared, she stood within the cover of the trees and brought the shotgun up to her head. She had to be careful. She didn't want the white box truck to catch fire and burn up all the priceless art inside. If that's what *was* inside, and she'd bet her sweet bullet-scarred ass it was.

She pressed her cheek firmly to the side of the stock and then mounted the gun high on her chest.

Aimed.

Fired.

Bingo.

Blew out the left rear tire.

She grinned in spite of herself.

Elvis rose to his feet but did not bolt. He barked once, as if to congratulate her.

"Good boy," she whispered.

The dog was alert and poised for action, but obedient. Just as he should be.

So far, so good. Maybe Martinez was his guardian angel. And hers. She hoped so.

A man in a black ski mask leaned out of the passenger window armed with a pistol, while the masked man at the wheel struggled to control his wayward vehicle.

"Now the fun is really going to start," she told Elvis. "Sit tight."

The electronic gates began to open, swinging away from her and Elvis and in toward the thieves and the estate.

But the chain held. The two doors did not part, they only slid about six inches away from each other, clanking against the chain but going nowhere.

The Ford F-150 still stretched lengthwise across the road between the stone gate posts. There was no getting through there without crashing through the fence and hitting Troy's truck. Whether they rammed it head-on or pushed it nicely ahead of them, she doubted he'd be pleased.

Mercy pumped the shotgun. She could feel Elvis brace himself against her leg. She cooed "good boy" while she kept her eye on the thieves and her finger on the trigger.

Where was Troy? Where was Susie Bear? Where was Thrasher?

She hated to admit it, but Troy was right: they should have waited for backup. Elvis's triangular ears perked, and he leaned far forward, as if he were ready to lunge.

"What is it?"

She saw Troy and Susie Bear hugging the opposite edge of the road just inside the tree line. They were on the inside of the estate grounds, behind the thieves and the gate, and she and Elvis were on the outside.

She wondered what his next move would be. If this were her operation, she'd blow out the other tires or the engine block and converge on the truck when the perps realized they weren't going anywhere. It looked like there were at least two bad guys—maybe more inside she couldn't see—but there were four good guys. Troy, herself, and the dogs. Good odds.

The thieves could always surrender the art, and try to steal the Ford F-150 and get out of there while there was still time. But the truck's doors were locked and the keys were in the front pocket of her cargo pants.

It was a fairly easy shot from here. She took it and hit a tire on her side of the white box truck. Troy did the same on his side. Great minds think alike, she thought.

Elvis whimpered but stayed put. Just like he was supposed to do. The perfect working dog. The perfect partner. Her partner.

Pistols fired from two windows, and she dropped to the ground, taking Elvis with her. They retreated into the woods and farther down the drive, away from the estate. She wanted to stay ahead of them.

The truck barreled forward, proving that driving on four flat tires was possible if the driver was determined enough. But what momentum the vehicle maintained was not sufficient to break through the fence. The gate held and the truck stalled. The driver started the engine again and floored it. The white box truck jerked forward, its nose straining against the chained doors, crushing it toward the Ford F-150—a screeching of metal on metal.

The fence gave way but only by about a foot. Sirens sounded in the background.

The driver bailed and made a run for it. He was a tall man but graceful for his size.

Max Skinner, thought Mercy.

He leapt onto the hood of the truck and over the gate. Using the fence as cover, the driver ran straight along the metal and stone barricade for the woods. He was fast, and he was armed.

"Stop! Game warden!" Troy stepped out of the trees but ducked when not one but two masked men fired from the truck. They opened their doors to make their own escape but thought better of it when three police cars roared up to the gate, sirens wailing. They slammed the doors again and stayed put. A black Cadillac Escalade followed in the wake of the law enforcement vehicles and parked at a discreet distance. Must be Feinberg and his bodyguards, Mercy thought.

She and Elvis kept moving, quiet as death, padding through the forest toward the point where the driver was on track to enter. The masked man approached the edge of the tree line. Almost out of sight, and into the woods.

Running straight for them.

CHAPTER FORTY-FIVE

G O GET HIM," SHE TOLD ELVIS and pumped her shotgun.
"Shoot my dog," she yelled at the surprised man, "and I shoot you."

Elvis did not hesitate. For the second time in two days, the sleek shepherd took down Max Skinner.

Only it wasn't Max Skinner, after all. Surrounded by cops, the two thieves in the white box truck surrendered and joined their colleague. Unmasked, the three of them looked like brothers. The Herbert brothers.

The tallest one looked like Paul and Louis, only leaner. Their big brother in every sense of the word.

"Wayne Herbert, I presume?" Troy grinned. "Your mother will be very happy to see you. She can visit you every week in prison."

"Where are Amy and the baby?" Mercy was angry, and she turned that anger on the Herbert brothers. "Where's Max Skinner?"

"The Major Crime Unit is in charge here, or will be shortly," said Thrasher. But he smiled at her as he said it. Maybe he liked her, after all.

"There were four of them, sir," Troy said.

Thrasher nodded at Detective Kai Harrington, who had just arrived in an unmarked car and was walking toward them with a scowl on his handsome face. "The cavalry has arrived."

"Where's Max Skinner?" repeated Mercy, ignoring Harrington as long as she could.

"That scumbag." Louis spat on the ground.

"Shut up," warned Wayne.

"Ms. Carr," said Harrington, in a voice that could freeze hell itself. "Remove yourself or I'll have you removed by force."

"Sir," said Troy.

Harrington shot him a look that said, *One more word and you're fired*.

"I'm going, no problem," said Mercy. She'd gotten poor Troy in enough trouble already.

She and Elvis retreated to the perimeter, where Feinberg and his bodyguards were watching the goings-on.

"Something's off," she told Feinberg.

"I must thank you for saving my collection. Anything you ever need, you just ask."

"I need to find Amy and Helena," she said. "And that means finding Max Skinner. I don't understand; I know he was part of this."

"It does seem unlikely that those dimwitted brothers plotted all this," said Feinberg.

"They did get caught," she said.

"Thanks to you and your game warden."

She sighed. "He's not my game warden."

Feinberg smiled and said nothing.

She looked past the billionaire to the white box truck.

"I'm afraid Amy and Helena weren't in the van. They're checking the house and the grounds."

"They must be with Skinner. We've got to find him." Mercy thought for a moment. "Is all your missing art there?"

Feinberg eyed her sharply. "I'm not sure yet. They're photographing it all now."

"I wouldn't be surprised if there's something missing. And Max Skinner has it. What's the most valuable piece in your collection?"

"Hard to say. There's the Hopper, the Pollock, the Wyeth, the Cassatt . . . but the jewel of my collection is probably the Winslow Homer."

Troy walked over to them. "You'll want to hear this."

"What about Harrington?"

Feinberg looked at them. "You're with me."

They followed him to where Harrington and the staties were interviewing the Herbert brothers. Thrasher was there, too, acknowledging them with a nod.

Wayne was maintaining his silence, but his little brothers were talking more than enough to make up for it.

"It was all Max's idea," said Paul. "He said he could get us inside. And he did."

"And then he disappeared," said Louis.

"Set us up," said Paul.

"Left us out to dry," said Louis.

"Shut up," said Wayne.

"Max planned it," said Paul. "Split up the rooms."

"We took the first floor," said Louis.

"Max took the upper floors," said Paul.

"He climbed up the stairs," said Louis. "And we haven't seen him since."

"Swear to God," said Paul.

"Shut up," said Wayne.

Feinberg leaned in toward Mercy. "The most valuable pieces in the collection are on the upper floors."

"We're searching the perimeter," said Harrington. "But the sun's going down soon."

"The dogs can find him," said Mercy, "even in the dark."

Troy smiled and pointed to the edge of the forest.

"It's Gunnar Moe," said Feinberg. "My groundskeeper."

"With Max Skinner."

A giant of a man, with long hair the color of straw and huge calloused hands, Gunnar pushed the tall man in black, sans ski mask, in front of him. Skinner grimaced as he limped forward, his hands tied behind his back. There was a bloody tear in his black pants, up along the meat of his thigh.

"Found him in the woods on an ATV," said Gunnar. "Didn't like the look of him."

"Where are Amy and Helena?" asked Mercy.

Skinner shrugged but said nothing.

"He took a shot at me," said Gunnar. "So I shot back."

"Where are they?" asked Mercy again.

Gunnar gave Skinner one last shove toward a couple of uniforms, and they cuffed him and took the tall man away.

The groundskeeper shrugged off his rifle case, and the fife case Max Skinner had carried in the parade. He handed the fife case to Feinberg. "He had this on him."

"Look in there," said Mercy.

"Hold on," said Troy and pulled a pair of plastic gloves from his pocket.

Feinberg slipped them on and opened the case. Carefully he pulled a rolled canvas out of the long cylinder. He unrolled it carefully, revealing a dark oil painting of two fishermen on a small boat in stormy waters. "*Lost on the Grand Banks.*"

"Winslow Homer," said Mercy.

CHAPTER FORTY-SIX

Iᴛ ᴡᴀs ᴀFᴛᴇʀ sᴇᴠᴇɴ ᴏ'ᴄʟᴏᴄᴋ when Troy dropped Mercy and Elvis off at the cabin. Her grandmother's convertible was still parked there at the side of the house.

He and Susie Bear insisted on walking them to the door.

"We're fine," she told him.

"Elvis was great." Troy smiled at her. "You, too."

"It was a team effort." She patted the shepherd with one hand and the Newfie mutt with the other. "You're a pretty good shot."

"Look who's talking."

Troy laughed, and Mercy was reminded again that he had a nice laugh.

"I loved the way Elvis took down Wayne Herbert," he said.

"And don't forget Max Skinner at the parade."

"Another great leap for canine kind." Troy grinned as he joined Mercy in spoiling the dogs with affection, scratching and rubbing and patting their ears, their tummies, that sweet spot just north of their tails. "It's been quite the Fourth of July."

"That it has."

He straightened up, and she followed suit. They stood there for a moment, looking at each other. Troy's short sandy-brown hair had fallen across his forehead, and without thinking she reached up to brush it back. He caught her hand and held it tenderly in his own warm palm.

It felt good. Way too good. She thought about asking him in but decided against it. They still had work to do. She gently pulled her hand out of his grasp and looked down at the shepherd beside her. "I am proud of Elvis. He was solid."

"Solid as a rock."

She rolled her eyes at him, and he laughed again.

"Seriously," said Troy. "He's cured of whatever ailed him."

Mercy nodded, too moved to speak. She'd fulfilled her promise to Martinez. She'd found his dog and adopted him and taken care of him until he was his old self again. Mission accomplished.

"Get some rest."

"We need to find Amy and the baby."

"You've done enough for one day." Troy nodded at Elvis. "You both have."

"But they're in trouble."

"Relax. Everyone's on it. Local PD, the sheriff's office, the staties, us. Even Harrington."

"They don't know where to look."

"And you do?" He shook his head. "Have you been holding out on me?"

"No." She frowned. "I don't know where they are, but I feel like I *should* know."

"Of course you do." Troy's voice was serious and quiet now. "And if anyone can figure it out, you can. Sleep on it."

"Okay," she said, knowing that was what he wanted to hear. "Good night."

"Good night."

She and Elvis watched Troy and Susie Bear go back to the truck. She felt bad that it was scratched up a bit, even if it did still drive fine. But she knew he'd want it back the way it was. Men were very sentimental about their trucks.

She watched as he backed his vehicle down her long driveway, remembering the feel of her hand in his. *A kind heart he hath . . .*

"Get a grip," she said aloud, and Elvis nudged her hand with a cold nose. She rubbed his dark muzzle. "I know, I know. I'm not fourteen anymore."

Elvis whined, leaning forward. He wanted to follow his friends in the truck.

"Easy, boy," she said as the Ford F-150 disappeared from view. "Come on. It's been a long day."

Mercy led the dog inside, and he settled onto the couch. He dozed while she took a shower and poured herself a glass of wine. She whipped up some ham and eggs and shared them with the hungry shepherd.

"We did good," she told him, scratching his handsome head. He licked her hand and trotted back to the sofa, settling onto his side with the teal quilt. He was snoring within minutes. No sign of nightmares now.

She should be sleeping, too. But she was restless. There was still no word of Amy and Helena, and Skinner insisted he didn't know where the young mother and her baby were.

He admitted to shooting at Elvis and ransacking the cabin, looking for the security key to the Nemeton estate, just like she'd thought. He also insisted that he didn't kill Adam Wolfe, whom he described as his "comrade in arms." But the Herbert brothers said Skinner was responsible for killing the artist and Don Walker.

Nobody seemed to know whose bones were buried in the woods. Based on the belt buckle and the broken femur and Flo Herbert's grief, they'd assumed that the vic was Wayne Herbert, but they were still waiting for the DNA tests to confirm that. Now who knew what the tests would reveal, and it would take weeks, Troy had told her. With any luck, they'd know more then.

Mercy was tired just thinking about it. So much about the past five days still didn't make any sense.

She sipped her Big Barn Red and wandered around the house in her pajamas, glass in hand, too restless to sit. She went to her bookshelves and stared at the spines of her beloved collection of Shakespeare and company. She pulled out the limited edition of *A Midsummer's Night Dream* that she'd shown Amy.

"I should have given it to her," she told Elvis, who snored on, ignoring her, as he always did when she talked Shakespeare.

Still thinking of the teenager, she replaced the book, thinking of that morning she'd met Amy and her conversation with her. She remembered that Amy, who'd named her baby after Helena in the Bard's most popular comedy, had been reading *Othello*—a far darker reflection of "Love is blind" than *A Midsummer's Night Dream*.

She found the slim volume of *Othello* on the shelf. When she held the paperback in her open palms, the book fell open to Act III, Scene IV.

Someone had folded down the corner of the page of the scene in which Emilia speaks to Desdemona about the nature of jealousy. The ink was smudged over the words *But jealous souls will not be answered so; / They are not ever jealous for the cause, / But jealous for they are jealous: 'tis a monster / Begot upon itself, born on itself.*

Mercy used bookmarks. She would never fold the corners of any pages of any of her books. As the book collector she was, she considered it a sacrilege. Just like Feinberg must feel about thieves who cut canvases out of frames and rolled them up to steal them.

Poor Amy was not an art thief, she was just a kid under a lot of stress who marked the pages of paperbacks by folding down the corners like most of the rest of the readers in the world liked to do. Which was why Mercy rarely loaned out her books.

It was obviously Amy who had marked this page and fingered Emilia's speech about the terrible curse that is jealousy. The distraught girl could have been drawn to this passage because of her boyfriend's possessiveness of her. *Stage-five clinger.*

But possessiveness was not the same thing as the sexual jealousy that drove people to murder. Amy had insisted all along that Adam was not a violent person.

If that was true—and so far it appeared to be—then maybe Amy's marking the passage was not a reference to him, but to one of his art groupies who hated her. An unhappy ex.

Like Dr. Winters.

She shut the book. Amy had never mentioned the professor specifically, but then, she hadn't appeared to take any of her boyfriend's former paramours seriously. And she was young enough that she probably dismissed any rival over thirty out of hand.

But Dr. Winters was not the sort of woman you should dismiss out of hand, Mercy thought. Amy was just too naïve to know that. And as far as Mercy knew, the professor was the only one of those groupies who was still hanging around the compound. She'd gone right there after Mercy and Troy paid her that little visit to question her about Adam Wolfe. And odds were she was still there when Mercy talked to the bird-watcher, aka Adam, about Amy and the baby. Still there when Mercy got hit in the head. Still there when Adam died.

The professor had the means and the opportunity to kill him.

And the motive. Maybe she wasn't over Adam Wolfe, after all. Maybe all of the merger-and-acquisitions attorneys in the world couldn't make up for the genius who enshrined you in art. Maybe she was the Othello to Wolfe's Desdemona. Or the Iago to his Othello. Either way, Amy was the Desdemona in this scenario, and that meant things could go very badly for her. And the baby.

If Mercy was right—and she knew she was—then they didn't have much time. Dr. Winters was supposedly on her way to the south of France. So she'd need to get rid of Amy and Helena before she left.

Mercy swapped her pajamas for her usual uniform of T-shirt, cargo pants, and hoodie, and pulled her hiking boots on over thick cotton socks.

"Come on, Elvis."

The shepherd jounced up, ready to go.

THIRTY MINUTES LATER she pulled the little red convertible onto the street where Dr. Winters lived in Bennington. She'd texted Troy, but she hadn't heard back from him yet. She was on her own, no gun and no vest.

But she did have Elvis.

Mercy stared up at the intimidating Victorian pile that the professor called home. The painted lady was dark tonight. Only the nineteenth-century lampposts framing the walk up to the house were lit. The sun was setting now and the place was falling into a deep gloom.

She and Elvis cased the property, but there was no vehicle in the detached garage out back and no sign of life in the house. She banged the angry-gargoyle knocker, but no one came to the door.

She considered picking the locks and taking a look inside, but she really didn't think the professor was there. This afternoon she'd been leaving the gala reception with the mergers-and-acquisitions attorney for what looked like a little merger of her own. She could still be negotiating her next acquisition, as the night was young. And this was still the Fourth of July weekend. The fireworks were just beginning.

But Mercy didn't believe that's what the professor was doing. She texted Troy again, and this time he called her back right away.

"What are you doing?" He sounded angry or frustrated or both.

"I'm at Dr. Winters's house."

"You're supposed to be at home. I promised Patience you would rest tonight. You promised Patience you'd rest tonight."

That was true. The only reason Patience hadn't come right over after hearing about the excitement at Feinberg's estate was because Mercy had abandoned her at the gala and run off in her car. Her grandmother said she'd get a ride home but not before exacting a promise that Mercy would go to bed and stay there. "I know, but this is important."

"What do you think you're going to find?"

"Nothing here. The professor's gone."

"She's probably out recreating. It's a holiday, remember?"

"I think she knows where Amy and Helena are."

"Why would she know that?"

"*Othello.*" She knew this was not an answer he'd like.

"What's *Othello* got to do with it?" From the tone of his voice, he didn't like it one bit.

He was going to like her explanation even less. She told him about finding the book and the quote. "She's jealous of Amy and the baby. I think they're in danger."

"I'm not sure that makes any sense."

"Think about it. She was probably still there at the compound when Adam was murdered and I was left for dead and Amy and Helena were last seen."

"True."

"I was wrong about her. She still loved Adam Wolfe. He dumped her for Amy, swapped her out for a younger Muse. That must have infuriated her."

"I can see that. But you've done enough for one day. Let me call it in."

"Harrington won't do anything about it. He'll say it's another wild-goose chase. And by the time you convince him otherwise, it could be too late. Remember the south of France."

Troy sighed. "She does have a lake house on Lake St. Catherine, and anyone with a lake house spends the Fourth of July weekend there."

Lake St. Catherine was a lovely lake about an hour north of Bennington in the Lakes Region of Rutland County. The popular destination bordered Lake St. Catherine State Park, and vacation cottages and four-season houses dotted its shores. This time of year the lake attracted summer people and year-round residents alike for its swimming and boating and fishing and every other kind of summer fun.

But even with all this activity, Mercy knew that many of the houses there were surrounded by trees and somewhat secluded.

"Not a bad place to hide a young mother and a baby," she said. "We need to go now."

"I'll meet you there. Don't do anything on your own. Wait for me."

"Over and out."

Troy texted her the address, along with another admonition to wait for him.

"Come on, boy," she said to Elvis. "Let's go to the lake."

The shepherd licked her face, and she laughed.

They got back into the convertible and headed for the professor's house on Osprey Point Road. She punched the address into the GPS. An hour and ten minutes.

But if she drove this little sports car as fast as her grandmother did, she might make it there in under an hour.

THE WOMAN WAS infuriating. Troy stared at his cell phone. She hadn't answered that last text he'd sent, which meant if she got there before he did, odds were she'd barge right ahead without him. Because she was stubborn and headstrong and reckless.

But she'd been right about practically everything so far.

Thrasher told him that Max Skinner still wasn't talking, and the Herbert brothers had finally shut up. But they all insisted that they didn't know anything about Amy and Helena. The captain thought the girl had just skipped town with her baby.

But Mercy didn't believe that, and neither did Troy.

He and Susie Bear were up at Branch Pond. It would take them about an hour to get to Lake St. Catherine.

If he drove fast enough, maybe he'd get there first.

CHAPTER FORTY-SEVEN

MERCY TURNED IN AT THE *DEAD END* SIGN and steered the convertible slowly down Osprey Point Road. Streetlights were few and far between. It was getting late and growing dark, and the only lights out on the lake were the fireworks people were setting off from their docks and on their boats.

Osprey Point was one of the more secluded areas on the lake. The houses on the narrow gravel road sat down by the water, and most were surrounded by trees that obscured them from the street. Not many had house numbers, at least not that she could see.

Thank goodness the navigation system was still working out here. According to the GPS, Dr. Winters's cottage was directly to her left. But she couldn't see the house.

She parked along the street, just shy of the driveway she hoped led to the professor's place.

"Come on, Elvis," she said.

Together they walked quietly down the dirt driveway to a little white farmhouse that was so different from the professor's Victorian that she thought for a minute that the GPS must have gotten it wrong. It seemed unlikely that the same woman could call such disparate places home.

They approached the unlit cottage carefully. It looked like no one was there, but Dr. Winters's SUV was parked out front so Mercy knew she must be home. They stepped up onto the small porch that fronted the farmhouse. She knocked on the door; no angry gargoyle here, just this plain white door with a small square window in the middle.

No one answered. The house was silent. All she could hear was the crackle of sparklers and the happy chatter of Fourth of July revelers and the slap of the current against the boats as the sound carried across the lake.

Elvis whined and took off, tearing around the cottage porch. She jogged after him, whistling softly to call him back. But he ignored her and raced past the SUV. He bolted down the backyard toward a small wooden boathouse by the water.

A burst of white and gold fireworks lit up the scene at the lake. The handsome shepherd froze—his sleek profile stark against the bright flashes of light—but just for that brief, illuminated moment. Then the dog sprang to life again and flew down to the boathouse. Mercy scrambled down the lawn after him.

The door to the boathouse was closed, but that didn't stop the determined shepherd. His triangular ears were perked, his stance military, his attitude *can do*. This was how he'd looked when he went outside the wire with Martinez, thought Mercy.

Elvis abandoned the boathouse. He barreled down to the shore of Lake Saint Catherine and plunged into the water. Stunned, Mercy watched as he swam over to the open end of the boathouse, the end that emptied into the lake. The dog disappeared inside.

She ran back up to the boathouse door and turned the knob. It was locked. She didn't have the light or the time or the inclination to pick it, so she backed up, took a running leap, and crashed into the door with her shoulder. Nothing. She tried again. This time the jamb splintered and the door gave way and she lurched into the dark room.

Her eyes adjusted, and she could see that the boathouse was tiny, just big enough for one boat. Oars and paddleboards leaned against one wall, and a canoe hung from the ceiling.

There was a twelve-foot bass boat in the single bay. Fireworks blazed and boomed outside, and in the light Mercy could see Dr. Winters in the boat with Amy Walker. The professor held a hunting knife at Amy's throat. A knife that looked very much like the Buck hunting knife that was sticking out of Rufus Flanigan, aka Adam Wolfe's, chest. And the one that killed Donald Walker.

"Corporal Carr," said Dr. Winters. "I see you're back to army surplus."

Amy's hands were bound together with rope at her wrists, and her feet were bound together with rope at her ankles. Her mouth was gagged with duct tape. The girl's eyes were bright with fear and tears. When she saw Mercy, those eyes widened with hope.

"Let Amy go."

The baby was there in the boat, too, wrapped in a blanket and sleeping on a curl of rope.

"Why would I do that?" The professor's huge eyes were wild with spite behind her thick black glasses.

Elvis swam into the boathouse and waded up to the dock. The water was shallow here, only a couple of feet deep. The shepherd leapt onto the dock.

"I loathe dogs," said Dr. Winters.

Most people who didn't like dogs were afraid of them. She didn't want Elvis scaring the woman into doing something terrible. Winters had done terrible things before—and she would do them again if Mercy didn't stop her.

"Come," she said. He cocked his head, then shook the water from his thick coat and came to sit beside her.

More fireworks exploded outside the boathouse. The baby slept on. Babies and dogs could sleep anywhere. Mercy envied them that.

Elvis, dripping wet, scooted to the edge of the boathouse dock, as close to Helena as possible without falling into the water or the boat himself. He was alert and ready for Mercy's next command. But she had no idea what to tell him to do next. She needed to try to talk the professor down.

"Why don't you put the knife down and tell me all about Adam Wolfe."

"She stole him from me." Dr. Winters did not drop the knife. The young girl squirmed and the professor tightened her grip. "Sit still, harlot."

"How did she do that?"

The professor ignored her and looked down at the sleeping child. "I wanted a baby. I begged him for a baby." She kicked at the coil of rope, just missing the infant's head.

Amy jerked toward Helena, and the knife nicked her throat slightly.

"Sit still, or you'll never see your baby again."

Mercy held her breath and watched as tiny drops of blood pooled at the cut on Amy's pale neck.

"It was the art," Dr. Winters said. "Always his precious art. He said it came first, that his art was his baby." She glared at Helena.

Mercy wept inside. The infant slept on, innocent and good and yet the object of such hatred.

"And then he has this . . . this, bastard child." She put out her foot again and jostled the coil of rope with the toe of her boot. "He left me for this abomination."

Mercy edge forward, her eyes on that boot.

"Don't move." Dr. Winters's voice was thick with rage.

Elvis growled, the low guttural warning that only a fool would ignore. Or a crazy woman. The baby stirred and began to whimper. Elvis snarled at the professor. The infant's whimpers became wails. The dog barked furiously. Another blast of fireworks rang out like shots.

"I told you, I don't like dogs." Dr. Winters yelled over the din. "Or bastards." She turned away and reached back with her free hand to turn on the motor. She held the button down for a second, then released it. The engine rumbled to life.

Mercy lunged for the knife. The professor let Amy go and slashed at Mercy, the blade shiny in the gleam of the fireworks. The weapon sliced Mercy's left shoulder, and she punched Dr. Winters in the stomach with a hard right. The professor dropped the knife, which clattered to the bottom of the boat. She collapsed in on herself, gasping for air and grabbing for the throttle.

The boat pitched forward, slamming against the dock. Dr. Winters pulled the throttle back, and the boat shot backward.

Amy toppled over, bumping her head against the edge of the boat.

"Elvis, go!" Mercy clutched at her bleeding arm.

The aggressive shepherd launched himself toward the moving vessel and landed onboard in the stern. Dr. Winters fell back and tumbled on top of Amy. The young mother kicked her away and tried to curl her bound body around her screaming baby.

The professor scrambled to escape Amy's jerking legs. She caught her breath and retrieved her knife and righted herself to attack again. But Elvis was faster. He chomped down on her wrist with his teeth and she dropped the knife.

Mercy ran after the boat as it plowed backward out of the boathouse. She leapt for the bow but missed by about six inches. She landed in about two feet of water and stumbled onto her knees into the silty muck of the lake bottom. Rising to her feet, she splashed through the boathouse.

Now the boat was moving forward once more. The professor must have pushed the throttle again. The water deepened, way over her head now. Mercy dove forward, swimming after the boat, desperate to catch up. But her aching shoulder was still bleeding and every stroke was an exercise in pain. The water was cold and her concussed head throbbed.

The lake was dark and choppy in the face of a light wind from the west. But by the staccato flash and thunder of the exploding fireworks overhead, she could spy Dr. Winters struggling with Elvis and trying to find the knife with her other hand. She watched Amy kick it away, and she swam harder. The sooner she got to the boat to help Amy, the better.

Mercy hoped that the baby was all right. She couldn't hear the infant's cries anymore. She couldn't see anybody else close by; Lake St. Catherine was large and the other boats were scattered across it like dark jewels on black velvet. But she could hear people laughing and talking and singing along to a radio blaring "Red Solo Cup."

Sound carried far across the lake, remembered Mercy. She started shouting for help as she pumped her arms and legs through the water, hoping a Good Samaritan would hear her.

The current was against her and the wake of the boat slowed her down. Mercy kept on swimming. Stroke after stroke, the lines from Shakespeare's *The Tempest* pounded in her sore head:

Sea-nymphs hourly ring his knell: Ding-dong
Hark! now I hear them,—Ding-dong, bell.

She saw Dr. Winters try to grab the tiller, and Elvis push his snout up to her face, barking furiously. His snarls echoed across the lake. The professor must have bumped the tiller to the side, because the unhinged boat was moving slowly in wide circles now, like a broken motorized toy in a child's bath.

Ding-dong.

Mercy was getting very tired. Her limbs were heavy, her injured arm floated limply at her side while she flailed forward with her right arm. But she couldn't give up. With the boat circling, she could close in on them now. She blinked the water out of her eyes as the fireworks intensified, lighting up the sky and filling the air with noise.

Elvis stayed on point, despite the sound and fury. She could see him straddling the professor, his teeth still clenched around her wrist. Good boy, she thought.

"Mercy! Mercy!" She heard Troy's voice calling her name over and over again, and she practically cried with relief. She couldn't see him, but hearing him was enough.

"Over here," she yelled, peering across the dark night and treading water until the next round of fireworks allowed her to spot him.

She didn't have to wait long. A torrent of red and blue and white sprays of light showered the night sky. A bellow and a splash, and she paddled round to see a black beast moving toward her with surprising speed. *Susie Bear.* Just the sight of the big shaggy dog, graceful as a seal in the water, gave her the strength to keep swimming.

"Come on, Susie Bear," she shouted, and powered against the current toward the bass boat. She looked over her shoulder to make sure the Newfie mutt was following her. There, silhouetted against the exploding sky, was a canoe manned by Troy Warner, who wielded his paddle like a sword and sliced through the water like a warrior on his way to war.

Ding-dong, bell.

Mercy was in reach of the bass boat now. She lunged for starboard as it careened past her, caught the side, and held on tight. She was exhausted, the adrenaline that had fueled her fading fast. She tried to heave herself onto the boat. Failed.

"I'm going to kill you and your dog," said Dr. Winters. Elvis was holding her down against her seat, his paws on her chest, his mouth still clamped around her wrist. Whenever she tried to strike him with her free arm, he clenched harder—and she pulled back her arm, moaning with pain.

"One more word and I'll order him to break your other wrist." Mercy breathed heavily, trying to prepare herself for another try at climbing aboard. She looked at the baby, who was sleeping again, still curled up on the coil of rope.

Amy maneuvered away from the professor, scooting across the boat on her butt to help Mercy. Her hands and feet were still tied together, and her mouth was still gagged. She shifted her feet and lifted herself to a standing position.

"No," Mercy said. "You'll fall."

Dr. Winters kicked at the rope where the baby lay. Helena whimpered. Amy turned to confront the professor. Elvis growled.

The boat tipped suddenly in the wake of a speedboat passing just far enough away not to notice the trouble they were in or Mercy screaming for help.

Amy lost her fragile footing and pitched backward, falling out into the water on the port side. The wrong side.

"Man overboard," Mercy yelled, hoping Troy at least would hear her.

With her hands and feet tied together, Amy would drown quickly. Mercy let go of the boat, hoping Elvis could forgive her for leaving him alone with a lunatic. She swam to Amy, who was kicking wildly with her legs but going down anyway.

Mercy was on the verge of going down herself. She needed to grab Amy under the arms from behind and help her float on her back, with the back of her head leaning against her own. But Amy's arms were tied together behind her back.

"Stay still." To her credit, Amy stopped kicking, and Mercy grabbed her by the shoulders as she went under, pulling her back up. "Stay still." She pulled the gag out of her mouth. Amy gasped for air and spit up water. "I'm going to turn you around. When I do, lie your head back against my chest, close your eyes, and float."

Amy moaned.

"Float," she ordered. "Float." Mercy's strength was fading, her cut arm and her concussion getting the better of her. She couldn't hold up Amy or herself much longer.

Where was Troy? She looked around but couldn't see anything. The dark sky was quiet now. Dr. Winters's boat lumbered on, circling them in the deep gloom. She could hear it, but she couldn't see it. She tried to untie the girl's hands, but she couldn't do it and keep them both afloat at the same time. She needed help. And nearly laughed out loud when she realized that Troy was right. She had to wait for backup.

She felt the big dog before she saw her. A cold nose, a wet shag rug she could hold on to for dear life.

"Good girl," she said.

Amy opened her eyes. "Big dog."

"Susie Bear," she said. "Search-and-rescue dog. We're going to be fine."

AMY CLOSED HER eyes. The fireworks started up again, and Mercy watched Troy's canoe reach Dr. Winters's boat. He climbed aboard and switched off the motor. Then he handcuffed Dr. Winters's free wrist and admonished Elvis to release her other one so he could handcuff that one, too. But Elvis was apparently reluctant to do so. She heard Troy say, "Drop it," two more times before the dog would relinquish his hold. But even once he'd let go of the professor, the shepherd continued to stand guard over his prisoner.

Mercy held on to Amy with one hand and Susie Bear's plumed tail with the other as the big dog swam toward the canoe. She smiled as Troy cradled little Helena and laid her carefully into the canoe. He tied the boat to the canoe and paddled over to them. Elvis kept an eye on Dr. Winters in the bass boat.

Without a word Troy helped Mercy get Amy into the canoe first. He untied her feet and wrists, then stripped off his uniform shirt and wrapped it around the young mother, who was shivering with shock.

"She killed Adam," stammered Amy. "She was going to kill us."

"You're safe now."

He pulled Mercy in next. "You're hurt."

Mercy had forgotten all about her injury. "Get Susie Bear up here first."

"We could, but it looks like she'd rather hang out with Elvis." Troy pointed behind the canoe, where Susie Bear was swimming alongside the boat, as close as possible to Elvis as he guarded the professor.

Troy paddled them quickly and expertly back to shore. As soon as they hit water shallow enough for Susie Bear to stand up in, she leaped onto the boat to join Elvis. The professor did not look pleased at the thought of two dogs guarding her now, the second even bigger than the first.

The dogs barked.

The professor cursed.

And the baby, happy again in her mother's arms, laughed.

FIVE DAYS LATER

CHAPTER FORTY-EIGHT

Patience ordered complete rest for Mercy, and she got a people doctor and a CT scan to back her up. Not that Mercy got much rest.

First, there was the matter of the cat. Patience came every day to check on her, bearing food and advice and, finally, the no-name kitten she and Elvis had rescued from the Walker place.

"Hello, kitty." She showed her grandmother into the kitchen, taking the carrier from her.

Elvis leaped up and trotted over to supervise the release of their new housemate.

The cabin was crowding up now. Amy and Helena had moved into the guest room, although in truth it was more like they had moved in everywhere. Astonishing how such a small infant could take over an entire house in no time at all. Child Protective Services had agreed that Helena could remain with her young mother under two conditions: that they live with Mercy, and that Amy finish her senior year and graduate.

They were in the living room now, the baby playing on a blanket spread out on the floor in front of the couch, surrounded by a growing mountain of toys supplied by all of her adoring fans—from Mercy and Patience to Mr. Horgan and Lillian Jenkins. Even Thrasher had presented the sweet little Helena with a new set of brightly colored blocks.

"The kitty's good to go. But still no name." Patience started pulling out covered dishes and groceries from her Vermont Country Store tote bag. "Any ideas?"

"Not yet."

The little tiger tabby—who'd been so worn and weary the last time Mercy had seen her—leapt out of the carrier with an excess of feline energy and greeted Elvis nose to nose.

"She's fattened up a bit."

"Poor thing was starving." Patience shook her head.

"I tried to take care of them," said Amy. "But there were so many of them. Mom never got them fixed, she said that was unnatural."

"Ridiculous." Patience had zero tolerance for people who did not spay or neuter their animals.

"I know." Amy's heart-shaped face flushed. "When I went to live with Adam, I couldn't take any of them with me. He is—was—allergic. I tried to sneak home sometimes, but it was hard to get away."

"You should have reported it," said Patience severely.

The teenager's dark blue eyes filled with tears. "I didn't want to get my mother in trouble."

Patience looked over Amy's head to catch Mercy's eye. She knew her grandmother was thinking what she was thinking: *She didn't mind getting you in trouble.*

Karen Walker had not been charged with anything to do with the murders, but Mercy knew that if Patience had her way she'd be found guilty of cruelty to animals and receive the maximum sentence, which could include jail time as well as hefty fines. Not to mention the forfeiture of all rights to the cats, which would enable the Cat Ladies to put them up for adoption. But she didn't tell Amy that.

"It's okay," said Mercy. "All's well that ends well." She told Amy all about the rescue, including the magpie Munchkin and his stash of collectibles.

"What kind of jewelry?" asked Amy.

Mercy described what she could remember of the items, including the pendant with the pine trees.

"My necklace." Amy gasped, and the tears that had pooled in the corners of her eyes rolled down her cheeks. "It was the first thing he ever gave to me. I thought Don stole it and pawned it." She wiped her cheeks with the back of her hand. "Do you think I could get it back?"

"I'll talk to the game warden about it," promised Mercy.

The three of them watched the baby on her blanket, mesmerized by Elvis and the cat playing together.

"Elvis is happy to see the kitty," said her grandmother, giving Amy a break and changing the subject.

"She's his little muse." Mercy smiled, and snapped her fingers. "Her name is Muse."

"A homophone," said Patience, rolling her eyes. "A homophone pun, no less."

"More specifically, a heterograph."

"I don't get it," said Amy.

"Don't worry, no one else will either," said Patience.

"*Mews* and *muse* are two words that sound the same but are spelled differently and have different meanings," explained Mercy.

"Cute," said Amy. "I think."

"Don't encourage her." Patience frowned at her granddaughter.

"You *are* kind of a word nerd," said Amy.

"Okay, okay." Mercy laughed. "I know it's lame. But in a good way."

"If you say so," said Patience. "I don't think Jade would approve."

"Jade?" asked Amy.

"She's the girl who helped out at the rescue. We invited her over to meet you and the baby, and little Muse."

"She *is* a very sweet kitty." Amy pointed to the kitten, who had danced over to the blanket. The baby laughed, her slate-blue eyes shining, as the kitty boogied through the blocks while Elvis supervised, a noble and vigilant babysitter alert at the edge of the blanket. Both were safe with this dog, for whom duty came first. Just like his sergeant.

Mercy excused herself to text Troy. She wanted to tell him about the necklace, but not with Amy around. And after nearly a week in the house she was desperate to get out. She bet Elvis was, too. Her Jeep was back, good as new with four brand-new all-terrain tires. She whistled for the dog, hoping to sneak out before her grandmother could stop her.

"Where are you going?" Patience called her out just as she and Elvis hit the front porch.

"Two Swords K-9 Training. I thought it would be good for Elvis." The truth was, the dog was just fine. She'd spent some time on the yoga mat with him, but she'd seemed to need it more than he did.

"Uh-huh."

"I thought you liked that place."

"I do. Jake is very good."

"So we'll see you later."

"Be home in time for dinner. We have guests coming."

No surprise there. Ever since word got out that Patience was coming over with dinner every day, everyone Mercy knew was dropping by to visit.

THE TWO SWORDS K-9 Training and Pet Resort was in a small converted strip mall about ten miles north of town on Route 7. She parked right next to Troy's Ford F-150, and Elvis knew the warden's truck when he smelled it. He barked his approval and jumped right out of the Jeep before she could get a lead on him. "Elvis! Down!"

He paid no attention, bounding for the front door, almost colliding with a lady carrying a white long-haired Chihuahua with a pink rhinestone collar in her big black purse. Realizing his mistake in the nick of time, he stopped just short of the woman, with only inches to spare. She shrieked, and her Chihuahua screeched and snarled and squirmed in her arms.

"Elvis! Get back here."

He came back to her, head hanging. He knew he was in trouble. She snapped on the leash and they waited while the lady dropped off her dog for grooming and returned to her Lexus sedan, glaring at them both as she drove off.

"Good going," said Mercy. "Maybe you need to go back to obedience school." But it was her fault. She'd isolated herself since moving home to Vermont, and in so doing isolated Elvis as well. The past ten days had been the most social interaction either of them had had in months, apart from visits with Patience—and it had challenged them both. One-on-one training and long walks alone in the woods were not enough. He needed more. Maybe she did, too.

The office and grooming rooms were housed in what looked a lot like a day-care center. Several chest-high enclosed cubicles were devoted to play, full of toys and cushions and small yapping dogs, most of whom seemed to be well-groomed poodles and shih-tzus and Yorkshire terriers and cocker spaniels. The back wall was lined with floor-to-ceiling kennel cages, where larger dogs who could scale the cubicles were kept—at the moment that meant a pair of harlequin Great Danes, a German shepherd, two black Labradors, a St. Bernard, and one lone Jack Russell terrier, who bounced up and down like a bungee cord.

The receptionist behind the long counter was a purple-haired young woman with a tattoo of a smiley pit bull on her slim upper arm. She wore a name tag that identified her as Kaitlyn. Kaitlyn grinned at her and Elvis, who paid no attention to her or to any of his fellow canines. His eyes were on the double doors on the back wall. "We're here to see Warden Warner."

"Sure. They're out back in the agility center." She pointed where Elvis was looking. "Through there to the right."

Elvis led her between the Great Danes and the leaping Jack Russell terrier and through the double doors to the outside into a large fenced rectangle of neatly trimmed grass the size of a football field. The space stretched all the way back to a line of maples and willows fronting a roaring creek. She could hear the rush of the water, even above the happy yelping and bellowing of the dogs of all shapes and sizes racing around the various obstacles that made up the agility course. There were several lanes, each with its own set of hurdles of different heights, cloth tunnels, seesaws, hoops, and weave poles. A small stand of bleachers anchored the far side of the field.

She spotted Troy and a good-looking, well-muscled guy with a shaved head on the sidelines, watching as a couple of assistant trainers in matching red shorts and T-shirts emblazoned with the Two Swords logo ran several dogs through their paces. She and Elvis trotted over to join them.

"Mercy Carr, meet Jake Wilder," said Troy.

"Great to meet you," said Jake, offering her a firm handshake. "And this must be the famous Elvis." He held out his hand for the shepherd to sniff. "Beautiful." Elvis wagged his tail and perked his triangular ears, as if they'd been friends forever.

Susie Bear bounded over, followed by a Bernese mountain dog, a border collie, two golden retrievers, and a feisty Pembroke Welsh corgi. They all sniffed and snorted Elvis and each other until Jake said, "Down!" in such a commanding tone that every dog on the field immediately dropped onto the grass. Even Elvis. Mercy was tempted to drop down herself.

The dog trainers ran over, and Jake laughed. "Go on back to work now." He looked at Mercy. "You can let him off the lead. He'll behave."

"I hope so." She didn't mention the incident with the Chihuahua.

The assistant trainers escorted all of the dogs back to the starting line, where they each took a lane and waited for their run at the course. She watched with Troy and Jake as the border collie went first, racing through the course like an Olympic athlete, cheered on by an assistant trainer yelling out the appropriate command before each test—*go, over, tunnel, seesaw, wee-wee-wee-wee-weave!*—and handing out goodies along the route for obstacles well met.

Each dog took a turn, and all performed well, although the corgi balked at the tunnel at first and had to be coaxed through with lots of high-pitched encouragement and treats. Susie Bear was up next. For her size, she was surprisingly fast—even if she looked more like a sumo wrestler than a track star. But what she lacked in grace, she made up for in spirit and strength.

Now it was Elvis's turn, and Mercy held her breath.

"Sniffer dogs are typically well trained in agility," said Jake. "This should be easy for him."

If he could read dogs as well as he read people, it was no wonder he was so good at his job, she thought.

"It's been a while," she said. "He's retired now."

At the command—*Go!*—Elvis was off. He sailed over the hurdles, streaked through the tunnels, skimmed the seesaw, and whipped through the weave poles. Mercy couldn't take her eyes off the sleek shepherd, and she found herself tearing up.

Because it was obvious that Elvis was having fun.

Fun.

The poor dog needed fun. He'd had fun with Martinez, as had she. In her grief she'd forgotten what a good time they'd all had together just hanging out whenever they got a break from the battlefield. *Live a little; comfort a little; cheer thyself a little.*

Elvis finished the course with a flourish to whoops and whistles—hers loudest among them—and raced past the finish lane and right to Mercy. She petted and praised him unabashedly. Susie Bear joined them, and for once Elvis seemed as chill and cheerful as his Newfie pal. Jake and Troy added their own plaudits of "Good job!" and "Good boy!" and "Good girl!" After another round of treats, the dogs ran back to join the others at the starting line to have another go.

"He did great," said Troy.

"He must miss agility," said Jake.

"I don't know. I mean, I wasn't his handler. I sort of inherited him."

"A Malinois is a one-woman dog." Jake looked at her. "Your dog."

HE EXCUSED HIMSELF to supervise the rest of the class, leaving Troy and Mercy alone.

"So why are you really here?" he asked.

Mercy smiled at Troy. "Maybe we just wanted to see you guys."

"Maybe." He waited.

"Okay, okay." She laughed. "I do have an ulterior motive. But we did really want to see you guys and meet Jake."

"Sure you did. Go on."

"Wolfe gave Amy the pendant. When it went missing, she figured her stepfather took it. Apparently he pawned anything that wasn't nailed down."

"What a lowlife. It's a wonder nobody killed him sooner."

"Did you find anything on Patrick O'Malley?"

"You were right. Patrick O'Malley, Irish jewelry designer and former IRA member, was living here in Vermont until about three years ago." He leaned toward her with a half smile. "Are you really going to make me ask?"

"The calla lily," said Mercy. "It fits." She explained how the maker's mark helped her identify the artist.

"He definitely left the area, but we've yet to confirm that he's in Ireland."

"You're not going to find him in Ireland."

"Why not?"

"He's our body in the woods."

CHAPTER FORTY-NINE

B Y DINNERTIME, MERCY WAS IN THE KITCHEN helping Patience prepare for their guests and Elvis was on the couch ready to bolt for the door when they arrived. When the doorbell rang, he raced to greet them, barking until she shushed him. She ushered in Thrasher and Troy, Susie Bear on their heels.

"We thought we'd bring you up to speed on the investigation," said the captain.

Behind him, Troy winked at her.

Mercy knew that their presence had as much to do with her grandmother's cooking as it did with any desire to keep her in the loop. In addition to her spectacular desserts, Patience was serving up her famous covered dishes—Vermonter favorites like salmon and peas, franks and beans, and Yankee pot roast as well as more exotic fare, like seafood lasagna and curried lamb and apricots. Tonight it was chicken and dumplings.

"Come on in and have a seat," said Patience. "You're just in time."

"Smells great." Thrasher handed Mercy two bottles of Big Barn Red and a four-pack of Heady Topper and promptly took up his place at the head of the table.

Troy had a Crock-Pot in his arms. "I brought Elvis some stew. You can keep the Crock-Pot. I've emailed you the recipe."

"I thank you," said Mercy, "and Elvis thanks you."

Troy grinned and joined his captain at the table.

At this rate, Mercy might have company for supper for the foreseeable future. But as long as the hungry bachelors kept her in her favorite red wine, she couldn't complain. She might have to learn how to cook, as she couldn't rely on her grandmother's superior culinary skills forever.

Amy and Jade helped Mercy set the table with her turquoise stoneware while Troy uncorked the wine. Susie Bear and Elvis greeted one another happily, sniffing in all the usual places, then took up their positions at either end of the baby blanket, the better to look after the infant and the kitten.

"The Herbert brothers have confessed to stealing Feinberg's art," said Thrasher. "Considering they were caught red-handed, they didn't have much choice. But they insist they had nothing to do with any murder."

"What about Wayne Herbert?"

"Wayne lawyered up. But we contacted the Canadian authorities, who confirmed that he's been living in Quebec under the name Pierre Darcy. He's suspected of a string of art thefts there. Mostly sculpture, sold for scrap metal."

"We've had similar thefts here in Vermont," said Troy. "Mostly up north, close to the border. The Herberts, no doubt."

"What about Max Skinner?"

"Skinner knew Wayne from Quebec. But he had much bigger ambitions." The captain licked his lips as Patience placed a steaming-hot casserole dish on a trivet in the middle of the table, along with a basket of warm Red Hen ciabatta bread. "As an artist himself, he had connections—connections that allowed him to fence the art he stole rather than scrap it. When he realized his pal Adam Wolfe was working for Feinberg, he recruited Wayne and his brothers to help him pull off the heist."

"We suspect that he was privately commissioned to steal the Winslow Homer painting by a rich Saudi prince," said Troy. "Feinberg says it happens pretty often these days."

"Just like Dr. Winters said." Mercy pulled over the high chair for Helena. "You remember, Troy. She told us that she hoped all of the other bronze sculptures Adam Wolfe did of her were in a sheik's harem somewhere."

"Imagine that," said Patience.

Amy fetched the baby and settled her into her seat. Thrasher pulled out chairs for Jade and Amy next to Helena. Helena banged a pink plastic spoon on her tray and both dogs, still watching the kitty explore the living room, perked their ears.

"All set," said Patience. "Let's eat."

Thrasher spooned a large helping of chicken and dumplings onto his blue plate, and passed the casserole on to Troy. "He didn't tell the Herbert brothers about the commission."

"We don't think he ever intended to share the lion's share of the proceeds with the Herbert brothers," said Troy. "That's why he told them to rob the lower floor. He knew that the most valuable pieces were on the upper floors."

"Wolfe must have told him," said Mercy.

"Adam would never have robbed Mr. Feinberg," said Amy. "He was not a thief."

Thrasher looked at Amy. "You're right. We don't think he had anything to do with the actual theft. But he had a security key to Nemeton because he worked for Feinberg. He must have grown suspicious and hidden the key so Skinner wouldn't find it."

"We found det cord in Skinner's pack on the ATV," said Troy.

"Det cord?" asked Amy.

"What's that?" asked Jade.

"Detonating cord," said Mercy. "We found a small piece of it at the compound. That explains why Elvis kept alerting to explosives."

"We think the det cord was Skinner's Plan B," said Thrasher between bites of dumpling. "We know it was used to blow open the doors to some of the storage facilities where the stolen sculpture was stored up north."

"But he ended up getting another security key card from the girl singer in the Green Mountain Boys band," said Troy.

"Sarah Lavery? The sous chef?" Mercy waved her wineglass at the game warden.

"Good memory." Troy toasted her with his Heady Topper. "Turned out she worked up at the Nemeton kitchens on a regular basis. So regular she had a key of her own."

"So he joined the band to get to Sarah. Skinner never cared about the Vermont Firsters at all?"

"Apparently not," said Thrasher. "Just a means to an end."

"Adam cared," said Amy. "But he would never hurt anybody. He really regretted blowing up those logging trucks when he was younger.

He said he'd never do anything like that again. He said his art was his message."

"But you left him," said Mercy.

"I didn't like living off the grid," said Amy. "I didn't think it was good for Helena." She smiled at her baby, who was still clanking away at her tray with the little pink spoon. "Adam got weird. I thought it was, like, because he wanted to hide me away from the world. You know, that living in the woods was making him crazy."

"What happened that day in the woods?" asked Patience.

"You mean, why did I leave Helena in the woods?" Her dark blue eyes filled with tears. "That's what the lady from Child Protective Services kept asking me." She took her baby's little hand in her own. "I would never hurt Helena. You know that."

"I do," said Mercy.

"No way," said Jade.

"Adam and Max had this big fight. They thought I was asleep, but I wasn't. Adam was yelling at Max that he couldn't do it. I didn't know what he was talking about but I knew it wasn't good. Max was really mad and when he got mad, he looked just like my stepdad. Bad news. I decided that I had to get Helena out of there right away." Amy sighed. "I just didn't know how. Then I remembered you and Elvis."

Mercy smiled. "I had no idea."

"One day we followed him back to you, just to make sure that he belonged to somebody. Otherwise we would have kept him for ourselves, huh, Helena?" She tickled the baby and Helena giggled.

"You still haven't told us why you left her in the woods." Patience was getting impatient.

"Tell them," said Mercy, who'd heard part of the story but wanted to hear it all this time.

"I was going to slip away on our walk. But Max insisted on coming with us. After a while, he told me he had to talk to Adam alone, and I should just go on back to the compound with the baby. So I took Helena away like we were doing what he said. But then I circled back to hear what they were saying. Adam was very upset. Max said something about taking care of loose ends. I figured me and Helena were the loose ends.

"Adam went off toward the compound, but Max stayed behind, as if he knew I really wasn't going back there. I could hear him following me. That scared me. So I took the baby as close to the trail as I dared and left her in the clearing." Amy looked at Mercy. "I knew if you didn't find her, Elvis would. Then I ran off in the other direction. If Max found someone, I wanted it to be me—not Helena."

"You did good." Patience smiled at her.

"Then what did you do?" asked Jade.

"I hitched a ride to East Dorset, and took the bus to Northshire. I thought you'd take Helena to the hospital, and you did." Amy smiled. "I hung around until they got so busy I could sneak in and get my baby back. I went to your place, because you seemed nice. You had to be nice with a dog like Elvis. I thought you'd help us."

"I was helping you. But you left."

"I didn't know what else to do. I thought I was safe at your house, but then he showed up." Amy looked at Troy. "I didn't know you were, like, a good guy."

"How did you know where Mercy lived?" asked Patience.

"I looked her up online."

"How?"

"Duh. On my cell."

"You have a cell phone?"

Amy looked at her as if she were a dinosaur. "Everyone has a cell phone. Even Adam knew that." She pulled a flip phone from her pocket. "I mean, it's a burner, but still. It got wet when I fell in the lake, but I dried it out and it's good as new."

"Give me that number right now," said Mercy, trying not to think how much grief they might have been spared if they'd known her cell number.

"You were right about Skinner being dangerous," said Troy, getting back to the subject at hand. "He killed your stepfather."

"I know."

"You were there," said Mercy.

"I found him dead in his chair. I saw Max driving away in his truck."

"How did you know that?" Troy frowned at Mercy.

"Elvis found a baby teether at the scene."

"You never told us that." Thrasher did not look happy.

"I was afraid Harrington would read it the wrong way."

"Back to your story, Amy," Patience said, silencing both Troy and Thrasher with a dark look.

"I was afraid he'd kill Adam next. So I went back to the compound to warn him. He told me to hide in one of the tents until he could get me out of there. Dr. Winters came and I told her about my stepfather. She told me to stay there with the baby. I didn't know she was crazy."

"So she knew how Skinner murdered Walker," said Troy. "That's why she killed Wolfe the same way, to throw suspicion back on Skinner."

"I suspect she was always good with a knife," said Mercy.

"But why did Max kill my stepfather?"

"We believe that Don Walker was blackmailing Skinner," said Thrasher. "He knew the Herbert brothers."

"They were hunting buddies," said Amy.

"And worse," said Mercy.

"Right," said Thrasher. "He knew them well enough to know that they'd stolen the sculpture and sold it for scrap. He may even have helped them do it."

"He was always stealing things," said Amy.

"Yeah," said Troy, "when he was a young man he was arrested a couple of times for petty theft, but he pled out for fines and time served. He was more careful about not getting caught from then on."

"When he figured out that his hunting buddies were up to something bigger, he wanted in on it," continued Thrasher. "But the Herbert brothers weren't in charge. Skinner was. And he wasn't having it. He tried paying Walker off, and when that didn't shut him up, he killed him."

"Paul and Louis aren't the brightest guys in the woods," said Mercy. "Did they even suspect their brother was still alive before he showed up for the robbery?"

"Apparently not," said Troy. "But I think Flo Herbert knew. That's why she was so surprised when she saw the photos of the belt buckle."

"But if it wasn't Wayne Herbert, who was it?" Patience passed the breadbasket to Thrasher, along with the pot of Animal Farm butter.

"Thank you." Thrasher buttered his bread as he explained. "We don't know. The DNA results could take weeks, if not months. And even then . . ."

"Go ahead, Mercy," said Troy. "Spill it."

"Patrick O'Malley."

"What?" Thrasher frowned. "The jewelry designer?"

Mercy explained the jeweler's mark and the research she'd done armed with its data. "O'Malley made the buckles and the necklace."

"And then disappeared," continued Troy. "Flo Herbert said he went to Ireland three years ago. About the same time the victim died. But the Irish authorities confirmed today that they have no record of that."

"Which gives my new theory some weight," said Mercy.

"Theories don't convict murderers," said Thrasher.

"Hear her out, captain. She's been right about everything else," said Troy.

"Think about it." Mercy took a sip of wine and went on. "Everyone who knew about this particular group of Vermont Firsters is dead or going to jail for art theft. Given the belt buckles and the tampering of the logging trucks, I think we can assume that originally Wolfe formed the group as a genuine activist organization, dedicated to preserving the best of Vermont."

"Saving trees," said Amy.

"Right," said Mercy. "If the jeweler was a believer—and given his past as an IRA supporter he may have been sincere about supporting their work—then he may have objected to the corruption of their mission."

"And paid for it with his life."

"So which one of them killed him?" asked Patience.

"Wayne Herbert," said Mercy and Troy in unison.

Mercy laughed "You go ahead."

"It would explain why he went to Quebec about the same time."

"Exactly."

"This all fits, I'll give you that," said Thrasher. "But even if DNA tests prove it's O'Malley, short of a confession there's no way to prove any of it. Harrington will laugh me right out of his office." He turned to Troy. "If he doesn't fire you first."

"Can he do that?" Patience looked worried.

"I don't think so. Mercy and Troy are golden at the moment. Which really pisses him off." The captain smiled. "Less glory for him and his staties. More for Fish and Wildlife."

"So you're safe, at least for now."

"Yes, safe and sound and free to enjoy your cooking." Thrasher tipped his head to her, and to Mercy's surprise, her grandmother blushed.

"Back to the case." Troy looked at Mercy. "Are you thinking what I'm thinking?"

She raised her wineglass to him. "If you're thinking that we've got the bullet from the skull and a shell casing found at Donald Walker's house, then yes."

Troy raised his beer mug to her and smiled.

"Shell casing?" asked Thrasher, between bites of dumpling.

"We know Donald Walker was a blackmailer," said Troy. "He could have been blackmailing Wayne, too. Maybe he was there when Wayne killed him, a hunting trip gone wrong. He found the shell casing and held on to it."

"Until the little magpie Munchkin stole it and hid it," said Mercy.

"We'll have that tested right away," said Thrasher. "If you're right, it would help to find the gun that fired it. With any luck it's one of the weapons we confiscated at Feinberg's."

"A lot has to fall into place," said Mercy.

"But we're closer than ever to wrapping this up." Thrasher smiled. "Great work."

"What will happen to Dr. Winters?" asked Amy.

"You don't have to worry," said Thrasher. "She's going away for a very long time."

"She confessed," said Troy. "She thought you and the baby were gone for good, and that she'd have a chance with Wolfe again. When she saw you back at the compound, she confronted him. She told him he was an idiot, and that thanks to Max he was going to end up dead or in jail, not in a love cottage with you. Only she could save him. He sent her home, but he realized that she was right about Max. He went off to find him and ran into Mercy."

"He thought I could get Amy and Helena out of there," said Mercy, "while he stopped Max from robbing Feinberg."

"But Dr. Winters didn't go home," said Amy.

"No," said Troy. "She was in a rage. She hit Mercy on the head. When Wolfe saw Elvis running alone on the trail, and circled back to see what happened to Mercy, the professor killed him."

"OMG," said Jade to Amy. "So you were there when she did it?"

"I snuck out of the tent cabin to see what was going on," said Amy. "I saw her hit Mercy. I wanted to help, but Adam got there first. She stabbed him." Her voice caught, and she looked away for a minute, wiping the tears from her heart-shaped face with the back of her hand. "I just ran. I didn't try to help him. I just ran."

"There's nothing you could have done," said Troy.

"I had to get Helena out of there. But she followed me and trapped us in the tent cabin. She said she'd hurt Helena if I didn't do what she said."

"Dr. Winters is capable of anything," said Mercy. "You did what you had to do."

"'Hell hath no fury like a woman scorned,'" said Thrasher.

"More Shakespeare?" Amy asked as she cleaned the baby's face and hands and took her out of the high chair.

"Actually, no," Mercy said. "It's William Congreve, from *The Mourning Bride*." She recited: "'Heaven hath no rage like Love to Hatred turned, nor Hell a fury like a Woman scorned.'"

"She's always like this," said Amy, bouncing Helena on her lap. "Total word nerd."

"When she's not tracking down murderers," said Troy, laughing.

The doorbell rang, and Mercy welcomed the opportunity to escape. This time it was a big guy in a dark suit. One of Feinberg's bodyguards. The taller one. He handed her a package wrapped in brown paper.

"Find the folly," he said.

CHAPTER FIFTY

O PEN IT," SAID AMY.
"Okay, okay. You can help me." Patience took the baby, and together Mercy and Amy carefully unwrapped the gift.

It was a framed sketch of a striking nude woman with a crescent in her hair, holding a bow in one hand and a staff and a quiver of arrows in the other, standing tall against a background of full-leafed trees.

"Diana," said Mercy.

"Goddess of the Hunt," said Thrasher.

"And the woods and the moon and animals and new mothers and babies," said Patience.

"She's so beautiful," said Amy.

"She's so *naked*," said Jade.

"Very appropriate." Troy grinned at Mercy.

"It's a Kenyon Cox," said Thrasher. "Wonderful."

"He wants me to find the other folly."

"Sounds about right," said Troy.

Mercy carried the sketch over to the fireplace and stood it on the mantelpiece. "Just until we can hang it properly."

"Perfect," said Patience. "Time for dessert."

Over her grandmother's triple-layered chocolate cake, they talked about everything from art and murder to the future of dairy farmers in Vermont. Mercy was content. Happy that there were so many people at her dining table, a prospect that would have mortified her even a month earlier.

"Other than interfering in our investigations," said Thrasher, "what is it that you actually *do*, Ms. Carr?"

"Please call me Mercy." The captain's formality disconcerted her and she suspected that was purposeful on his part. Always the commanding officer. She wondered if anyone ever got the better of the man—and lived to tell about it.

"Mercy." He turned those extraordinary blue-green eyes on her.

"I've been taking some time since my retirement to consider my options."

"She helps me out at the animal hospital," said Patience. "She'd make a fine vet. But her parents are pushing for her to finish her degree and go to law school. Join the family firm."

"Really." Thrasher raised an eyebrow.

Troy laughed. "The captain is not a big fan of lawyers."

"Although your parents are lovely people," Thrasher said.

Mercy smiled. "So far I've resisted that siren call."

"It would be more productive if you worked with us rather than against us," said the captain. "There's a shortage of good working dogs and dog handlers."

"We're retired," she said.

"Could have fooled me."

THE LITTLE PARTY broke up. Patience packed up the dirty casserole dishes and cake pans and promised to come back the next day with new delights. Thrasher offered to drop Jade off at her grandparents' on his way home, and Amy settled the baby down for the night. *Bath, book, bed.* Just like her grandmother ordered.

Mercy and Troy did the dishes and then took Elvis and Susie Bear outside. Usually she took visitors out to the back deck, but tonight she felt the need to sit out front, where she could see the flag. So much had happened over the past ten days that she felt alienated from Martinez, from the life they'd shared and the life they'd planned, from his memory and from her continued remembrance of him and what they were to each other. She didn't want to forget him or get over him or move on with her life without him. But she had a terrible feeling that was just what she was doing.

While the dogs ran around the yard, Mercy and Troy settled onto the wide front porch. She sat in her grandfather's white cedar rocking chair, and he sat in her grandmother's matching one. Patience had given both of them to her when she'd moved in here. "You always need a pair," her grandmother had told her. "One for you, and one for your guest."

Troy was her first guest.

"Been quite a July so far," he said.

"Yeah."

"You and Elvis make a good team."

"We're working on it." She smiled as she watched Elvis bound down to the barn, Susie Bear on his heels. "He's certainly my better half."

"I'm not sure about that."

"Oh, it's true. All this time I've been so worried about taking care of him, while he's actually been the one taking care of me." For the first time it occurred to her that maybe that was what Martinez had intended all along.

"Dogs are like that."

"I thought I was helping him get better."

"You were. He is better."

"Yes, he is."

"Maybe it's your turn now."

"Maybe." They looked out across the garden as the two dogs raced up from the barn and around the flower beds, brushing by the lavender and filling the air with its sweet scent as the sun set and the stars appeared in the dark summer sky.

"'Blessed be the man that spares these stones,'" she quoted quietly. "'And cursed be he that moves my bones.'"

"Shakespeare again. You said that in the woods when we found the bones."

"Seems like a lifetime ago." She felt like she'd lived several lifetimes since that day in the woods.

"Which play is it from?"

"It's not from a play. It's his epitaph," said Mercy. "The assumption is that he wrote it. But no one knows for sure."

"Right."

"I was just thinking about the bones we found in the wilderness. No epitaph for him."

"Not yet. But soon, thanks to you."

"I hope you're right. I'm sure Patrick O'Malley would prefer to spend eternity at home in Ireland."

Troy stopped rocking and turned toward her. "May I ask you a question?"

"Sure." She stopped rocking, too, but kept her eyes on the dogs.

"What's up with all the Shakespeare?"

Mercy laughed. "Amy asked me the same thing."

"What did you say?"

"I told her the truth. That reading his stories made me feel better about being human."

"Pretty heavy for an eighteen-year-old." Troy paused. "But it makes sense to me."

He leaned back in his chair, and she followed suit. They sat there in silence for a moment, the only sound the panting of the dogs and the squeaking of the rockers and the hooting of the owls.

"So I guess tomorrow you'll be back out looking for people lost in the wilderness."

Troy smiled. "I've got patrols."

"Right." She smiled back. In his own way, the game warden was a rebel, just like his famous ancestor.

"So I guess tomorrow you'll be back out looking for art lost in the wilderness."

"Trade you," she said.

He laughed. The man had a nice laugh.

"Martinez told me this story once about a monk who was lost in the wilderness. He came to this river too wide and wild to swim across. So he built himself a raft out of downed limbs and vine, and used it to ford the turbulent waters safely to the other bank. He continued his journey, carrying the raft with him. He carried it for a long time, until he could no longer smell the scent of water in the air. Then he put the raft down and set it on fire. After the flames burned out and nothing was left but smoke and embers, he went on his way. Ultimately he left the wilderness and went back home."

Troy thought for a moment. "Why burn the raft? Why not leave it for the next guy who gets lost in the wilderness?"

"I asked the same questions."

"And?"

"Sometimes you need to build your own effin' raft."

He laughed, and she laughed with him.

THEY SAT THERE together for a long time. Not saying anything. It seemed to Mercy that everything had been said, at least for now. Elvis and Susie Bear tired eventually, and came running back to the porch, curling up on either side of the rocking chairs.

It was a perfect warm summer night, filled with the deep sweep of starlight and silence. The sweet seesaw of the rocker lulled Mercy to sleep, and when she woke up, she found herself covered with a quilt, the handsome shepherd still at her feet. Troy and Susie Bear were gone.

Dawn was breaking, and she could see Orion rising over the horizon. Orion the hunter, beloved of Diana, goddess of the hunt, who was so distraught over his death that she turned him into the brightest constellation in the sky.

She gathered the quilt around her, and stood up. She glanced up at the flagpole, where the flag rippled gently in the slight wind from the south.

Mercy saluted. "Martinez."

She whistled, and the shepherd hustled to his feet. As the sun rose slowly over the mountains and cast the cabin in shadow, Mercy and Elvis went inside.

ACKNOWLEDGMENTS

The way I came to write *A Borrowing of Bones* is a serendipitous one. I was working on *The Writer's Guide to Beginnings* for Writer's Digest Books, and I needed an opening chapter of a story that I could use as an example, one that I could take through several revisions, illustrating the many iterations required to nail those first pages.

So I wrote a scene inspired by the military and law enforcement working dogs I'd met at Leo Maloney's swell fundraiser for Mission K9 Rescue (www.missionk9rescue.org), which I'd been invited to attend thanks to the lovely Michaela Hamilton of Kensington Publishing. I was so impressed by the dogs, their handlers, and Kristen Maurer and Louisa Kastner of MK9R that I went home determined to rescue another dog. Michael and I somehow ended up with our son's cranky old beagle, Freddie, and rescued a torby tabby named Ursula, but our beloved rescue mutt Shakespeare had died a couple of years before and I hadn't had the heart to adopt another dog. Yet. But now I was ready.

And along came Bear, the goofy and gregarious Newfoundland retriever mix we adopted sight unseen from Alabama, with the help of Chey Ottoson of the fabulous Double Dog Rescue (www.doubledogrescue.org). Bear is simply the best—and, as you've probably guessed, Susie Bear is his female doppelgänger.

All this found its way into that sample chapter for *The Writer's Guide to Beginnings*. That might have been the end of it, but my dear friend, agent, and mentor Gina Panettieri read it and persuaded me to finish what I'd started—and she sold it as the first in a series to the indomitable Pete Wolverton of St. Martin's Press/Minotaur.

So thank you to everyone who contributed to this fortuitous turn of events, including the aforementioned folks as well as Phil Sexton, Cris Freese, and Rachel Randall.

A special shout-out to my Scribe Tribe—Susan Reynolds, Meera Lester, John K. Waters, Indi Zeleny, Mardeene Mitchell—and my pal Michael Neff, for their support and encouragement. And to the magnanimous and magnificent Lee Child, Jane Cleland, Hallie Ephron, Lisa Gardner, Larry Kay, William Martin, Spencer Quinn/Peter Abrahams, and Hank Phillippi Ryan, all of whom were kind enough to say nice things about this book.

But back to Pete, who asked me during the rather rigorous revision process if "everything in Vermont had to be the best." Maybe not, I conceded at the time, but here I state unequivocally that her people (and dogs) are the best, most notably Susan Warner, Director of Public Affairs for the Vermont Fish & Wildlife Department, who introduced me to the generous and knowledgeable Vermont State Game Warden Rob Sterling and his magnificent K9 Crockett. Much appreciation also to the energetic and empathetic Donna Larson, founding member and VP of the New England K9 Search and Rescue (nek9sar .org), the always engaging and enlightening Gardner "Bud" Browning and Scott Wood of the TSA, wicked-smart author and retired homicide detective Brian Thiem, the fabulous folks at the splendid Northshire Bookstore, dog trainer extraordinaire Michael MacCurtain of Five Rings K9 services, and the delightful Stasia Tretault, innkeeper at the Seth Warner Inn. All shared their expertise freely and graciously, and any mistakes are solely my own.

And back to Pete again: Best. Editor. Ever. And to Pete's aide de camp, the ever-cheerful and talented Assistant Editor Jennifer Donovan, the brilliant Andy Martin, the inimitable Kelley Ragland, the indefatigable Martin Quinn, the vigilant Karen Richardson, and all of the swell folks at St. Martin's Press/Minotaur, my dearest thanks and appreciation.

To Mom and Dad, my children Alexis, Greg, and Mikey, and Michael—my endless love and gratitude for, well, everything.

And a final heartfelt thanks to the wonderful community of readers, writers, editors, and publishers that make up the literary universe in which I have worked and played and dreamed all my life. I would not wish for any companion in the world but you . . .